Praise for

BLESSING OF THE LOST GIRLS

"Jance proves she's still at the top of her game in this tense crossover of her Joanna Brady and Walker Family series. Nearly four decades into her career, Jance is still finding new ways to thrill her readers."

—*Publishers Weekly*

"An intriguing read guaranteed to keep audiences engaged from first page to last."

—*Booklist*

"Jance returns to her Southwest roots in this gripping tale that combines characters from her Joanna Brady books and the Walker Family novels."

—*Mystery Sequels*

Praise for
Joanna Brady and New York Times
Bestselling Author J. A. Jance

"Fans of police procedurals with a Southwestern flair will love Joanna's determination to manage marriage, motherhood, and policing."

—*Library Journal*

"J. A. Jance does not disappoint."

—*Washington Times*

"J. A. Jance is one of the best at combining mystery and family dynamics."

—New York Journal of Books

"Jance starts her books fast . . . and keeps things moving with cinematic panache. . . . You want an accessible thriller? Jance is your gal."

—*Los Angeles Times*

BLESSING OF THE LOST GIRLS

By J. A. Jance

Joanna Brady Mysteries

Desert Heat
Tombstone Courage
Shoot Don't Shoot
Dead to Rights
Skeleton Canyon
Rattlesnake Crossing
Outlaw Mountain
Devil's Claw
Paradise Lost
Partner in Crime
Exit Wounds
Dead Wrong
Damage Control
Fire and Ice
Judgment Call
Remains of Innocence

The Old Blue Line
(novella)
No Honor Among
Thieves: An Ali Reynolds
and Joanna Brady
Novella
Random Acts: A Joanna
Brady and Ali Reynolds
Novella
Downfall
Field of Bones
Missing and Endangered
Blessing of the Lost
Girls: A Brady and
Walker Family Novel

J. P. Beaumont Mysteries

Until Proven Guilty
Injustice for All
Trial by Fury
Taking the Fifth
Improbable Cause
A More Perfect Union
Dismissed with Prejudice
Minor in Possession
Payment in Kind
Without Due Process
Failure to Appear
Lying in Wait
Name Withheld
Breach of Duty
Birds of Prey

Partner in Crime
Long Time Gone
Justice Denied
Fire and Ice
Betrayal of Trust
Ring in the Dead (novella)
Second Watch
Stand Down (novella)
Dance of the Bones:
A J. P. Beaumont and
Brandon Walker Novel
Still Dead (novella)
Proof of Life
Sins of the Fathers
Nothing to Lose

Walker Family Novels

HOUR OF THE HUNTER
KISS OF THE BEES
DAY OF THE DEAD
QUEEN OF THE NIGHT

DANCE OF THE BONES:
A J. P. BEAUMONT AND
BRANDON WALKER NOVEL
BLESSING OF THE LOST
GIRLS: A BRADY AND
WALKER FAMILY NOVEL

Ali Reynolds Novels

EDGE OF EVIL
WEB OF EVIL
HAND OF EVIL
CRUEL INTENT
TRIAL BY FIRE
FATAL ERROR
LEFT FOR DEAD
DEADLY STAKES
MOVING TARGET
A LAST GOODBYE (novella)
COLD BETRAYAL

NO HONOR AMONG
THIEVES: AN ALI REYNOLDS
AND JOANNA BRADY
NOVELLA
CLAWBACK
RANDOM ACTS: A JOANNA
BRADY AND ALI REYNOLDS
NOVELLA
MAN OVERBOARD
DUEL OF THE DEATH
THE A LIST
CREDIBLE THREAT
UNFINISHED BUSINESS
COLLATERAL DAMAGE

Poetry

AFTER THE FIRE

ATTENTION: ORGANIZATIONS AND CORPORATIONS
HarperCollins books may be purchased for educational, business, or sales promotional use. For information, please e-mail the Special Markets Department at SPsales@harpercollins.com.

J. A. JANCE

BLESSING OF THE LOST GIRLS

A BRADY AND WALKER FAMILY NOVEL

wm

WILLIAM MORROW

An Imprint of HarperCollinsPublishers

BLESSING OF THE LOST GIRLS. Copyright © 2023 by J. A. Jance. All rights reserved. Printed in the United States of America. No part of this book may be used or reproduced in any manner whatsoever without written permission except in the case of brief quotations embodied in critical articles and reviews. For information, address Harper-Collins Publishers, 195 Broadway, New York, NY 10007.

First William Morrow premium printing: March 2024
First William Morrow hardcover printing: September 2023

Print Edition ISBN: 978-0-06-302267-6
Digital Edition ISBN: 978-0-06-301011-6

Cover design by Richard L. Aquan
Cover photographs © Getty Images

William Morrow and HarperCollins are registered trademarks of HarperCollins Publishers in the United States of America and other countries.

24 25 26 27 28 BVGM 10 9 8 7 6 5 4 3 2 1

For James and his War Pony

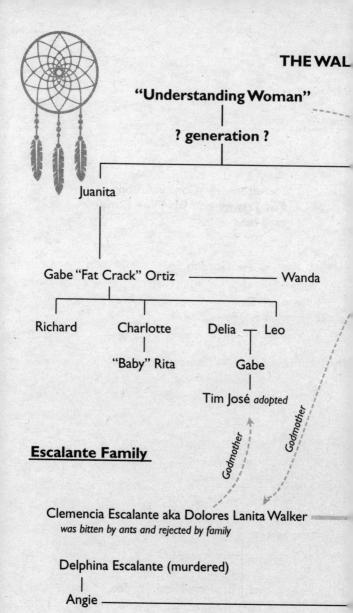

"Understanding Woman"

? generation ?

Juanita

Gabe "Fat Crack" Ortiz ——————— Wanda

Richard   Charlotte   Delia ⊤ Leo

"Baby" Rita   Gabe

Tim José *adopted*

Godmother   *Godmother*

Escalante Family

Clemencia Escalante aka Dolores Lanita Walker
was bitten by ants and rejected by family

Delphina Escalante (murdered)

Angie ——————

...MILY

...aises

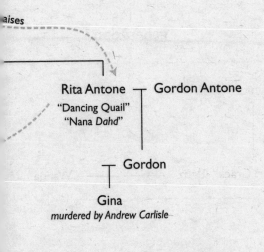

Rita Antone ── Gordon Antone
"Dancing Quail"
"Nana *Dahd*"

── Gordon

Gina
murdered by Andrew Carlisle

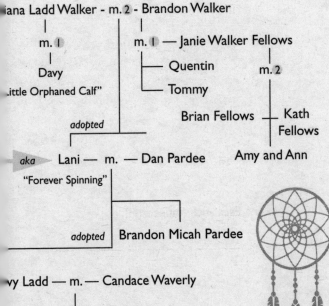

...iana Ladd Walker - m. 2 - Brandon Walker

m. ❶   m. ❶ ── Janie Walker Fellows
│   ├── Quentin   m. 2
Davy   └── Tommy
...ittle Orphaned Calf"
                               Brian Fellows ── Kath
                adopted   Fellows
                               Amy and Ann
aka   Lani ── m. ── Dan Pardee
"Forever Spinning"

        adopted ── Brandon Micah Pardee

...vy Ladd ── m. ── Candace Waverly

        Tyler

PROLOGUE

April 2022

FOR RV NOMADS FROM ALL OVER THE COUNTRY, Charles Milton was always something of an enigma. There was nothing about him that stood out. He was unassuming enough—someone you could walk past on a sidewalk and never have him register. His rig, a Thor Omni BT36, wasn't one of the showier ones in the RV parks he frequented. And yes, although the vehicle he towed behind it happened to be a Lexus, his 350 GS sedan was also seven years old. Although he wasn't a flashy dresser, his Dockers and cotton Polo shirts were a lot more conservative than the Bermuda shorts and Hawaiian shirts favored by most of his neighbors.

He seemed fit enough and carried almost no extra weight on his lean body. His close-cropped silver hair and wire-framed glasses gave him an intellectual appearance, but he never seemed to put on airs on that score. He was pleasant enough—always greeting people with a friendly wave and a casual "How's it going?" Occasionally he'd invite people over to have a beer or share a smoke under his RV's roll-out awning. Female visitors often admired the pair of gaily painted maracas that was front and center on his small, fold-up patio table.

"They came from a street fair in Guaymas," he'd tell anyone who inquired about their origin while giving the instruments a satisfying rattle, which usually was enough to allay their curiosity. Of course, Charlie had never been to Guaymas, and he didn't know if the town even had a street fair, but it seemed plausible enough, and since he always told the story the same way, no one ever questioned it.

Occasional visitors aside, however, Charlie mostly kept to himself, not suspiciously so, but as though he preferred his own company to palling around with others. Nonetheless, if someone in the park needed a hand with getting their various antennas deployed or stored away, he was always glad to help out.

Of course, his very separateness gave rise to a good deal of speculation. Some suspected that he was a retired spy. Others thought he must have been a small-town banker or accountant although there was never any hint as to the location of that small town. His vehicles both carried South Dakota license plates. Had anyone studied his driver's license, they would have noticed that his listed home address was in Yankton, SD. But when South Dakota ex-pats gathered to discuss their good old days of growing up on a farm, or visiting Rapid City for the first time, or stopping off at Wall Drug on the way to Mt. Rushmore, or fishing on Big Stone Lake, or having a 4-H bull win a blue ribbon at the state fair in Huron, Charlie's participation was limited to nods, grins, and chuckles. The assumption became that although he officially listed South Dakota as his place of residence, he probably did so for similar reasons lots of other people were doing the same thing these days—to save on taxes.

When RV womenfolk got together over coffee, Charlie's name came up often enough because they couldn't figure him out. Over time, several widows had targeted him; after all, he was a good-looking guy for his age and seemed to be fairly well fixed financially. But none of those relationships panned out. It wasn't a matter of whether or not they were his type, Charlie simply wasn't interested. That gave rise to another whole kind of gossip. He didn't wear a ring, so clearly he wasn't married. If there had been a previous wife or even more than one along the way, he never mentioned them. Was he one of what Garrison Keillor used to refer to as "Norwegian bachelor farmers"?

A lot of those guys were just naturally shy people who didn't like to mingle while others were closeted gays who didn't care to go through the complex process of "coming out." They were happy to stay where they were and be who they were. But one woman in particular, Helen Snowdon from Aberdeen, who considered herself far more worldly than her compatriots, insisted that Charlie couldn't possibly be gay—he just wasn't "limp-wristed enough." Had Helen's grandchildren heard her say that out loud, they would have been scandalized.

The one thing they all knew for sure about Charlie was that he loved rodeos. Other than wearing a Stetson, he didn't dress like a cowboy or act like a cowboy, so that was a bit puzzling. While most snowbirds followed the weather in their migrations, Charlie followed rodeos from city to city and region to region. He attended professional competitions and collegiate ones, too. Since he never discussed having any kids or grandkids who might be participating, that was also mystifying. Nonetheless, when rodeos came to town, he was right there day after day, sitting in the bleachers, watching.

And that was how things stood in the RV ranks for a very long time. Then on an April day when mug shots of Charlie's face were suddenly on TV newscasts all over the country, no one was more surprised than his former friends and neighbors. They all recognized Charlie's face all right, but not his name—Ronald J. Addison. But the thing none of them could believe was that the stories were true. How was it possible that such an unassuming, totally forgettable man— someone they had all known on a first-name basis—had just been unmasked as a serial killer?

Initially all of Charlie's former friends and associates were in complete denial. Surely law enforcement was mistaken. How could someone so ordinary be so evil? But when the grieving families of his six victims looked at that same mug shot they saw someone else entirely—they saw the devil incarnate, and they all wanted him dead.

CHAPTER 1

TUCSON, ARIZONA
Saturday, February 16, 2019

AT TUCSON'S BUCKEROO BAR AND GRILL, THE
Fiesta de Los Vaqueros was in full swing. That
was hardly surprising since it was the closest watering hole to the rodeo grounds. It was a divey
kind of place where waitresses cooked customers' steaks more or less to order on a well-worn
indoor grill positioned just inside the front door.
The bar came complete with bad lighting and
peanut shells scattered on the sticky surface of
a grimy floor. There were plenty of rodeo fans
crowding the place, but a goodly number of the
guests that night were rodeo participants—bull
and bronco riders, the guys who looked after
the livestock, groomers, and even a rodeo clown
or two.

Since the Tucson Rodeo was only a few miles
down the road from Charlie Milton's current
RV park north of town, just off I-10 at Ina Road,

he could hardly turn up his nose at that, and naturally he stopped by the Buckeroo afterward. Anywhere people were prepared to let their hair down and party hearty was a happy hunting ground for him. They made it easy for him to settle in on a stool with his camera bag casually placed on the bar next to him, while he kept an eye out for whatever sweet young thing might catch his fancy. Once he spotted a likely prospect, the next task at hand was finding a way to cut her out of the herd.

Tonight he waited around until he was able to grab the stool at the very end of the bar. He wasn't here for casual conversation, and being next to the wall halved the risk of his being caught up in some drunk's idle chitchat. Once settled in, he ordered a small pitcher of sangria. He knew from experience that he could sip on that all night long without getting tipsy, because unlike most of the Buckeroo's other patrons that evening, Charles Milton had no intention of getting drunk. And now, with his camouflage camera bag on display, he settled in to see what opportunities might present themselves.

Charlie's BA, from Harvard no less, was in psychology, and he considered himself to be a keen observer of people. He studied them from afar, watching for what made them tick—for what might make them vulnerable and/or available. He always focused on young women because, generally speaking, young also meant stupid. Good-looking was fine as far as it went, but he especially liked them young and trusting.

When a waitress came around, he ordered a

medium-rare steak and a baked potato. Steaks at the Buckeroo were somewhat problematic. Since each waitress was responsible for grilling her customers' steaks, and since some waitresses were better at that than others, it was a crap-shoot whether or not your indifferently prepared Buckeroo rib eye would come to the table as ordered. Of course that wasn't a problem for Charlie. He hadn't come to the establishment looking for fine dining any more than he had come in search of engaging conversation. He had a different kind of red meat in mind.

Eight o'clock that evening found Charlie still at the bar, eating his tough, overdone steak, working away at his pitcher of sangria, and still keeping an eye out for likely prospects. The first one was a shapely young blonde who was obviously an out-of-towner. While the locals were all wearing long pants topped by sweaters and/or jackets, Blondie was decked out in a pair of very short shorts and an equally skimpy top. In honor of the rodeo, she wore a pair of rhinestone-studded cowboy boots. From the way she tossed her mane of long platinum hair and the up-close-and-personal manner in which she interacted with the guys gathered around the two pool tables, Charlie soon realized she was a pro in search of a john.

Most of the time, Charlie chose to avoid prostitutes, although on occasion he'd had to settle for what was readily available. Generally speaking, whores were too damned worldly-wise, and he had learned from experience that someone like Blondie might have a switchblade tucked inside one of those fancy boots and a pimp standing guard outside. Charlie couldn't fault the woman on her looks, but he preferred his potential victims to be on the innocent side and most definitely unarmed. Besides, whores expected to have sex, and sex just wasn't his thing.

As time passed, Charlie began to worry that his evening at the Buckeroo was going to be a bust. Couples came and went. He observed their interactions although they held no real interest for him. One couple in particular engaged in a hell of an argument, which ended with the woman tossing her full glass of beer right in the poor guy's face. After that, she got up and stalked out. Had Charlie been less experienced, he might have been tempted to get up and go after her, but he didn't—and a good thing, too. Less than a minute after their altercation, the guy involved paid his tab and hurried out of the room, hot on her trail. Had Charlie opted to target her, he would have had to deal with her boyfriend as well.

Then, just as he was about to give up and head home, three new arrivals entered. As soon as Charlie saw them he thought, *That's more like it.* They were young—old enough to get past the security guard checking IDs at the door, or maybe they just had top-drawer fake IDs. They were in high spirits and out on the town with no male escorts in sight. All three were good-looking, with shapely bodies decked out in proper rodeo attire—western shirts, tight jeans, and cowboy boots—none of which sported a single rhinestone. All three had long, jet-black hair. Judging by that and by the stunning pieces of silver and turquoise jewelry they wore, Charlie pegged them as Indians. If prostitutes were at the bottom of his list of favorite candidates, Native American women were at the top.

When young women of color disappeared, and most especially those from Indian reservations, there was a good chance they would never resurface. For one thing, the various law enforcement agencies involved spent so much time bickering about who was supposed to handle the case, that investigations generally went cold before they ever started. As far as Charlie Milton was concerned, unsolved missing persons investigations were just what the doctor ordered.

Fortunately for Charlie, the new arrivals settled into a booth that was only one table away from his perch at the bar. That made it possible for him to keep them under observation without it being obvious. He had no intention of interacting with them—of buying them a drink or challenging them to a game of pool. That would be too blatant, and Charlie had no doubt the room was well equipped with video surveillance.

Soon after the trio placed their beverage order, what showed up was a pitcher of beer and two chilled glasses. Two of the girls shared that while the third settled for what appeared to be a soda of some kind—Coca-Cola, most likely—accompanied by a slice of lime. Charlie spent some time evaluating what it might mean that two of the girls were drinking and one wasn't. Was she the designated driver?

Shortly after eight the music fired up—a three-man band complete with a drummer, a piano player, and a guitar player who also fancied himself a singer. At that point a few of the guys from the pool table migrated over to the booth and struck up a conversation with the girls. Two of them—the beer drinkers—accepted invitations to dance and left the booth with their newly designated partners. As for the girl with the soda? She stayed put, passing on every invitation with a firm shake of her head. When her friends returned to the booth and shot glasses appeared on the table—compliments of the pool players turned dancers—the beer drinkers washed theirs down with relish while the girl with the soda pushed hers aside. And the longer her companions danced and drank and carried on, the more unhappy Soda Girl became.

Charlie remained where he was, keeping the goings-on in the girls' booth under discreet observation. Clearly the three were having a difference of opinion. Soda Girl kept looking at her watch and seemed impatient to leave. Each time one of her gal pals returned to the booth, an animated discussion ensued. Once the dancer resumed dancing, Soda Girl would purse her lips and shake her head. She was obviously impatient to leave while her friends were busy having too much fun. Realizing the situation would soon come to a head, Charlie called for his tab, which he paid in cash. Then, without a glance back toward his target, he left the bar. As far as police investigations are concerned, people who leave bars after victims are far more likely to be considered suspects than individuals who depart earlier.

When Charlie had arrived at the Buckeroo, the parking lot had been virtually empty. Nonetheless, he had parked on the far perimeter. Parking on the fringes of a property greatly enhanced the possibility that his Lexus would be well beyond the range of the Buckeroo's surveillance cameras.

Once outside the bar, Charlie walked purposefully to his vehicle and drove it away, leaving the lot but not going far. Two blocks away, he executed a quick U-turn, parked on the shoulder of the street in front of what appeared to be a defunct car wash, and spent the next few minutes ditching his customary Stetson and retrieving some essential equipment from the camera bag—a black hoodie, a pair of latex gloves, and a pair of high-powered night-vision goggles. His weapon of choice was a fully loaded syringe, which he tucked into the hoodie's right-hand pocket. The hypodermic was filled with xylazine, a horse tranquilizer, which he'd purchased for cash from a local feedstore two weeks earlier. After donning the hoodie and the gloves, a now fully equipped Charlie headed back toward the far edge of the Buckeroo's parking lot where he took a seat on the battle-scarred bench of a trash-littered bus stop. From there, the magnification in his night-vision goggles gave him a clear view of the area surrounding the bar's front door.

As if on cue, Soda Girl emerged a few minutes later. She had arrived at the bar with friends, but she was leaving alone. Charlie fully expected her to head for a vehicle, and he hoped he'd have time enough to retrieve the Lexus and follow. Instead, Soda Girl threaded her way through rows of parked cars, walking straight in his direction. From the glow illuminating her face, he suspected she was using her cell phone. It seemed likely she was in the process of summoning either a cab or an Uber. He hoped she wasn't calling a friend for a lift. That might cause complications.

As she came closer, seemingly oblivious to Charlie's presence and the danger he posed, his heart rate ramped up. He glanced anxiously back at the bar entrance. A few people remained clustered around the door, smoking and talking. No one else appeared to be leaving right then. At that precise moment, traffic on South Sixth was blessedly light, but he understood that once he launched his attack, it would have to be quick, brutal, and absolutely silent.

Soda Girl emerged from the unpaved parking lot and stepped determinedly onto the sidewalk as though fully prepared to hoof it back to wherever she was going. At that point Charlie pushed his goggles up under his hood, leaned back on the bench, closed his eyes, and pretended to be asleep, counting on the sound of her boots on the sidewalk to keep him apprised of her movements. He remained where he was, seemingly out cold, until she passed by. Then, after one last check for oncoming traffic, he hurtled after her.

He closed the distance between them in two quick steps. She never saw it coming. There was no time for her to cry out in alarm or even raise her hands to fend him off. After slamming his left hand over her mouth, Charlie landed a powerful closed-fist blow just over her right ear. Temporarily stunned, she crumpled toward the ground. By the time she landed, he'd managed to wrest the syringe out of his pocket and plunge the needle into the bare flesh at the back of her neck. Then he hefted her limp body into his arms and bodily carried her back to the waiting Lexus where he opened the trunk with the punch of a button.

As Charlie lowered Soda Girl into the trunk, she began to stir. In preparation for that eventuality, he had left strips of duct tape hanging on the interior surface of the trunk door, ready and waiting to be deployed at a moment's notice. Before his victim could scream, he slapped one of the shorter strips of tape over her mouth. Then, overpowering her struggles, he used the longer ones to bind her hands and feet.

Once, when Charlie had still been a novice at this game, he'd made the nearly fatal mistake of binding his captive's arms in front of her rather than behind with nearly disastrous consequences, and that was a mistake he hadn't repeated. Once Soda Girl was fully restrained, he returned the hoodie and glasses to the camera bag. It took a few moments for him to locate her cell phone and tuck that into the pocket of his jeans.

After closing the trunk lid, Charlie returned

to the bus stop. Without the aid of the goggles, he was unable to make out any details of the smokers still gathered around the Buckeroo's front entrance, but none of them exhibited any alarm or seemed to be moving in his direction. Using the flashlight on his own phone, Charlie searched the sidewalk until he located the plastic lid that had covered the needle on the loaded hypodermic.

That was one thing Charlie knew for sure— the whole trick to surviving in this business was following one cardinal rule: Don't leave behind any incriminating evidence. Once in his car, he headed straight for the nearest entrance to I-19. Somewhere between Tucson and Green Valley, while still wearing his latex gloves, he rolled down the passenger window of the speeding Lexus and tossed his victim's telephone out onto the pavement. If and when someone bothered to go looking for her phone, that's the last place it would ping, on the shoulder of the southbound lanes of I-19, presumably in a vehicle headed for Nogales. At the next available exit, Charlie left the freeway, crossed over the traffic lanes, and headed north.

CHAPTER 2

TUCSON, ARIZONA
Sunday, February 17, 2019

WHEN LAST CALL CAME AT THE BUCKEROO BAR and Grill that night and with Rosa Rios nowhere to be found, Amanda Lewis and Evangeline Rodriguez were pissed—in every sense of the word. They were both more than slightly drunk, and they were mad as hell that their friend Rosa had taken off by herself without so much as a word to either one of them.

Yes, Rosa wasn't drinking these days and they were, but did she have to be so mean about it? Back in the old days at Fort Thomas High, the three of them had called themselves the Three Musketeers. Considering they were all San Carlos Apaches and girls to boot, that was pretty hilarious, but at the time, they'd been inseparable and had done everything together. That ended in the spring of their senior year when Rosa had shown up drunk at school. The night before there had been a big party in the desert outside Bylas. Rosa had stayed later than almost everyone else, and she'd still been inebriated the next morning when Thomas, her then-boyfriend, had dropped her off at school. He and his friends thought it was a big joke, but Mr. Winston, the school principal, had other ideas.

Matthew Winston was a hard-ass if ever there was one. He didn't give a damn that this was the first of May and just weeks prior to Rosa's scheduled graduation. Rather than give her a suspension, he expelled her that very day and sent her home. Rosa's widowed mother, Ida Rios, had tried appealing the principal's decision to the school board, but they had backed Winston instead. Two weeks before graduation, Rosa filled a backpack with her worldly goods and left town. For the next three and a half years she seemed to have vanished from the face of the earth. No one on the San Carlos heard a word from her. Over time, all of them, including Rosa's mother, concluded she was dead. Then, a little over a month ago, an overjoyed Ida had called both Amanda and Vangie at work to tell them that she had just heard from Rosa who was alive and well and living in Tucson.

By then Rosa's friends had gone on with their lives. Amanda had moved in with her longtime boyfriend, Jacob. They lived in Fort Thomas where she worked as a clerk for the BIA. Vangie, who lived at home with her mother and younger siblings, was a teacher's aide at Mt. Turnbull Elementary in Bylas. According to Ida, Rosa had straightened out her life. She had gone through treatment. She was now clean and sober and working at a Taco Bell. Once Ida passed along Rosa's phone number, Amanda and Vangie hatched a plan to go visit her.

Back in the day, Rosa had been a talented barrel racer who had expected to go far on the rodeo circuit. That whole future had evaporated when her trailered horse, a pinto named War Paint, had been involved in a horrific traffic accident on the way home from a junior rodeo event and had had to be put down. The terrible loss of her beloved mount took the competitive wind out of Rosa's sails, and she never barrel raced again. But back when rodeos had been a regular occurrence in their lives, the three girls had attended them together—with Rosa as the performer and Amanda and Vangie as her cheering section. And that was why, with the Tucson Rodeo coming up only weeks after Rosa resurfaced, they decided to have their reunion there and then.

Jacob, Amanda's boyfriend, hadn't been thrilled at the prospect of her being away for a whole weekend. He remembered all too well the scandal that had surrounded Rosa's abrupt departure from Fort Thomas High. He didn't really believe that Rosa's drinking days were over, and he was a little worried about Amanda's drinking, too. Eventually, however, he had grudgingly agreed. When Amanda and Vangie finally set off for Tucson, they did so with Amanda behind the wheel of Jacob's shiny Toyota Tundra.

Their visit hadn't lived up to expectations. For one thing, Rosa's tiny studio apartment on South Fourth wasn't big enough for all of them. Amanda and Vangie had had to cough up money for a hotel room. And much to their dismay, Rosa wasn't at all the high-spirited, take-no-prisoners girl she used to be. She was serious now—seriously serious. She was going to Pima Community College with the expectation that she'd transfer over to the University of Arizona in the fall. She had a job at a nearby Taco Bell where she earned enough to pay for food and rent, but not enough for her to own and operate a vehicle. And although the hours at her job were flexible enough for her to attend classes, when it came to Rodeo Weekend, she was only able to get Saturday off. So that evening, as they headed out, Rosa made it clear that if the others wanted to drink, that was fine, but she wouldn't be joining them, not in drinking, or, as it turned out, in dancing, either.

When Amanda and Vangie finally left the bar that night, they looked around for Rosa. Since Amanda had left the truck unlocked, they assumed they'd find her sleeping in the pickup, but no such luck. They tried calling her phone. No answer. In fact not only was there no answer, the call went straight to voice mail. More than a little worried about being picked up on a DUI, Amanda nonetheless drove to Rosa's apartment. When they knocked on the door and she didn't answer, they assumed that either she wasn't home or else didn't want to have anything to do with them. Finally they gave up and went to their hotel.

That had taken the blush off Amanda and Vangie's getaway weekend. They had expected it to be a fun time for all three of them, and without Rosa, there wasn't much point. By noon the next day, still unable to connect with Rosa, Amanda and Vangie gave up and went back to the San Carlos. On the way they talked about what they should do—tell Ida Rios or not? In the end, they decided that telling was the only option.

"Back so soon?" a mystified Ida asked when they turned up on her doorstep. "I thought you were going to stay the whole weekend."

That's when they explained what had happened.

"You've tried calling her again today?" Ida asked, when Amanda finished telling the story.

"Our calls go straight to voice mail," Vangie replied.

"Did you contact the police to report her missing?"

Amanda shook her head. "We thought she just got mad because we were drinking and having fun and she wasn't."

At that point, Ida picked up her own phone. Amanda and Evangeline sat there while Ida Rios called the Tucson PD. All they heard was Ida's side of the conversation, and it didn't last long.

"My daughter Rosa's gone missing," Ida reported. "She went out with some friends in Tucson last night. They went to a place called the Buckeroo, drinking and dancing. When the bar closed, they couldn't find Rosa anywhere, and she isn't answering her phone. I know it hasn't been that long, but . . ." Ida fell silent, and a long pause followed. "So that's what I'm supposed to do—wait forty-eight hours and then call you back? But what if—"

Whoever was on the other end of the line must have cut Ida off in midsentence. Because another long period of silence followed.

"Well, I suppose something like this did happen once before," Ida resumed at last. "She ran off when she was a senior in high school, and we didn't hear from her for a long time, but back then she'd had some trouble at school and—" Once again, Ida was interrupted by someone on the other end of the line. "All right," she agreed finally, "if I haven't heard from her by then, I'll call back."

Amanda and Vangie looked at Ida expectantly, but she shook her head. "After," she said, biting her lip. "I'll have to call them later. Tomorrow, he said. Today is too soon."

Amanda and Vangie left Ida's house then, but as they climbed back into the pickup and closed the doors, a black cloud of dread filled the cab around them. At that point, although neither of them said anything aloud, they both knew that their friend Rosa Rios was gone, and this time they doubted she'd be coming back.

CHAPTER 3

WHEN MAUREEN HUDDLESTON CAME INTO THE kitchen at six o'clock that Tuesday morning expecting to start the coffee, she was surprised to see that the Mr. Coffee was almost done dripping, and her husband, Jack, was working away at the kitchen counter. After all, her spouse of some thirty-odd years wasn't exactly the domestic type.

"What are you doing?" she asked.

"Making a couple of sandwiches," he answered.

"For the kids?"

"No, for me," he said. "I'm gonna take Waldo and go check the fences."

Maureen took a critical gander at his sandwich workmanship while she poured her own coffee. His end product consisted of white bread, Miracle Whip, salsa, ketchup, and bologna, without a single shred of lettuce. Had she been in charge, she would have added lettuce and fresh tomato slices to the mix, but these were his sandwiches and his choices.

"Why not use the ATV?" Maureen asked. "Wouldn't that be faster?"

Jack's shoulders stiffened. "I'm too old for all this crap," he said. "Sometimes a man needs a little peace and quiet."

Maureen understood exactly what "crap" he had in mind. Months earlier, when their daughter, Doreen, and her latest and by far most-worthless boyfriend had been picked up on drug smuggling charges with all three of their kids in the back seat of their soon-to-be-impounded vehicle, Child Protective Services had come calling. Of course Maureen and Jack said yes, they'd take the kids. What else could they say? But now, at ages fifty-three and fifty-eight, respectively, she and Jack were back to raising kids—ages six, eight, and ten—with all that entailed—feeding them, clothing them, making sure they brushed their teeth, getting them out the door in time to catch the school bus, overseeing homework, and keeping track of after-school activities. It was way more than either of them had bargained for.

"You're not the only one who could use some peace and quiet, you know," she told him. "Maybe I should go check out the fences while you get the kids ready for school."

Jack turned to face her. "Look," he said, sagging against the kitchen sink, "I know I'm the weakest link, and you're not far short of sainthood, but if you look at the results, I wasn't such a hotshot at fatherhood the first time around, and I doubt I'm going to be any better at it now."

"You did the best you could," she assured him.

"We both did. Dory made her own bad choices."

"And we're the ones reaping the consequences."

"Since Dory's in jail, she's suffering some consequences, too," Maureen said. "Besides, where would our grandkids be if we hadn't stepped up?"

"Exactly," Jack told her, "which is why I'm going to take my sandwiches and my horse and spend the day trying to get my head screwed on straight."

"You do that," she said, giving him a forgiving peck on the cheek in passing. "In the meantime, I'm going to go wake the galloping herd so they can get dressed while I make breakfast."

Half an hour later, Jack and Waldo headed out. Huddleston Ranch was a family-owned operation, and Jack was the third generation to run it. The place, located halfway between Bowie and San Simon, included 650 deeded acres and another 400 of federal leased land.

Ten of those acres were devoted to Maureen's truck farm where she grew fruits and vegetables that she sold at area farmers' markets throughout the spring and summer. Another two hundred irrigated acres were used to grow alfalfa. The rest was devoted to pastureland where Jack ran a herd of grass-fed beef. The truck garden was a cash-only business and the source of a good portion of their annual income. Jack couldn't help but wonder how that would work this year when school let out for the summer and Maureen was stuck watching three kids as well as doing her gardening.

Jack realized that Maureen understood his checking fences was nothing more than an excuse. He was pretty sure the fences were just fine, but he really needed to get away. As he left the house, barn, and garden behind, Jack simply gave Waldo his head and let him go where he pleased while Jack wrestled with the disaster their daughter's life had become and wondered what he could have done differently to bring about a better outcome.

Waldo plodded along, happy to be out and about and moving with no real purpose or direction. When they came to the first fence, the horse stopped and waited for Jack to dismount and open the gate before they moved on into the leased part of the ranch. Once inside, Jack turned Waldo's head to the left and east to where his property was bordered by Wood Canyon Road, although calling that rough dirt track a road was being far too generous.

Heading south again, still following the fence line, they came to a spot where a clump of mesquite had grown up next to the fence. Rather than plow through the thorny barrier, Waldo veered around it. In the clearing behind the mesquite Jack spotted the charred remains of a fire. Serious drought conditions had persisted throughout the Southwest for years, and Jack was instantly incensed. Who the hell would start a fire out here in this dry grassland? What were they thinking? What if they had started a brush fire? If that had happened, everything Jack owned might well have gone up in flames.

Pulling Waldo to a stop, Jack dismounted. Only when he examined the ashes more closely did he see a charred rib bone protruding from the ash. His first thought was that someone had set fire to one of his calves, but a closer examination told him otherwise. What he was looking at was a rib bone, all right, but a distinctly human one, which was confirmed by the item he spotted next—a human skull complete with several teeth still attached to the lower jaw.

Feeling half sick, Jack wrestled his cell phone out of his pocket. A year or so ago, he wouldn't have had a signal out here, but over the past few months an additional cell tower had been built along I-10 between Bowie and San Simon. With shaking hands, he struggled to punch in the number.

"Nine one one, what are you reporting?"

"I just found a dead body," Jack managed. "It looks like someone's been burned to death."

"What is your location?"

"A couple miles south of I-10 between Bowie and San Simon, just off Wood Canyon Road."

"And your name, sir?"

"Huddleston," he said, "Jack Huddleston. I was riding my fence line this morning and just now found it."

"Are there any vehicles nearby?"

"No, the body's lying out in the open all by itself with no sign of anyone else."

"Please stay on the line, sir," the woman said.

"There's a Cochise County Sheriff's Department deputy currently in your area. I'll dispatch him to your location as soon as possible."

The 911 operator may have directed Jack to stay on the line, but he wasn't someone who always did as he was told. He hung up and called Maureen. He needed to tell her what was going on before a string of cop cars came roaring past the house. Fortunately, it was late enough in the day that the school bus had already picked up the kids. His calling home on his cell was unusual enough that Maureen was already on high alert the moment she answered.

"What's wrong?" she demanded. "Are you all right? Is Waldo?"

"We're both fine," Jack assured her, "but somebody isn't. I just found a dead body."

"A dead body?" she echoed in dismay. "Are you sure?"

"I'm sure."

"On our property?"

"Yes, just inside the fence line along Wood Canyon Road. I already called the cops. A deputy's on his way."

"That's awful. How long has the body been there? Who can it be?"

"No idea," Jack told her. "That's probably the first thing the cops will need to figure out."

"Do you want me to come there?"

"No, better not," he said. "The fewer people around a crime scene, the better."

CHAPTER 4

BISBEE, ARIZONA
Tuesday, April 16, 2019, 8:00 A.M.

SHERIFF JOANNA BRADY SAT AT HER DESK IN the Cochise County Justice Center and stared at the front page of that day's *Bisbee Bee* in utter disbelief. Front and center was a bylined article from her least favorite reporter, Marliss Shackleford. The headline read:

MISMANAGEMENT ISSUES
PLAGUE SHERIFF'S DEPARTMENT

Positioned next to the article to bolster that claim was a photo of the front door to her office's public lobby with a County Health Department citation slapped on the glass declaring the place to be a public health hazard. On Saturday at noon her weekend off had been interrupted by a panicked call from her jail commander telling her that cells were filling up with sewage, forcing Joanna to spend the remainder of the weekend dealing with a problem that turned out to be a literal shitstorm.

Jail inmates had been immediately evacuated to a collection of hastily procured tents that had been erected in the jail's exercise yard, while a squad of plumbers—all delighted to be working weekend overtime—had been summoned to clear up the problem. What they discovered had left Joanna seething. When she learned the blockage had been caused by dozens of towels being flushed down inmates' toilets, Joanna and her investigators went to work, studying surveillance footage.

They soon discovered that flushing had occurred in several different cells almost simultaneously, late on Friday night. One by one the inmates involved had been summoned for interviews, and eventually several of them caved. It turned out the scheme had been dreamed up by a fairly new and now disgruntled jail guard who had taken exception to his first ever annual employee review.

When he came to work that afternoon, Joanna had confronted him with what his cohorts had said. Once he admitted it, he had been fired on the spot, but Joanna's whole weekend had been shot. She had spent hours rehousing inmates, overseeing the plumbers, and making arrangements for a certified biohazard crew to come in and do a thorough cleaning of all the affected areas—one of which happened to be the kitchen. Until that area had been remediated, she also needed to make arrangements for inmate food to be brought in from outside suppliers.

Summoned from home, Joanna had been on duty dealing with that complicated mess for the remainder of the weekend. By the time she arrived in the office on Monday morning, she was already exhausted, and finding that Health Hazard citation taped to the door had added insult to injury. Now, a day later, Marliss's piece piled on more. Gritting her teeth, Joanna forced herself to read the whole thing. The article mentioned that part of the plumbing issue over the weekend had been caused deliberately, but the underlying message was that negligence on the part of administration was also responsible. In other words, Sheriff Brady herself had contributed to the problem by not properly maintaining the Justice Center's aging infrastructure, including its plumbing.

Joanna's first instinct was to get Marliss Shackleford on the line and give her a piece of her mind. That's when her phone rang.

"Sheriff Brady," Joanna answered.

"Good morning, Sheriff," Tica Romero, the department's daytime dispatcher, told her. "We've got a reported dead body found on Huddleston Ranch between Bowie and San Simon. Deputy Creighton was just finishing a traffic stop south of Willcox, but he's en route to the scene."

"Natural causes?" Joanna asked hopefully.

"Sounds like a homicide," Tica replied. "Jack Huddleston, the guy who called it in, said it looked like the victim had been incinerated and could've been there for some time."

These days, Joanna kept a daily duty roster on a sheet of paper next to her computer. "Looks like Detectives Howell and Raymond are next up," she said.

Deb Howell was a longtime detective at this point. Recently promoted Garth Raymond was still a newbie.

"I'll let them know, along with the CSIs," Tica said.

"And also Doc Baldwin?"

Kendra Baldwin was Cochise County's resident ME.

"Yes, ma'am," Tica said. "After the bullpen, she's next on my list."

"You might also give Marianne Maculyea a call," Joanna added. "The guy who found the body may be in need of some emotional support."

Reverend Marianne Maculyea was not only Joanna's pastor, she was also her best friend. In addition, she served as the Cochise County Sheriff's Department chaplain.

"Tell everyone I'm on my way."

Years earlier, Joanna had been married to her first husband, Deputy Andy Brady, who had been in the process of running for the office of sheriff against his boss. Shortly before the election, Andy had been murdered, shot dead by a drug cartel hit man. In the aftermath of her husband's death, Joanna had been persuaded to run for office in his stead even though she herself had never been involved in law enforcement.

Once she won, most people had assumed she'd be little more than a figurehead. Instead, she had sent herself through police academy training and learned how to be a professional law enforcement officer. From the start she had considered it part of her duty as sheriff to personally visit the scene of every homicide that occurred inside her jurisdiction. Now well into her third term in office, she still did.

Pushing away from her desk and all its attendant paperwork, she walked as far as the door leading to the reception area where her secretary, Kristin Gregovich, held sway, accompanied by Spike, the department's now retired K-9, who was sleeping peacefully on a dog bed stationed next to her desk.

"Homicide up by San Simon," Joanna announced.

"You're going?" Kristin asked.

Joanna nodded. "No idea when I'll be back."

She left via her office's back door, one that opened directly on her reserved parking place. Even though the victim may have been deceased for some time, Joanna used lights and sirens to get there. San Simon was located in the far northeastern corner of Joanna's jurisdiction. At posted speeds the trip would have taken more than two hours. With lights and sirens, she arrived in just under an hour and a half.

CHAPTER 5

THEY SAY IT HAPPENED LONG AGO THAT THE *Spirit of Goodness, I'itoi, was out walking with Tash—the Sun. I'itoi looked back and saw that a man and woman were following them.*

I'itoi waited for the man and woman and showed them which way Sun would travel. He explained to them that some of the paths traveled by Sun made things hot while others made them cold.

All that day the man and woman traveled with I'itoi and Tash. At the end of the day, I'itoi told the man and woman that they must always live among the Desert People, the Tohono O'odham, and watch them to make sure Sun didn't make things too hot or too cold. Since this did not seem to be very hard work, the man and woman agreed.

This man and woman happened to have four sons. The two older ones always played together and never had anything to do with the younger ones except to tease them and pick on them. The mother had to watch all the time to keep the two little ones from being hurt. As the years passed, the children became more and more quarrelsome. Eventually the mother died, and the father had no peace in his house because of all the quarreling.

By now there were many people on Earth, and they began complaining. Some thought there was too much sun and not enough rain. Others said that every day was too much like the other days.

The four brothers heard all the people talking, and they began planning how they would change things once it came time for them to take their father's place.

DAN PARDEE SAT ON THE FOOT OF THE BED, watching his wife, Lani, weave her hair into a long silver braid, which she then pinned in a circle at the back of her head. He loved watching her do that and always had. When they'd first met and married, Dr. Lani Walker-Pardee's shoulder-length hair had been jet black. She was only in her late thirties now, but two years of doing hand-to-hand combat with Covid at the Sells Indian Hospital in Sells, Arizona, had taken its toll. Initially she'd tried to hold off the encroaching gray by dyeing her hair, but then Madeline Juan, the town's sole beautician, had fallen victim to Covid. Once her shop closed, Lani's all-black hair had gone completely gray.

She was good-natured about it. She sometimes jokingly referred to herself as "Old White-Haired Woman," the hero of the family's favorite

Tohono O'odham legend, but Dan knew it bothered her even if she pretended it didn't. Truth be
told, these days touches of gray were appearing
at Dan's own temples. He had seen the com-
mercials about men retouching their hair. Some
other time he might have been tempted to give
one of those products a try, but out of loyalty to
Lani, he hadn't succumbed.

"I wish you didn't have to go," she said, quietly catching his eye in the reflection of the
bathroom mirror.

"I do, too," he agreed, "but Rosa Rios has
been dead for three years. Now that her remains
have finally been identified, I need to talk to the
officers who investigated the crime scene. Once
I do that, I'll need to go to Bylas and see the victim's mother. I want to be the one who delivers
the news."

"You're a fed these days, you know," Lani reminded him as she finished with her hair. "What
makes you think whoever's in charge down in
Bisbee will bother giving you the time of day?"

"There is that," Dan agreed thoughtfully.

While Lani headed for the kitchen to make
breakfast, Dan climbed into the shower where
he continued to consider the problem under a
stream of hot water. Unfortunately there was a
good deal of truth in what Lani had implied.
In his current position Dan Pardee really was a
fed—a field officer for a newly formed branch of
the US government called the Missing and Murdered Indigenous People Task Force, or MIP,
for short. The agency had been created at the di-

rection of the Department of the Interior secretary. Its main purpose was to investigate and put right how law enforcement agencies all over the country had dealt with both solved and unsolved cases involving the deaths and disappearances of Native American victims.

Everyone seemed to agree that this was a problem long in need of being addressed, but MIP was the first-ever broad-based, systematic attempt by the federal government to actually do so. To come to grips with the extent of the issue, law enforcement agencies throughout the country had been asked to provide information on all applicable cases. At that point MIP investigators, dubbed "field officers," would then examine the submitted materials and take whatever course of action they deemed necessary. As a consequence, MIP arrived on the scene as a fully operational cold case unit operating on a massive scale. Current and former law enforcement officers of Indigenous descent were encouraged to apply to be field officers, and Dan Pardee had been among the first to submit an application.

For years he had worked with the Shadow Wolves, a Border Patrol unit made up entirely of Native American officers who patrolled the challenging stretch of international border inside the boundaries of the Tohono O'odham Nation. It was rough, desolate terrain where the Shadow Wolves, all of them experienced trackers and often patrolling on horseback, attempted to control illegal border crossings. Some of the crossers were ordinary migrants in search of the

American dream, but others were armed and dangerous criminals engaged in various cartel-sponsored smuggling operations.

Smugglers of both drugs and people had little regard for human life. Their so-called mules, the people who traveled the burning desert carrying drug- or cash-laden backpacks, were totally expendable and were often abandoned to die of heat and dehydration. The same thing happened to many of the hopeful migrants who, after forking over exorbitant fees for being transported to the US, were left to die in the unrelenting desert. More often than not, the Shadow Wolves, while dodging bullets from cartel-paid snipers, ended up supplying emergency medical care to migrants who otherwise would have perished.

Initially, Dan had been gung-ho about working with the Shadow Wolves, but over time he had lost heart. For one thing, while the never-ending stream of human suffering continued, no one in government seemed the least bit interested in doing anything about it. And while the officers struggled to make ends meet on their less than generous salaries, they had almost daily encounters with the vast amounts of money changing hands along the porous Mexican border. More than once they had found what they presumed to be a backpack filled with illegal drugs only to discover it was stuffed with bundles of hard cold cash.

A number of years earlier, one of the Shadow Wolves, a man named Henry Rojas, had fallen victim to the temptation posed by all that money and had become involved in a scheme transporting blood diamonds into the States. Henry's participation had ultimately resulted in the deaths of three young brothers from the reservation, but his involvement hadn't come to light until after Henry himself had been found shot to death by the woman running the illicit operation.

Henry, someone widely respected on the reservation, had been Dan's immediate supervisor. His unexpected fall from grace had hit everyone hard. From that moment on, Dan's participation in the Shadow Wolves had turned into a job rather than a mission. When a chance for him to jump ship had come along, he had done so. He was one of the first of the sixty or so MIP field officers to sign on. Each was assigned to work cases from a particular area. As one of the first hirees, he'd had his choice of location, and Dan had opted to handle Arizona, a decision that allowed him to accept the job without disrupting Lani's already well-established career path with the Tohono O'odham Nation.

MIP had officially opened for business in January of 2022. At first cases had barely trickled in. Some agencies and jurisdictions had responded immediately. Others had been much slower on the trigger. However, now with the threat of the loss of federal funding hanging over their heads, previously reluctant agencies were beginning to comply, and Dan's trickle of cases was fast becoming a flood. He happened to know that the Cochise County Sheriff's Department had been one of the last of his agencies to comply. That suggested Dan's arrival on the scene was likely to be less than welcome.

By the time he entered the kitchen, he'd made up his mind about how to handle the situation. "I'll stop by Brian's office on my way to Bisbee," he told Lani. "I expect he'll be able to give me a hint about the lay of the land down south."

The Brian in question was the newly elected Pima County sheriff, Brian Fellows. In what Lani sometimes referred to as her "duct-taped-together family," Brian was someone who, without being a real blood relation, was none-theless considered to be not only Dan's brother-in-law but also his kids', Micah and Angie's, beloved uncle.

"Good idea," Lani said. "He'll set you straight." After a pause, she added, "Do you think you'll be back tonight?"

Dan shrugged. "That depends on what goes on in Bisbee. I'm pretty sure I'll head for Bylas directly from there. I may or may not end up staying over. What about you?"

"As soon as I get off work, the kids and I will head into town to Mom's," Lani answered. "I've asked Lucy to heat the pool. That way, the kids can swim, Lucy can have a break, and I'll . . ."

Lani's voice drifted away into silence, and Dan understood why. He barely remembered his own mother. Lani's mother, Diana Ladd Walker, was still alive, but increasingly frail and in need of care.

Lucy Rojas, Diana's hired caretaker, was actu-ally the widow of that disgraced Shadow Wolf, Henry. At the time of her husband's death, Lucy had been a nurse at the hospital in Sells, but once Henry was gone, overcome with shame,

Lucy had left the reservation; however, she and Lani had remained in touch. For a time Lucy had worked at Kino Community Hospital in Tucson, but once the Covid burden was more than she could handle, Lani had asked if she would consider becoming Diana's caretaker. Lucy had accepted the position and now occupied the part of the Walker/Ladd household where Lani's beloved but long-departed godmother, Rita Antone, had once lived.

Lani was standing at the kitchen stove with her back to Dan. He crossed the room and put his arm around her waist.

"Gotcha," he said quietly. "Every moment you can spend with your mom right now is precious."

CHAPTER 6

PIMA COUNTY SHERIFF BRIAN FELLOWS SAT AT his desk and breathed in the peace and quiet. When former Sheriff Jack Abernathy had resigned while under investigation by the FBI on federal corruption charges, Brian Fellows had decided to take a run at the office himself. He'd been elected in a blowout, leading his nearest competitor by a ten-point margin.

Brian was hardly a newcomer to law enforcement—he'd practically cut his teeth on it. The idol of his life had been his stepbrothers' father, Brandon Walker, a man who had previously occupied this very office. Brian's mother, Janie, had been Brandon's first wife. When he had shipped out to Nam, although she was already the mother of two boys, she hadn't exactly kept the home fires burning while her husband was gone. In fact, she was pregnant with Brian before her Brandon returned from overseas. Since the number of months involved didn't exactly measure up in the paternity department, a divorce soon followed.

Brian's first memories of Brandon had been when he came by the house to pick up his own sons, Quentin and Tommy, to take them on non-custodial parental weekend outings. Brian didn't know how many weekends he had stood there, brokenhearted, watching the three of them drive off to wherever they were going. Then one day, something magic had happened. Brandon had gotten out of the car, walked back up the sidewalk, and asked Brian if he wanted to come along. Boy, did he ever! And from then on, if Brandon took Quentin and Tommy for a ride, Brian went, too.

Naturally, his stepbrothers had hated Brian's guts. Then something else wonderful happened. Brandon married a woman named Diana Ladd, a widow with a son of her own. Diana's Davy and Brian became such close friends that they could just as well have been brothers. Later, when Brandon and Diana adopted a little girl they named Lani, Brian had regarded her as his "little sis."

Considering Brian's very real case of hero worship for Sheriff Brandon Walker, it was hardly surprising that he had gone into law enforcement, joining the Pima County Sheriff's Department while Brandon still was at the helm. Brian had stayed on first as a deputy and later as a detective long after Brandon was voted out of office despite the fact that Bill Forsythe, the next sheriff, had made Brian's life as miserable as possible.

Forsythe had still been sheriff when, assigned to work without backup, Brian had gotten caught up in a carjacking that had evolved first into a high-speed chase and eventually a freeway wreck. The carjacked woman and her baby, having managed to escape from their vehicle, had suddenly found themselves in the path of another speeding vehicle. Brian had succeeded in pushing them out of the way, thus saving their lives but at great cost to himself.

After the incident he had spent months first in the hospital and later in rehab. When it was made clear that he'd never walk again, he thought his life was over. But then his wonderful wife, Kath, had given him a swift and much-needed kick in the butt. "Are you going to use that wheelchair as an excuse to be a bump on a log for the rest of your life," she had demanded, "or are you going to do something about it?"

Brian had chosen the latter. He had gone back to school and earned a master's degree in public administration from the University of Arizona. That degree combined with his previous experience in law enforcement had landed him a job as assistant chief of police in Tucson, and that was what he had been doing when Forsythe retired. For a moment, Brian had considered standing for election, but he had let the urge pass, and Jack Abernathy, a guy Brian had regarded as a worm, was elected sheriff. Two years later, under FBI investigation on police corruption charges,

Abernathy had been forced to resign. That was more temptation than Brian could resist. He had run and won handily. Brian's only regret was that Brandon Walker was gone by then and didn't live to see it. The old guy had passed away months earlier, succumbing not to Covid, but to a massive stroke.

A special election had been held in November 2021, and Brian had been sworn into office in early January. His office at the sheriff's department came equipped with a private restroom, but no one had anticipated that at some point in time the duly elected sheriff would also be a paraplegic. He soon discovered that the facilities reserved for his private use were anything but handicapped accessible. Correcting the situation had been the start of a three-month ordeal during which his office was in a constant state of construction. It may have been a county building, but numerous permits had to be obtained, posted, and signed off on. Brian's attempts to do his new job had been complicated by the steady parade of plumbers, electricians, carpenters, drywall installers, and painters meandering through his office. Today at last, the job was finished. Earlier that morning the final inspection had been signed off on, and Brian was relishing a few moments without disruption. That's when his phone rang.

"There's a man out here asking to see you," Donna announced. Donna Loper had been secretary to four different Pima County sheriffs so far, starting with Brandon Walker. Brian expected she would probably outlast him as well. He wished, for the hundredth time, that she'd be kind enough to mention the waiting guest's name when she made those cryptic notifications, but that would have required teaching a very old dog a new trick.

"Fair enough," Brian said. "Send him in."

Since standing wasn't an option, Sheriff Fellows generally rolled his chair around the desk to greet arriving visitors, and he was nothing short of delighted when Dan Pardee strode into the room.

"Why, Dan!" Brian exclaimed. "What a surprise! How the hell are you, and how's your new job?"

"I could ask you the same thing," Dan replied with a grin. "Looks like you landed a pretty posh gig yourself."

"Today it's fine," Brian returned, "but it hasn't been easy. For the last three months they've been trying to fix the bathroom so it would work with my wheels here," he said, patting the arm of the chair. "That has been quite the undertaking, and I'm glad it's finally over. Have a seat. What's up? You MIPWhatevers—I can never remember all those initials—got our list of cases, right?"

"Just did," Dan answered. "It came in sometime last week." As he recalled, there were twenty-seven cases on the Pima County Sheriff's Department list, and he was only starting to look into them.

"Is that why you're here?" Brian asked.

Dan nodded. "The victim is from the San Carlos. Her charred remains turned up in Cochise

County three years ago and remained unidentified until just now when her dental records,
newly submitted to NamUs, matched those of
the homicide victim found in 2019. That's where
I'm headed today," Dan added. "I'm on my way
to Bisbee to talk to both the sheriff whose officers discovered the body as well as the ME
there, the one who did the autopsy."

"What does any of this have to do with me?"
Brian asked.

"Sheriff Brady only reported one MIP-related
case, and I'm on my way there to discuss it, but I
was wondering what you could tell me about her.
Will I be walking into a situation that's likely to
blow up in my face?"

By then Brian had rolled his chair back to the
far side of the desk. "I doubt it," he said. "As far as
I know, Sheriff Brady's a pretty straight shooter.
When I went to my first sheriffs' association
meeting last month, she wasn't there—some
kind of scheduling conflict, but some of the
guys in attendance couldn't wait to tell me how
at a meeting up in Page years ago, she played
poker with the boys. I don't know if it was Texas
Hold'em or Five Card Draw, but she beat the
socks off Old Bill Forsythe—really cleaned his
clock. As far as I'm concerned, it couldn't have
happened to a nicer guy."

"Since she beat some random guy at poker,
you think she's okay?" Dan asked.

"Bill Forsythe was a jerk, and she whipped his
ass in public in a roomful of his peers. As far as
I'm concerned, it doesn't get much better than
that. However, I've yet to hear anyone running

her down, except for the guy who ran against her last election and lost. She beat the crap out of him, too, by the way, but tell me about your case."

"Her name was Rosa Rios," Dan began. "She grew up in Bylas. Left there for Tucson right out of high school. Had some drinking issues at one time, but she'd apparently cleaned up her act. In 2019, she and a couple of friends from back home went to the rodeo in Tucson on Saturday and then ended up at a happening place near the rodeo grounds, a joint called the Buckeroo. Her friends were evidently living it up that night. Rosa wasn't. There was some kind of disagreement over that. When closing time came around, Rosa was nowhere to be found and was never heard from again. A couple of months later her charred remains turned up on a ranch between Bowie and San Simon."

"Couldn't they have identified the body from dental records?"

"Tried, but didn't get a match."

"You say all this happened back in 2019?" Brian asked.

"Yes, over Rodeo Weekend."

"And she disappeared from the Buckeroo?" Brian asked. "That place isn't exactly the Ritz, but it's inside the Tucson city limits. Was Tucson PD notified?"

"Ida Rios, Rosa's mother, told me she called in to report that her daughter was missing."

"She did?" Brian asked with a frown. "I don't remember hearing a thing about it."

"I'm not surprised," Dan told him. "Rosa was from a reservation. My guess is you never heard about it because no report was actually taken. That's the whole reason behind MIP," he added. "Indigenous people disappear all the time, and nobody gives a rat's ass."

"But you do," Brian observed.

"Yes, I do," Dan agreed.

Brian picked up a nearby Post-it pad and a pen. "What did you say the victim's name was again?"

"Rosa," Dan replied, "Rosa Elena Rios, from Bylas, Arizona."

Brian jotted it down. "Where the hell is Bylas?"

"On the far side of Safford, over near the New Mexico border."

"Never heard of it," Brian said.

"It's not exactly a bustling metropolis," Dan told him. "Less than two thousand people live there."

Brian pushed the note aside. "I still have some connections inside Tucson PD," he said thoughtfully. "I'll make a couple of calls."

"Thanks," Dan said, standing up to go. "Appreciate it."

But Brian stopped him before he could leave. "With both Davy and Brandon gone now, how's Diana doing?"

Davy Ladd had been Brian's best friend growing up. Three years earlier, in the aftermath of a bitter divorce, Davy's former wife, Candace, had taken their son, Tyler, and headed back home to

Chicago. Lani, Davy's adoptive sister, had never been especially fond of Candace, and she had always considered Tyler to be a spoiled brat.

Shortly after the divorce was finalized, Davy had perished in a one-car rollover driving back to Tucson from Phoenix on I-10. Both Lani and her mother had been devastated by the loss. Diana had loved her daughter-in-law and doted on her grandson. When neither Candace nor Tyler had bothered to return to Tucson to attend Davy's funeral, Diana had been crushed.

Davy's death was eventually ruled to be accidental, but privately Lani maintained it was a suicide. At the time of the wreck, her brother had been driving drunk without bothering to engage his seat belt. Since he hadn't gotten around to changing the beneficiary designation on his life insurance policies, Candace had made out like a bandit.

Diana's steady decline had started with Davy's death and worsened from there. When Brandon died two years later, it seemed as though she simply gave up on living. The spinning pottery wheel in Diana's studio that had once given her so much joy was now still. Like his wife, Dan Pardee believed Diana Ladd wasn't long for this world, but he didn't want to say that out loud.

"Not very well," he allowed, responding to Brian's question. "Losing them both has been really hard on her. I doubt she'll ever completely recover."

Brian nodded sadly. "Kath and I will try to stop by soon, I promise."

"Don't wait too long," Dan cautioned. "Lani

and the kids will be here in town over the weekend. I know they'd love to see you."

"We'll do our best."

At that point, the two men shook hands. "Safe travels," Brian said, "and good luck with Sheriff Brady. I think you'll be pleasantly surprised."

CHAPTER 7

AT LAST THE FATHER WEARIED OF ALL THE *talking and arguing. He called his four sons together and told them that it was time for them to take his place and watch to see if Tash was making things too hot or too cold. Each boy was supposed to have his own regular turn, and each turn would last for the same length of time. During that time, the days would be the same ones he wished for, and the youngest son would take the first turn.*

When the youngest son set off with Tash that morning, he was a quiet, gentle child. Along the way he stopped and looked at every tree and bush. Under his gaze the leaves—hah hahhag—turned green— chehthagi—and beautiful—kehg.

The boy whistled and called to U'u whig, the Birds. They came in great numbers. They were very happy. They all sang and began building nests—ko'kosh. The boy loved the earth—Jeweth—and wherever he touched the ground it became covered with green while the skies above turned blue. If the sun became too hot, the boy called Juhk O'othham—Rain Man, Chewagi O'othham—Cloud Man, and Hewel O'othham—Wind Man to cool things off, and all the people were happy.

And even to this day, this time of the younger brother is called Shonkam, Spring.

LEAVING BRIAN'S OFFICE, DAN STOPPED FOR gas. The powers that had created MIP had somehow failed to include any kind of motor pool arrangement. Dan's territory, which included literally thousands of square miles, required a lot of driving. At the time Dan had signed on, Lani had suggested that they purchase a new car to go along with his new job, but he had refused, preferring to stick with his beater, an almost ten-year-old Tahoe.

Admittedly, the aging vehicle was a gas guzzler, but that was hardly a problem since he was reimbursed for every mile driven for work purposes as long as he maintained meticulous records. In his opinion, as long as the Tahoe's AC continued to work, he was keeping it. Once the AC gave out, it would be time for a trade-in, but in terms of practicalities, driving an older, ragtag vehicle was exactly what was called for. On the various Indian reservations Dan visited in the course of his work, driving a battered SUV made his presence less conspicuous.

As Dan Pardee left Tucson and drove toward Cochise County, the irony of his situation wasn't lost on him. The desert landscape, stretching as far as the eye could see on either side of I-10, had once been home to free-ranging Apaches. The Chiricahua Mountains, which had once been home to the Chiricahua Apaches, rose up out of the Sulphur Spring Valley to the east. Cochise Stronghold was also nearby. In that rock-bound part of the Dragoon Mountains the great Apache chief, Cochise, had once taken refuge with his people. Geronimo, too, had roamed these parts, but nowhere was there any hint of that Indigenous history. It was as though the county bearing his name had completely erased all evidence of that long-ago warrior and leader. As for the Chiricahua Apaches who roamed these hills and valleys? They were now housed in other locations, including on the San Carlos—the same place Rosa Rios had once called home.

Ironically, the Chiricahua Apaches and the San Carlos were both part of Dan Pardee's personal history, too—at least on his mother's side. It seemed likely that Adam Pardee, his father— the Anglo Hollywood stuntman who murdered Dan's mother, Rebecca Duarte Pardee—had emerged fully formed from the depths of hell itself. It seemed odd to Dan that this desolate stretch of desert from which his forebears had sprung could be so foreign to him. After his father was sent to prison, Dan had been raised by his grandparents, Micah and Rachel Duarte, in an English-speaking household near the town of Safford, where his grandfather had lived and worked and where Dan himself had attended school. Although the San Carlos was a mere thirty miles away, there had been almost no mention of the Apaches in his classes there, and nothing at all about their culture or language.

Dan recognized the plants and wildlife he drove past along the way, but he had worked among the Tohono O'odham for so long that he knew them by their TO names rather than their Apache ones. Among the Desert People, the single word *ohb* means both Apache and enemy, so naturally, when he had first started working there, the people had distrusted him. They had called him the *Ohb* and given him a wide berth. Now, though, he was sometimes called *S'Ohb*, which means Apache in a good way, or even *Nawoj Ohb*, which means Friendly Apache. A major part of Dan's level of acceptance on the TO was due to his marriage to Lani. She was a doctor, yes, not to mention the chief medical officer of the only hospital on the reservation, but she was also an honored and greatly respected traditional medicine woman.

Lani's university education had been bought and paid for with assistance from the tribe, on the condition that she come home and use her medical schooling to benefit her people. The medicine woman part had been carefully passed on, one generation to another by a line of previous holders of that title—including Lani's beloved godmother, Rita Antone, also known as Nana *Dahd* but who, as a child, had been called Dancing Quail. The stories and teachings Rita passed on to Lani were the same ones Dancing Quail had learned at the knees of her grandmother, *Oks Amichuda*, Understanding Woman.

Those two had provided the foundation of Lani's medicine woman training. The rest had come via a blind old medicine man named Looks at Nothing, and from Rita's nephew, Fat Crack Ortiz.

Lani was generous about sharing those ancient stories and traditions with anyone who cared to listen, and most especially with her own children. When it was time for her to pass along the TO's Winter Telling Tales to an enthralled Angie and Micah, Dan often listened in as well, always feeling remorseful that he had no Apache stories of his own to share with them.

Halfway to Benson, when a black-winged buzzard abandoned a choice piece of carrion on the blacktop and rose slowly into the air in front of the speeding Tahoe, Dan knew that, among the Desert People, that particular bird was called *nuhwi*. As for that poor, tire-flattened jackrabbit? He was *mikithwuikd*. And was *Ban*, the Tohono O'odham's Coyote, the same kind of trickster for the Apaches that he was for the TO? And although Dan knew all those animals by their Tohono O'odham names, he regretted that he had no idea what the Apaches called them.

The same held true for passing vegetation. The last week in March a small rainstorm had blown through southern Arizona. As a result the ocotillo along the road sported a bright green covering of tiny green leaves, ones that sprouted overnight after that first drop of moisture hit the ground and which dried up almost as fast. For the Desert People, ocotillo was called *melhog*, mesquite *kukiu*, prickly pear *nahkag*, and saguaro *hahshani.* So what did his own people call these things?

But, of course, his own people weren't really his, either. Half Anglo and half Apache, he didn't quite fit in anywhere. He barely remembered his mother. Dan knew now that she had once been strikingly beautiful, but that hadn't been obvious in the early school-age photos of her that had adorned the walls of his grandparents' home. Over time the photos had changed; the girl in what was clearly a senior portrait had been an absolute knockout. Shortly after graduation and hoping for a career in the movies, Becky had packed her bag and hitched a ride to Bowie where she had flagged down an LA-bound Greyhound bus, heading for California to make her fortune.

Unfortunately, Rebecca Duarte's Hollywood accomplishments hadn't measured up to her dreams. She landed a few bit parts here and there, mostly in TV westerns, but that was about it. On the set of one of those, she had caught the eye of a handsome stuntman named Adam Pardee. They had married quickly and had a son, but their stormy, tumultuous marriage had come to a tragic end, with Rebecca lying shot dead on the living room floor of their apartment while her terrified four-year-old son cowered under the bed in his room.

Years later, a true crime writer wrote a book entitled *Return of the Stuntmen*. It recounted the stories of three different Hollywood stuntmen who, after being convicted of murdering their wives or girlfriends, had all, after serving their individual sentences, simply resumed their lives and careers almost as though nothing had happened. The book briefly provoked a small amount of outrage, but what it had done for Dan was provide an image of his mother—a glamorous publicity headshot—that he would never have seen otherwise. The photo had predated his mother's involvement with Adam Pardee. There had been no hint of glamour in the woman Dan remembered. Her husband had stolen all of that away.

Lost in thought, the miles of highway unspooled in front of him, with the voice of his dashboard-mounted GPS issuing occasional directions. He was jolted out of his reverie when he entered the short tunnel at the top of Mule Mountain Pass. Exiting the tunnel, he drove down a stretch of highway carved into gray limestone cliffs, while on the far side of what was evidently a narrow canyon with small houses, many of them still wearing tin roofs, perched precariously on steep hillsides covered with red shale. Dan didn't know what exactly he had expected Bisbee to look like, but he hadn't anticipated that so much of it would be hidden from view.

A mile or so from the tunnel, the highway wound its way around a flat curve that was clearly part of a long defunct open-pit mine. After passing behind what must have once been a small business district, the GPS directed him around a traffic circle. Exiting that he drove for what seemed like another mile beside an enormous copper-colored tailings dump—a long flat mesa made up of dirt and rock extracted from the gigantic hole in the ground he had seen minutes earlier. Dan was no stranger to those ugly man-made mesas. He had seen them near other Arizona mining communities—Clifton, Morenci, Safford—so he knew exactly what this one was.

Moments later, Dan was out in the desert and driving on relatively flat ground. Just as he began to believe he had missed the Cochise County Justice Center, the voice from the GPS offered him reassurance. "Your destination is half a mile ahead on the left."

Okay, Dan said to himself, switching on the directional signal. *Let's see how this goes.*

CHAPTER 8

ONCE AGAIN, SHERIFF JOANNA BRADY WAS NOT having a good day at the office. It was April Fools' Day, all right, and the joke was on her. Two of her deputies were out for today and most likely for the next several days as well. One had taken a bad fall while out hiking with his son's Cub Scout troop, setting a bad example as far as hiking safety was concerned, but giving his boys the opportunity to practice some of their newly acquired first aid skills. Fortunately, with the scoutmaster's cell phone handy, the boys had also been able to summon help.

The second one was in Tucson where his wife, who had suffered through a very challenging pregnancy, was now undergoing an emergency cesarean. Joanna's fingers were crossed that both mother and child—a boy—would come through fine, but with a department that was chronically shorthanded, covering the missing officers' shifts in the immediate future was a big problem. Some of her deputies were going to end up having to work overtime, and paying overtime always took big bites out of her budget.

Joanna had delegated Tom Hadlock, her chief deputy, to stand in for her at an emergency Board of Supervisors' meeting while she did hand-to-hand combat with revising the duty roster. She was closing in on finishing that when Kristin poked her head into the office.

"Someone to see you," she said.

Joanna glanced at her watch. It was almost noon. She had planned on having lunch with Marianne Maculyea that day. The two women tried to have lunch together at least once a week, just to help keep each other on an even keel. These days, as often as not, Kendra Baldwin, the ME, made it a threesome.

"Who is it?" Joanna asked.

Kristin shrugged. "Beats me," she said. "The front office says his name is Daniel Pardee. His business card says he's a field officer for some kind of agency that comes with a whole lot of letters."

"So a fed of some kind?" Joanna asked.

"Probably," Kristin agreed.

"All right," Joanna said with a resigned sigh. "Send him in."

From her previous experiences with the alphabet soup guys, some good and some bad, the sheriff more than half expected some smarmy suit-clad little guy who would give her a half-assed smile full of too many too white teeth, flash a shiny badge in her face, and assure her he was "here to help." What she didn't antici- pate was the tall, dark, and handsome hunk Kristin ushered into her office. He wore a blue plaid western shirt, well-worn Levi's, and a very snazzy pair of Tony Lama boots. His eyes were a striking gray-green hazel. His left hand car- ried a white Stetson while his right hand was extended in greeting.

"I'm Daniel Pardee," he said apologetically. "Sorry to drop in unannounced."

Joanna rose from behind her desk and stepped forward to greet him. Shaking hands had gone out of style for a while, but she, for one, was glad it was coming back.

"And I'm Sheriff Joanna Brady," she said after exchanging handshakes and before sitting back down. "Have a chair," she invited. "What can I do for you, Mr. Pardee?"

He fumbled in the pocket of his shirt and pulled out a business card that he passed across the desk to her. The somewhat crooked grin that accompanied his words suggested that he prob- ably hadn't had an up-close-and-personal rela- tionship with an orthodontist back when he was a kid.

Joanna studied the card. It identified Daniel Pardee as the Arizona field officer for an agency called MIP—Missing and Murdered Indigenous People, a division of the Department of the Interior. The card listed two phone numbers and a PO box in Sells, Arizona.

"Your office is in Sells?" she asked.

"No," he replied. "My office is the interior

of the old Chevy Tahoe that's parked outside. I actually live in Sells."

"You must be an Indian then?"

He nodded. "Half," he said, "but enough that they let me stay there. My wife is a doctor who runs the hospital on the reservation."

"Presumably you're here about that dental records hit on Rosa Elena Rios?" Joanna asked.

The question seemed to surprise him, as though he hadn't expected Joanna to have any idea about why he'd come calling on this day in particular. And he wasn't far from wrong. Only half an hour earlier Kendra Baldwin, Cochise County's ME, had called to advise Joanna that the charred remains of an unknown female homicide victim found near San Simon years earlier had just been matched to a missing person case from Bylas, Arizona. At the time the body had been found, the remains had been so badly burned that there had been no way to obtain a DNA profile, and imprints of the victim's teeth had yielded no results.

"Yes," Dan replied after a moment. "I'm here about Rosa. She's one of my lost girls."

"Your what?"

"That's what I call the victims in my casebook," he said. "I refer to them that way because that's usually what they are—girls in their teens or young women in their twenties who make bad choices and end up missing, dead, or both."

"I know the statistics," Joanna interrupted, cutting him off, "and they're appalling. And you guys—you MIP people—are out to solve them."

"As many as can be solved," Dan asserted.

"We've had requests from there to provide information on applicable cases. I knew about Rosa's, of course," she said, holding up a Post-it with Rosa's name on it, "but we've been too shorthanded to research any cases that might have predated my time in office. Our ME notified me of the NamUs match a half hour or so ago. Sells is what, four hours from here?"

"Three."

"So how did you find out about it before we did?"

"Our agency has been focused on collecting information—cataloging victims, generating familial DNA, and gathering dental records wherever possible. Whenever a hit comes in on one of our victims, on either CODIS or NamUs, the MIP field officer assigned to that case is automatically notified right along with all other applicable agencies. Rosa's dental record match turned up on my computer overnight, and I'm an early riser. I came here in hopes of having a chance to see whatever evidence you may have on file and to speak to the original investigators."

"That would be Detectives Deb Howell and Garth Raymond," Joanna answered. "Garth had just been moved up to investigations from patrol. I believe this was his first homicide. I was about to dispatch the two of them to Bylas to do the next of kin."

"That won't be necessary," Dan said. "Since I have a personal connection to Rosa's mother, Ida, I'd rather do that myself. I'll head over to the San Carlos as soon as I leave here."

"That'll be tough," Joanna observed.

Dan shook his head. "I doubt it. The first time I went to visit her, right after I was assigned Rosa's case, she was thrilled beyond words to know that someone besides her still gave a damn about her daughter."

Joanna picked up her phone. "Kristin," she said, "would you please give Casey a call and ask her to bring me the evidence box for the charred remains for that Jane Doe found near San Simon in 2019. I believe Detectives Howell and Raymond were assigned to the case. At the same time, please let her know that, as of this morning, the victim is no longer a Jane Doe. She's Rosa Elena Rios of Bylas, Arizona." Then, after putting down the phone, she added for Dan's benefit, "Casey Ledford is my lead CSI."

"Thanks for your prompt attention to all this," Dan said. "Some jurisdictions aren't nearly so . . . well . . . responsive."

"We do our best," Joanna said, smiling now that the initial tension in the room had evaporated. "I'm curious, though," she added. "It's my understanding that MIP field agents are required to be Native American. If you'll pardon my saying so, you look a lot more like a cowboy than you do an Indian."

Dan laughed. "You're not the first person to mention that," he said agreeably. "As for me? I didn't expect a sheriff to be so . . ."

"So what?" she asked. "You mean you didn't expect me to be a woman?"

"No," he replied. "I didn't expect you to be so short."

Together they both erupted into laughter. After that, the ice between them was officially broken.

Casey Ledford arrived a few minutes later with an evidence box and a murder book, both nearly empty. Between them the two contained precious little material. In terms of physical evidence all that remained were melted bits of a zipper from a pair of off-brand jeans and a few misshapen rivets that came from what was left of a leather purse, which had evidently been emptied before being tossed on the fire.

Casey waited patiently while Dan studied the contents of the box and shuffled through the pages of the murder book. During the autopsy, Dr. Baldwin had determined that the young female was approximately eighteen to twenty years old and five six to five seven in height. She was most likely of Native American descent and had never borne a child. She was missing several teeth, which Kendra indicated had probably been removed postmortem. The investigators who worked the case had reached out to neighboring jurisdictions for a missing person case that might be a match to theirs, but they had come up empty.

"What about the remains themselves?" he asked.

"Those are stored at the ME's office up in old Bisbee," Joanna explained. "I'll be glad to give you directions when you're ready to go there. Dr. Kendra Baldwin, the ME, found that the hyoid bone had been broken, so most likely the victim died of manual strangulation. There were no signs of stab wounds or bullet wounds on any of the bones, but Kendra says our guy probably wasn't a first-timer. Most of the time, when killers attempt to burn their victims in hopes of destroying evidence, they fail to take into account how much of the human body is made up of water, and they end up burning only the side that shows. This guy hung around long enough to make sure both sides burned to ash."

That comment was followed by a moment of silence. "Are you suggesting Rosa's murderer might be a serial killer?" Dan asked.

Joanna nodded. "You can't take that to the bank, but it's what Dr. Baldwin thinks, and it's what I think, too, but maybe that's just women's intuition talking."

"Or maybe it's the voice of experience," Dan supplied.

Joanna's cell phone rang. It was her friend Reverend Marianne Maculyea. "Kendra and I are already at Daisy's," she said. "Are you coming or not?"

"Sorry," Joanna said. "An unexpected visitor showed up. Just a sec." She held her hand over the mouth of the phone and asked Dan, "Have you eaten?"

"Not yet," he answered. "Why?"

"It turns out I'm supposed to have lunch with my pastor and the ME today. Why don't you join us?"

"Sure," Dan said, "I guess."

Joanna uncovered the mouthpiece. "I'll be

there in a few," she said, "and I'll be bringing a guest."

"Who is it?" Marianne asked.

"His name is Dan Pardee," Joanna said into the phone. "He's either a cowboy or an Indian or maybe a little of both."

CHAPTER 9

YOUNGEST BROTHER WAS HAVING SUCH A *good time with the blue skies and green earth that he forgot that his time was over. That's when he met up with his next elder brother, the one who had always played with him. Now it was this brother's turn to have things the way he wanted them.*

Youngest Brother showed the new brother all the things he had done. They visited all the birds in their nests and looked at all the trees and plants. Because the trees and plants loved Youngest Brother, they gave them fruit to eat. But then, because the next elder brother liked things hot, everything that was green turned yellow, and that's when the two brothers fell asleep.

And to this day, nawoj, my friend, the time of the second elder brother is known as Toniabkam, Summer.

————

LATER ON, WHEN DAN WAS TELLING LANI about his lunch in Bisbee, he said it reminded him of one of those old jokes where a priest, a rabbi, and a minister all walk into a bar together. In this case, it wasn't a bar but an old-fashioned diner, and the attendees in question were an Indian, a county sheriff, a medical examiner, and a Methodist minister. And although he had originally thought he was being invited to some kind of girly hen party, that wasn't the case at all.

Initially, Dan had been disappointed to learn that neither of the two detectives directly involved in Rosa's case would be available to him that morning, but shortly after sitting down in the booth at Daisy's, he learned that he'd hit the jackpot. All three of the women seated with him at Daisy's had been at the crime scene the morning Rosa's remains had been discovered. It made sense that Dr. Kendra Baldwin, the medical examiner, would be there. That was only to be expected. He found it commendable that Joanna Brady felt it was her duty to personally be in attendance at the scene of every homicide that occurred inside her jurisdiction. As for Reverend Marianne Maculyea? It turned out she was Bisbee's resident police and fire chaplain. That was why she, too, had been on hand in San Simon the morning Rosa's charred body was found.

Dan had expected lunch would be a casual dining experience where they'd all be tiptoeing around the subject at hand. Instead, over what Dan considered to be top-notch Mexican food, they discussed the case in considerable detail. Like Joanna, Kendra was amazed that an investigator from MIP had shown up almost immediately once the remains had been identified. Now that they had an ID, and once the death notification had been done, the ME needed to know the family's preferences about final arrangements.

"I can release the remains to a mortuary here in Bisbee and have them transport them to Bylas," she explained, "or perhaps it would be better for someone from a mortuary there to come and collect them."

"There isn't a mortuary in Bylas," Dan explained, "or in Fort Thomas, either. The nearest one is thirty miles away in Safford, but when I speak to Ida, Rosa's mother, I'll have her get in touch with you."

"What, if anything, can you tell us about when Rosa disappeared?" Joanna asked.

Since Dan knew more about the case than anyone else, he passed along what he could. "She dropped out of high school without graduating and was living and working in Tucson at the time of her disappearance. Two of her girlfriends from back home—from Fort Thomas High School—showed up in Tucson for Rodeo Weekend. On Saturday, the three of them went out for a night on the town. The two friends were more into partying than Rosa was. When she was ready to go home, they weren't, and there was evidently some disagreement about that. Later on, when closing time came around, Rosa was nowhere to be found. The other two assumed she had just gone home, but that wasn't the case."

"Did Rosa have a boyfriend?" Kendra asked.

"Not that I know of," Dan replied. "When I went to see her mother, that first visit was simply to introduce myself and let her know that Rosa's case had been assigned to me. At the time I collected Ida's DNA, I also asked if she had ever considered having Rosa's dental records sent to any investigative agency. When she said no one had ever mentioned that might be useful, I suggested sending them to NamUs, and she indicated she would."

"And evidently did," Kendra added.

"After that, Ida gave me something of an overview of what was going on around the time Rosa went missing but she made no mention of a boyfriend. However, without knowing for sure if Rosa was dead or alive at that point, I felt it would have been premature to start doing official interviews. As of today that's no longer the case."

"And since the two girlfriends were the last people to see her alive—" Joanna began.

Dan cut her off in midsentence. "Ida insisted that neither of them could possibly have been involved. Given what I've learned about the condition of Rosa's body when it was found, I'm pretty sure that's true. Now, though, things have changed. I plan to have a long talk with both her friends about that weekend on the off chance that they might remember something else from that night, some small detail, that would be helpful, and from here on out, I'll be sharing anything I learn with you and your people."

"Good," Joanna said. "Appreciate it."

Before ordering, the group had informed their waitress that they'd need separate checks. Once the meal ended and they'd paid at the register, Joanna and Dan headed out to the parking lot. Because Dan had followed Joanna from her office to the restaurant, their vehicles were parked side by side. Dan paused at the door of the Tahoe. Standing next to Joanna, the height discrepancy between them was even more pronounced. The top of her red head barely reached his elbow.

"Am I to assume you'll be running lead on this case from now on?" Joanna asked.

Dan nodded. "I'll be able to bring some federal resources to that table that wouldn't necessarily be available to you or your people. But as I said, earlier, I'll keep you apprised of whatever I find. Now, what's the quickest way for me to get from here to Bylas?"

"Go back the way we came," she advised. "Take the first left beyond the Justice Center and then follow the signs north to Willcox and I-10. From there you're on your own. Be advised, it's a long way, probably a good three hours at least."

"I'd best head out then, but thanks for all the help. Now let's solve this thing."

"I think we will," she replied. "At least now we have a starting place, and I'm especially glad someone like you is on the case. You seem to take this personally."

That last comment caught Dan Pardee off guard. It was as though she had somehow peered into his soul and glimpsed what was hiding there.

Because he did take what he was doing personally. His mother's body may have been found, but she, too, had been yet another lost girl.

"Somebody has to," he said.

Minutes later Dan Pardee was back on the road. This morning he had driven to Bisbee with no idea of what to expect. Now as the narrow two-lane highway to Bylas stretched out ahead of him, he knew exactly what awaited him at the end of the road—a mother's heartbreak and desolation.

CHAPTER 10

WHEN EVERYONE HAD STARTED TALKING ABOUT the coming Covid pandemic in early 2020, Charles Milton hadn't paid much attention. As a retired bachelor, he didn't have to go to work every day. He lived alone, traveling the highways and byways in his motor home. He was a serial killer after all. Yes, the media was in full-scale panic mode, pushing people's fear buttons twenty-four seven for all kinds of reasons. Finally he got so tired of it all that he simply pulled the plug on watching the news. Because he had every streaming service known to man loaded into his RV's entertainment center, he watched movies instead—police dramas and true crime shows, especially. He loved all those. And when it came to choosing RV parks, that was always his number-one priority—their Wi-Fi connection. If they didn't have the capacity to support his streaming addiction, he stayed elsewhere.

But it turned out Covid was as bad for serial killers as it was for everyone else, and 2019 had been his last good year. It was a full two years before he made it back to Tucson again, and when he did, things weren't the same. While he'd been away, a lot of his favorite watering holes had dried up and closed. Restaurants he'd once frequented had shut down for good. As for the Sears store where he used to shop for tires? It had turned into a bowling alley, for Pete's sake! So here he was getting ready to head out because the weather was already getting too hot. In the meantime, rather than worrying about the one who had gotten away, Charlie occupied himself by revisiting his past exploits.

Rosa Rios's case had been textbook perfect. He hadn't known her name at the time he was choking the life out of her—and strangling victims was his whole deal. Charlie was a predator all right, just not a sexual one. What he loved was holding some young woman's dainty little throat in his hands and squeezing it until she was nearly to the point of death, usually not just once but several times in a row, until both Charlie and his hands tired of the game. That's when he would go for dessert and finish her off, staring into her agonized face until the light finally went out of her eyes. That was what he lived for— the exact moment when the spark of life was extinguished and the eyes went blank. Somehow screwing women had never quite worked for him. Killing them did.

His mother—damn her soul to hell!—had always told Charlie that he'd never amount to much, but she had been oh so wrong about that! Every time he took one of his victims to the brink and beyond—whenever he was in the throes of those powerful sensations and emotions—he saw himself as godlike if not God himself. After all, he was someone with the power of life and death in his hands. What could be better than that?

He hadn't known Rosa's name at the time he was strangling her or when he was dousing her body with a gallon of Clorox. As far as Charlie knew, bleach was the only remedy that would ensure none of his DNA lingered on her skin or clothing. Nor had he known her name while he'd been using a pliers to yank several trophy teeth out of her mouth. And she'd still been nameless when he soaked her body with gasoline and lit her on fire. Only while standing by the burning pyre, waiting to turn the body over, had he taken the time to sort through the contents of her purse. That's how he had learned her name.

A tribal registry card indicated that she'd been born in Safford, Arizona. At the time it had worried him that, although he was pretty sure San Simon was in a different county, Safford was just up the road from the burn site and a little too close for comfort. He'd flipped a coin about heading east or west on I-10 to dispose of her body. Now he knew heading west on I-10 would have been a better idea. By then, however, the fire was already burning full blast and there was no going back.

Afterward he had hung around Tucson until his usual departure date in April. Leaving early might have raised an eyebrow on the off chance investigators had somehow been keeping an eye on Charlie's comings and goings. Staying on also enabled him to follow local newscasts to determine if the body had been discovered. Almost two months later, just before his departure date, his diligence was rewarded. Stories out of Cochise County reported that unidentified human remains had been found outside the town of San Simon. And that was it. Other news stories followed for the next several days, but nothing that offered any further details or that indicated investigators were making any headway in identifying either victim or perpetrator. And, despite numerous online searches, he found no mention about a missing person named Rosa Rios who had disappeared during Tucson's Fiesta de los Vaqueros.

By the time he left Tucson in 2019 the temperatures were starting to soar. That seemed to be happening earlier and earlier each year, so maybe there was something to all this global warming crap after all. Charlie headed north, all right, but not that far north. His next stopping-off place was at an RV park in a place called Prescott Valley. The community was located on the far side of the Verde Valley, which was not only green at this time of year, it was a hell of a lot cooler than Tucson. Once again, the park he chose was one with an adequate Wi-Fi connection. It was also a place where the on-site manager gave him a hell of a good deal since he always paid in cash and stayed for several months at a time, and that's exactly what he intended to do this time around—stay for a while.

His next targeted venue happened to be the oldest rodeo in the world—Prescott, Arizona's annual Fourth of July celebration, and the scheduling for that was perfect. He liked to separate his "events," as he called them, in terms of both time and distance. Hitting the pause button for five to six months was about right in terms of timing. And not wanting to advertise the presence of a serial killer, he thought it best to vary the ways in which he disposed of bodies.

As a result, during the months he lived in Prescott Valley, he occupied his days by exploring the neighboring wilderness areas. As far as his RVer neighbors were concerned, he was out walking and getting his daily constitutionals. In actual fact, he was searching for exactly the right spot to get rid of his next victim's body. Eventually he found what he needed—an old glory hole, one of millions of abandoned test mining shafts dug and later abandoned by the hopeful prospectors who had scoured the Old West searching for mineral wealth. This one was located in a particularly empty stretch of desert known as Skull Valley, southwest of Prescott proper.

When Independence Day finally rolled around, bringing with it the Prescott Rodeo, Charlie was more than ready. Wearing his face-shielding Stetson and with camera bag in hand, he was right there on Whiskey Row, whooping it up with all the other out-of-control partygoers. He spent a lot of time meandering around town, locating various surveillance cameras. Those on banks and around the courthouse were plentiful and easy to spot, and the bars and restaurants on Whiskey Row and Gurley Street were full of them. But just a few blocks away on South Granite Street, the area around Jefferson Park was virtually devoid of surveillance.

On Saturday afternoon, with his Lexus decked out with a license plate stolen from an almost identical vehicle, he arrived early enough to grab a prime parking spot. This time, rather than targeting someone inside the bar, he'd have to take potluck and see if any likely subjects happened to come his way. He spent most of the evening visiting one rowdy drinking establishment after another, always with the Stetson on his head, but as closing time approached, he headed out.

In terms of electronic surveillance, cameras weren't the only problem he had to take into consideration. Once back at the Lexus, Charlie got rid of his phone. After turning the device to silent, but leaving it turned on, he hid it away in the park, tucking it into an empty Styrofoam cup he had brought along for that precise purpose. He tossed the cup under a thorny bush where it looked for all the world like a piece of discarded trash. Charlie figured that as long as he made it back to collect it before someone got around to cleaning the park on Monday morning, he'd be fine. And, in case anyone ever bothered to study his cell phone's location, it would say that he had been right there in downtown Prescott the whole time and nowhere near Skull Valley.

After that he suited up, donning his hoodie and gloves. Then, after slightly reclining the front passenger seat, Charlie settled in to wait. He was looking for a solo girl, preferably one who was more than slightly tipsy. The first prospect who walked past the Lexus showed up within minutes. Unfortunately for him but fortunately for her, she was far too tall—five ten or so. Taller automatically meant heavier. Since Charlie himself was only about five eight, he generally looked for victims who were on the small side. Generally speaking, tiny girls were easier to overcome and much easier to carry.

After allowing Tall Girl to pass unharmed, he waited for another candidate. It didn't take long, and this one wasn't nearly as lucky. She was suitably alone and far more inebriated. She shambled along the sidewalk, wobbling unsteadily from side to side. Once she staggered past, Charlie opened the door and sprang out after her. In a matter of seconds he overpowered her from behind, dosed her with a rag soaked in chloroform, and manhandled her into the trunk. Once she was properly gagged and zip-tied, he relieved her of her cell phone and car keys. A press of the button on her key fob caused a pair of taillights to flash on a vehicle parked cars ahead of his on the same street.

After depositing her cell phone in that, he returned to his own car and started the engine. By then the chloroform had worn off enough that she had started thumping the trunk lid with her bound feet. The ungodly pounding was worrisome, but as Charlie turned down Whiskey Row to head out of town, there were enough noisy revelers out raising hell in the streets that no one paid the slightest bit of attention. By the time Charlie hit the highway, the kicking ceased.

It's something of a tradition in Arizona that the first monsoon of the season usually arrives on or around the Fourth of July, and one was certainly brewing at this point. As Charlie headed for Skull Valley, he spotted steady glimmers of lightning over the horizon ahead of him. Obviously a storm was on its way, but how soon would it arrive? On the one hand, rain after the fact would be a good thing because it would wash away any telltale tire marks, but rain that came too soon or too hard might leave him stranded either in or on the wrong side of a flooded wash. With his phone still stashed in Jefferson Park in Prescott, if Charlie needed to call a tow truck, he'd literally be up a creek.

By the time he pulled off the road within walking distance of the glory hole, a jagged fork of lightning flashed across the sky above him, followed almost immediately by an earsplitting crack of thunder. The mine shaft was a good half mile across the desert. That's why he had used chloroform to subdue her rather than horse tranquilizer. He had known in advance that he'd need his victim to walk that far under her own steam. But as rain began pelting, the idea of walking seemed out of the question. Skull Valley Wash lay just on the far side of the roadway, and he'd have to make do with that.

As soon as Charlie opened the trunk, his victim was wide awake, and she came out fighting.

Anticipating the removal of at least one of her teeth, he'd stuffed a pair of pliers into the pocket of his hoodie. He used that to smack her hard on the back of her head. Once she went limp from the blow, he dragged her across the road and into the wash.

Charlie had been around the desert long enough to understand the nature of flash floods. In a water-starved desert, you could be standing in a dry, sandy riverbed one minute and be overwhelmed by a twelve-foot wall of water the next. Fearing that possibility, Charlie decided to get things done and over with. Yes, he strangled her all right, but she'd been out cold at the time. Since he'd been unable look her in the eye as it happened, the experience was less than optimal. Later, removing her teeth with the rain-soaked pliers had been incredibly difficult. Once the teeth and the pliers were stuffed in his pocket, he collected one last trophy by yanking a heart-shaped locket from around her neck.

By then, however, the very real possibility of a flash flood roaring downstream negated any attempt to bury the body. Hoping a wall of on-coming water would do the work for him, Char-lie simply left her lying in the wash. Even so, by the time he made it back to the car, the shoulder of the road had already changed to muck and he had a hell of a time negotiating the necessary U-turn that would allow him to head back the way he'd come. With the engine running, steam from his drenched clothing made it almost im-possible for him to see out through the wind-shield, even with the defroster going full blast, while sheets of water covering the glass rendered the wipers virtually useless. The drive back to Prescott was a white-knuckled affair all the way.

Once back in town, Charlie parked on Granite, directly behind his victim's rickety Ford Fiesta where he used the reading lamp to locate her purse and sort through the contents. It contained a package of tissues, two tubes of lipstick, a compact, a package of tampons, a package of condoms, a pack of Marlboros, a lighter, and a wallet. Inside the wallet he found a driver's license that indicated his victim's name was Annika Wallace. She was twenty-nine years old and lived on South Butte Street in Dewey, Arizona. She was five two, blue-eyed, blonde, and weighed a hundred and ten pounds.

In addition to the driver's license, the wallet held twenty-two bucks in cash, and a debit card containing an unknown amount of food stamps, so obviously Annika had been down on her luck long before she'd had the misfortune to walk past Charlie's car. And that was exactly what he needed—another throwaway girl who could disappear without a trace and no one would be the wiser. And if her body ever was found, there'd be no way for law enforcement to link her to Charlie.

Before exiting the Fiesta, he carefully moved the seat setting back to where she'd had it. He left the vehicle, taking both the purse and phone while leaving the keys in the cup holder. Next he collected his own phone from where he'd left it. The cup had done its job and kept it dry throughout the storm, and there had been no missed calls.

Back in the Lexus, Charlie left Granite Street and drove straight back to his RV park in Prescott Valley. There he took his phone inside, noting that it was just after three A.M. when he turned it off and put it on the charger. As far as anyone would be able to tell from his digital footprint, he was home sawing logs for the remainder of the night.

His clothing was still damp from being caught in the storm. After changing into dry duds, Charlie made himself a cup of coffee and then headed out once more. This time he drove as far as Cordes Junction where he turned south on I-17. Ten miles south, he pulled into the Sunset Point rest stop where he dropped Annika's purse, IDs, and cell phone into a dumpster located behind the restrooms. Knowing tie wraps could be traced back to a manufacturer or a retailer, Charlie had collected all the ones he'd used on Annika before leaving the scene. Now he moseyed over to the dog walking area, slipped them into one of the green plastic doggy-doo bags, and dropped that into the appropriate refuse container. It seemed unlikely that anyone in his right mind would go sifting through bags of dog shit to see what else might be hidden there.

With those details handled, Charlie headed home for the night. He was exhausted. On the way, he opened the windows and let rain-dampened desert air blow through the car, noticing as he did so that it was starting to get light in the east. Before the sun rose, he peeled off his latex gloves and tossed them out the window and onto the still-dark shoulder of the highway. For the remainder of the drive, coming down off his adrenaline rush, he had to struggle to stay awake.

It was full daylight by the time Charlie fell into bed. Unfortunately, his all-night adventure with Annika Wallace hadn't been quite the peak experience he'd expected, but it would hold him until the next one came along. What he didn't know right then and what would take months for him to realize was that after Annika, Charlie Milton was in for a long dry spell.

Once the pandemic hit full force in early 2020, grocery stores weren't the only ones who would be faced with supply chain issues. So would serial killers.

CHAPTER 11

NOW IT WAS THIRD BROTHER'S TURN, BUT *when he came looking for his siblings, he could not find them because they were fast asleep. This made Third Brother very angry, and he sent Wind Man to find them. Once they were awake, he drove them home, scolding them every step of the way. Wind Man heard Third Brother's angry scolding, so he began scolding and screeching, too, the same way he does to this day when it is time for Third Brother to have his turn and have things the way he wants them.*

Then this angry Third Brother took a stick and beat Wind Man because he was not working. Tash was making things too hot, and there were no storms. So Wind Man tried to hide, going low to the ground where he dried up all the leaves and all the green cover of the earth. The Birds were frightened. They hid and did not sing for this brother as they had for

*Youngest Brother. That caused the people to begin
complaining again. The Desert People have no name
for this time of the Third Brother—the time between
Summer and Winter, but the Milghan, the Whites,
call it Autumn, even to this day.*

IT WAS COMING UP ON 5:30 WHEN DAN PARDEE
pulled up in front of Ida Rios's drab home on
Ocotillo Circle in Bylas. The only sign of vegetation in her barren yard were two straggly
mesquite trees that flanked a peeling front door
that may have once been painted a cheerful
shade of turquoise but was now a sun-faded
bluish gray. Dan knew from his first visit that
the doorbell no longer worked, so he knocked
instead with a firm police knock rather than the
kind of gentle tap a visiting neighbor or friend
might have used.

"*Dah-goh-taaah*," Dan said when Ida opened
the door. "How are you?" At least he remembered that much Apache.

She peered up at him. "Do you have news?"

"I do," Dan said, nodding grimly, "and it's not
good. May I come in?"

Without another word Ida held the door open
and beckoned him inside. In the world of Native
Americans, being granted entry into someone's
home is a real privilege. Dan couldn't help but
wonder what his welcome would have been had
not both his grandparents and his mother been
buried less than a mile away in the town's dusty,
sunbaked cemetery.

Ida waited for Dan to take a seat on a butt-sprung sofa. Only when she was settled in a nearby rocking chair did she speak again. "You found her then?" she asked quietly. There were no tears. It seemed likely that so much time had passed since her daughter's disappearance that all the tears in her body had long since dried up.

"Somebody else did," Dan told her. "Rosa's skeletal remains were found a little over three years ago. Her body was dumped in the desert outside San Simon and set on fire. This morning they were identified due to a match with the dental records you forwarded to NamUs. After checking in with the Cochise County Sheriff's Department, I came straight here."

For a moment Ida sat quietly with her hands in her lap while she internalized what he'd just said. "Where?" she asked at last. "Where was she found again?"

"In a patch of pastureland south of I-10 between Bowie and San Simon. The property owner—a rancher—was out checking fence lines when he spotted the remains. He's the one who called in law enforcement."

"And how did she die? Did somebody shoot her?"

Dan shook his head. "I've spoken to Dr. Kendra Baldwin, the Cochise County medical examiner. According to her, Rosa's hyoid bone was broken. That suggests that she was most likely the victim of manual strangulation." Dan paused long enough to extract Kendra's business card out of his pocket and held it out to Ida. "Here's her contact information. Dr. Baldwin would like to hear from you concerning final arrangements."

Ida took the proffered card and studied it silently for the better part of a minute. She seemed to be staring at it, but Dan wondered if she was seeing anything at all.

"I always knew she was dead," Ida murmured at last. "Other people said I should hope that she was still alive and would come home one day, but I always knew she wouldn't."

Another silence followed. Dan was the one who broke it. "Will you bring her home to be buried?"

Ida nodded.

"I can give you the name of the mortuary in Safford, the one that handled my grandfather's funeral," Dan offered.

"I know who to call," she said. "Only one mortuary in Safford does any work here on the res. So what happens next?"

"As of today, Rosa's case is now officially a homicide investigation. I'll be working it in conjunction with the Cochise County Sheriff's Department. They're the ones who were called in on the case when the body was found, although it seems unlikely that the homicide occurred there."

"You mean she was already dead and that's where the killer left her?"

"Yes."

"If you're in charge of the investigation, what will you do next?"

"I didn't interview Rosa's friends the last time

I was here—the ones who were with her in Tucson that weekend. This time I need to speak to them. I won't try to contact them tonight, but if you could give me their names and numbers, I'll reach out to them tomorrow."

"Of course," Ida said. She stood up and disappeared into the kitchen, returning minutes later with a piece of paper that she gave to Dan. On it, written in pencil, were the names Amanda Moreno and Evangeline Joaquin.

"They're both married now and live in Fort Thomas," Ida said. "They used to be Amanda Lewis and Vangie Rodriguez. These are old phone numbers, so I don't know if they still work. Do you want me to call and tell them you're coming?"

"No," Dan said. "Don't bother. It would probably be better if I showed up unannounced."

"Well," Ida said, "if the numbers are disconnected, just ask around town. Someone will know where to find them, and since you don't look like a cop, they'll probably talk to you." The last was accompanied by a hint of a smile.

"Thank you," Dan said, folding the paper and stowing it in the same pocket from which he'd extracted Dr. Baldwin's business card. "Is there anyone I can call for you right now?" he asked. "You probably shouldn't be alone tonight."

"There's really no one," she said. "Besides, I've been alone with this for a long time. Where will you stay?"

"Safford, probably. You're sure there's nothing more I can do for you?"

"No, you've been very kind, and I know you'll do your best to find out who's responsible."

"I will," Dan agreed.

"But there's one more thing I want to know," Ida added. "I want to know why he did it."

"Believe me," Dan said, "so do I!"

Dan let himself out through the front door while Ida remained seated where she was, once again holding the business card, staring at it, and rocking back and forth. He left the house, but he didn't leave town, at least not right away. Instead he drove to Bylas's weedy, barren excuse for a cemetery. It was surrounded by barbed wire meant to deter hungry livestock.

One slow step at a time, Dan made his way through the cemetery to a far corner plot where three small granite headstones were clumped together. His grandparents, Micah and Rachel Duarte, were buried there as was his mother, Rebecca Duarte Pardee. He paused briefly in front of each headstone. Even though he'd only been four at the time, he'd always felt guilty that he'd been unable to save his mother. Pausing in front of her marker Dan said aloud, "I want you to know that because of what happened to you, I'm trying to help others."

Next came his grandmother's headstone. Rachel Duarte had cared for him, but with a certain indifference. He had felt that the things she did for him were more out of a sense of obligation rather than love. Now he suspected that every time she had looked at him, she'd been forced to come face-to-face with someone who looked just like her daughter's killer, but she had fed and clothed him nonetheless. In fact, Rachel was the one who had taught him to drive, so what Dan said to his grandmother was different from what he'd said to his mother. "Thank you for taking me in," he said, "and thank you for everything you did."

Finally he stopped in front of Micah Duarte's headstone and stood there for a very long time. When he spoke at last, what he said was more of a prayer than it was a comment. "You taught me how to be a tracker, Grandpa. Now please help me find the son of a bitch who murdered Ida Rios's daughter."

CHAPTER 12

IT WAS FRIDAY NIGHT AT THE BUTCH DIXON/ Joanna Brady household. When it came to TGIF, there was something to be said for having a former restaurateur/bartender on hand. The chores were done. Butch had grilled steaks for dinner. The dishes had been cleared and loaded into the dishwasher. The kids were bathed and in bed, and now it was time for just the two of them, Butch and Joanna.

Butch had blended Joanna's favorite—a frozen margarita—for her. As for Butch? He was having coffee. Once Joanna went to bed, he'd be retreating to his study to work on his next book. The deadline for that was rapidly approaching, and his best writing time was after the kids' bedtime.

All through the pandemic, he had been the one who kept things at home on track. Once schools shut down, he'd been in charge of over-seeing Denny's switch from in-person to virtual primary school while also supervising two-year-old Sage. He'd had some help from their nanny, Carol Sunderson. Unfortunately she'd been dealing with the same kinds of issues with her own brood—the abandoned grandkids she was raising on her own.

Now, though, with school back in session and Sage enrolled in preschool, things were a little better on the home front. Nonetheless, Butch continued to find that his best writing time came when the rest of the household was asleep.

Butch handed Joanna her beverage. Then, sitting down next to her and putting one arm around her shoulder, he asked, "How was your day?"

Joanna took a sip, smacked her lips appreciatively, and said, "You go first."

"All right then," Butch said. "I suppose I'd better tell you what went on at preschool today."

Every other Friday, parental units at the preschool were required to "volunteer" their services. With Joanna usually having to attend the Board of Supervisors' meeting on Friday mornings, the family's preschool obligations fell on Butch's shoulders. As far as Joanna knew, he was the only father pulling that duty. The other volunteers all were mommies.

"What?" Joanna asked. "Did Sage spill her Kool-Aid again?"

"Nope," Butch said. "The other Friday morning volunteer is Allison Hobbs."

Joanna knew that already. Allison's husband,

Derek, was a newly hired doctor at Bisbee's Copper Queen Hospital.

"Anyway," Butch resumed, "Allison and I were putting out snacks, and she asked how things were going. I told her I was having a devil of a time with chapter eleven. She stopped pouring a pitcher of Kool-Aid, gave me a strange look, and said, 'I'm so sorry. I had no idea you were having financial difficulties.'"

For years, Butch had been writing and publishing cozy mysteries. He was now an acknowledged solid midlist author. His series of books, set in a fictional version of Bisbee called Copper Creek, featured a small-town sheriff named Kimberly Charles whose exploits sometimes bore a surprising resemblance to his wife's. Joanna had learned through experience that when it came time for Butch to write a book, the most difficult part was figuring out how to start. After that, if a story was going to hit a snag and refuse to move forward, that misfortune often occurred somewhere around chapter 11.

Joanna snorted a sip of margarita. "Don't tell me she thought we're declaring bankruptcy."

"I tried to explain I was talking about chapter eleven in the book I'm working on, but I'm not sure she really heard."

"Let's hope she did," Joanna murmured.

"Indeed," Butch said, "let's hope. Now tell me about your day."

So she brought him up-to-date, telling him all about Dan Pardee's unexpected visit to her office. In the process she mentioned that the remains of a murdered female, found near San

Simon some three years earlier, had finally been identified.

"Who was she?" Butch asked. "Someone from around here?"

"Not from here, from Bylas," Joanna answered.

"Where's that?" Butch asked.

"Up near Safford. Her name is Rosa Rios. She went out on the town during Rodeo Weekend in Tucson in February of 2019 and was never seen again. Now we know she's dead."

"Rosa Rios," a frowning Butch repeated thoughtfully. "Why does that name ring a bell?"

Joanna almost dropped her drink. "It does?"

"I think we may have met her."

Now Joanna was utterly dumbfounded. "We did? Where? When?"

"Over in Silver City—at the rodeo there. I'm pretty sure Rosa was the girl who beat out Jenny and Kiddo in the barrel-racing competition that time. I believe Jenny even introduced us after the competition was over."

Joanna felt a lump form in her throat. That Silver City Rodeo had been held years earlier when Jenny and her first horse, Kiddo, had still been competing in junior rodeo events. Joanna had made the trip there, but she'd been called away by some emergency that had caused her to leave before Jenny and Kiddo had taken center stage. It was one of the many instances where she'd regrettably chosen job over family, a shortcoming she was striving not to repeat with the two younger kids.

"Rodeo's a pretty small, tight-knit circle,"

Joanna said, reaching for her phone. "By now Dan has notified Rosa's mother, but I should call Jenny and let her know about this before someone else does."

"By all means," Butch said, standing up to pour another cup of coffee.

Jenny, studying criminal justice at Northern Arizona University in Flagstaff, was in the last two months of her college career.

"It's Friday night," Joanna said when Jenny answered. "Are you at home or out and about?"

"Are you kidding?" Jenny replied. "I've got a huge research paper due first thing Monday morning. What's up?"

Joanna had participated in numerous death notifications over the years, but this was the first time she had ever delivered that kind of news to her own daughter. As far as Joanna knew, Rosa and Jenny hadn't been close, but they were contemporaries and participants in the same sport. Joanna wanted to be sure Jenny heard about Rosa's death from her and not from some TV newscaster.

"Our ME identified some human remains today," Joanna began. "They belong to someone who died three years ago. Unfortunately, Dad and I believe the victim is someone you know."

Joanna heard her daughter's sharp intake of breath.

"Oh, no," Jenny murmured. "Who?"

"Her name is Rosa Rios."

"Rosa?" Jenny repeated. "You mean Rosa from Bylas?"

Joanna knew in that moment that she had

been right in making the call. Jenny had known exactly who Rosa was the moment she heard her name.

"Butch told me he thought you knew her, and I can tell now he was right," Joanna said. "Were the two of you close?"

"Not close," Jenny said, "but we knew each other. She and War Paint beat the socks off Kiddo and me at that junior rodeo over in Silver City. A few months after that, there was a terrible wreck up in Tucson—a semi versus a horse trailer. War Paint was badly injured and had to be put down. I sent Rosa a card after that. It's hard to find sympathy cards for someone who's lost a horse. Jeannine Phillips helped me find one. I never heard back from Rosa, and as far as I know, after that she never competed again. What happened to her?"

"According to the ME, she was strangled. After that her body was burned."

"Couldn't they have identified her from dental records?" Jenny asked.

"They did, but only just now after her mother finally submitted them to NamUs—the National Missing and Unidentified Persons System."

"I know about NamUs, Mom," Jenny said, sounding aggrieved.

"Of course you do," Joanna responded quickly. "I keep forgetting you're a criminal justice major these days. But that's how we made the ID. Rosa's dental records were uploaded to the NamUs database overnight, giving us the hit."

"If somebody strangled her and then burned the body, we're talking about a real sicko," Jenny said. "Are your guys going to be able to track him down?"

"Since my department was involved in locating the body and since Dr. Baldwin succeeded in identifying it, we'll certainly be involved, but probably not primary. It's likely the homicide didn't occur inside county lines and that the San Simon location was just the dump site. A guy named Dan Pardee will be running point. He's with a new federal task force inside the Department of the Interior called Missing and Murdered Indigenous People—MIP for short."

"I've heard about MIP," Jenny said. "It focuses on crimes against Native Americans, and it sounds cool. I looked into it, but people just graduating from college with criminal justice degrees and no experience can't even apply. They only hire people with previous investigative experience with some other jurisdiction."

Joanna knew that her daughter's heart was set on joining the FBI eventually, but that would entail her working for some other law enforcement agency beforehand. She had also heard about some other MIP hiring requirements as well.

"Not only that," Joanna added, "to work for them, you have to have a fair amount of Native American blood in your background. Unfortunately, you don't qualify on that score, either, but have you heard back on any of your internship applications?"

Wanting to avoid the appearance of nepotism, mother and daughter had mutually agreed that when it came to internships, Jenny would no apply with the Cochise County Sheriff's Department.

"Not yet," Jenny replied, "but that's okay. For right now I'm focused on finals and graduation."

"Then I'm sorry to disrupt your concentration with such bad news."

"I'm glad you did," Jenny told her. "I'm pretty sure I met Rosa's mother a couple of times, but I don't remember her name. If you could send me her name and address, I'd like to send a sympathy card."

"Will do," Joanna said. "You'll have it in the morning. Good night."

"Night, Mom," Jenny replied. "Sleep well."

Butch had been quiet throughout the call. Now, after the women ended their call, he spoke up. "What are you going to do when Jenny flies the coop, graduates from a police academy somewhere, and starts serving as a newbie patrol officer in somebody else's jurisdiction?"

"What do you think I'll do?" Joanna asked back. "I'll be in the same boat as every other cop's mother—I'll be worried sick."

CHAPTER 13

FINALLY THIRD BROTHER WENT HOME AND gave up his turn to Eldest Brother. Now this oldest brother had always been mean and overbearing. He was forever telling everybody what they must do. He went to Tash and told him that he was on the wrong path and needed to go some other way. That made Sun angry, so he went on a path that was farthest from Earth. Wind Man and Cloud Man were both working very hard, but Sun had walked away so far that there was not enough heat. So the winds were cold and when the rains came down from the clouds they were not soft but hard and cold.

Eldest Brother did not like the ground. He would not listen when Jeweth—Earth—called to him. When he saw anything growing out of the ground he stamped on it. That is why, when Eldest Brother has his way, the earth is hard and cold.

And this time of the Eldest Brother is what we all know as Hehpch'edkam—Winter.

TRAVELER'S INN IN SAFFORD WAS OFF-BRAND, which meant it was old and a bit on the dowdy side, but it was easy on Dan's per diem. The phone system was ancient enough that you had to go through the office to get an outside line. That wasn't an issue since Dan was able to use his cell. There was no sense in trying to call Lani until the kids were in bed and settled down for the night. In the meantime he busied himself in writing a detailed report of everything he had learned on the Rosa Rios case in the course of one day. When that document was typed into his laptop and safely saved, he turned himself to the other part of his homework— locating Amanda Moreno and Evangeline Joaquin.

In the end, that process proved easier than expected. He picked up the phone and called what passed for law and order in Fort Thomas. When Dan explained to the nighttime supervisor who he was, who he worked for, and that he was there looking for information to advance the investigation into Rosa Rios's disappearance turned homicide, he was immediately given the police chief's home number. It turned out the chief's daughter had attended Fort Thomas High School with Rosa and her two friends. One call to the chief's daughter, Melissa, was all it took for Dan Pardee to have everything he needed to contact Amanda Lewis Moreno and Vangie Rodriguez Joaquin the next day—cell numbers, work numbers, and street addresses as well. He'd cautioned the chief that he didn't want either of his witnesses told in advance of his upcoming visit. Now he had to trust that those wishes would be honored.

With all that handled, he dialed Lani's number. "How are things?" he asked when she answered.

"I'm worn out," she answered. "How can Mom be so stubborn? I can see she's losing ground every day. She's refusing to eat. She claims nothing tastes right, so she doesn't eat. Not only that, she told me today that she's done and just wants to be with Dad."

When it came to stubborn, Dan suspected Lani ran a close second to her mother, but he was smart enough not to say so.

"Losing your dad has been tough on her," he counseled. "If something happened to you, I'd probably feel the same way."

Lani thought about that for a moment. "Thank you, I think," she said a bit dubiously, "but it doesn't make what I'm dealing with any easier. I'm a doctor. I'm supposed to help people. I'm not supposed to just stand on the sidelines and let it happen."

Dan remembered his grandfather voicing similar sentiments when Rachel, his grandmother, had been on her way out, and all Gramps could do was watch it happen. But Micah Duarte hadn't been a doctor. Dan understood that what was going on with Lani right now was tearing her apart. Unfortunately, he was as unable to help her as she was stymied about helping her mother. Suddenly Dan was stricken with a pang of guilt that, instead of being in Tucson helping her deal with this looming crisis, he was literally more than a hundred miles away in a dead-end motel.

"Where are you?" Lani asked, changing the subject.

"Safford," he answered. "I drove over to Bylas to do the death notice, and I have a couple of possible witnesses to interview in the morning, then I'll head home."

"Good," she said. "It turns out we're having company. You must have rattled Brian's chain when you stopped by this morning. Kath called this afternoon and asked if they could come by for dinner tomorrow and bring food from Barrio Anita. I said yes, because I thought if someone else brought the food it might guilt Mom into eating. I told Kath that the pool is heated if they want to bring the girls, but with a houseful of company, I hope you can be here."

"I'll make a point of it," he said.

They spoke for a few more minutes before signing off. It had been a long emotional day, and Dan fell asleep as soon as his head hit the pillow.

THE NEXT MORNING, AFTER TAKING A QUICK shower and grabbing breakfast at the Main Street Cafe, Dan headed to Fort Thomas. Since Evangeline Joaquin's mobile home was located on the way into town, he stopped there first. The woman who answered the door was more than slightly pregnant with a toddler of indeterminate age clinging to her leg.

"Ms. Joaquin?" Dan asked.

"Yes," Evangeline answered warily. "Who are you and what do you want?"

Obviously the police chief's daughter hadn't spilled the beans.

"My name is Dan Pardee, and I'd like to talk to you for a few minutes," he said, holding out his ID wallet. "I'm here investigating the death of Rosa Rios. Her mother gave me your name."

Evangeline took a step backward. "She's really dead then?"

"I'm afraid so. Her remains were located back in 2019, but they've only just now been identified."

Evangeline hesitated, and Dan was afraid for a moment that she was going to slam the door in his face. Instead, she bent down, scooped up the little one, and perched the child on her hip. "You'd better come in then," she said.

Once inside, Dan negotiated his way through a minefield of toys and took a seat on a sagging leather sofa. Vangie sat down opposite him with the child balanced on what remained of her lap.

"Now, Ms. Joaquin . . ." Dan began.

"You can call me Vangie," she said. "You said they found Rosa? Where was she?"

As with Ida Rios, there were no tears here, either, just quiet questions.

"Her body was found in pastureland south of

San Simon. She had been strangled and then set on fire. The ID occurred after her mother submitted Rosa's dental records to a national missing person database."

"Was she dead before the fire?"

Dan couldn't say for certain, but the alternative was too horrifying to consider, so he fudged. "We believe so," he said.

"What do you want from me?"

"Information," he said. "I'm hoping you and Amanda will be able to tell me whatever the two of you remember about your visit to Tucson that weekend and about the night she disappeared."

"Amanda's not home right now," Vangie said. "She and her husband, Jacob, are in Lordsburg for his cousin's wedding."

That was disappointing, but Dan went with the flow. "Well, then," he said, "I'll just talk with you for the time being. Do you mind if I record what you have to say?"

Vangie shook her head. "Go ahead." She waited patiently while Dan set his phone on record.

By the time he was ready to start the recording, the child—a little girl—had fallen asleep in her mother's lap.

"What do you want to know?" Vangie asked.

Dan had already decided that he would take a soft approach in the interview rather than a hard-nosed one. "I'd like you to tell me about your friend Rosa."

Vangie sighed. "We were good friends— Amanda, Rosa, and I—all through school. We were a little wild back then, you know, with drinking and stuff. I guess you knew she got expelled from school just before graduation?"

Dan nodded. "I believe her mother mentioned something about that."

"It was just a few weeks before graduation. She showed up drunk at school. It was really her boyfriend's fault, but she's the one who got expelled. It wasn't fair, and that's when she took off. She left home without a word, and nobody heard from her for a long time after that—for a couple of years at least. Then all of a sudden she got back in touch with her mom. Ida told us she was living and working in Tucson and going to Pima Community College."

"By then she'd gotten her act together?" Dan asked.

"Seemed like," Vangie agreed. "So after we knew she was in Tucson, Amanda and me got this bright idea to go visit her over Rodeo Weekend. We always used to like hanging out together at rodeos, back when Rosa was still barrel racing, and we thought it would be fun to do that again. We borrowed Jacob's pickup and off we went. We showed up at her place on Friday evening. Her apartment was tiny, so me and Amanda stayed in a hotel. Rosa had Saturday off work, so we went to the rodeo during the day and partied that night."

"At the Buckeroo."

Vangie nodded. "It was a fun place. Amanda and me were having a good time. Rosa? Not so much. She had gotten sober once she moved to town, and it was like since she wasn't drinking, she didn't approve of us drinking, either—like if she was sober, we should be, too. And just when the party was getting good, she was ready to leave because she had to work the next day. She got mad. While we were out on the dance floor, she took off without a word. All of a sudden we noticed she was gone. We thought she'd caught a cab home, but when we went to her apartment, she wasn't there."

"Was there anyone hanging around her at the bar that night?" Dan asked. "Anyone who seemed to focus on her or show her too much attention?"

Vangie shrugged. "Not really," she said. "I mean a couple of guys tried to get her to dance with them, but she said no. She wasn't interested."

"Did she have any romantic entanglements in Tucson—a boyfriend maybe?"

"Could be," Vangie allowed. "I mean she talked a lot about some guy named John. She made it sound like he was something special."

"Did she happen to mention John's last name?"

"Not that I remember," Vangie replied. "She said he was part of something called the Circle. She made it sound like the people in that group were the ones who helped her sober up."

"The Circle?" Dan repeated with a puzzled frown. "Did she go into any detail about what or where that was?"

"Not really; she said it was just a bunch of Indians sitting around talking and helping each other."

"Any idea where this Circle thing was located

or who might have sponsored it—the University of Arizona perhaps or maybe even Pima Community College?"

Vangie shook her head. "She never said."

"Is it possible she had some friends there," Dan suggested, "friends who might know more about her life and activities in Tucson than either you or Amanda?"

"Maybe," Vangie agreed.

The little girl in her lap suddenly stirred awake, opened her eyes, took one look at Dan, and let out an earsplitting howl. As Vangie tried to quiet her, Dan decided it was time to pull the plug on the interview. It seemed likely that he had already learned everything there was to know. He turned off the phone.

"Thank you so much," he told her, as the little one settled once more. "I'll be heading out. I'll try to get in touch with Amanda next week."

"She won't be able to tell you anything more than I did."

"That's likely," Dan conceded, "but I'll probably give her a call anyway. I like to cover all the bases."

"Okay," Vangie said. "I hope you find out who did this."

"So do I," Dan said, dropping one of his business cards on the coffee table. "And if you think of anything more, please give me a call."

CHAPTER 14

FLAGSTAFF, ARIZONA
Saturday, April 2, 2022, 1:30 A.M.

ONCE JENNY GOT OFF THE PHONE WITH HER mother, work on the research paper went out the window. Rosa Rios was someone she had known. Rosa had been older than Jenny and in many ways, she was a role model—a girl from a small town who showed up at rodeos in a run-down pickup hauling an equally run-down horse trailer, but, boy, could she ride! Jenny remembered that Rosa had hoped to receive a rodeo scholarship to go on to college, but the last media mention of her name was in the aftermath of the terrible wreck after which War Paint was put down. After that, Rosa's online and social-media presence simply disappeared.

If Rosa went missing and was murdered three years ago, Jenny wondered, *how come there weren't any news articles about her disappearance? Shouldn't someone have noticed? Shouldn't someone at least have mentioned it?*

At the time Jenny had been interacting with Rosa, her life had been all about rodeo. And now so was her death. She hadn't been competing when she was murdered, but she had still been interested enough to be a spectator and a fan. And that's where she was when someone had taken her life. Did that mean that whoever had done it also had something to do with rodeos?

Jenny had met Rosa on the junior rodeo circuit. Since then she'd been involved in intercollegiate rodeos, but she knew a lot of the pros. She had done pro-am events with some of them and idolized others, and the rodeo in Tucson was a pro affair. Did that mean the killer was someone Rosa had met along the way? Some of the guys involved with rodeo were fine. Others were more than slightly rough around the edges. And what about rodeo clowns? If regular clowns could be bad news, couldn't rodeo clowns be just as bad or worse?

Jenny's heart began to race because she suddenly remembered something that had happened fairly recently. A little over a month earlier, in late February, she'd been in Albuquerque to participate in the 2022 Mountain States Intercollegiate Rodeo Championship. It was the last rodeo competition scheduled for that academic year, and for some of the graduating seniors it would be their last rodeo ever. A few of them intended to turn pro, but most, Jenny included, were getting ready to hang up their competitive spurs.

When she had told people that this was probably her last rodeo, several had asked if Maggie was up for sale. Jenny had already figured out that it wouldn't be fair to Maggie for Jenny to head off to police academy training and leave Maggie stuck in some boarding facility. Nonetheless, she told all the prospective purchasers that Maggie was already spoken for.

Maggie loved competing, yes, but she also loved people, and she was used to interacting with them on a daily basis. While attending NAU, Jenny and her boyfriend and fellow rodeo-team member, Nick Saunders, had boarded their horses—her Maggie and Nick's Dexter—at the Lazy 8 in Munds Park, south of Flagstaff. But the Lazy 8 was also home to Equine Helpers, a horse therapy facility for special needs kids. The four of them, Nick and Jenny along with their horses, had put in a lot of volunteer hours taking mentally and physically challenged kids on slow-moving trail rides and helping them learn how to care for and groom horses. Maggie had been wonderful with each and every one of those people. And that was where Maggie would be going once she retired from barrel racing—to Equine Helpers where she'd spend her retirement years taking developmentally and physically disabled kids on leisurely trail rides.

After graduation, Nick was bound for vet school at Washington State University in Pullman, Washington. Dexter would be going along, and Nick would probably continue to do some rodeo competitions, but not Jenny. Rodeo had been a huge part of her life for years, but if she was abandoning the sport, she wanted to make a clean break of it. With all that looming on the horizon, the rodeo held in late February in Albuquerque had been an especially emotional one for her.

The host team, the University of Albuquerque, had walked away with first prize. NAU's team had come in a clear second, but the surprise of the weekend was that Snow College, a small junior college in Ephraim, Utah, had beaten out far larger schools to capture third.

With only a two-second difference between them, Deborah Russell and her sorrel mare, Daisy Mae, the competition had pushed Jenny and Maggie into a second-place finish in barrel racing. Deborah was young and bright. She was also a good Mormon girl with a boyfriend named Eddie Willis. Everybody thought Eddie was a bit on the sketchy side, and the party he'd taken Deborah to on Saturday evening certainly wasn't on any activity list approved of by Snow College's straitlaced collection of coaches.

At the party, the couple had made arrangements for a late-evening assignation in a loft-style bunk room in a barn where horses from visiting teams were stabled. Armed with a condom, Eddie had left the party half an hour before Deborah did. She had been on her way there, threading through the fairgrounds from the party to the barn, when she was attacked from behind. As her unknown assailant grabbed for her, he slipped, missing her throat and knocking her purse to the ground. That inadvertent stumble meant that his chloroform-soaked rag missed her mouth, and Deborah had been able to let out a single bloodcurdling scream. Her attacker quickly stifled another scream by wrapping both hands around her throat. As Deborah struggled to breathe, she had managed to jab the guy's face, knocking his glasses to the ground, but that was it. He was far larger and stronger than she was. Devoid of oxygen and seeing stars, she knew she was dying, and that's when Eddie showed up.

Barefoot and wearing nothing but his Fruit of the Looms, he had charged out of the barn yelling at the top of his lungs and pointing the flashlight on his phone directly toward the melee.

"What the hell do you think you're doing, asshole?" he shouted as he raced forward. "Let go of her, you son of a bitch!"

Eddie Willis may have been sketchy, but even barefoot, he was fast on his feet. As he sprinted toward them, the attacker glanced briefly in his direction and then took off running. Rather than chase after the assailant, Eddie chose to stay with Deborah who had sunk to her knees, choking and coughing. As she clung to his neck, sobbing, they both heard a car start up somewhere in the distance and race away.

"Are you all right?" he asked.

"I think so," she croaked. "He was trying to kill me."

"I know," Eddie said grimly.

Deborah's purse had fallen open on the ground, spilling its contents everywhere. Once Deborah caught her breath, they gathered up what they could find and stuffed everything back into the purse, then they hurried to the barn so

Eddie could get dressed before anyone came by and saw him. By the time he had his clothes on, Deborah had stopped shivering and was finally getting a grip. Together, they walked back to the party because that's where he'd left his pickup. Eddie drove her to her hotel and walked her up to her room.

The next morning, word of the attack spread like wildfire through all the teams, and not just the one from Snow College. In the photo of the three winning teams, Deborah Russell wore a bright red bandanna around her neck. The kids in attendance all knew it was there to hide the purple bruises on her throat. The coaches, however, were left completely in the dark.

When Jenny first heard about what had happened, she was appalled. "Did Deborah call the cops to report it?" she asked.

"She didn't bother," one of Deb's teammates replied. "I mean, nothing happened really."

"Something did happen," Jenny insisted. "She may not have been raped or murdered, but she was bodily assaulted. It's a serious crime that needs to be reported."

"But she can't go to the cops," someone else said.

"Why not?" Jenny asked.

"Because she'd been drinking," was the answer. "She's Mormon. Her parents would disown her."

"No, they wouldn't," Jenny argued. "Lots of parents say stuff like that, but they never mean it."

"Hers would," the first girl said. "You don't

know her father. He's a bigwig in the church, and he's also Dean of Students at Southern Utah University in Cedar City. He'd toss her out in a minute."

As a result, no report about the attack was ever made, at least not as far as Jenny knew. But was it possible that the guy who had attacked Deborah was the same rodeo-connected guy who had murdered Rosa Rios? Suddenly Jennifer Ann Brady needed to know a whole lot more about what had happened that night in Albuquerque. To get those details, she did what any right-thinking member of her generation would do—she went straight to her computer and started combing through social media, looking for Deborah Russell.

CHAPTER 15

ONE DAY WHEN ELDEST BROTHER WAS OUT *hunting Wind Man who was hiding from him, I'itoi found him and sent him home. Then I'itoi went back to the house of the father of the four brothers where he called out the first brother, the youngest one, and told him it was once again time for him to take his turn.*

Then the father and Spirit of Goodness talked things over. Some of the people had complained about each son while others had liked each one. So I'itoi decided that from that time forward, the four brothers should continue to take turns just the way they had done the first time.

And that, nawoj, my friend, is why even to this day, every year we have four seasons—spring, summer, autumn, and winter. And, of course, that is as it should be, for all things in nature go in fours.

———

WITH AMANDA OUT OF TOWN AND UNABLE TO be interviewed, Dan Pardee left for Tucson as soon as he finished speaking with Evangeline Joaquin. Driving west he mulled over everything he'd been told. He was struck by what Vangie had said about the Circle. It sounded like a self-help organization of some kind, one designed to focus on young Native Americans. Dan suspected it was probably run by a group of well-meaning but possibly misguided Anglos who, in Dan's experience, often did more harm than good. The Circle might turn out to be religiously based, but Dan thought it was likely to have a physical presence on the campus of one or the other of the two government-based institutions of higher learning located in the area—the University of Arizona or Pima Community College.

And that's when Dan hit on Gabe Ortiz, Lani's godson. Gabe was the grandson of Fat Crack Ortiz, the medicine man who had been Lani's good friend and mentor. Now she was slowly training the boy so he'd be ready to step into Lani's shoes when, as she sometimes smilingly said, she herself was ready to give up her "feather shaking" responsibilities. Gabe and his adopted brother, Tim José, were both seniors at the U of A now, due to graduate with honors in two months' time. If there was an Indigenous People's organization operating on campus, one or the other of them would know about it.

As always, any thought or mention of Tim's name took Dan straight back to the specter of Henry Rojas. Henry, Dan's immediate supervisor in the Shadow Wolves, had actually been the inside man who had pulled four fatherless boys—Tim and his three older brothers—into a lucrative blood diamond smuggling operation.

At the time, Gabe had been in his midteens and was starting to act out. His best friend, Tim José, was the youngest of four brothers. Suspecting that the José brothers were headed in a bad direction and worried their son might be sucked into whatever the others were doing, Gabe's parents, Leo and Delia Ortiz, had asked Lani to intercede. In true medicine woman fashion, she had taken him on what was supposed to be an intervention-style campout under the stars on Ioligam, I'itoi's sacred mountain. She had hoped that two nights of storytelling under the stars might point the boy in the right direction.

The expedition turned out to be a total bust as far as its original purpose was concerned. At about that same time, one of the shipments of smuggled diamonds went astray. Believing the José brothers to be responsible for the loss, the woman in charge had ordered Henry to clean house. He had done so by shooting and killing the three older brothers in cold blood. By the time all was said and done, both Tim and Gabe had been placed in serious jeopardy as well. Only Dan Pardee's timely intervention had spared the two of them from certain death.

Shortly thereafter, when Tim's mother and only surviving parent passed away, leaving him an orphan, Gabe's parents had taken Tim in, officially adopting him as their own. Since then both Tim and Gabe had walked the straight and narrow. After that initial campout failure, Lani and Gabe had made several more trips to Ioligam, where under the stars she had finally been able to teach him in the same way the boy's grandfather had once taught her.

Surprisingly enough, those long frigid nights of sharing ancient Tohono O'odham legends and lore had paid off in a way Lani had never anticipated. When Gabe went off to the University of Arizona, he had enrolled as an astronomy major. Four years later, he was due to graduate with honors in just a few weeks' time and had already been accepted into a coveted intern program at Kitt Peak's nationally renowned observatory.

Members of the Tohono O'odham tribe had been employees at Kitt Peak for years—as maintenance men, mechanics, and food service providers. Gabe Ortiz would be the first one serving in a scientific capacity. Meanwhile, Tim, Gabe's relatively new brother, was also a senior honors student at the U of A, graduating with a degree in business and accounting. Delia had told Lani and Dan more than once that she thought Tim might have what it took for him to run for the office of tribal chairman someday.

Yes, if the Circle was something operating from the University of Arizona, either Gabe or Tim would be in the know about it, and if Dan played his cards right, maybe he could touch base with one of them and find out more while still showing up at Gates Pass in time to serve as backup for Lani and her houseful of dinner guests.

With Gabe's number in Dan's Contacts list, he picked up his phone and pressed the button.

"Hey, Siri," he said aloud. "Call Gabe Ortiz."

As he waited for the call to go through, Dan Pardee couldn't help thinking that here in this vast empty desert, being able to use a cell phone beat the hell out of sending smoke signals.

Moments later, Gabe's cheerful voice came on the phone. "Hey, Dan," he said. "What's up?"

"Hi, Gabe. I'm working a case at the moment, and maybe you can help."

"How's that?"

"Have you ever heard of something called the Circle in Tucson?"

"Sure," Gabe replied. "It meets every Saturday afternoon. Why? What about it?"

"Who sponsors it?" Dan asked. "Is it run by the U of A?"

Now Gabe seemed puzzled. "As far as I know it isn't sponsored by anybody."

"Who runs it then?"

"A guy named John Wheeler. He's not local, by the way. He's Lakota originally from Pine Ridge. We all call him Chair Man."

"So he runs it, the same way your mother is tribal chairman and runs the TO Nation?"

"He runs it, but not as chairman," Gabe replied. "We call him the Chair Man because he's in a chair—a wheelchair—one of those fancy electric things. Years ago, he was in an accident that messed up his legs really bad—turned him into a paraplegic—sort of like what happened to Brian Fellows."

When Vangie Joaquin had mentioned John's mysterious connection to Rosa Rios, the idea that the man might be a paraplegic hadn't crossed Dan's mind.

"And you say this Circle meets on Saturdays? Where? And what is it exactly?"

"It's sort of like a support group for Indians. If you're one of the People, no matter what kind, young or old, you're welcome. During the winter the Circle meets in the park at Twenty-Second and South Fourth Avenue, but as of today, with the weather turning, we'll be at the Santa Cruz Catholic Church at the corner of Twenty-Second and South Sixth. In the spring and summer when it's too hot to meet outside, the school lets us use their cafeteria. Some ladies from the res usually show up with popovers and tamales to sell, so no one goes away hungry."

"What time does it start?"

Gabe laughed aloud at that. "It starts on Indian time," he answered. "Chair Man is usually there from noon on, but people come and go whenever."

"And what goes on?"

"What do you think?" Gabe replied. "We sit around in a circle and talk. It's a lot like doing the Peace Smoke but without the sacred tobacco. As for beverages? We mostly stick to coffee or sodas. The popover ladies bring those, too."

Dan knew all about the Tohono O'odham's Peace Smoke custom, one that had nothing at all to do with pipes. He had heard Lani explain it to Angie and Micah countless times. According to the story, after the Evil People had killed Wise Old Grandmother, and even though her grandsons Little Bear and Little Lion were dead, she called them home. She told them where to find her body and explained how, if they handled it properly, a powerful plant called *wiw*, what the Whites—the Milghan—call wild tobacco, would grow out of her grave. She taught them how to harvest the *wiw* and dry it and roll it into sticks. She directed that people should sit in a circle, smoking the tobacco and passing it from hand to hand, always saying the word *nawoj*— Friendly Gift—as they did so.

"A Peace Smoke," Dan repeated.

"Yup."

"Are you planning on going today?" Dan asked.

"I wasn't but I can if you want me to. Do you want to go?"

"Yes, I do," Dan said, making up his mind on the spot.

"When?"

Dan glanced at the screen on his GPS. "I'm driving back from the San Carlos, so I'm about an hour out."

"Okay," Gabe agreed. "As I said, the church is at the corner of South Sixth and Twenty-Second Street. It's all white. You won't be able to miss it. The school and gym are directly behind the church. And don't worry about showing up at a certain time. During the course of the afternoon people drop in and out. It's not like someone's there taking attendance or marking people tardy."

"See you then," Dan said.

"Okay," Gabe replied, "I'll be there, but remember, I'm talking Indian time here. I've got some stuff I need to do first."

CHAPTER 16

FLAGSTAFF, ARIZONA
Saturday, April 2, 2022, 10:30 A.M.

JENNY MAY HAVE STARTED HER INTERNET search for Deborah Russell the night before, but the effort didn't pay off until late the following morning. In between, once in bed, her restless sleep had been plagued by one evil mask-wearing rodeo clown after another. Finally at five o'clock on Saturday morning, giving up on sleeping altogether, she got out of bed, padded over to the kitchen corner of her studio apartment, and made a pot of coffee.

For her senior year, in hopes of dodging the drama that had surrounded some of her previous college roommates, Jenny had opted to live solo. Her apartment, formerly a two-car garage, was located within easy walking distance of campus, and her landlady, an elderly widow, reminded Jenny of Eva Lou Brady, her beloved grandmother back home in Bisbee.

Armed with coffee, she settled in to do battle with her research paper—one dealing with the impact of community policing in preventing violent crime. Having grown up in a small town with a mother involved in law enforcement, Jenny's ideas on the subject were often at odds with those of her classmates, especially ones who had grown up in more urban environments. Nor was she on the same wavelength as many of her professors, few of whom had ever actually worked as sworn police officers. That was especially true of the professor teaching Current Trends in Law Enforcement. In writing her research paper, she had to walk a fine line between saying what she believed to be true and what she needed to say to get a decent grade.

It was midmorning when her cell phone dinged with an incoming message, a response from one of Deborah Russell's rodeo teammates who was glad to supply Deb's cell phone number. The caller was under the impression Jenny wanted to talk or text Deb about the possibility of her purchasing Maggie, and Jenny went along with that program. She suspected that Deb's friend wouldn't have been nearly as forthcoming if she'd known the real reason for contacting Snow College's star barrel rider.

Armed with the number, Jenny could have initiated contact by sending a text, but she didn't. The situation she wanted to discuss with Deborah Russell was dicey enough that Jenny wanted their encounter to be either face-to-face or else over the phone. She couldn't risk leaving behind any retrievable digital messages.

Before making the call, Jenny decided to clear the mental debris of the research paper out of her head. Donning a light jacket, Jenny took herself for a brisk walk. Yes, it was early April, but in Flagstaff, Arizona, situated at an elevation of seven thousand feet above sea level, spring had not yet arrived. Piles of melting snow still lined the streets and sidewalks. As she strode along, Jenny considered calling home and asking her mom for advice, but she didn't. She couldn't be sure which Joanna Brady would answer the phone—Joanna the mom or Joanna the sheriff. Jenny was pretty sure the sheriff's advice would come through under the heading of MIND YOUR OWN BUSINESS. And if she had called her dad, she was reasonably sure Butch Dixon would tell her to go for it. In that case it was likely he'd end up in the doghouse right along with Jenny. The upshot was, Jenny returned to her apartment without calling either of them.

Back home and with a new cup of coffee in hand, Jenny settled down on her couch, folded her legs under her, and punched Deb's number into the phone.

"Hello," Deborah said uncertainly. "Who's calling?"

"It's Jenny, Jennifer Brady. You know, barrel racer number two?"

"Oh, you," Deborah replied, with a relieved laugh. "Daisy Mae and I managed to get a two-second head start on you, that's all. How are you, and what's going on?"

"I wanted to talk to you about what happened

that night, about the attack out by the horse barns."

The laughter went out of Deborah's voice and wariness returned. "I don't want to talk about that," she said quickly. "I'm going to hang up now."

"Please don't," Jenny begged. "I'm asking you about it because of someone else—another barrel racer, another one who beat me."

As Jenny hoped, the mention of barrel racing caused Deborah to bite. "Who?" she asked.

"Her name was Rosa Rios. She was a San Carlos Apache from Bylas, Arizona. The last time I raced against her was at a junior rodeo event in Silver City. She beat me all hollow, but she's dead now. She disappeared three years ago over Rodeo Weekend in Tucson. They found her charred remains a few weeks later outside a town called San Simon in Arizona. The autopsy showed that she'd been strangled."

"If this happened three years ago, why are you calling me now?"

"Because they've only just now been able to use dental records to identify her."

A long pause followed. When Deborah spoke again, her voice was little more than a whisper. "Did they catch the guy who did it?" she asked.

"No, they haven't," Jenny answered. "Not yet."

"And you're thinking the guy who murdered her might be the same one who attacked me?"

"It's just a gut feeling," Jenny said quickly, "and it's all because of the rodeo connection. I don't really know much of anything about what happened to you. I just heard what people were saying at the time."

"The gossip, you mean?" Deborah asked.

"Yes," Jenny agreed, "the gossip. That's why I wanted to talk to you directly—to get the real story."

FOR THE BETTER PART OF THE NEXT TWENTY minutes, Deborah Russell told her story.

"What happened to you was appalling," Jenny said, when Deb finished. "You were violently attacked and could easily have been killed, so why didn't you call the police and report it?"

"Because of my parents," Deborah answered hopelessly. "They're beyond strict and nosy, too. If they'd found out from a police report that Eddie and I were at the barn together in the middle of the night, they would have figured out that our being there had nothing to do with our horses, and they would have pitched a fit. They probably think I'm still a virgin, and I'm not, by the way. If I hadn't been going there to meet up with Eddie that night, the attack might never have happened, but then again, if he hadn't been there to scare the guy away, I'd probably be dead."

"It sounds like Eddie's a bit of a jerk, but you're still giving him a pass?"

Jenny was surprised when Deborah's response to that question was a short burst of laughter. "He is, but I guess I am," she said.

"Okay," Jenny said. "I can understand why you didn't want to report the incident, but because you didn't, any evidence related to your case and possibly to Rosa's, too, is gone. For example, you mentioned hearing a vehicle drive away, right?"

"Yes, I was still coughing and choking at the time. I didn't see a car anywhere around. It was probably hidden behind one of the barns, but I heard it speed off."

"I don't remember seeing any surveillance cameras near the barns," Jenny continued, "but I'm sure there are some at the entrance to the fairgrounds. One of those might have caught a plate number as the guy drove away. That footage would have been retrievable at the time, but it's gone now. The same goes for DNA. The crime of manual strangulation is up close and personal. A forensic examination at the time might have located touch DNA on your neck or clothing. And if you managed to scratch him, there would have been DNA under your fingernails."

"I didn't scratch him," Deborah said. "As for leaving DNA on my throat? That didn't happen because he wore latex gloves, but all the same, I might still have some of his DNA."

"Are you kidding?" Jenny gasped in surprise. "How? Where?"

"Like I told you, when he came after me, he hit me so hard that he knocked my purse off my shoulder. It went flying. It ended up popping open when it landed. Everything inside it fell out. After the guy left, Eddie and I gathered up all my stuff and put it back into the purse. Two weeks later, when I was cleaning out the purse, I found a pair of glasses that weren't mine. At first

I couldn't imagine whose they were, and then I remembered. During the struggle, I must have knocked the guy's glasses off. While Eddie was helping gather my stuff, he must have picked up the glasses, assumed they were mine, and put them back in the purse along with everything else."

Jenny was beyond excited. "You actually kept them?"

"I did," Deborah admitted. "You'll probably think it's silly, but I felt like his glasses were a kind of trophy, one that said he lost and I won."

"Where are they now?" Jenny demanded.

"In the bottom of my underwear drawer," Deborah said.

"Have you told anyone else about them?"

"No, you're the first. Why?"

"Because those glasses may have retrievable DNA on them," Jenny told her. "Since you and Eddie both handled them, your DNA profiles would most likely be there, but so would your assailant's."

"Even this long afterward?" Deborah asked.

"It's only been just over a month," Jenny told her. "The glasses have been inside and out of the weather, so the DNA is probably still good."

"I see," Deborah said.

But Jenny wasn't really listening. Her mind was going a mile a minute. If there was even the smallest chance that Deborah's attacker and Rosa's killer were one and the same, those glasses needed to be in the hands of someone from MIP as soon as possible, and that had to be accomplished in a way that wouldn't jeopardize

Deborah's relationship with her parents. At the same time, since there were most likely three DNA profiles on the glasses, Jenny needed to provide a way for investigators to differentiate Eddie's and Deborah's from the assailant's. She was pretty sure Deborah would be willing to provide a sample. Getting one from Eddie Willis might be a problem.

"From what you said about Eddie earlier, I assume the two of you aren't an item anymore?"

"We're not," Deborah answered. "Turns out he was playing me for a fool because he already had a steady girlfriend, one I didn't know about. I learned about her right after we got back from Albuquerque. But why are you asking me about Eddie?"

Jenny answered Deborah's question with one of her own. "What do you know about genetic genealogy?" she asked.

"I'm Mormon," Deborah answered, "so I know about genealogy, but what does that have to do with any of this?"

"It's a way of using family history to identify unknown killers. It's how law enforcement finally nailed the Golden State Killer in 2018."

"Who's the Golden State Killer?" Deborah asked.

Obviously she wasn't a devotee of true crime.

"When cops find DNA at a crime scene, once they have a profile, they run it through CODIS—the Combined DNA Index System—a national database that includes DNA of all kinds of people, including ones arrested for and convicted of violent crimes. The Golden State Killer was a rapist and murderer who operated in California for decades. Cops had his DNA but his profile wasn't in CODIS. Then they asked for help from a genealogist who went to the public databases . . ."

"Like Ancestry.com?" Deb asked.

"Yes, sites similar to that one," Jenny agreed. "She located a familial match, a partial match, to a distant relative who had submitted his DNA just to trace his own roots. Once she found that first relative, she was able to go back and create a family tree that finally, generations later, led to the killer. Some jurisdictions call it genetic genealogy while others call it forensic genealogy. Both work."

"Wait," Deb said. "Are you saying, if the cops have the DNA of the guy who attacked me, they might be able to do that kind of family search to locate him?"

"I am," Jenny said.

"And he might be the same guy who killed that other girl? Was his DNA found at that crime scene, too?"

"Unfortunately it wasn't," Jenny answered. "Not even Rosa's DNA was found at the crime scene, but if this does turn out to be the same guy, once law enforcement identifies him, they can go about seeing if they can find any evidence linking him to Rosa."

"How do you know so much about all this stuff?" Deborah asked after a moment.

Jenny understood that whatever answer she gave to that question would put her on shaky ground as far as Deborah Russell was concerned.

If she told the truth, the conversation was liable to blow up in her face, but if she didn't . . . After a moment she decided she was better off going with the truth.

"Because I'm a criminal justice major," Jenny admitted at last. "And my mom happens to be the sheriff in Cochise County, the jurisdiction where Rosa's body was found."

Deborah exploded. "So that's what this is all about!" she exclaimed. "You're grilling me about what happened to me so you can turn my information over to your mom? I already told you, no cops!"

"What I'm trying to explain is this," Jenny said patiently. "Obtaining DNA profiles is complicated and expensive. You can't just walk into the nearest Walgreens and ask for one. If you wanted to, you could send your own sample in to Ancestry and get a profile back, but you can't submit anyone else's. Not only that, in this case we need the profiles of every person who handled the glasses—you and Eddie Willis as well as your assailant. That means we'll need a sample from you and one from Eddie. We'll also need the glasses themselves, which might end up becoming evidence."

"Meaning I lose my trophy?"

"Correct," Jenny said.

"And by *we*," Deborah continued sarcastically, "I suppose you mean you and your mother?"

"We may need to go through my mother, but her department won't be running point on this case. I think we should take this to someone else. Rosa was Apache. These days there's a new federal agency out there called Missing and Murdered Indigenous People—MIP for short. Mom told me that someone from there is taking over the case."

"So?" Deborah asked.

"The guy's a fed," Jenny explained. "That means he's likely to have more latitude in obtaining DNA profiles than local cops do. He'll also be less interested in taking what a certain random coed might have been doing with her not-exactly-upstanding boyfriend a few weeks ago and reporting that back to her parents."

"You think he'd be more interested in solving the case than in ratting me out?"

"I do," Jenny answered.

A long silence followed. Jenny's upper-division class on conducting interrogations had stressed the power of silence—of simply staying quiet and letting the other person fill in the blanks.

"What do we do now then?" Deborah asked at last.

Jenny had been holding her breath. Now she let it out. "First tell me everything you can remember about your assailant," she said.

"He was white," Deborah said definitively. "And older, like a grandfather older, and I don't think he was really strong because I managed to get my arm loose enough to hit him in the face."

"Did you see his face?"

"All I saw were his hands. But when Eddie came charging at us and the guy took off in the opposite direction, his hoodie came off. Eddie's flashlight app was turned on, and there was enough light for me to see that his hair was either white or silver, and he wore it short—in like a buzz cut."

"How tall was he?"

"About my height, or maybe a little taller. I'm five six. I'd say he was maybe five eight, so not very tall. Way shorter than Eddie."

"Speaking of Eddie," Jenny said. "Do you still see him?"

"Here and there," Deborah answered with a sigh. "As a matter of fact, I'll probably see him tonight at the rodeo team's end-of-year banquet. He's team captain, so he'll be there, and so will his girlfriend."

"What about you?"

"I earned the right to go and I will," Deborah answered. "I'm not going to be aced out of taking part in the celebration because Eddie Willis is a jackass."

"Okay then," Jenny said. "Here's the deal. As I said, there'll most likely be three separate profiles on those glasses. The two known ones will belong to you and Eddie. The unknown one will belong to the perpetrator."

"Are you suggesting that I show up at the banquet with a cotton swab in hand and tell Eddie to open his mouth?"

"It would probably be best to leave the cotton swab at home, but take along a small paper bag. If you can lay hands on something that Eddie has used—like a straw or a paper cup or even a cigarette butt. Whatever it is, grab it and bag it. Ditto for the glasses along with a cotton swab of your own, and ship all of it to me. My dad has a FedEx account that he lets me use. I'll do my best to get them to the guy with MIP. I may have to go through my mother to make that happen, but I'll do my best to keep your name out of it."

"I don't know," Deborah Russell said. "Let me think it over."

That's when she hung up, leaving Jennifer Brady talking into an empty phone.

The sudden disconnect left her feeling like a complete failure. She'd had a possible lead, but now she'd blown it. Rather than sit there feeling sorry for herself, she punched Nick's number.

"What are you doing?" she asked.

"Trying to study but running on empty at the moment. Why?"

"How about heading down to the Lazy 8 and taking Dexter and Maggie out for a spin?"

"When?"

"How about now?"

"Would you like me to come pick you up?"

"Yes, please," Jenny said. "I'd like that very much."

CHAPTER 17

DAN PULLED INTO THE CHURCH PARKING AREA where his aging Chevy fit right in with the other well-used vehicles in the lot. The only exception to the mix was an almost new white Dodge Pacifica minivan with a handicapped license that read CHR MAN. Obviously John Wheeler had already arrived on the scene.

When Dan stepped out of his SUV into blinding sunshine, the familiar scents of woodsmoke cooking assailed his nostrils. Obviously the refreshment ladies were already on hand and doing their popover magic the old-fashioned way— over a hot wood fire on the school playground. Once pieces of hand-flattened dough were dropped one at a time into blackened metal pots full of simmering lard, what emerged a minute or so later was a flour-tortilla-sized piece of puffed, crispy pastry, which was then slathered with either shirt-staining red chili or a light dusting of powdered sugar, depending on the preferences of the person at the head of the line.

Dan supposed that the ladies had all heard about the dietary benefits of using vegetable oil, but hot lard was what they knew, and they stayed with that. Knowing Kath and Brian were bringing dinner to the house in Gates Pass only a few hours down the road, Dan bypassed the popover line and beelined toward a young woman who was dispensing coffee for a mere dollar a pop. Then, coffee in hand, he headed for a door marked GYM.

This was actually a dual-purpose facility that served as both gym and lunchroom. Rolling tables had all been pushed to one side next to a pair of doors that probably accommodated cafeteria serving lines at lunchtime. The absence of tables left the center of the room bare except for a circle of forty or so metal folding chairs that had clearly seen better days and all of which were empty. If the Circle supposedly started at one, Gabe's warning about Indian time was on the money.

Other than Dan, the only person in the room was a man sitting in a motorized wheelchair. Despite the heat, his legs were covered with what, to Dan's unpracticed eye, looked like an authentic, handmade Navajo blanket. His shoulder-length black hair was shot through with streaks of white, and one side of his face was horribly disfigured. Dan had seen similarly damaged but still bloody flesh on battlefields in the Middle East.

Wanting to take advantage of a private moment, Dan walked over to introduce himself. "You must be John Wheeler," he said, holding out his hand in greeting. "My name is Dan Pardee. I'm from out on the TO. Gabe Ortiz is a friend of mine."

The wheelchair-bound man held out a frail and badly mangled left hand. "Wheeler's my name," he said with a lopsided grin, "but most people around here call me Chair Man, for obvious reasons. Glad to meet you, Mr. Pardee."

"Please call me Dan." Then with a nod toward the chair, he added, "I was in Afghanistan. Were you there, too?"

Chair Man shook his head. "Nope, Iraq," he said. "I was in Desert Storm. Came home from there safe and sound. What you now see happened to me only a mile or so from here. Some young punk from up in the foothills who happened to hate Indians got high on his dad's marijuana and decided to push me under a moving train. The train dragged me for half a mile before it stopped. At first everybody thought I was dead.

"I was in the ICU for weeks after that, and hospitalized for the next six months, most of it in the VA Hospital here in Tucson," he continued. "While I was there, my best friend turned out to be a Navajo named Josiah Lone-tree who was a code talker during World War II. He told me a lot about the *Dine* culture and got me interested in my own. He also helped me relearn how to talk and read. Once I did that, I made it my business to learn about my own roots—the Oglala

Sioux. As for the kid who hit me? He went to juvie for six years until he turned twenty-one. He's been out now for ten—but I sued his parents and won. I ended up with a ton of money, but I'd rather have working legs."

"I can see why," Dan said, digging out a business card and handing it over. "I came here hoping to have a word or two about someone who used to be part of your Circle."

"Rosa Rios by any chance?" Chair Man asked.

Dan was stunned.

"Don't look so surprised," Chair Man said. "News about her murder was all over the TV news first thing this morning. When she disappeared without a word and never came back, I figured she was dead, and now we know that for sure. Are you working the case?"

Dan nodded. "I am."

"You're what, Apache maybe?"

Dan was taken aback. Generally speaking people didn't think of him as an Indian at all to say nothing of guessing which kind.

"Half," he admitted. "Half Apache and half white."

"Half Wasi'shu, then," John concluded.

"Half what?" Dan inquired.

"That's what Lakotas call the Whites," Chair Man explained. "What kind of Apache?"

"San Carlos," Dan said. "Originally we were Chiricahua."

"You're one of the People then, so you qualify," Chair Man said with a grin. "You're welcome to stick around. That's the wonderful thing about circles—there's always room for one more." Then, as the grin morphed into a frown, he added thoughtfully, "San Carlos. Isn't that where Rosa Rios came from originally?"

Dan nodded. "It is. I grew up near there, but not on the reservation."

"Rosa was part of the Circle for a time," Chair Man said, "but she left several years ago. Still, there might be someone here today who'll remember her. She was troubled when she first arrived, but she was doing much better by the time she disappeared. I seem to remember that the last time she was here she was all excited about meeting up with some old friends from the res who were coming to visit."

"They came all right," Dan told him, "but it didn't go well. Her friends were deep into partying, and she wasn't."

"No surprises there," Chair Man said. "When Rosa decided to sober up, she was dead serious about it. That's why it was so strange when she just vanished."

"I understand you were helpful with her getting sober," Dan said.

Chair Man nodded. "When our young people get caught up in the White world and lose their way, they often turn to alcohol and drugs, so the first step in getting them back on the right path is getting them off whatever they're on."

Two new arrivals approached and were waiting their turn to speak with Chair Man, so Dan excused himself and went looking for a place to sit. When he did so, he was surprised to find that a crowd had gathered while he was talking to John Wheeler, and the circle of empty folding chairs was more than half full. In the course of the next few minutes, most of the rest of them were occupied as well. Eventually Chair Man moved to an empty spot in the circle that was evidently reserved for him and his bulky chair.

"Welcome," Chair Man said as a hush fell over the room. "Let's begin with a moment of silence during which we can all address the Great Spirit by whatever name we may call him and invite him to join us in this circle."

And that was when Dan Pardee realized that in coming to this humble school gymnasium, he had also stumbled into an unlikely holy place. Lani would be right at home here, and he planned on telling her all about it the moment he got back to the house in Gates Pass, only that didn't happen.

BY THE TIME DAN ARRIVED AT HIS MOTHER-in-law's home at a little past four, there was way too much going on. The four kids—Micah and Angie as well as Brian and Kath's twins, Ann and Amy—were all out by the pool, hunkered around a table on the shaded patio, and playing some kind of video game on their phones. Dan found a tight-lipped Lani in the kitchen where, with Kath's help, she was busy emptying plastic bags of food and laying out a Barrio Anita feast on the kitchen island. There were bowls of red and green chili and refried beans as well as a platter of tamales. Included was a stack of Anita

Street Market's signature, paper-thin flour torti-llas, which, in Dan's opinion, were the best Tucson had to offer. Brian's wheelchair, the lightweight one he used indoors, was parked at one end of the breakfast nook. Diana Ladd Walker was nowhere to be seen.

"Where's your mom?" Dan asked.

Lani shot him an exasperated look. "She just announced that she's not hungry, and she's going to bed. That means she'll be up prowling around the house about the time the rest of us are ready to go to sleep."

"So your ploy of using company to get her to eat didn't work?" Dan asked.

"I guess not," Lani replied.

"What ploy?" Kath asked.

"Diana's been off her feed, and Lani was hop-ing to use your presence to guilt her mother into actually eating a meal for a change."

"Really," Lani said, "it's a lot worse than that. The only reason we've been able to make this work is by having Lucy Rojas living here and looking after Mom. But this afternoon, Lucy's niece called from Window Rock saying her mother is deathly ill and asking if Lucy would please come home and look after her. I told her, of course. By all means she should go, and she plans to leave early tomorrow, but I don't have any idea what we're going to do without her, and there's no telling how long she'll be gone. I can take a few vacation days next week, but what happens after that? We can't bring Mom home to Sells. Our place isn't big enough, and there's no way I can commute sixty miles one way back and forth to the hospital and still look after her and the kids at the same time."

"Have you ever thought of assisted living?" Kath inquired gently.

There wasn't a drop of blood relation among the four people gathered in the Gates Pass kitchen, and yet they were all kin in a way that allowed for speaking one's mind on occasion even when it meant stepping on someone else's toes. This time it did.

"I've suggested that more than once," Lani said. "To no good effect. Mom more or less said no way in hell would she go live in one of those places!"

"She's already been in hell," Kath observed. "First she lost your brother and then your dad. I can see how it must seem as though she's got nothing left to live for."

"Because I'm not good enough?" Lani asked bleakly.

"Because she can't see any way forward right now," Kath replied.

"That makes two of us," Lani muttered. Dan could see that his wife was close to tears, and that was something that almost never happened. The Tohono O'odham weren't supposed to cry—ever.

"Then I suggest you pull up your big girl panties," Kath said. "The same thing happened to my grandmother after Grandpa died. She insisted on moving into my mother's retirement condo, and it's a miracle the two of them didn't come to blows. And Grandma said the same thing Diana's saying, that there was no way she'd go. Finally Mom put her foot down and said, 'You're going or else.'"

"What happened?"

"She ended up loving it."

"So you're saying I should just lay down the law—my way or the highway?" Lani asked.

"I am," Kath said.

"But how do I go about finding a place like that? And how much do they cost?"

"They can be fairly expensive, but your mom's fairly well off financially, isn't she?"

"She is," Lani agreed.

"Since you have your hands more than full right now, let me do some recon work for you," Kath offered. "I'll find out what the local options are and let you know. You'll probably have to pull rank on her to make it happen, but you really don't have a choice."

Dan and Brian had listened to this whole exchange in dead silence. Dan had raised the subject of assisted living more than once only to have Lani shut him down. Kath Fellows had somehow managed to bypass all of Lani's objections.

"All right then," Lani agreed finally. "Thank you. Now let's call the kids and tell them soup's on."

Dan picked up a paper plate and began filling it. Today had been nothing short of mind-blowing. First he had visited a humble school gymnasium that turned out to be a holy place.

Now Kath Fellows had just delivered a miracle. It didn't get any better than that.

After dinner, while Lani and Kath cleaned up the kitchen, Dan had a chance to talk to Brian about what he'd learned over the past two days, while Brian, after checking with sources at the Tucson PD, was able to supply the unwelcome news that whoever had taken Ida Rios's initial phone call hadn't bothered to generate an actual report.

"That's exactly why we need people like you out there doing what you're doing," Brian said.

"Thanks," Dan replied. "Coming from you, that means a lot."

It wasn't until Dan and Lani were in bed in the guest room that had once been Brandon Walker's study before Dan was finally able to share what he'd learned with Lani. She was particularly interested in what he had to say about John Wheeler, aka Chair Man.

"You say Gabe and Tim go to this Circle thing on a regular basis?" she asked.

"Seems like," Dan replied. "When Gabe finally showed up, he and John Wheeler greeted each other like old friends."

"I wonder why Gabe's never mentioned him to me," Lani mused aloud.

"Maybe he thought that having another medicine man encroaching on your territory might pose a problem."

"You're saying you think this Chair Man guy is a medicine man?"

When Dan had first shown up on the scene, he had discounted what he called all that supposed "feather shaking" stuff. He considered Lani's question for a long time before he answered.

"I do," he concluded finally. "I think he's the real McCoy, same as you."

"That's a major concession," Lani said.

"Yes, it is."

"In that case I'd like to meet him some time."

Within minutes, Lani's breathing steadied, letting Dan know she had fallen asleep. When that happened, it wasn't lost on Dan that they had talked at length about the Rosa Rios case and Chair Man, all the while ignoring the elephant in the room—what were they going to do about Diana Ladd Walker?

Dan was smart enough to let that sleeping dog lie.

CHAPTER 18

TUCSON, ARIZONA
Saturday, April 2, 2022, 1:30 P.M.

FOR TWO WEEKS AFTER HIS COMPLETE SCREWUP in Albuquerque, Charlie Milton had barely slept a wink, spending his sleepless nighttime hours going over and over what had gone wrong. For one thing, he never should have picked her in the first place. She was a cute little blonde who had set his mouth watering the moment he saw her. From then on he'd admired her from afar, including her stunning win in barrel racing.

That evening, official parties and unofficial ones were held by rodeo teams at several locations on the fairgrounds. The unofficial ones had included plenty of underage drinking and a good deal of marijuana use as well, and that was the kind Blondie had attended along with a tall lanky guy who was evidently her boyfriend. When the boyfriend had taken off early, Charlie could barely believe his luck. He'd eagerly followed her as she left the party and headed for the barns.

It was cold as hell that night. And the path between the barns had been pitch-black. It should have been an easy takedown, but it wasn't. The moment he grabbed for her, he slipped on something—frozen horse shit, as it turned out. He'd learned much later when he scraped the mess off the sole of his shoe. He had managed to right himself by the time he grabbed her again. She was larger than expected, and harder to handle, and she had managed to pierce the frigid night air with a single earsplitting scream. It took bare seconds for him to have his hands around her neck, but she fought like crazy, kicking his shins and knocking off his glasses.

Just as she started to weaken, her boyfriend had shown up, charging out of the barn and yelling at the top of his lungs. With no other choice, Charlie let go of Blondie's neck and took off. He was in the car and driving away when he realized he'd left his glasses behind, but he hadn't dared go back to look for them. Fortunately, he made it to his hotel without incident. He would have headed out of town right then, but driving in the middle of the night with only a pair of prescription sunglasses seemed like a bad idea. He had spent the remainder of the night kicking himself for disregarding the advice of the ophthalmologist who had recommended he consider having cataract surgery sooner than later. From where he was that night, earlier would have been better.

As soon as the sun came up, Charlie headed

south, keeping an eye on his rearview mirror, terrified he might see blue lights flashing there. He'd left the barns and driven straight out through the rodeo ground's front gates, for Pete's sake! No doubt there were surveillance cameras coming and going at the entrance. As soon as the little bitch reported what had happened, they'd check the footage, and Charlie would be toast.

The GPS said it would be a little more than a six-hour drive to get from Albuquerque to his RV park in Tucson. By midafternoon the next day, he was back home and in familiar territory, thankful that the following day he'd be able to go back to Costco and order a replacement pair of glasses. Nevertheless, he knew he still wasn't out of the woods. The license plate he'd used that time had been stolen in Tucson, and the cops might get lucky and come looking for him anyway.

Once he was safely home, Charlie got on the computer and started checking Albuquerque news sites, where he found no mention of any trouble at the rodeo grounds. Maybe there were enough more-serious assaults in Albuquerque that attempted ones merited zero coverage. Either that, or maybe Blondie hadn't made a police report. Why would that be?

And then Charlie hit on a possibility. Maybe she hadn't reported it *because* of the boyfriend. Obviously the two of them had been planning on hiding out in the barn to do the dirty. Why else would the asshole have come racing out the door of the barn wearing nothing but his tighty-whities and yelling bloody murder? Snow College was a junior college. What if the girl was underage? What if her folks got wind of what had been going on and decided to go after the boyfriend for statutory rape?

That realization allowed Charlie to hope that he might get away with it after all. Even so, it hadn't made it any easier for him to sleep that night and for many nights thereafter.

After Charlie's long pandemic-enforced dry spell, obviously he'd been out of practice. He'd been too eager, and he'd made mistakes. That couldn't happen again. In the meantime, with his ever-worsening itch remaining unscratched, every time he passed the maracas, he gave them a serious shake, just for luck. He spent an hour or two almost every day, reminiscing over his treasures—Adele's wedding ring, Rosa's belt buckle, Makayla's diamond nose stud, Yolanda's class ring, Coreen's opal birthstone ring, Annika's heart-shaped locket, and Marcella's handmade beaded bracelet. The Snow College barrel racer, whatever her name was, would have been number eight. With her he had come away empty-handed, but each time he held one of those items in his hands, he recalled the girl's name and remembered the exact moment the light and life had gone out of her eyes.

Gradually, he'd started feeling better. Until today. This very morning everything had come to a screeching halt when Rosa Rios's name had been plastered front and center on every local TV newscast. Although her remains had evidently been found years earlier, they had only just now been identified. That was the whole reason Charlie had dropped her off in Cochise County as opposed to Pima. At the time Charlie had correctly assumed that human remains found in Cochise County would be of little interest for media outlets in Tucson. But now word was out that Rosa had gone missing in Tucson over Rodeo Weekend 2019. She'd last been seen at the Buckeroo Bar and Grill. With the unwelcome knowledge that Tucson would now be ground zero for the Rosa Rios investigation, Charlie Milton's world shifted on its axis.

For several moments after seeing the story for the first time, he didn't move a muscle. He simply sat there in stunned disbelief. How had this happened? As far as he knew, obtaining a DNA profile from charred remains was impossible, but maybe Rosa's bones hadn't been charred enough, although they should have been. He had taken his sweet time with killing her without allowing enough of a margin for getting rid of the body. With the sun coming up, he'd rushed the job, hurriedly extinguishing the fire by covering it with a layer of dirt. The remaining cinders should have maintained enough heat to do the job, but maybe he'd been wrong about that, and she hadn't been completely cooked. The same thing had happened with Annika Wallace. He'd done fine in terms of planning the initial takedown but hadn't paid enough attention to weather conditions when it came to disposing of the body.

What was it his mother used to tell him?

"Haste makes waste." In both instances, haste had actually left waste behind.

Eventually, however, Charlie began to reassess his current situation. Sitting out on his tiny patio, having his morning smoke, he decided that maybe this wasn't as catastrophic as it could have been. He'd always known DNA might be his downfall. That was why he'd always been so diligent about wearing gloves; why, whenever possible, he soaked each of his victims with bleach before leaving them behind. But he must have screwed up somewhere along the way because a DNA match was most likely what had made the identification possible.

On the plus side, the three-year delay in making the identification definitely worked to his advantage. Even if interior surveillance cameras at the Buckeroo had captured Charlie's image, he'd made sure there had been no personal interactions between him and Rosa. In addition, even if he'd gone over to her table and chatted her up before heading out of the bar, that footage would be long gone by now. Had someone been aware of her disappearance at the time, the cops might have collected it and kept it for future reference, but this late in the game it was in the ethers.

With that realization, Charlie began to breathe easier. The identification of Rosa's remains constituted bad news, all right, and it certainly provided a serious warning about how he would need to conduct himself in the future, but this wasn't the end of the world. With that in mind, he hauled his computer and his precious maracas out to the shade-covered table on his patio. There with the desert morning heating up around him, he did some online research into recent advances in DNA technology. Sure enough, it was right there in the second link he checked. With advances in forensic science, usable DNA could now be extracted from *some* but not *all* charred human remains. The whole trick was making sure you didn't rush the process.

Charlie paid extra to have a search engine that automatically deleted his online history. With that in mind, he went ahead and worked through his list. He checked Annika Wallace first. The only items he could find were about her being reported missing in 2019, but there was nothing since then mentioning that her body had been found. The fierce storm that had blown through that night, causing areawide flash flooding, must have worked its magic, allowing Skull Valley Wash to continue living up to its name. The remains or partial remains of one of his other victims—Yolanda Darlene Larson—had been found and identified, but so far no suspects had been identified, and the case had gone cold. The others remained exactly where he'd left them, and hopefully that's where they would stay—out of sight and out of mind.

Just then, Melody Baxter, whose RV was parked directly behind Charlie's, came around the far end of his rig walking her miserable dog.

"Morning," she called cheerily. "Are you heading out soon?"

Charlie actively disliked Melody. She was far

too chatty for his taste, and her dog—an obnoxious little poodle named Hazel—never failed to bark her head off at him, which was what the dog was doing that very moment, from right there in his own yard. If he ever caught that little mutt outside on her own, he'd strangle the life out of her, too. With those thoughts rumbling through his head, it took a moment for him to realize that the woman was waiting for an answer of some kind and he had to struggle to recall the question.

"Maybe in a week or so," he said at last. "And you?"

"We'll probably leave sometime early next week," she said. "Earl likes to be back home in Indiana when it's time for the income tax dance, but we're going to take it slow and easy this time around and do some sightseeing along the way. Both the Grand Canyon and Zion are still on our bucket list."

Good riddance, Charlie thought. What he said aloud was, "Have fun."

"Oh, we will."

Fastening the dog's leash to a fence post, Melody meandered over to Charlie's table. Then without so much as "Mother, may I," she picked up one of his maracas and gave it a shake. This wasn't the first time she had shown an unhealthy interest in those. She'd even offered to buy them on more than one occasion. He had told her quite firmly that they were not for sale. On this occasion, Charlie had to restrain himself to keep from snatching the one she was holding out of her hand.

"Are you sure you won't let me buy these?" she inquired. "They're really unusual. Back home I have a collection of unique instruments from all over the world. These would fit in perfectly."

"Sorry," he said, forcing a smile. "A now-deceased friend of mine made them, sentimental value and all that. They're not for sale at any price."

As soon as he said the words, Charlie realized his mistake. With her standing right there he'd forgotten about the street fair in Guaymas. Crap!

Fortunately Melody left then—finally. Charlie stubbed out his cigarette in the black marble ashtray he had inherited from his father. The ashtray and the empty box from the Zegna tie he'd worn to Adele's funeral were the only things he'd taken with him when he'd abandoned his previous life. Then, as he always did, he used his foot to raise the lid on the small metal trash can he kept next to his front steps and emptied the ashtray into that. Smiling to himself, he went inside. Adele had never allowed him to smoke inside the house. Even though she'd been gone for the better part of a dozen years now, he still followed that rule. It was the one thing she'd been right about. RVs were too damned small for indoor smoking!

CHAPTER 19

FLAGSTAFF, ARIZONA
Sunday, April 3, 2022, 1:30 A.M.

DECIDING HER COMMUNITY POLICING PAPER
was as good as it was going to get, Jenny finally
called it done and went to bed around midnight.
She was awakened almost an hour later by her
cell phone. Her phone actually rang, unlike her
mother's, which, no matter how many times
Jenny objected, still crowed like a rooster. But
given that her mother was in law enforcement,
a middle of the night call sent Jenny into a mo-
mentary panic until she saw Deborah Russell's
name in caller ID. She had added Deb's number
to her contacts list as soon as their earlier phone
call ended.

"Deb," Jenny exclaimed when she answered.
"Are you all right?"

"I'm fine," Deb answered with a giggle that
hinted that maybe a bit of partying had occurred
after the end of season banquet. "And I did it."

"You did what?"

"I got a sample of Eddie's DNA. Actually I stole it, and I've never stolen anything before in my life!"

"You stole it?" Jenny demanded.

"I did, and I'll probably go to hell for it, but I'm not sorry. Seating assignments were based on overall rankings, so Eddie and I were at the same table. I knew his girlfriend was going to be there and that would be awkward, so I had planned on trading places with someone else. But then I changed my mind and decided to go for it. After dinner, they called us up onstage for team photos, and I had to walk past the place where he'd been sitting. His dessert plate and fork were right there in plain sight next to his dirty napkin. So I acted like I had tripped and sat down on his chair long enough to check the strap on my shoes. You'll never guess what happened next. When I stood back up, both his napkin and dessert fork had somehow ended up in my evening bag. His stupid girlfriend didn't even notice."

"Good job," Jenny told her, cringing a bit when she realized how much that remark sounded like her mother who was currently attempting to potty train Sage. "But why are you calling me in the middle of the night?"

"Because I'm afraid I might lose my nerve and not go through with this," Deb replied. "If I spend all day tomorrow thinking about packing them up to send to you, I might end up changing my mind. So I was wondering if you'd meet me in Vegas tomorrow afternoon. That way, I can hand the stuff over to you and be done with it. It'll be more like giving it to a friend than giving it to the cops. At least it'll feel that way to me. And since I'll be coming from Ephraim and you'll be driving from Flagstaff, that'll be about a three-and-a-half-hour drive for you and a little over five for me."

Jenny had planned to spend the whole day studying, but if there was a chance the DNA comparison might solve Rosa Rios's homicide, her studies would have to wait.

"Where and when?" she asked.

"Do you know the Railroad Pass Casino?"

Jenny had to think about that for a moment. "Isn't that the first one after you cross Hoover Dam?"

"That's right. I've been there with friends a couple of times—you know, for parties and stuff," Deb replied vaguely.

Jenny did know, and she was beginning to think that Deb Russell wasn't nearly the kind of straitlaced perfect Mormon girl she was purported to be.

"My folks wouldn't go there on a bet, and neither would any of their friends," Deb continued, "but the casino has a nice little coffee shop. I could meet you there, say around noon?"

"Done," Jenny said. "I'll meet you in the coffee shop at Railroad Pass at high noon. Now go to bed. You'll have to be up early to meet me there. You don't want to fall asleep along the way."

Jenny started to go back to bed, too, but thought better of it. Her worst class all semester had been History of American Policing. The material itself was boring, and Professor Roger Smedley was dry as dust. Not only that, it had been an afternoon class that met on Fridays. Travel to rodeo events often led to Jenny's missing class completely. And more often than not, even when she'd been in attendance, she'd had difficulty staying awake. The grade on her midterm exam had made that abundantly clear.

Recently she'd heard about a guy who called himself the Pied Piper of NAU. Carson Green was a senior working on a double major in computer science and sound engineering. He had masterminded a scheme where, during the pandemic, he had prevailed on individual students in various disciplines to record professors' virtual lectures for many of the university's most challenging courses. Carson could probably have made a fortune had he decided to monetize it. Instead, calling it his Underground Railroad, as a public service, he created a free-use audio library where students could download lectures from the previous year, which didn't seem to vary all that much from year to year.

Dreading having to face the final, Jenny had recently learned that History of American Policing happened to be listed in the Underground Railroad's catalog. Before going back to bed, she ordered up the first six lectures and downloaded them into her phone. This time, if she listened as she drove, there'd be no sleeping in class.

BY SEVEN THIRTY THE NEXT MORNING, EGG McMuffin in hand, Jenny was underway with Professor Smedley's raspy voice droning in her ear, but her strategy worked. She had no other option but to listen, all the while hoping that some of what she was hearing would still be in her head in a few weeks' time when finals rolled around.

Crossing the bridge high over Hoover Dam, Jenny was appalled by the low water level in Lake Mead. For people whose drinking and irrigation water depended on the reservoir behind Hoover Dam, that was worrisome.

The hotel/casino was only a few minutes' drive beyond the bridge. Walking through the casino area to locate the coffee shop, Jenny was appalled by all the cigarette smoke. It seemed gambling and smoking went hand in hand.

As soon as Jenny set foot inside the coffee shop, she spotted Deb seated in a nearby booth with a menu and a filled coffee cup situated on the table in front of her. Coffee would count as yet another no-no for a devout Mormon girl.

"You beat me here," Jenny said, slipping into the opposite side of the booth.

Without a word of greeting Deborah Russell reached down, retrieved something from the bench seat beside her. The item turned out to be a small beaded handbag. She laid it on the table and then pushed it across to Jenny.

"There," she said. "I did it. Now it's in your hands. My own cotton swab is in there, too."

"Are you relieved?" Jenny asked.

"I guess," Deb said, but she didn't sound relieved.

Jenny studied the handbag. She had seen tiny purses like that one once before—in a locked display case at a high-end store. The ones in the display case had all been well above Jenny's purse-shopping price point.

"I don't need the handbag," she said, "just the napkin and the fork. Don't you want to keep it?"

Deb shook her head. "I don't want it."

"Thank you, then," Jenny said, slipping the purse into her backpack.

Their waitress appeared. After handing Jenny a menu, she refilled Deb's coffee cup without bothering to ask if a refill was wanted.

"Can I get you anything?" the waitress asked, turning to Jenny.

"A tuna melt, please," Jenny answered, "and coffee for me, too."

"I'm not supposed to drink coffee," Deb said once the waitress walked away.

Jenny smiled. "I know, and I suspect there are a lot of other things you're not supposed to do, either, including stealing dessert forks."

Deb actually laughed aloud at that. "You've got that right. My folks would be shocked."

"Your folks are probably very nice people."

"I guess," Deb agreed. "I just wish sometimes..." she added wistfully.

"What do you wish?"

"That they were less strict."

"Maybe they would be if they knew you better," Jenny suggested.

"What do you mean?"

"You're here, aren't you?" Jenny asked, with a gesture that encompassed the entire room. "You're someone who fought back and survived a brutal assault. Maybe you didn't report it at the time, but you're here now because you're willing to do what you can to aid law enforcement in getting a dangerous creep off the streets."

"What are you saying?"

"That maybe it's time to show your parents who you really are. You're not their little girl anymore, but a responsible young woman who's willing to put herself on the line to help others."

"I didn't file a police report at the time because I didn't want my folks to find out about Eddie."

"And why didn't you tell them about him?"

Deb shrugged. "I guess I knew they wouldn't approve."

"And there's a reason you knew that," Jenny suggested. "Because, even before you found out about Eddie's girlfriend, you already knew he was bad news, and now the jerk is history. You were smart enough to put him in your rearview mirror, so take credit for that. And take credit for this, too."

"You're saying I should tell my folks about what happened?"

Jenny was probably less than two years older than Deborah Russell, but in that moment, it seemed as though there was a world of difference between them in terms of life experience. What if the advice Jenny was about to dish out ended up being totally wrong? Still, after a pause, she said what was on her mind.

"I think you need to tell them about the attack," Jenny asserted, "or, at the very least, tell your mother."

Deb looked up in alarm. "Why?"

"Something terrible may have happened to you, but you're still her daughter. You'll always be your mother's daughter, no matter what. And I can tell you, if you were my daughter, I would want to take you in my arms and hold you and tell you how sorry I was about what had happened to you, but I'd also be incredibly proud to think that you'd be willing to take that terrible experience and use it to help someone else and give answers to a grieving mother who's still suffering over what happened to her own daughter."

Deb listened without comment. Finally, after a long pause, she spoke. "I'll think about it, but I'm not making any promises."

Their food came then. Deb attacked her chiliburger as though she were starving. Jenny looked at her food without touching it for a long moment.

"There's another reason I think you need to tell your parents about what happened," Jenny admitted.

"Which is?"

"Because if we're right, and if the guy who attacked you is responsible for murdering Rosa Rios, like it or not you're going to end up being dragged into an official homicide investigation. When that happens and things get tough, your mother will be the person you'll want to have in your corner."

"That's easy for you to say," Deb replied. "Your mother's a cop. Mine's just a mom."

"Maybe so," Jenny allowed, "but one who loves you more than anything."

After lunch, they didn't linger. A little after one, Deb headed north, and Jenny headed south. On her way back to Flagstaff, Jenny didn't listen to Professor Smedley, at least not at first. She was too busy replaying, analyzing, and second-guessing everything she'd said to Deborah Russell. Was the advice she'd given good or bad, right or wrong? And just how much of that same advice could as easily be applied to Jennifer Ann Brady?

So far she hadn't shared any of her suspicions about the Deborah Russell/Rosa Rios connection with her own mother. Initially she had assumed that any information she managed to glean would be sent along to MIP through the Cochise County Sheriff's Department. But maybe it was time for her to do the same thing she had suggested Deborah Russell should do and let her mother know exactly who Jenny was.

She was the one who had made the possible connection between the two cases—between what had happened to Deb and what had happened to Rosa. Right or wrong, this was her lead. The DNA evidence inside that beaded hand-bag constituted her physical evidence, not her mother's. If it turned out to be a great big noth-ing, that, too, would be on her head, with no reflection on Sheriff Joanna Brady or her depart-ment.

Jenny remembered that her mother had mentioned the name of the MIP investigator working the case, but she'd been too preoccupied with the news about Rosa to pay close attention to the background details. She could have called her mom right then and asked for the guy's name and number, but she didn't. She needed to handle this on her own. Instead of leaning on her mother for credibility, she'd do what anyone else with a possible tip on one of MIP's cases would have to do—go through regular channels to obtain the man's contact information and supply the tip without any outside help. Whatever information she provided had to be able to stand up to the investigator's scrutiny on its own and not because the sheriff of Cochise County had vetted it beforehand.

Jenny suspected her parents might be disappointed upon learning Jenny had inserted her game-changing information into the investigation without asking for help, but she was pretty sure of something else. When push came to shove, both Joanna Brady and Butch Dixon would be incredibly proud of her taking that action under her own initiative.

Jenny reached that conclusion just as she arrived at the first Kingman exit. With a good three hours of driving yet to do, she firmly put Rosa Rios and Deb Russell aside and turned on Professor Smedley. With any kind of luck she'd be able to plow through the better part of three more lectures before she made it back to Flagstaff.

CHAPTER 20

AS DEB RUSSELL HEADED BACK NORTH ON I-15, she did so with a strange mixture of relief and dread. At least she didn't have to worry about those damned glasses anymore. They really were out of her hands. Still, she couldn't help wondering what would happen next. What if she really was dragged into the Rosa Rios homicide investigation? If the guy who had attacked her turned out to be the same one who killed Rosa, Deb might be called upon to testify against him in open court. Eddie Willis might be required to testify, too, and that prospect brought her right back to her parents—James and Edena Russell.

Jennifer Brady knew nothing at all about Deb's family, but she was right about her mother being the one person Deb could always count on. It had been true for as long as she could remember. From the start, her father had made it plain that she was a disappointment. He had wanted a boy. Not only was Deb a girl, but due to some kind of gynecological complication suffered by her mother during the delivery, she was the only child he got.

James Russell, PhD, was a smart man who viewed himself as an intellectual. He'd been a professor of English literature at Southern Utah University for years before being appointed Dean of Students. He always expected that his daughter would follow in his academic footsteps. Unfortunately that hadn't come about, either. From kindergarten on, Deb had struggled at school. It wasn't until third grade when her teacher finally figured out Deb was dyslexic. With that diagnosis in hand, Edena Russell had done everything in her power to fix the problem, including procuring the tutoring and extra help that eventually made it possible for Deb to read well enough to get by even if she wasn't especially proficient at it. When it came time for standardized tests, she never once finished any of the reading comprehension segments before time was up. Other kids would already have completed their work and be staring off into space, but not Deb Russell.

Oddly enough, James Russell had also expected his daughter to grow up to be a girly girl. She didn't. Dolls and dresses were of no interest to her. Instead, she was all in for horses. James had derided her wanting to join 4-H, and he'd been 100 percent opposed to Deb's having her own horse or taking up barrel racing, and yet all those things had happened. Why? Because of her mom. Not only had Edena won each of those rounds, she had eventually convinced her husband that they needed a pickup truck and a horse trailer to get Deb and her barrel-racing horse, Daisy Mae, from competition to competition.

By senior year, when other kids were discussing plans for college, Deborah Russell was all too aware of her intellectual shortcomings. Those early years in school had left her with a permanent deficit as far as learning the basics was concerned. She had struggled all through high school. She could do math all right, but things like English and history—which were long on reading and reading comprehension—were incredibly difficult. She graduated in the lower third of her class having eked out passing grades but not stellar ones.

When it came to college enrollment, James's expectations were clear. He wanted his daughter to enroll in SUU. Worried that her academic abilities wouldn't measure up to university-level standards, and not wanting to embarrass her father in front of his colleagues, Deb had opted for Snow College, a small junior college in Ephraim, Utah, a hundred and sixty miles north of Cedar City. Not only did she think the smaller school would be more in keeping with her skill set, the Snow College athletic department offered her a place on their rodeo team. Once again James had raised strenuous objections, but once again, Edena had sided with her daughter and carried the day.

On the way to Vegas and focused on her meeting with Jenny, Deb hadn't even taken her foot off the gas pedal as she drove past the Cedar City exits. Going back, though, having spent more than three hours contemplating her lifetime's worth of interactions with her parents, once Deb hit the first Cedar City exit, she turned off. Of course, it helped that she knew her father was out of town for a four-day church leadership conference in Salt Lake. But even as she drove down the exit ramp, and later as she turned up the driveway to her parents' house, Deb still wasn't sure whether or not she'd tell her mother the whole story.

Parking in the driveway, Deb let herself into the garage with her clicker and then entered the house through the door that opened into the kitchen.

"Jimmy, is that you?" Edena called from the family room. "What are you doing home?"

The entire rest of the world called Deb's father James. Only his wife referred to him as Jimmy.

"No, Mom, it's me."

"Deb? Really?" her beaming mother called out in delight as she rushed into the kitchen and pulled her daughter into a welcoming embrace. "What in the world are you doing here?"

Deb was always taken aback by how lovely her mother was. She may have been home alone on a Sunday afternoon, but she was dressed in a pair of white slacks topped by a vividly flowered long-sleeved blouse. Not a hair was out of place, and her makeup and nails were perfection itself.

"I came down to see a friend," Deb said, pulling away.

"What friend?" Edena asked.

"A girl I know from rodeo," Deb said dismissively. Yup, the jury was still out as to how much of the real story she'd be telling.

"Are you hungry?" Edena asked. "Can I get you something to eat?"

"No," Deb said. "We had lunch just a little while ago."

Taking her daughter's hand, Edena led the way into the family room. "Come join me," she said, sitting down on the oversized sectional positioned in front of a huge flat-screen TV. "I'm here watching the Masters all by my lonesome, but I can turn it off if you like. I've spent so much time watching golf with your dad that I've actually learned to enjoy it. You don't need to tell him that though," she added with a grin. "What he doesn't know won't hurt him."

"You can leave it on," Deb said, dropping onto the sofa, too, but in a spot that was slightly more than beyond arm's length as she grappled with what her mom had just said. The last had been little more than a throwaway line, a supposedly meaningless joke—but, under the circumstances, it was exactly what Deborah needed to hear—a tiny hint that there could be things between mother and daughter that didn't include Deb's father. Although that was what eventually pushed her over the edge, she didn't launch into it immediately. Instead, she sat in silence for a time, watching the action on the screen.

The Masters wasn't exactly exciting. A lot of time was spent watching golfers walk silently from place to place with banks of colorful flowers forming a backdrop. And all the while, the announcers' subdued voices were punctuated by the sharp calls of birds populating the trees lining the course. The sliding door that led from the family room out to the patio was wide open. No doubt the bird calls being broadcast nationwide from Augusta, Georgia, could be heard by the ones native to Cedar City, Utah. Deb wondered if they spoke a common language and if the birds in Utah ever wondered who these strange interlopers could be and where they were from.

"How are things?" Edena asked, interrupting Deb's train of thought.

If she was going to tell the story, now was the time. "Not so good," Deb murmured.

"Oh, no," Edena exhaled. With a click of the remote the foreign bird calls were silenced, and the Masters vanished from the screen. "What's going on?"

"Something bad happened to me, Mom," Deb admitted, "and I need to talk to you about it."

"What?" Edena asked, with one hand pressed against her chest. "Don't tell me you're pregnant!"

So much for her parents still thinking their daughter was a virgin. "No," Deb said at once. "I'm definitely not pregnant."

Edena sighed in relief. "What then?" she asked.

Deb took a deep breath. "Someone tried to kill me."

Edena was aghast. In the silence that followed

all color drained from her face. "Oh, no," she managed. "Where? When? How did it happen?"

After a moment Deb continued. "While we were in Albuquerque for the regional finals, I was leaving a party when a guy came up behind me and tried to strangle me. He might have succeeded if my boyfriend hadn't shown up and chased him away."

That's when the tears came—the tears Deborah Russell had been holding at bay for weeks. Edena rose from where she was sitting, moved over, and took her daughter in her arms, holding her close and consoling her until the storm of tears subsided.

"Tell me about it," Edena said finally once Deb regained her composure.

"I was walking back to the barns to meet up with Eddie, when this guy I didn't know came up and tried to grab me from behind. I couldn't get away, and I managed to let out a single scream before he wrapped his hands around my throat and started choking me. Fortunately Eddie had heard the scream. He came on the run and chased the guy away. But by the time he got there, I was already losing consciousness. If he hadn't arrived when he did, I'd probably be dead."

Somehow Deb failed to mention the fact that, at the time, Eddie had been barefoot and dressed in nothing but his underwear.

Edena was aghast. "You must have been scared to death!"

Deb nodded. "I was."

"And this boyfriend—Eddie. What's his last name? I don't think you've ever mentioned him."

"His last name is Willis," Deb answered. "The reason I've never mentioned him is he didn't last long. Turned out he already had a girlfriend, and he was two-timing her with me. I ended up dumping him a few days later."

"He may have turned out to be a jerk, but at least he was there when you needed him," Edena declared. "Thank God for that. What did the police do? Were they able to catch the guy?"

"They didn't do anything, and, no, they haven't caught him."

"Why not?"

"Because I didn't report it," Deb admitted. "I knew if I brought in the cops, you'd end up knowing all about it, and I was afraid . . ."

"Afraid of what?"

"Mostly that the two of you would find out about Eddie," Deb said in a small voice. "But that's why I'm telling you now—because the cops may have to be involved after all."

"How come?"

"When the guy attacked me, he knocked my purse off my shoulder and everything fell out onto the ground. Eddie helped me gather up my purse and everything in it, but in the process he picked up something that belonged to the bad guy instead of me—a pair of glasses. I didn't find out about them until much later on when I cleaned out the purse."

"What does any of this have to do with the police?" Edena asked impatiently.

"I'm getting to that. Although I didn't report it to the cops, word about what had happened spread like wildfire among all the kids who were there. One of them, a girl named Jennifer Brady—the one Daisy and I aced out of first place in barrel racing that weekend—is from a small town in southern Arizona where her mother is the county sheriff. Last week they identified the remains of a murder victim, a girl named Rosa Rios. Turns out, before she died, Rosa used to be a barrel racer, too. And since she disappeared during Rodeo Weekend in Tucson, Jenny wondered if the guy who killed her might have been the same one who attacked me."

"Albuquerque and Tucson aren't exactly next-door neighbors," Edena observed. "And when did it happen, before you were attacked or after?"

"Way before," Deb answered. "Rosa died in 2019, and her body was found soon afterward, but it was just now identified. Jenny contacted me about a possible link. When I told her about having the guy's glasses, she went nuts because she thought that if it was the same guy, maybe the cops could get a DNA profile off them and be able to identify him from that. And that's what I was doing today. I drove down to Vegas, met up with Jenny, and gave her the glasses. She suggested I tell you what was going on because, if it does turn out to be the same guy, I might end up being called on to testify against him in court. That's why I'm telling you now, so if that happens it won't come as a surprise."

Another silence followed. "This is a lot to take in," Edena said at last. "Will Jenny's mother's department be the one investigating the case?"

"No, it's somebody else—some federal agency that investigates crimes against Native Americans. Rosa's an Indian—an Apache from San Carlos."

"Then let's hope those glasses help them nail the guy," Edena said. "He's a monster who needs to be locked up for good."

Deb's heart overflowed with gratitude. Had her father been home, the reaction to her story might have been far different, but her mother's calm acceptance of what she'd just heard came as a huge comfort.

"I'm really sorry for keeping all this a secret," Deb apologized. "I should have told you about it as soon as it happened."

Edena nodded. "Keeping secrets is always harder than telling the truth," she said softly. "Believe me, I know."

That wasn't at all what Deb had expected her mother to say, and the statement left her puzzled. "What do you mean?" she asked.

"Have you ever noticed that I only have three of my high school yearbooks?"

Now it was Deb's turn to nod, but she was puzzled by this sudden change of subject. "I figured you'd just lost it or something."

"No," Edena said. "I burned it."

"You burned it? Why?"

"My then-boyfriend and I were Homecoming King and Queen our senior year. He was a big man on campus—the star quarterback—and being king and queen seemed like a really big deal, but after the dance that night, on the way home, we stopped off to neck, and he raped me."

Deb suddenly felt as though the world had stopped spinning. "No!" she whispered.

"Yes," Edena said. "It was awful. When I got home from the dance that night, I burned the dress, too. I told Grandma that somebody had spilled a drink on it and ruined it, but that was a lie. Fortunately, I didn't get pregnant, but just like you, I never told my parents about it or anyone else, either. I told my friends that we had a big fight after the dance and broke up."

Deb was taken aback. "Did you tell Dad?" she asked.

"Not at first. We met two years later when I was a sophomore in college. He was an old-school kind of guy who didn't believe in premarital sex, so I just let it slide and led him to believe I was still a virgin. Then, our senior year, when he popped the question, I knew I had to tell him, and I did."

"What happened?"

"He took me in his arms and told me how sorry he was that I'd had to endure something so awful. Then he said it wasn't my fault and that we'd never talk about it again. We got married six months later, and I've never spoken to anyone else about it until today when I told you."

Deb was stunned. That kind of kindness and understanding wasn't something she would ever have expected from her father. She was still sitting there wondering about it when her mother stood up in a fashion that indicated that, as far as Edena was concerned, the conversation was over. Deb was relieved because she really didn't want to answer any more questions.

"Where are you going?" Deb asked.

"To thaw out some pork chops from the freezer," Edena said. "You're here now, and you're not leaving until I've fixed you a decent dinner."

Deb was glad to go with the flow. Later, while her mother cooked, they talked about other things, less troubling topics like how school was going and what her plans were for the summer. Only as they were cleaning up the kitchen did Edena steer the conversation back into bumpy territory.

"Did you sleep with Eddie Willis?" she asked.

That time Deb couldn't bring herself to tell the truth. "No!" she exclaimed. "Absolutely not. I think I was headed there. If it hadn't been for the attack, it might have happened that night, but it didn't. It was the next week, after we got back from Albuquerque, when I found out about his other girlfriend."

"I'm grateful he saved you that night," Edena said, "but you weren't wrong in thinking we would have disapproved of him. In fact, I probably would have hated him the moment I laid eyes on him, so I'm happy you found out about the girlfriend and uncovered his true colors on your own."

"So am I," Deb agreed.

"But let me give you a word of advice," Edena continued. "When you get back to school, the next time you go looking for a boyfriend, don't go looking for some flashy jerk who wants the whole world to know how important he is. Go looking for someone who's serious about his schoolwork and who's shy about blowing his own horn; someone who'll take a job and keep it, and bring his paycheck home every single time. That may sound boring, but when it comes time to choose someone to spend your life with, there's a lot to be said for boring."

"Like Dad, you mean?" Deb asked.

"You might think your father is boring," Edena said fondly. "I suspect a lot of people do, but my Jimmy is also honest and true, steady, and trustworthy. Stubborn? Yes. Opinionated? Yes, again, and is his first instinct always to say no to everything? Absolutely, but you have to remember that when he was growing up, his family was dirt poor. That's why, whenever you ask him for something, his first answer is always going to be no—because that's the way it always was for him."

"Like when I asked him for a horse?" Deb asked.

Edena smiled. "Yes, and ditto when I told him we needed a horse trailer. And ditto when you told him you wanted to go to Snow College. The thing is, your father is also someone who can be reasoned with, and I've got more than twenty years' worth of experience in talking him down out of his 'no' tree. The real trick is finding a man who's worth reasoning with. Once you hit on one of those, you'll know you have a keeper."

"So what should I do about what happened in Albuquerque—do I tell Dad or not?"

"Don't worry about that," her mother assured her. "I'll tell him. I'll also tell him about the possibility that you might be drawn into a homicide investigation. I'm guessing he'll feel the same way I do about that—happy that you're willing to help Rosa's poor mother, someone who isn't able to help herself."

That was almost exactly what Jennifer Brady had predicted—that Deb's parents would be proud of her for what she was doing rather than disappointed. And in that moment Deborah Russell realized that something terribly important had just happened between her mother and her.

Deb had planned on leaving to head north again as soon as dinner was over, but she stayed on for several more hours, chatting with her mother in a way that had never been possible before. They talked about anything and everything and nothing in particular. It was far later than it should have been when Deb finally left Cedar City for that last two and a half hours of her drive home, but she did so with a happy heart. Between the guy who had attacked her and the mess with Eddie Willis, she had lived through something bad, but with Jenny Brady's help, she had come out of it on the other side in better shape than ever before. That was all to the good, and if she could somehow help the authorities track down Rosa Rios's killer, it would be that much better.

CHAPTER 21

Sunday, April 3, 2022, 9:30 P.M.

SUNDAY WAS A QUIET DAY AT DIANA LADD
Walker's river-rock house in Gates Pass. No
cooking was necessary since there were plenty of
Anita Street Market leftovers from the day before to suit everyone's dietary fancy. While the
kids splashed in the pool, Lani spent the morning both on the phone and on her computer,
making arrangements to take five days' worth of
vacation to look after her mom.

Shortly after noon, and wanting to give Lani
and Diana some time alone, Dan packed up the
kids and headed back to their place in the hospital housing compound in Sells. Both Micah
and Angie had homework that had been put off
until Sunday afternoon. While they set about
doing that, Dan caught up with the week's worth
of laundry. He and Lani shared those kinds of
chores, and he didn't mind picking up the slack,

especially since laundry was something Adam Pardee wouldn't have done in a million years.

The kids were showered and in bed by nine. He was considering settling down in front of the TV set to see what was saved on the DVR, when his cell phone rang. The number was blocked on caller ID, which meant it was probably work.

"Field Officer Pardee?" an unfamiliar female voice asked.

"Yes."

"This is Molly from the MIP's tip line."

Having a round-the-clock fully operational tip line was only one of MIP's many bells and whistles. The agency had been created out of "discretionary funds," which meant there was little or no oversight. Local sheriffs and police chiefs were answerable to their voters. Not so with the secretary of the Department of the Interior, and since the new agency was designed to address literally decades of official neglect, she had taken full advantage. MIP headquarters was located in Denver, Colorado. It came equipped with the latest and greatest in terms of DNA profiling and had a fully staffed crime lab on call to analyze whatever evidence local field officers were able to submit. Criminalists working in the lab had full access to all outside DNA databases that were willing to work with law enforcement. In view of the fact that most of the cases were already cold, there was also a team that included several trained genetic genealogists who could be called upon as needed.

Unsurprisingly, the tip line was equally top-of-the-line. If someone dialed into the tip line, the call was answered twenty-four hours a day by trained former 911 operators who took the information and immediately passed it along to the applicable field officer. They were able to respond to both phone-in and online tips.

"What's up, Molly?" Dan asked.

"I just received an email from someone who claims to have information on the Rosa Rios homicide. I believe that's one of yours."

Dan could barely believe his ears. Rosa's remains had been identified only a few days earlier. "It is one of mine, but you're saying there's already a tip?" he asked in astonishment.

"There sure is," Molly said.

"What have you got?"

"It came in as an email," Molly replied. "Do you want me to read aloud or just send it?"

"Send it," he said. "If it's something I can respond to tonight, I will."

The email arrived seconds later:

To whom it may concern.

My name is Jennifer Brady. I believe I have important information relative to the Rosa Rios homicide. Please feel free to contact me at any time. My contact details are listed below.

Dan studied the contact information. Jennifer's email address came with an NAU.edu tag line. That meant she was either a student at Northern Arizona University in Flagstaff or else was an employee there. The phone number listed had a 520 prefix. That meant the cell phone was based in southern Arizona somewhere, most likely in Cochise County. That seemed like a bit too much of a coincidence. Was it possible this Jennifer Brady might somehow be related to Sheriff Joanna Brady? Maybe, but eager to find out what might be on offer, Dan simply dialed the number, and the phone was answered after the first ring.

"Hello?"

The voice sounded young, leading Dan to assume the speaker was most likely a student.

"My name is Daniel Pardee," he told her. "I'm a field officer with the Missing and Murdered Indigenous People Task Force, an agency inside the US Department of the Interior. Is this Jennifer Brady?"

"Yes, it is. That was fast," she added. "I sent an email to the MIP tip line just a few minutes ago."

"Well, Ms. Brady," Dan said, "we aim to please. What do you have for me?"

"Call me Jenny," she said. "And are you sure you want to go into this right now? It's a pretty long story."

"I'm all ears," he said, "and take as long as you like. I've got all the time in the world, but do you mind if I record our conversation?"

"Not at all," she said. "Record away."

For the next forty-five minutes, Dan listened. At first he had his guard up. Jenny sounded young enough that at first he wondered if this might be some kind of undergraduate prank, but the more he listened, the more fascinated he became. Jenny Brady was not just a disinterested bystander. Like Amanda Lewis Moreno and Evangeline Rodriquez Joaquin, Jenny was someone who had known Rosa Rios prior to her death.

Dan was determined to let Jenny tell the story at her own pace and without interruption. Once she related the part about the attempted strangulation of Deborah Russell in Albuquerque, Dan became downright excited. There were common denominators here—first the rodeo connection and followed by the attempted manual strangulation. Jenny would have had no way of knowing about the latter detail unless someone had told her about the autopsy results. That's the point when Dan did interrupt.

"Hold up, just a sec," he said. "Your last name is Brady. You wouldn't happen to be related to Sheriff Joanna Brady, would you?"

Jenny paused. "I am," she said somewhat defensively. "Sheriff Brady is my mother. Does that matter?"

"Did she discuss the details of Rosa's case with you?"

"No, she called to tell me Rosa was dead because she knew I knew her and didn't want me to find out about it from the news," Jenny declared. "She said Rosa's remains had been found years ago, but that they had only just now been identified. That's all she told me."

"And she made no mention as to cause of death?"

"Mom's a cop," Jenny said, sounding irritated, "a professional police officer. She doesn't discuss active cases with anyone, not even me. Why do you ask?"

"Never mind," Dan assured her. "It's no big

deal. But getting back to this attempted strangulation. Do you happen to have a case number from Albuquerque PD regarding that incident? Having that in hand would be a big help."

"That's what I'm trying to tell you!" Jenny said, sounding downright irate. "There isn't any case number! Eddie Willis, Deb's boyfriend at the time and the guy who broke up the attack, was someone her parents would have disapproved of if they'd known about him. She was afraid if she filed a report about the incident, word about her relationship with Eddie would get back to her folks."

"How did you hear about it?" Dan asked.

"What do you know about rodeos?" Jenny countered.

Dan had attended the Tohono O'odham All-Indian Rodeo and Fair a couple of times, but that was about it. "Not much," he admitted.

"Rodeo in general and intercollegiate rodeo are worlds apart from other sports, like football or baseball, for example. It's a small world. The people involved tend to know one another, and we stick together. There may not have been an official police report, and I'm sure the coaches were completely in the dark that anything out of the ordinary had happened, but by the next day all the kids in attendance, regardless of what team they were on, knew about the attack."

"All right, then," Dan said. "Please continue."

So she did. By the time Jenny got to the part about having obtained both the perpetrator's eyeglasses as well as comparison DNA samples for both Eddie Willis and Deborah Russell, Dan Pardee was downright dazzled.

"Where are those three DNA samples now?" he asked.

"Here in my apartment in Flagstaff," Jenny said. "I was wondering if you'd like to drive up here tomorrow and collect them."

Dan considered the logistics of a driving trip to Flagstaff. With Lani in Tucson and the kids in school and needing to be looked after, there was no way he could schedule a daylong trek back and forth to Flag. Besides, those samples didn't need to be in his possession—they needed to be in the hands of MIP's technicians in the DNA lab in Denver.

"Could you do me a huge favor?" he asked.

"What's that?"

"I can't drive up tomorrow, but I can give you my FedEx account number along with an address in Denver. If you could send them there overnight express directly from a FedEx office in Flag, they'll be in the lab a whole day sooner than if I come to collect them."

"What if I ask for a favor in return?" Jenny asked.

Here goes, Dan thought. *No telling what she's going to want.* "What kind of favor?" he asked.

"Would you try to leave Deb Russell's name out of this? Let's just say her parents might be upset to find out about what happened without her telling them about it."

"I'm not sure I can promise that," Dan answered. "If we get a hit on the DNA, there are likely to be questions about chain of evidence and how we obtained the sample."

"Could you maybe treat her as a confidential informant?"

"Possibly," Dan conceded. "This is all circumstantial at the moment—two rodeo-connected attacks, both of them featuring either manual strangulation or attempted manual strangulation. It may turn out that the two incidents are entirely unrelated, but for right now, let's proceed as though they're connected. If your hunch is right, I may not be able to protect Deb's anonymity, but let's jump that fence when we get to it."

"Okay then," Jenny said. "What do we need to do first?"

"Get those glasses shipped to the lab ASAP."

"All right," Jenny agreed.

"I have one more question," Dan said. "Since you contacted me via the tip line on the website rather than getting my information through your mother, I'm assuming Sheriff Brady doesn't know anything about this?"

Jenny hesitated, but only for a moment. "Correct," she answered, "she doesn't."

"Do you mind telling me why?"

"Because I need to stand on my own two feet on this," Jenny told him. "If it ends up turning into something real, then you'll be welcome to tell her. If it doesn't, I'd rather she didn't know about my sticking my nose in somewhere it didn't belong."

"Fair enough," Dan replied. "If this all comes to nothing, my lips are sealed, but you weren't wrong in seeing a possible connection between these two incidents. If it turns out your hunch is right, your mother is bound to find out about it eventually."

"I know," Jenny said, "but don't tell her until I'm ready."

Jenny hung up then, leaving Dan feeling far more enthusiastic than he'd let on. Deb Russell wasn't part of his official brief. She was Anglo not Native American, and it sounded as though she was anything but marginalized, but the rodeo connection and the assailant's modus operandi were chillingly similar.

To Dan's knowledge, most killers use guns or knives or even garrotes as their weapons of choice. Individuals who can look their victims in the eye during the minutes-long process of compressing their necks until they die were a breed apart and far more evil. With that in mind, the DNA on the eyeglasses Jennifer Brady was about to ship to the lab in Denver might possibly unmask a stone-cold killer who could have been doing this for years—killing helpless women and getting away with it.

CHAPTER 22

WHEN THE PHONE CALL WITH DAN PARDEE ended, Jenny wasn't entirely sure how to assess what had just happened. It seemed as though he had taken her information seriously enough. The fact that he wanted her to ship the purse directly to the lab in Denver to speed up the testing seemed to be a mark in her favor. But would he keep his word about leaving Deb's name out of the investigation? On that score there was no way to tell.

Jenny picked up her phone and checked for incoming texts. Before she and Deb had left Railroad Pass, they had agreed to text each other once they arrived home. She had done so, but so far Deb had not returned the favor. Jenny and Nick had exchanged several texts over the course of the evening, but Jenny was beginning to be concerned about Deb's ongoing silence.

They had left the hotel/casino just past one in the afternoon. Now it was after eleven. That was more than enough time for Deb to have made it back to Ephraim. Maybe she'd had car trouble along the way.

Feeling a bit exasperated, Jenny sent another text asking if Deb was okay. Once again no response was forthcoming. With an early morning class on tap, Jenny had no choice. She set the alarm and went to bed, but not to sleep. Instead, she lay awake, worrying about Deb. If something terrible had happened on her way home, Jenny would never forgive herself.

WHEN JENNY AWAKENED THE NEXT MORNING she found a brief text from Deb that had arrived at 3:30 A.M.:

> Just got home. Sorry to worry you. Thanks for everything.

There was no explanation as to why it had taken her so long to drive home from Vegas, but with her safely back where she belonged, Jenny could finally stop worrying. After submitting her research paper and attending her two morning classes, Jenny went straight to the FedEx office where she packaged the purse. While copying the address Dan Pardee had given her onto the shipping label, Jenny assumed that the addressee, Anna Rae Green, was someone who worked in MIP's forensics lab.

With that out of the way, and with several

hours to spend before the start of a live History of American Policing lecture, she popped over to Munds Park and took Maggie out for a ride. Between now and the end of school, she was determined to spend as much time as possible with her horse. While traversing a familiar trail, Jenny turned on her phone and listened to two more recorded lectures.

You had to stay awake to ride, the same way you had to stay awake to drive. With a little more help from Maggie, Jenny might be able to get a passing grade in that class after all.

CHAPTER 23

DAN PARDEE SAT HUNCHED OVER HIS COM-
puter keyboard, cursing his much younger self
who, at age sixteen, had told his school coun-
selor he had zero interest in keyboarding and
had opted for auto mechanics instead. In the
years since, he'd hardly ever worked on his own
vehicles, but he'd spent hours hunting and peck-
ing his way through the creation of countless
reports, first as a Shadow Wolf and now as a field
officer for MIP. He was getting better at the
task, but it didn't help his ego that both Angie
and Micah could type circles around him.

It took well over an hour and a half for him to
finish the written report that would now become
part of MIP's digital file on Rosa Rios. After
editing it to the best of his ability, he sent it off
to the Records Department at MIP. This wasn't
like his old Shadow Wolf days where the only

person who would lay eyes on a written report would have been his immediate supervisor. MIP didn't work that way.

The agency's director, Anna Rae Green, PhD, was a full-blooded Cherokee from Oklahoma. She had come to MIP for reasons very similar to Dan's. She'd been little more than a babe in arms when her mother and father had gone off to a weekend dance. Her father had returned alone, claiming that he and his wife had quarreled. Her mother's dumped remains had been located days later, and although her father was never charged in the homicide, most people on the reservation had assumed he was responsible. All that changed finally when, years later, DNA analysis linked her mother's homicide to a truck-driving serial killer who had been arrested in 2005. To avoid the death penalty, he confessed to murdering seven women in Kansas, Oklahoma, and Texas during the eighties and nineties. Anna Rae's mother had been one of his victims.

Anna Rae had grown up with the shadow of those twin family tragedies hanging over her young life—the death of her mother and on-going suspicion surrounding her father. While attending the University of Oklahoma she had majored in chemistry with a double minor in criminal justice and computer science. When she graduated from college, she had landed an entry-level job in the Forensics Services Department of the Oklahoma State Bureau of Investigation where she quickly became a rising star.

While working there she came face-to-face

with the grim reality—far too many individuals shared tragic family histories all too similar to hers. And although her mother's murder had eventually been solved, the homicides of countless Native American women often went unsolved forever. Over time, Anna Rae made a national name for herself by advocating in public for all those victims for whom justice had never been served. While doing so, she became more and more convinced that computer science might hold the key that would eventually provide answers for many of those underserved victims and families.

Given all that, when the Interior secretary set about creating MIP, it was hardly surprising that she had come looking for Anna Rae Green. She was the one who was ultimately responsible for envisioning the agency as it was now—an agency that came complete with all the latest forensic technology available in house. Her handpicked field agents were primarily of Native American descent, and she encouraged them to work in a collaborative fashion. As a result, once a field officer's written reports went into his or her individual case files, they were put through a program in which an algorithm analyzed them for key words or phrases that might be common to other ongoing cases.

That was why, half an hour after Dan finished submitting Rosa's report, a text came through from Martha Little Calf Dobbins, the MIP field officer responsible for cases originating in Montana and Wyoming. Martha, a full-blooded

Arapahoe, was originally from the Wind River in Wyoming. She now lived in Missoula where her husband, a Paiute from southern Utah, was a professor of Native American Studies at the University of Montana:

> Hey, Dan. Big Sis says the key word is RODEO. If you'll tell me about your case, I'll tell you about mine. I'm driving right now, so give me a call when you can.

Dan had been out in the kitchen microwaving one of yesterday's tamales for lunch and had missed the original computer-generated email specifying that the key word *Rodeo* was common to his case and one being handled by Martha. "Big Sis" as opposed to "Big Brother" was how field agents referred to the computer program that was forever keeping a watchful eye on their individual caseloads.

Dan dialed Martha's number immediately. "Hey, Martha," he said. "Dan here. What have you got?"

"My vic's name is Yolanda Darlene Larson. She was a member of the Blackfeet Nation, born and raised in Kalispell, Montana. From what I've been able to learn, she was a bright young woman from a loving family. She was twenty-one years old, living, working, and going to school in Butte. Shortly before her disappearance in August of 2018 she had attended the Northwest Montana Rodeo in Kalispell where her younger brother was a bronc rider. She left the rodeo grounds late in the afternoon to head back to Butte but never made it that far. Her vehicle was found abandoned two weeks later on a forest service road near Beaver Lake. Damage to that suggested that it might have been forced off the road at some point. The following summer, two guys out trout fishing found her skull washed up on the banks of the Yellowstone River. It was identified through dental records."

Dan had been listening to Martha Little Calf's summary with a growing sense of excitement, right up until she mentioned the dental records.

"Wait," he said. "Did Yolanda have all her teeth?"

"Several teeth that should have been there weren't," Martha replied. "The ME said they may have been knocked out while the body was in the river. The Yellowstone can be pretty rough in spots. The point is, there were enough teeth present to make a positive ID. But why did you ask about her teeth?"

"Because my victim was missing several, too," Dan said.

"You think her killer removed them?" Martha asked.

"Maybe, maybe not. When the ME in Cochise County took dental impressions from the skull, she noted in the autopsy that several of Rosa's teeth were missing. With nothing to compare them to, those impressions went nowhere in identifying the victim. Once I caught the case, I did an initial interview with Ida Rios, Rosa's mother, and urged her to submit Rosa's dental records to NamUs. She did so, and those have just now been uploaded into the system. That's how we finally established the ID, but when I spoke to Ida again earlier this week, she told me that, at the time Rosa went missing, all her teeth were present."

"So the missing teeth might have come out in the course of a physical assault," Martha suggested. "Or else . . ."

"Or else her killer deliberately removed them," Dan suggested grimly. "You might want to check with Yolanda's survivors and see if her teeth were present and accounted for at the time she disappeared."

"I will," Martha agreed.

After that, Dan went on to pass along everything he'd learned so far about Rosa's case, including the bits that hadn't made it into the initial report.

"Big Sis is right," Martha said when he finished. "There's definitely a rodeo component in both cases."

"And I may have found another," Dan told her. With that he launched into what he had learned about the unreported attempted strangulation of Deborah Russell in Albuquerque, including the fact that he had submitted the assailant's glasses in hopes of coming up with a DNA profile.

"But Deborah's not Indigenous, right?" Martha asked when he finished.

"No, but with the rodeo connection and a similar MO, what happened to her might just be the key to the other two."

"Maybe so," Martha agreed. "Three's supposed to be the charm. All the same, don't be surprised if you end up getting into hot water for investigating something outside our purview."

"It's worth the risk," Dan replied, "and if that case ends up leading back to ours, I'll be sure to let you know."

The phone call ended after they had agreed to exchange all relevant information on the two cases. For a long time after that, Dan simply sat at his desk staring at his computer screen and thinking. Something Martha had said about the fact that, since Deborah was Anglo, the attempt on her life wasn't MIP's problem. That was true, and it was why what had happened to her would never have surfaced on Big Sis's algorithm radar. What if there were similar cases against other Anglo victims that might lead back to the same perpetrator?

With that, Dan turned to his keyboard and called up his own search engine. The first search he tried was "rodeo and homicide." That yielded several hits having to do with a shootout between two rodeo riders, duking it out Old West style over the same woman in which one of them died and the other went to prison. In other words, nobody had a happy ending, including Dan Pardee who realized early on that the two bronco-busting gunfighters had nothing to do with his cases.

He was about to give up on the search idea, when he decided to try a different word combination—"Rodeo and disappearance." Much to his astonishment, the first item on the list hit pay dirt. The article was time-stamped July 14, 2019.

> The Yavapai County Sheriff's Department and the Prescott Police Department are jointly investigating the disappearance of Dewey resident Annika Wallace who disappeared after leaving the Lucky Strike, a bar located on Prescott's Whiskey Row on Saturday, July 6. The missing woman was last spotted on surveillance video leaving the bar shortly before one A.M. after an evening spent partying with revelers celebrating this year's Prescott Rodeo.
>
> On Tuesday morning, Dewey resident Matilda Hancock, Ms. Wallace's next-door neighbor, contacted the authorities asking for a welfare check at the Wallace residence. Ms. Hancock told officers that she'd been kept awake all night long by the constant barking of Ms. Wallace's dog. When she went over to complain about the noise, no one came to the door.
>
> Officers responding to the residence found the dog there alone and exhibiting signs of severe dehydration. The animal was turned over to Animal Control. A further check revealed that Ms. Wallace's vehicle, a Ford Fiesta, had been parked on Granite Street only a few blocks from the bar. It had been cited for several parking violations during the course of the day on Monday and had eventually been towed to the city's impound lot earlier on Tuesday morning.
>
> Ms. Wallace is reported to weigh approximately

a hundred and ten pounds. She's five foot two with blue eyes and short blond hair. Anyone having information about her possible whereabouts is urged to contact either the Prescott Police Department or the Yavapai County Sheriff's Department.

As he finished reading the article, Dan knew he was onto something. *And Annika makes four,* he said to himself, *but they have yet to find her body.*

Within minutes he was on the phone to the Yavapai County Sheriff's Department, asking to be connected to whoever was assigned to the case. "One moment, please," he was told.

A minute or so later the call was picked up by a female. "Detective Lauren Tucker," she said. "Who's calling please?"

"My name is Daniel Pardee. I'm a field officer with the MIP—a federal agency charged with investigating cases of missing and murdered Native Americans. I was hoping to speak to whoever is handling the Annika Wallace missing persons case."

"I'm not really up to speed on missing persons cases," Detective Tucker said. "Can you tell me more about it?"

Despite knowing little about the case at the beginning of the call, Detective Tucker did her best to be helpful. Over the course of the next forty-five minutes, she gave Dan everything she could find from the Annika Wallace file—which wasn't much. Permanently estranged from her family back home in Ohio, she had come to Arizona with a boyfriend who had moved on to greener pastures soon thereafter, leaving Annika to fend for herself.

Plagued with drug and alcohol problems, she'd managed to find occasional work here and there, enough to keep body and soul together. After her disappearance over Fourth of July weekend 2019, investigators had learned that she'd been involved in numerous acts of prostitution as well as occasional drug dealing. At the time she went missing, she was several months in arrears in terms of rent on her residence, which, according to Detective Tucker, was little more than an old miner's shack. No sign of foul play had been found in her vehicle, which had been left parked on the street with the keys still in the cup holder. Without a body, there had been nothing to warrant moving the investigation from missing persons to homicide.

"Although," Detective Tucker concluded, "considering how long she's been gone, it's easy to believe that she's probably deceased. Had family members been around pushing, her case might have received more attention, but based on what I'm seeing here, the last time anyone even looked at the file was more than a year ago."

That made sense to Dan. That's how many serial killers got away with doing what they did for years at a time—by focusing on vulnerable, throwaway victims no one of influence cared about. And although he doubted there was a hint of Native American blood in Annika Wallace's background, he was nonetheless convinced that she, like Deborah Russell, was part of his case.

Everyone else may have closed the book on her, but Dan was about to reopen it.

"Whatever happened to Annika may or may not be related to my cases, but I'd really appreciate it if you could forward me everything you have, including Annika's next of kin. I may need to speak to them."

"Of course," Detective Tucker agreed. "Where would you like me to send the info?"

After giving her his address, Dan ended the call. A glance at his watch told him it was almost three in the afternoon. It wouldn't be long before Angie and Micah got home from school. If he was going to have a challenging conversation with his boss, Anna Rae Green, he wanted to do so before the kids were in the house listening in on every word, but before he had her on the phone, he wanted to confirm that his DNA bombshell was in transit.

He sent a text to Jenny Brady: Is it done?

Her reply was instantaneous: On its way.

Good, he told her. Wish us luck.

With that he squared his shoulders, picked up his phone, and dialed. Once again he was surprised when the director answered her own phone. "Anna Rae Green," she said.

"It's Dan Pardee," he said.

"Good afternoon, Dan. How are things?"

"All right," he told her. "I'm making some progress on the Rosa Rios case, and I wanted to bring you into the picture."

"Shoot," she said.

He spent the better part of the next half hour telling her about everything he had learned on all four cases—Rosa's, Deborah Russell's, Yolanda Larson's, and finally Annika Wallace's. Since two of the possible victims were anything but Indigenous, he expected his boss to hit the roof about his impending request for DNA profiling on the material Jenny had sent to her. That didn't happen.

"Wow," Anna Rae breathed when he finished. "This is exciting. When's that FedEx package due to arrive?"

"Tomorrow morning by eleven," he responded.

"All right then," she said. "I'll put a rush on it with the lab. Since our perpetrator seems to have been active for years and getting away with it, I doubt we're going to get a hit on his profile from CODIS."

"That occurred to me, too," Dan agreed.

"If we do come up with a profile, I'll put our forensic genealogy team on it right away. If any of our perpetrator's relatives have ever signed up on a participating ancestry site, we'll be in a position to figure out who he is and where he is. Any idea how old our perp might be?"

"Deborah Russell told Jenny that he seemed to be on the older side, forties or fifties, or maybe even older."

"All right then," Anna Rae said. "I'll also make arrangements to send any resulting profile through Parabon NanoLab's phenotyping division to see if they can give us an age-enhanced composite sketch. I have to say, Dan, you've done amazing work here."

"Thank you," he murmured.

"And pass my regards on to that young woman who brought this possibly game-changing evidence to our attention. What's her name again?"

"Jenny," he said. "Jennifer Brady. Her mother, Joanna Brady, is the sheriff of Cochise County."

"Like mother like daughter then," Anna Rae said. "Good for her."

CHAPTER 24

THEY SAY IT HAPPENED LONG AGO THAT A BOY *and a girl were left all alone. Their mother and father had died, and all their people were dead. They lived in the southern part of the lands of the Desert People, but they felt very lonely there because everything around them reminded them of their mother and father. So they moved to a village in the North called Uhs Kug, which is near the place the Milghan—the Whites—call Casa Grande.*

Because they had no fields, the boy went hunting all day. The girl, after grinding her corn, would go out into the desert to find plants for cooking and drying and to gather seeds for planting, but because they had no fields of their own and because they seemed very sad, their new neighbors in the village thought they were Pad O'odham—Bad People.

It happened there was a man in this village of very great influence. He had large fields and many cattle, which meant he also had great power. One day Big Man noticed that this new girl, this sad stranger who was so unlike other girls in the village, was also s'kehegaj—very beautiful. He fell in love with her, but because she was always grinding corn or gathering seeds, he couldn't see her very often.

One day Big Man called Ban, Coyote, and asked him for help. Ban, as you will remember, nawoj, my friend, is often filled with the Spirit of Mischief. Big Man gave Coyote some beads and told him to go to the village and slip them onto Beautiful Girl's wrist.

The next morning Ban did just that. He went to the house where the brother and sister lived and found Beautiful Girl cooking. When he tried to slip the beads onto her wrist, she burned herself. This made Beautiful Girl very cross. She told Ban to go away. She scolded him, saying she wanted no beads and no husband, and she wanted nothing more to do with any coyote.

WHEN LANI PARDEE OPENED HER EYES ON Tuesday morning, she was momentarily confused. Instead of being in her own home on the hospital compound grounds at Sells, she awakened in the guest room at her mother's place in Gates Pass. Her first impulse was to jump out of bed and get ready for work, but of course she didn't have to go to work that day. She was on leave—for this whole week at least—and charged with looking after her mother rather than looking after a hospital. As the chief medical officer on the reservation during Covid, Lani had dealt with plenty of difficult patients and complex family problems, but the one facing her right now was by far the most challenging.

If Davy were still alive, she'd at least have someone she could turn to and ask for advice in dealing with this current situation. As for discussing it with her husband? The fact that Dan's mother had been murdered when he was a little boy made Lani reluctant to lean on him about the situation. Having a difficult situation with a living mother was a far cry from having no mother at all.

She had slept fitfully at best. Once again, her mother had taken to her bed at five o'clock the previous afternoon, which meant she'd been up roaming the house in the wee hours of the morning. Lucy Rojas, well aware of Diana's tendency to roam the house overnight, had asked Lani and Dan to install a series of baby monitors throughout the house. Lani had always been a light sleeper, and as her mother wandered from room to room, she was able to follow her movements. Diana finally settled down in the easy chair in her pottery studio, and when she seemingly dozed off, so did Lani. As a consequence, the Lani Pardee who rose from her bed to do battle with whatever was coming that day was short on sleep, and her usually composed bedside manner was in very short supply.

Lani found her mother in her studio, watching the morning news on TV. During the course of Covid, Lani had looked so much bad news in the face on a daily basis that she had stopped watching news of any kind—local or national. She didn't feel as though she needed daily doses of poison from ever-smiling news personalities who told their dire stories of death and destruction while seated safely in studios and doing their reporting in front of robot-operated cameras.

"Mom," she said, poking her head into the room, "what do you want for breakfast?"

"I'm not hungry," Diana replied.

"You're not hungry because you're starving yourself," Lani snapped, "and you know what? I'm sick and tired of it. Remember how, when I was little and hated green peas? You told me I had to try them at least, and refusing wasn't an option. This is the same thing. This morning you're having eggs. Do you want them scrambled or fried?"

"Scrambled."

"Bacon and toast?"

"Toast no bacon."

Amazed that her tough-love act seemed to have borne fruit, Lani went to the kitchen and began rattling pots and pans. Once the food was prepared, she set it on the kitchen table and called out, "Soup's on. Come and get it."

Lani had it on good authority that Lucy Rojas had brought her mother's meals on trays to wherever Diana happened to be at the time. Lani wanted her mother to understand that there was a new sheriff in town and things were going to be different.

Once Diana was settled at her customary place in the breakfast nook, she stared down

at her plate without picking up her fork. Lani
was tempted to tell her "eat it or wear it," but
she didn't. Instead, she opted for something less
confrontational.

"What shall we do today?" she asked.

"Do?" Diana asked vaguely.

"Yes, do," Lani insisted. "I'm off work for the
entire week, and I have no intention of sitting
around the house doing nothing."

"I have no idea," Diana replied, but by then
she had picked up her fork and was absently poking away at her pile of scrambled eggs.

"Well, I do," Lani said determinedly. "After
Dad died, you had us empty all his stuff out of
the study so you could use it as an extra guest
room. The problem is, everything was all tossed
into boxes willy-nilly and hauled down to the
root cellar. We need to sort through all of it and
decide what to keep and what to let go."

Diana's forkful of scrambled eggs stopped
in midair, halfway between her plate and her
mouth. "I'm not going into the root cellar!" she
declared.

Lani knew all about the root cellar. Long
before she was born, the cellar was where her
brother Davy and Nana *Dahd* had been held
prisoner during the life-and-death struggle between Diana and Andrew Philip Carlisle, the
vengeful serial killer the two women—Rita
Antone and Diana—had helped send to prison
years earlier. By the time the physical confron-
tation was over, Carlisle lay writhing in agony
on the floor, permanently blinded by the frying
pan full of overheated bacon grease Diana had

flung into his face. No doubt, for her mother, the very words—*root cellar*—conjured up that whole nightmare scenario.

"Of course you're not," Lani agreed soothingly. "I'll bring the boxes up here. Where do you want to do the sorting, here or in the living room?"

Lani's assumed-close tactic worked. She hadn't given her mom a choice about participating in the unwelcome task, allowing instead a choice of where to do it.

"Here," Diana said at once. And then, maybe because of the unfamiliarity of actually being caught up in an actual conversation, she finally went ahead and put that first forkful of scrambled egg into her mouth. After swallowing that first bite, she picked out another.

Won that round, Lani thought to herself. It wasn't much, but it was a start.

CHAPTER 25

JENNY USUALLY SLEPT IN ON TUESDAYS. HER first class that day didn't start until late in the morning. She made coffee, then, iPad in hand, she scrolled through her email and social media. As long as she'd been away at school, she'd made a point of checking in with various news sites in southeastern Arizona on a daily basis. Her mother wasn't especially forthcoming about what was happening in her life, and Jenny liked to keep track of what was going on in Bisbee and the surrounding towns.

During Covid, the town's only print newspaper, *The Bisbee Bee*, had finally closed its doors for good, putting their star columnist, Marliss Shackleford, out of a job. Somehow she had managed to wangle enough startup money to launch a news website called the *Cochise County Courier*. What had once been her signature crime column, Bisbee Buzzings, was reborn as a local events calendar where people could post news about church potlucks, rummage sales, school plays, and garage sales. But that didn't mean Marliss was done with her self-appointed role as the county's star crime reporter. Her twice-weekly column, now dubbed Cochise Crime Central, often took aim at her favorite target, none other than Sheriff Joanna Brady. That was why, although Jenny had forked over thirty bucks of her own money for a yearlong subscription, she hadn't exactly admitted that fact to her mother.

That morning the headline on her column took Jenny's breath away.

IS SHERIFF BRADY IN FINANCIAL HOT WATER?

Undisclosed sources are reporting that thrice-elected sheriff, Joanna Brady, and her mystery-writing husband, FW "Butch" Dixon, are experiencing financial difficulties and may be close to filing for bankruptcy.

No irregularities surfaced in her financial disclosure forms from the last election, but if the couple is now on the verge of Chapter 11, it does cause one to wonder what's changed between then and now.

That was typical Marliss—drop a controversial bombshell sentence, ask a question or two, and then leave it up to her readers to figure out what the hell was really going on.

Jenny put down her iPad, picked up her phone,

and dialed her mother's office. "Is it true?" she asked when her mom answered.

"Is what true?"

"Marliss's latest column," Jenny answered.

"Good lord," Joanna groaned. "I've been too busy to check. What's she saying now?"

"That you and Dad are about to file for bankruptcy."

To Jenny's amazement, her mother burst out laughing. "You've got to be kidding," she said.

"I'm not," Jenny replied, "and this isn't funny. It says right there in black and white that you and Dad are about to file Chapter 11."

Joanna stopped laughing. "What does Dad do?" she asked.

"He's a writer," Jenny began, "but . . ."

"And when you write a book, what chapter comes after chapter ten?"

"Chapter eleven," Jenny said, "but . . ."

"But nothing," Joanna interrupted. "Last week during his volunteer stint at Sage's preschool, he was partnered with someone who's new to town. The book he's working on has been giving him fits. The story hit a wall in chapter ten, and he hasn't been able to get it moving again. When the woman asked how he was doing, he said he was having trouble with chapter eleven, which, as it happens, is absolutely true. He realized what was going on at the time and tried to straighten out the misunderstanding. Obviously that didn't work, and she must have gone straight to Marliss with the story."

"What are you going to do about it?" Jenny asked.

"Nothing," Joanna replied, "not a single thing. Marliss's loyal readers can hang around waiting for me to go belly-up until hell freezes over. In the meantime I'm going to keep on doing my job."

"Aren't you going to call her out on this?"

"No, I'm not. Her credibility is on the line, not mine. Why get into a public pissing match? She's in the business of getting attention. For someone like that, nothing hurts worse than being ignored, and that's what I'm going to do—ignore her completely and hope she goes away."

"Do you want *me* to call her out in a comment?"

"Please don't," Joanna said. "The best thing to do about fake news is refuse to give it the slightest amount of credibility."

"There are already comments from several people who obviously believe everything she writes," Jenny said.

"What other people say doesn't matter in the least. Please don't get sucked into the middle of this. All right?"

"Okay," Jenny agreed reluctantly.

"So what did you do over the weekend?" Joanna asked. "After getting that bad news about Rosa on Friday, I thought we'd hear from you. Are you okay?"

Jenny most definitely didn't want to go into the details of her weekend activities. If it was okay for Marliss Shackleford to tell fibs and get away with it, maybe it was okay for Jennifer Ann Brady to do the same.

"I had a big paper that was due on Monday," Jenny replied. "I spent a lot of time working on that."

CHAPTER 26

WHEN COYOTE CARRIED HIS BEADS BACK TO Big Man and told him what Beautiful Girl had said, he was very angry. He was used to having his own way and didn't like it when someone disagreed with him. Big Man told Coyote that he must return to Beautiful Girl the next day and tell her that if she didn't accept his beads, he would kill both her and her brother.

The next day Ban returned to the home of Beautiful Girl and her brother. This time he found her wearing her *giwho tho'ag*, her burden basket, because she was ready to go out and gather plants. This time she refused to even listen to Coyote. Instead, she walked away.

When Big Man heard this, he was even more angry. This time he went to Hewel O'odham—Wind Man, and asked for his help. The next time Beautiful Girl was out in the desert gathering plants, Wind

*Man came and found her. With a loud whoop, he
gathered her up and took her to the top of a steep
mountain that stands all alone in that part of the
country. This is the one the Milghan, the Whites,
call Picacho Peak, but the Desert People call it Cloud
Stopper Mountain. As everyone knows, it is not very
tall, but it is very steep.*

*That evening, when Beautiful Girl's brother,
Tobitham—Hunter—came home, the house was
empty. He could not find his sister anywhere. Finally
he went to the village and told the people what had
happened and asked for their help in finding her.*

*The next day the people went out to the mesa where
Beautiful Girl had been gathering plants. They found
her burden basket filled with plants, but she was not
there, and that's where her tracks stopped.*

ON TUESDAY MORNING, DAN GOT UP, MADE
breakfast, sent Angie and Micah off to school,
cleaned the kitchen, loaded the dishwasher, put
one load of clothes in the dryer, and another in
the washer. When Lani did these things, she
made it all look easy and seamless. Not so for
Dan, especially when he had to go back to the
dryer and remove the half-dozen marbles that
had been noisily rattling around inside it. Obviously he hadn't been as attentive to pockets as he
should have been when he was loading clothing
into the washer.

He was finally sitting down at his computer
just as two texts came in. The first contained a
color photo of a lovely young woman, clearly of
Indian descent, wearing a cowboy hat fitted out

with a rhinestone tiara as a hatband. The second text said: Henry Wilcox here. I'm driving. Call me.

Once Anna Rae Green had finished the hiring process and before the official launch date, she had summoned all her troops to Denver for two weeks of in-depth training that had been accompanied by a good deal of socializing. That's where Dan had learned that most of his fellow MIP field officers had been selected to work in places where they lived on the assumption that operatives living in the same area and with some of the same background might be more well received by nearby Indigenous populations than total outsiders would be.

That was certainly true for Henry Wilcox, the hand-chosen MIP field officer for the state of Oklahoma. Hank and Dan had met during that initial training session. Despite a twenty-year age gap between them, the two men had hit it off like gangbusters and had spent several long evenings talking into the early morning hours.

Henry, a full-blooded member of the Osage Nation, had been born and raised in Pawhuska, aka White Hair, Oklahoma. He related how his distant forebears, once known as the Thorny Valley People, had fought against the Americans during the French and Indian War. During a battle in Ohio, when the chief went to scalp one of his fallen opponents, the man's white wig had come off in his hand. Struck by the way the wig had protected his enemy from being scalped, the chief kept both the wig and the name *Paw-Hiu-Skah* and passed both down the line for several generations.

After graduating from Pawhuska High, Henry had joined the Marine Corps. Having done his duty, he returned to Oklahoma and hired on with the Oklahoma City PD where he had retired years later after a career that had included ten years as a homicide detective. His wife, Charleen, had taken to retirement like a duck to water, spending her time doing volunteer work that kept her engaged and busy. Henry, bored to tears, had been thrilled to land a job that would most likely focus on cold cases. That suited him to a tee.

Dan immediately picked up his phone and returned the call. "Hey, Hank. Dan here. What's up?"

"Did you see the picture?"

"I did," Dan replied. "Who is she?"

"You mean who *was* she," Hank corrected. "Her name is Marcella Andrea Sixkiller. I think her dad is a second or third cousin of that Sixkiller guy, the one who was in *The Longest Yard*."

"You mean Sonny Sixkiller?" Dan asked.

"Yeah," Hank said. "That's the one. Anyway the photo I sent was of Marcella in 2013. At the time it was taken, she was a sophomore at Wichita Falls High School in Wichita Falls, Texas where she had just been chosen to be their rodeo queen. Four years later, in 2017, while living on the streets in Oklahoma City and working as a prostitute, she disappeared, never to be heard from again. I was working Missing Persons for OCPD back then."

"Was her case one of yours?"

"Unfortunately it was," Hank said wearily. "She was one of mine back in the day and she's one of mine now."

"What's her story?"

"The family's Cherokee from Tahlequah, Oklahoma. When she was little, the family moved to Wichita Falls where her dad worked in the oil fields and her mother had a job in a school cafeteria. It looked like Marcella had everything going for her, but then, during the summer between her sophomore and junior year in high school, her mom died unexpectedly of a brain aneurysm. That's when her father shipped her back to the res to live with his mother. That ended up being a disaster.

"The grandmother enrolled her in the only high school in town, Tahlequah High, which happened to be a boarding school. Most of the kids there had gone through grade school in a Cherokee Immersive program. That made for huge language and social barriers between Marcella and everyone else. She ran away two months into her junior year and ended up on her own in Oklahoma City, doing drugs and working the streets."

Unfortunately Dan Pardee knew exactly how Marcella must have felt back then—like a fish out of water.

"She got busted a couple of times for soliciting," Hank continued. "If you saw her mug shots, you wouldn't believe it was the same girl."

"Meth mouth?" Dan asked.

"Yup," Hank agreed. "Anyway, the guy who reported her missing turned out to be her pimp, and he didn't call it in until three days later. He thought she'd run out on him. He was pissed and thought he could track her down on his own. We traced her to one of her usual hangouts, a dive bar in a bad part of town. The joint had surveillance cameras everywhere, but by the time we showed up asking questions, the footage from that night had been overwritten. The bartender said he thought he saw Marcella leaving with an older white guy, someone who'd been sitting at the bar all night—wearing a Stetson, drinking sangria, and paying his tab in cash. That's all he could tell us about him. Oh, and he wore glasses. We had him do a composite sketch, but we never identified the guy."

"And you never found Marcella or her body?"

"Nope, Marcella's case happened to be one of the first ones in my MIP caseload," Hank continued, "so one of my first family visits was to drive over to Tahlequah to pick up a DNA sample. George, Marcella's dad, got hurt on the job a couple of years ago, so he's living back home in his mom's old place. While I was there, I noticed that he keeps a framed copy of the rodeo queen photo on his living room wall.

"As soon I saw the Big Sis notice about the rodeo connection, I remembered that photo, and it made me wonder if Marcella's case might be related to yours. Yesterday afternoon, I called in to OCPD to check the dates. Turns out Marcella disappeared on Friday, October 13, 2017. By some strange coincidence, according to the internet, the Pro Rodeo Oklahoma was in town that same weekend. First thing this morning

I drove over to Tahlequah and asked George if he'd allow me to scan the photo so I could send it to you."

Mention of the rodeo queen photo had gotten Dan's undivided attention, but that last bit took his breath away.

"Well?" Hank asked. "What do you think?"

"I think you're onto something," Dan said excitedly. "And if these are all connected, we may be about to get a DNA profile for our killer. Can you lay hands on that original composite drawing and send me a copy?"

"Sure thing," Hank said. "Will do."

Great, Dan thought. *Maybe now we're getting somewhere.*

CHAPTER 27

THAT NIGHT THE PEOPLE HELD A COUNCIL TO
decide what to do, but no one could suggest anything.

At last Coyote spoke up. He told them that as he had been passing Cloud Stopper Mountain, he heard a noise that sounded like a woman crying for help. Everyone at the council knew that this was very bad trouble because the mountain was so steep that Beautiful Woman could not come down, and no one could climb up to help her.

At last Hunter, Beautiful Girl's brother, decided to ask I'itoi for help. He prepared a messenger, dressed all in white and wearing eagle feathers on his head. I'itoi received Messenger—Ah'atha—and asked him what the trouble was. Once Messenger told the story, Great Spirit told him he would help. He took some seeds from a gourd and traveled with Messenger to Cloud Stopper Mountain. At the bottom of the peak, he planted some gourd seeds under a big rock. Then he began to dance and sing.

This is the song I'itoi sang:

> *Come little gourd seeds, grow big;*
> *Let your vines grow big and strong.*
> *Send your vines up and send them far.*
> *Grow, little gourd seeds, grow fast.*
> *Climb up these rocks and grow strong.*

As I'itoi sang and danced the gourd vines began to grow. Before the end of the day, the vines had reached the top of the mountain, and Beautiful Girl was able to climb down safely.

Her brother was waiting. Hunter offered to pay I'itoi and Messenger, but all that was asked of him was a bobcat skin to hold arrows. After that Hunter and Beautiful Girl went home.

DIANA LADD'S LATE-NIGHT WANDERINGS MEANT that soon after breakfast, she needed a nap. That was fine with Lani. Once breakfast was cleared away, having her mother back in her bedroom gave Lani a chance to call the hospital, see how things were going, and attend to a complex staffing problem. Dr. Walker-Pardee wasn't a fan of working remotely. She expected to be hands-on all the time, but for now, remote was best she could do. Only then did she finally head for the root cellar.

As she switched on the single light bulb dangling in the middle of the room and started down the stairs, she felt a sudden sense of unease. The relative coolness of the basement should have been pleasant rather than chilling, but in this room Andrew Philip Carlisle's evil presence still cast a lingering shadow. Had he succeeded in murdering her mother, no doubt Lani's brother Davy and Nana *Dahd* would have been slaughtered here as well, bleeding out their lifeblood into the cool earthen floor.

And yet, the moment Lani picked up the first of her father's banker's boxes, the uneasiness seemed to dissipate. Brandon Walker and Diana Ladd were not yet an item at the time of Carlisle's brutal attack, but her father had been on the scene that night, doing his best to protect an endangered woman and her vulnerable son. Now, his possessions—the mementos and papers he had once handled—seemed to act as a buffer between Lani and Andrew Carlisle's evil presence.

There were ten boxes in all, and they were densely packed, most of them too heavy for Lani to carry more than one at a time. Some obviously contained nothing but books, probably the set of Great Books that had accompanied a long-ago discarded set of *Encyclopaedia Britannica*. The books had sat unopened on the shelves in her father's study for decades. After wiping the boxes clean of dust and cobwebs, she lined them up in a neat stack next to the breakfast nook with the book boxes at the bottom.

She was just finishing that when her mother showed up in the doorway, pausing there, staring at the assembled boxes, and frowning in distaste.

"Good," Lani said. "You're here. I was about to come wake you."

"Do we have to do this?" Diana objected.

Lani was adamant. "Yes, we do. Let's get started."

The first carton, the lightest one, was the easiest to sort through. It contained the trophies, wall plaques, and awards Brandon Walker had received through the years. In the end, there were only three of those Diana chose to keep— her husband's badge, the Montblanc pen given to him by his officers as he was leaving office, and his national Detective of the Year award. Everything else went back into the box to be disposed of by Lani and Dan at a later time.

Two cartons contained stacks of crumbling newspapers. Those in the first box featured stories about Brandon Walker's exploits over the years, including his work as a homicide detective for the Pima County Sheriff's Department. The other dealt with his years as sheriff, including coverage of both elections—the one he had won and the one he had lost. Lani found it interesting that her father had made no effort to separate good publicity from bad—it was all there. Some of the pieces were laudatory, but many were highly critical. After scanning through a few of the articles, Diana pushed them all aside.

"Fake news isn't exactly new," she said. "I've got no reason to hang on to any of this."

One box held what appeared to be an entire file drawer's worth of records. They were devoted to the cases Brandon had worked on for The Last Chance (TLC)—a volunteer cold case organization he had been involved with during retirement, some of which, Lani realized, might still be active.

"What about these?" she asked.

"We should probably consult with Ralph Ames on those," Diana said. "He'll know if they should be sent along to someone else or simply shredded."

"You have his contact information?"

Diana nodded. "In my computer," she said.

The next carton was devoted to the all-too-public history of Brandon's troubled son Quentin. There was nothing happy to be found there—no perfect attendance certificates from Sunday school or straight A report cards, for example, and no programs for grade school or high school band concerts, either. Instead, it was a box full to the brim with parental heartbreak framed in the transcripts of courtroom proceedings and various parole board hearings.

Diana sorted through the top layer and quit shaking her head as she did so. "Brandon was such a great father to you and Davy and even for Brian Fellows. Why neither of his own sons ever appreciated all his efforts, I'll never understand, but his failure with them was something he never got over. It broke his heart. Shred all of this."

Nodding, Lani moved that box to the discard heap.

The next carton turned out to be a mixed bag. The top layer was made up of several photo albums where the pictures, some of them faded over time, were held in place by layers of clear plastic. Seated side by side, Diana and Lani paged through those together. The photos were the same as those found in any family history—kids playing kickball and swinging on swings, grade school headshots, Little League teams, Christmas celebrations, Easter egg hunts. Quentin and Tommy were there in photos that predated their parents' divorce and in later ones as well, but so were Lani, Davy, and Brian.

Seeing those made Lani's heart hurt. Here was Brian running toward first base, decades before he ended up in a wheelchair. And here was Davy sitting next to a smiling Nana *Dahd*, proudly showing off a basket he had just finished weaving.

"I never knew your father kept all these photos much less put them in albums," Diana said.

Lani was taken aback. She understood that, in the days before digital photography, mothers had usually been the ones in charge of maintaining familial photo collections. In this family, her father had been charged with that task.

The album at the bottom of the pile had a pink plastic cover and turned out to be Lani's baby book, although she wasn't really a baby in any of them. The first page contained a single photo. In it, Nana *Dahd* and Diana stood side by side to the left of a black-robed female judge who was clearly a Tohono O'odham. Brandon stood to the judge's right with a dark-haired little girl, a toddler, perched on his hip and clinging to him like a burr. Her face, buried in his neck, was invisible. What took Lani's breath away was the joyous expression on her father's face. He was literally aglow as he smiled into the camera's lens, and it was something she had seen on only one other occasion—the day she graduated from medical school.

"My adoption day?" she asked in a small voice.

Diana nodded. "Molly Juan was the tribal judge at the time. We were Anglos, and you were Tohono O'odham. If we hadn't had Nana *Dahd* along with Fat Crack and Wanda Ortiz in our corner, I don't think the adoption would have gone through."

"May I keep the albums?" Lani asked.

"Of course," Diana agreed.

Lani removed the three oversized photo albums and set them aside, but the box wasn't empty. Beneath the albums was a complete set of Diana's own books, still in pristine jacket covers. They were all there, books in which Diana had set down her engaging telling of the history of the American Southwest, starting with her groundbreaking bestseller, *The Copper Baron's Wife*. But there was also a copy of Diana's Pulitzer Prize–winning true crime bestseller, *Shadow of Death*. In that she had told both sides of the Andrew Philip Carlisle story, using his words to tell the killer's version of events and hers to portray the victim's point of view. That book had become a true crime phenomenon, right up there with *In Cold Blood*, and it had made Diana Ladd a household name.

When Lani lifted the books out of the box and handed them over, it was Diana's turn to be gobsmacked. "I'm surprised," she said. "I never knew Brandon kept any of these for himself."

When Lani hefted the next box to the table, Diana shook her head. "I don't want to look at that one," she said, physically distancing herself from it.

"Why not?" Lani asked, removing the lid.

"That's what Candace sent after Davy died."

A brown eight-by-eleven envelope lay on top of everything else. Lani flipped it open and pulled out the single photo—a picture of a radiant young woman wearing a tiara and a rodeo queen sash. Lani looked first at the photo and then at her mother. The resemblance was there, but Lani wasn't sure what she was seeing.

"You were a rodeo queen?" she asked in disbelief.

Diana looked stricken. "I thought sure I had thrown that one away. Nana *Dahd* must have rescued it and given it to Davy."

"But where was it taken?" Lani wanted to know. "When?"

"St. Joseph, Oregon," Diana said faintly. "When I was in high school."

"But don't rodeo queens have to be able to ride horses?" Lani asked.

"Oh," Diana Ladd said. "I could ride all right. George Deason saw to that."

Lani was mystified. This was a name she had never heard. "Who's George Deason?" she asked.

"My biological grandfather," Diana whispered. "His son and my mother fell in love. She was pregnant with me, and they were going to get married when my birth father died. I ended up being raised by the godawful son of a bitch who saved my mother from disrepute by marrying her and giving me his last name, but from that moment on he made both my life and my mother's a living hell. It probably would have stayed that way if George Deason hadn't turned up at our house dragging a horse trailer with a horse in it behind his truck. That changed everything."

Suddenly it was as though someone had pulled a plug and all of Diana's long buried story came pouring out, including things Lani had never heard about before—the abusive childhood Diana had endured, one that had left her permanently damaged and unable to be the kind of loving mother she had wanted to be. Suddenly Lani had answers to all the questions she had never been able to ask. She could see why her mother had always seemed so distant and unreachable—a void that Nana *Dahd* and Brandon Walker had both tried valiantly to fill.

While Diana talked, the three bottom boxes—the book boxes—sat untouched on the floor. When she finally ran out of steam, more than an hour and a half had flown by unnoticed.

"Why haven't you told me any of this before?" Lani asked at last.

"I'm not sure," Diana said. "I guess I just couldn't." She looked around the kitchen then, as if surprised by her surroundings. Then she turned back to her daughter. "Are there any Barrio Anita tamales left?" she asked. "I'm feeling hungry."

CHAPTER 28

CHARLIE SPENT THE DAY MULLING OVER HIS next move. Eight years earlier a guy named Ronald J. Addison had taken a sailboat rented in Puerto Vallarta, Mexico, far out into the Pacific Ocean. Five days later the boat was found abandoned. On board, authorities had discovered what was believed to be a handwritten suicide note.

I am not going to jail. This is better for all concerned. So sorry.

Ron

Of course he wasn't sorry at all. The fact that he had cheated many of his so-called investors out of their life's savings didn't bother him in the least. The great thing about Ponzi schemes was that they were so easy to set up. People believed what they wanted to believe, and if you offered them a chance to get in on the ground floor of a good thing, they practically lined up to hand over their money, especially if you offered them choices that included funds with "safe" returns as well as those with "aggressive" returns. Guess which ones most people picked?

He'd been careful to have safeguards in place. To ensure that his SEC filings had been flawless, he'd kept a well-respected accounting firm in his pocket, one that had alerted him of upcoming audits in a timely fashion, thus allowing him to move money around as needed and have each separate fund looking great whenever bean-counting auditors showed up.

Those early investors, especially the ones in the "aggressive" accounts, made money hand over fist. Naturally, they went bragging to all their friends and relations. The problem was, by the time latecomers went looking for their returns, they weren't there—at least not for them—because everything they'd deposited had gone straight into Ronald J. Addison's pocket and later into one of his many offshore numbered accounts. Once everything about Addison Investments went south, those supposedly lucky early investors discovered to their dismay that all their windfall earnings would be clawed back by the bankruptcy court.

As for Ronald J. Addison? Faced with real federal oversight, he had opted for that last-minute vacation trip to Puerto Vallarta, never to return, and making that happen had taken some doing.

Ron had hired a first-class ID-changing specialist who had been extremely costly but also full service. When Ron's rented sailboat set off from Puerto Vallarta, for a princely sum, a small motorboat had followed. After transferring to the second vessel, he was taken back to shore where, under the dark of night, he'd been transported to an off-the-books medical facility in Guadalajara. There, Dr. Octavio Madrid—which may or may not have been his real name—had performed his facial reconstructive magic. Three months later, a new man entirely, one bearing the name Charles Milton, had emerged. As Charlie, Ronald Addison had had a good run, but maybe it was time for someone else to take his place.

Charlie couldn't help but be concerned. The first time around it had taken months to put his exit plan in place. But now speed was of the essence. With a full-blown well-publicized investigation into Rosa Rios's death underway, there was a heightened risk that one of Charlie's other cases might bubble to the surface. Charles Milton along with his RV and his aging Lexus all had to disappear into the woodwork before some nosy cop came around asking questions. To that end, on Tuesday afternoon, Charlie Milton sent a discreet inquiry to a so-called travel agency in New York City inquiring about the availability of their specialty high-end spa getaway in Guadalajara.

Charlie knew in advance that any response to his request would most likely be slow in coming, and it would happen through a personal connection rather than via some kind of electronic transmission. Once he sent the request, all he could do was settle in to wait, knowing that, in this case, his patience would be rewarded. No matter what it cost, he'd be able to pay the fare. His only hope was that Dr. Madrid was still in business and available on a moment's notice.

CHAPTER 29

BEFORE MANY DAYS BAN RETURNED WITH
*another message from Big Man in the village. This
time Hunter was home, and he called out to his sister,
"Do not listen to that Coyote," he said. "He probably
has mange from hanging around kitchens so much."*

*That made Coyote very angry. He said that Beau-
tiful Girl must marry Big Man or he would come
with all the men in the village and kill both the girl
and her brother. After delivering the message, Coyote
went away.*

*Beautiful Girl told her brother that she did not
want to marry Big Man. She did not want to marry
anyone. She said that if trouble came she would go far
away into the Eastern Sky and stay up there, only
showing herself to those people who rose early in the
morning to do their work. She said she would smile
on those people and make them glad.*

Hunter, too, said he would rather live in the air,

but that sometimes he would like to come back to the earth. When he did return, he said he would do so with a bounce and a bang that would shake things up so people would know he had returned.

THAT NIGHT WHEN DAN TRIED TO DO A LOAD of laundry, the washing machine quit. It wouldn't spin or drain. Naturally, the outfit Angie needed to wear to school the next day was in that particular load. He plucked that set of clothing out of the machine. After wringing it out by hand, it took several cycles through the dryer before it was dry enough to iron. The kids were already in bed when he went searching for the iron and ironing board. The iron was found under the sink in the laundry room and the ironing board tucked away out of sight in a bedroom closet.

He was reasonably adept at ironing and did what he considered an acceptable job, but as he was doing so, he kept thinking about a story his grandmother, Rachel Duarte, had read to him once when he was a kid. It was something about a man who told his wife he could do her job way better than she did. When she took him at his word and he assumed the housekeeping chores, everything went to hell in a handbasket. Eventually he had ended up with a goat stuck up on the roof. The goat on the house was the only detail from the story Dan remembered. The other thing that made it memorable was that his grandmother had seldom read to him. He seemed to recall that earlier that day his grandparents had quarreled about something. He now suspected that perhaps his grandfather Micah, rather than Dan, had been the target audience for that story.

Once the iron and ironing board had been stowed in their proper places, Dan returned to the kitchen to clean up that as well. He had just finished loading the dishwasher when Lani called. "How are things?" he asked.

She promptly burst into tears. Dan expected that her reaction to the question had something to do with Diana's continual refusal to eat. Instead it turned out to be something else entirely. Bit by bit Lani retold her mother's story. Dan had often regarded his mother-in-law as distant and almost cold, but now as he learned the painful details of her upbringing, all that made sense.

"Knowing this explains a lot of things about your mother that I never understood," Dan said once Lani finished.

"It does for me, too," Lani agreed. "But why am I just now hearing this for the first time? Why didn't she ever mention it?"

Dan wasn't blind to the irony that, at a time he was investigating a series of homicides with rodeos front and center, the thing that had caused Diana to unburden herself had been her daughter's unexpected glimpse of her mother as a long-ago rodeo queen.

"She probably just wasn't ready," Dan suggested. "For some reason, today she was."

"And when she finished, the first thing she asked for was a tamale," Lani said.

"She was finally willing to eat something?" Dan asked.

"Yes," Lani replied.

"Then count that as a win."

"I'll try," Lani said. "How was your day?"

He was in the midst of telling her about the broken washing machine when call waiting showed an incoming call on his phone with Anna Rae's name in caller ID.

"My boss is calling," he told Lani. "I'll call you back."

"Not tonight," Lani said. "I'm beat and going to bed. I'll talk to you in the morning, and tomorrow will be time enough to deal with the broken washer. Before we buy a new one, I'll see if Richard can stop by the house and take a look at it."

Richard Ortiz, Fat Crack's other son, was a wizard not only with automobiles, but with all things mechanical. He served as the Tohono O'odham's honorary and only appliance repairman.

When Dan switched over, the voice on the other end of the line did indeed belong to his boss.

"You're not going to believe this," Anna Rae said. "We got a hit. The guy's name is Ronald J. Addison, formerly of San Francisco, California."

Dan was astonished. In the world of DNA profiling, results never came in this fast. It couldn't have been more than a matter of hours since Jenny's FedEx package landed in MIP's lab.

"That's got to be the fastest DNA hit in the history of CODIS!" Dan exclaimed.

"It wasn't CODIS," Anna Rae corrected. "It was AFIS. The lab got a partial fingerprint off one of the lenses in the glasses. Our hit was on that."

"Amazing," Dan breathed.

"That's the good news," Anna Rae said. "Do you want to hear the bad?"

"What's that?"

"Addison disappeared from a rented sailboat off the coast of Puerto Vallarta, Mexico, in 2014 and was officially declared dead by court order in Dallas late last year."

"Wait," Dan said. "That makes no sense. Dead men don't leave fingerprints."

"No, they don't," Anna Rae agreed. "I suggest you do what you can to get to the bottom of this. The boat was found abandoned with what was presumed to be a suicide note on board."

"A fake suicide note," Dan put in.

"Obviously," Anna Rae agreed. "No body was ever recovered."

"Was he married?" Dan asked.

"At the time he disappeared, yes," Anna Rae replied. "His former wife, Michelle, divorced him on the grounds of desertion soon after he disappeared, but she's evidently the one who initiated the court proceedings to have him declared dead."

"Was there any life insurance involved?" Dan asked.

"Some," Anna Rae answered. "Something north of a quarter of a million dollars' worth."

"So maybe his disappearance is nothing more

or less than a case of insurance fraud, possibly with the ex-wife in on it. She may even know where he is."

"My thoughts exactly," Anna Rae agreed. "That's why someone needs to interview her as soon as possible. As far as I'm concerned, that someone is you. The sooner you contact her, the better—tomorrow, if you can make it happen."

"Do other agencies know about the AFIS hit?" Dan asked.

"I haven't been in touch with any of them," Anna Rae said, "but notifications may be sent out automatically. In any event, I'd like you to be the first law enforcement officer to turn up on the ex-wife's doorstep."

Dan didn't want to admit to his new boss that his mother-in-law was having health issues, his wife was dealing with those, and he himself was up to his eyeteeth with childcare.

"What about the DNA issue?"

"We're still going full tilt on that," Anna Rae said. "Once we have a profile, I'll send it through Parabon's genotyping process and have them do an age-enhanced composite sketch so we'll have some idea of how he might look in his forties, fifties, and sixties. We'll be able to compare that to the bartender's composite drawing Hank Wilcox just sent me with regard to the Marcella Sixkiller case."

"Wouldn't it be easier to just age enhance a photo of the actual guy?"

"Easier and less expensive," Anna Rae countered, "but maybe not as effective. We know that although Addison disappeared in Mexico, he's currently operating in the States, apparently with no fear of being recognized. That suggests he somehow altered his appearance, most likely with reconstructive surgery. Phenotyping won't give us an exact image of the man as he looks now, but it may reveal bits of facial structure that aren't necessarily altered by plastic surgery."

"And someone might pick up on that resemblance more than on his former exact features."

"It's worth a try," Anna Rae said.

"Getting back to my interview issue," Dan said. "I believe you mentioned that the court declaration occurred in Dallas. Is that where the ex-wife is located?"

"Outside of Dallas, in Plano; she remarried three years ago. She's Michelle Barlow now. Her new husband's name is William. I'll text you her details."

"Okay," he said. "I'll get right on it."

Suddenly Dan Pardee felt very much like that poor guy in Switzerland—the one with the goat on his roof. Knowing Lani was physically and emotionally exhausted, he abided by her wishes and didn't call her back. Instead he went online, looking for flights from Tucson to Dallas—without much success. They were all milk runs, with intermediate stops in either Denver or Albuquerque, neither of which were places he wanted to go at the moment. There was a noontime nonstop from Phoenix to Dallas, so he booked a ticket on that. It was still reasonably early—not quite ten—so he picked up his phone and called his and Lani's best friends, Delia and Leo Ortiz. Delia was the longtime tribal chairman, and Leo and his brother, Richard, sons of Fat Crack, still owned and operated the only automotive garage and tow truck operation on the TO.

Delia had returned to the reservation as Fat Crack's protégée. At the time, the medicine man was also mentoring Lani, and that had given rise to a serious case of sibling rivalry between the two women. After the birth of Delia's son, Gabe, however, the two women had bonded over the child and were now the best of friends.

"Hey, Leo," Dan said. "Hope it's not too late to call."

"Nope," Leo replied. "We're about to watch the ten o'clock news. What's up?"

"I need a favor," Dan said. "Lani's stuck in town looking after her mom, and I'm being called out of town on business."

"MIP business?" Leo asked.

When Dan had decided to leave the Shadow Wolves in favor of the new job, Leo and Delia were the first people he told after telling Lani and the kids. Understanding the seriousness and extent of the problem, both of them had been enthusiastic about his signing on.

"Yes," he answered. "I've got a lead on a guy who may be a serial killer, but it means I have to go to Dallas. With any kind of luck I'll be able to come back the next day, but I haven't booked a return flight in case there's some kind of delay with doing the interview. Could Micah and Angie come stay overnight with you tomorrow? I can get them to school in the morning and then drop their overnight stuff off at your place on my way to the airport."

"Sure," Leo said. "I'm sure my mom will be delighted to look after them."

Fat Crack's widow, Wanda, still lived in the Ortiz compound in a single-wide mobile home tucked in between those belonging to her two sons. She tended to regard Angie and Micah as an extra pair of grandkids.

"Thanks," Dan said. "I owe big on this one."

"No problem," Leo replied. "Glad to help out."

And that, Dan told himself as the call ended, *is how you get the damned goat off the roof.*

CHAPTER 30

SELLS, ARIZONA
Wednesday, April 6, 2022, 10:00 A.M.

WHEN COYOTE WENT BACK TO BIG MAN AND
*told his story, Big Man was very, very angry. He
went out and called all his friends together. Then,
early the next morning, Big Man and his friends
armed themselves with bows and arrows and went
looking for Hunter and Beautiful Girl.*

*The girl saw them coming and called out a warn-
ing to her brother, but he didn't seem to care very
much. As Big Man and his friends came closer, Beautiful Girl saw there was no hope, so she hurried off
to the Eastern Sky just as she had said she would do.*

*Big Man and his friends came to the house and
called out to Hunter. When the brother came out, Big
Man and all his friends aimed their arrows at him.
But as the arrows flew, he jumped up into the air, and
they did not hit him. Then the people mocked him,
asking where his feathers were. They said he should*

*have wings, but the people noticed that when Hunter
came back to Earth, the earth trembled.*

*Three times the people shot their arrows at the
brother of Beautiful Girl. Three times Hunter
jumped and returned to Earth, and each time when
he came down, the earth trembled.*

THE NEXT MORNING DAN WAS UP AT THE CRACK
of dawn—packing his own clothes as well as
those for the kids. Before they climbed out of
bed, he had also managed to sort out both a car
rental and a hotel reservation in Dallas. While
waiting for the kids to emerge from their rooms,
he went looking for Michelle Barlow on the internet. Since she was something of a social media
presence, she wasn't hard to find. As he went
along, Dan made notes of questions he wanted
answered.

Michelle Barlow, age thirty-four, was a first-
grade teacher at Daffron Elementary School in
Plano. That was good news for Dan. It meant
that she would most likely be working during
the day and at home in the evening after Dan's
plane landed in Dallas. From the information on
Ronald Addison that Anna Rae had forwarded to
him, Dan knew that he'd been born in 1959. Dan
did the math and realized that made Addison
almost three decades older than Michelle—old
enough to be her father. So where and when
and how had they met? From the photos she
posted, he saw that Michelle was gorgeous now
and would have been even more so back when

she was in her twenties. Most likely, Ronald had been happy to show her off as trophy-wife arm candy. Given that, Dan couldn't help but wonder what had become of Mrs. Ronald Addison, 1.0.

Michelle's current husband, William Barlow, age thirty-six, was a good-looking dude himself and the owner of a local construction company. They were both graduates of BYU and were active in alumni events occurring in the Dallas area. So how had William and Michelle met? When? They were now the parents of twin sons, Aiden and Arthur, who had recently celebrated their second birthday. And the whole family was evidently made up of bicycling enthusiasts since there were numerous posted photos showing the four of them on bikes, with the two helmet-clad little ones strapped into infant seats behind their parents.

The family home looked to be an ordinary tract house—probably three or four bedrooms in a nice-looking neighborhood. But that would have been a big step down from the high-rise penthouse condo where Michelle had been living while married to Ronald Addison. According to the information supplied by Anna Rae, at the time he went missing, he'd been the CEO of a much-vaunted tech-centric investment company based in San Francisco. But even if the house in Plano was a big step down from the penthouse, photos of Michelle as she was now showed someone who appeared to be blissfully happy.

For comparison's sake, Dan was about to go looking for images of Ronald Addison and Michelle together when Micah turned up asking for breakfast. From that point on it was a footrace to get the kids to school, their goods dropped off at the Ortizes' place, and Dan headed north to Phoenix. On the way he touched bases with Lani and told her he was on his way to Dallas.

"Why didn't you call me?" she demanded. "I would have come straight home."

"I didn't call because you don't need to come home," he replied. "You need to be with your mom right now. I'll only be gone for one night, and I've made arrangements for the kids to stay over with Leo and Delia. Leo said Wanda will be thrilled to look after them, and I should be home sometime tomorrow. In the meantime, how are things with your mother?"

"Two steps forward, one step back," Lani replied gloomily. "I thought after yesterday we'd made some forward progress, but she's back in isolation mode this morning. I'm baffled."

"You'll figure it out," Dan assured her, "and that's exactly why you need to stay on in Tucson right now instead of heading back home."

"But I'll still check in with Richard on the washer situation," she said.

Glad to have that issue off his list, Dan made it to Sky Harbor with just enough time to clear security and board his plane.

Once the aircraft's Wi-Fi was up and running, Dan resumed his internet searching, this time focusing his efforts on Ronald Addison, and there was plenty of material to be found. Dan located literally dozens of articles reporting on his disappearance off the coast of Mexico, but the vast majority of the links were devoted to what had happened afterward. Within weeks of his going missing, his supposedly successful tech-based fund at Addison Investments had gone belly-up. A subsequent investigation revealed that the high-earning investment fund had been nothing but an outrageously successful Ponzi scheme. By the time investigators came looking for the money, it had vanished, right along with Addison himself. Since his body was never recovered, the suicide had been thought to be faked, but no sign of the missing man had ever turned up.

Michelle had left the family home in San Francisco a few weeks before Addison himself disappeared, so a good deal of investigative effort had been devoted to finding out what, if any, involvement she might have had not only in the Ponzi scheme but also with regard to her husband's very suspicious disappearance. As far as Dan could tell, the authorities had eventually cleared her of having participated in either one. In yet another article Dan learned that although Michelle had indeed initiated the process of obtaining a legal declaration of Addison's death, she had done so at the behest of the bankruptcy court seeking to retrieve any and all remaining assets for the benefit of Addison's duped clients.

Close to the bottom of the list of Dan's search links, he finally discovered what had become of the first Mrs. Ronald Addison. Unlike Addison himself, she really was dead. He learned that from a short article in the obituary section of the *Pleasonton Times* dated May 15, 2008.

Pleasonton native Adele Renquist Addison, age 47 and wife of tech investment entrepreneur Ronald Addison, was laid to rest in Pleasonton's Garden of Hope Cemetery. Late last week she was found unresponsive and floating in the pool at the family home in Santa Clara County outside Los Gatos. Her death has been ruled accidental.

Adele and Ronald, high school sweethearts who graduated from Pleasonton High School two years apart, had recently celebrated their twenty-fifth wedding anniversary with a river-boat cruise down the Danube. The couple had no children.

Long an advocate for women's education, Mrs. Addison was active in P.E.O. A higher education scholarship benefiting young women graduating from Los Gatos High has been endowed in her name.

In addition to her husband, Adele is survived by her parents, John and Helen Renquist, of Pleasonton, and by her three brothers and two sisters.

Dan read through the article twice more. Obviously his initial arm-candy assumption was correct. If Addison had taken up with Michelle shortly after the death of his first wife, he would have been in his fifties by then with Michelle in her early twenties.

That was about the time the flight's Wi-Fi was turned off and the seat back announcement came on. Dan stowed his computer, but he didn't turn off his brain. Considering what he now knew or thought he knew about Ronald Addison, what were the chances that Adele Addison had actually died of an accidental drowning? He was pretty sure Anna Rae Green would say that wasn't any of MIP's business, but Dan Pardee thought otherwise.

Once on the ground, it took time to negotiate the car rental and set the Dodge Durango's GPS to sort out the most direct way to drive the twenty or so miles from Love Field to the Barlows' place in Plano.

IT WAS CLOSE TO SEVEN P.M. BY THE TIME DAN pulled up in front of the Barlows' house. He hadn't called ahead because he wanted both his visit and the news he had to impart to come as a surprise.

When he rang the doorbell, a man he recognized as William Barlow came to the door. "May I help you?"

Dan held out his badge. "I'm Dan Pardee, an investigator with the MIP," he said.

Barlow frowned. "The what?"

"Missing and Murdered Indigenous People," Dan told him. "We're an investigative agency inside the Department of the Interior. Does your wife happen to be home?"

"I think there's some kind of mistake," Barlow objected. "Indigenous—as in Native Americans? There's nobody here like that."

"Will?" a woman's voice inquired from the background. "Who is it?"

"A police officer of some kind," Barlow answered. "Something to do with a murdered Indian."

"I'm actually looking into the deaths of several murdered Indians," Dan corrected, "all of them young women. But my purpose in coming here tonight is to speak to Ms. Barlow concerning her former husband, Ronald J. Addison. We have reason to believe he's still alive and that he may be involved in our homicides."

At that point the door was yanked all the way open, revealing the presence of Michelle Barlow herself. "Are you saying he's alive?" she demanded.

"We're reasonably sure he is," Dan replied. "A partial of one of his fingerprints was found on a pair of glasses left at the scene of an attempted homicide that occurred in February of this year. Dead people generally don't leave fingerprints."

"You'd better come in then," she said. Then she turned to her husband. "Do you mind putting the boys down?"

"Sure thing," Barlow said, giving Dan a dubious look, but he set off to do as he'd been asked without any protest.

Michelle led Dan into a comfortable living room, cluttered with toys and child gear. She moved a basket of unfolded laundry from the sofa to clear a place for him to sit.

"You didn't seem surprised to hear that he's alive."

"I'm not," Michelle said. "I never for one moment believed the bastard was dead. That's why I divorced him. I wanted him completely out of my life, and getting a divorce was the best way to do that. What's he done now?"

Dan knew that in interview situations he was the one who was supposed to ask the questions, but from the vehemence in Michelle's voice he knew instinctively that asking questions wasn't the right way to proceed with this one. Michelle was already on Dan's side, suggesting that Addison had victimized her as well, and telling her what his investigation had so far revealed about her ex might encourage her to share her own story.

"I'm investigating the homicides of several young Indigenous women who have died over the course of the last decade. I call them my 'lost girls,'" Dan explained. "The earliest victim we know of died in 2017. At least three of them are members of various Native American tribes, and all of them seem to have had some connection to rodeos."

Michelle's eyes widened. "Rodeos?" she echoed. "Ron adored rodeos. He went to rodeo events all over the country. At first I went with him, but one time, during a calf roping contest, the poor little calf's neck got broken. I never went to another."

Ka-ching! Dan thought. *Addison loved rodeos. We're getting warmer.*

After that he told Michelle about the girls one by one—Yolanda Larson, Rosa Rios, Annika Wallace, and Marcella Sixkiller, finishing with the unsuccessful attack on Deborah Russell in Albuquerque, mentioning along the way how each attack had occurred in close proximity to a local rodeo.

"As far as we know," Dan finished, "Deborah is the only victim who managed to get away."

"What happened to her?" Michelle asked.

"She was going to a barn located on the rodeo grounds in Albuquerque to meet up with her boyfriend. An assailant grabbed her from behind and tried to strangle her. Fortunately she was able to call out for help. Her boyfriend came running and chased the guy away. During the struggle, Deborah's purse was knocked to the ground and fell open. While Deborah and her boyfriend were putting her things back in her purse, a pair of the assailant's glasses, which must have been knocked off his face during the struggle, were mistakenly put into the victim's purse. Later on, when she found them, she realized they must have belonged to her attacker. Fortunately for us, she set them aside in a safe place. It was only after she turned them over to law enforcement that we found the partial fingerprint."

When Dan looked at Michelle, he was startled to see that her face had suddenly gone stark white. "Is that how they died?" she asked faintly. "They were strangled?"

"Yes," he answered, "at least for the ones whose remains have been found so far. Autopsies have identified broken hyoid bones. Those are usually indicative of manual strangulation."

"That's what he did to me, too," Michelle Barlow whispered hoarsely. "He attacked me for no reason and tried to strangle me. I was trying to fight him off. Then, all of a sudden he just let go of me, and I was able to breathe again. Afterward, he said he was sorry, and that he didn't mean it. I told him I was fine and acted like it was no big deal. I went to bed and pretended to be asleep. When he came to bed, I waited for him to start snoring. As soon as he did, I snuck out of bed, got dressed, called a cab, and went to the airport. I didn't even pack a bag. I left with the clothes on my back and nothing else.

"I called my folks on the way to the airport. They had always disapproved of Ronald because he was so much older than me. As soon as I told them what had happened, they bought me a plane ticket home to Salt Lake. I had a credit card, but I didn't want to use it for fear Ronald would know where I'd gone. That was stupid, of course, because he tracked my phone."

"Did he come after you?"

"He tried to. He showed up on my folks' doorstep demanding to see me. He didn't leave until my father threatened to call the cops. Then he started sending me texts and emails begging me to come back to him. I finally told him I was done and that I was filing for a divorce."

"What happened then?"

"He reminded me of the prenup and told me I wouldn't get a penny. I told him there were lots worse things than being broke, and that if he didn't leave me alone, I'd go to the media and tell them what he'd done to me. Threatening him with exposure must have done the trick. I never heard from him again. The next thing I knew, the cops showed up to let me know that he'd gone missing in Mexico."

"Did you tell your parents what had happened?"

"Not at first," Michelle admitted. "I tried to cover the bruising around my neck with makeup and high-necked sweaters, but I'm sure they had their suspicions. They were so glad to have me safe at home that they gave me the time and space to sort out my next step. By the time I was finally ready to tell them, Ronald had already gone missing. Later on, when Ronald's business blew up—when it turned out he had cheated all those poor people and stolen their money—my parents had an army of reporters parked on their doorstep. I told my folks at the time that I didn't believe Ronald was dead, and they were the ones who encouraged me to get a divorce—so I could put all of it to bed and move on with my life. And I'm glad I did. Two weeks after my divorce was final, I was the matron of honor at my best friend's wedding. Bill was the best man. We met and clicked. Six months later we got married."

The man himself chose that moment to return to the living room. "They're finally down," Bill told his wife. "What did I miss?"

"I was telling him about what happened to me," Michelle replied, "about how Ronald tried to strangle me."

"You told him about that?" Barlow asked. "Why?"

"Because it turns out I was right. According to Mr. Pardee here, Ronald Addison is still alive, and there's a good chance he's a serial killer. If there's any way I can help bring that evil son of a bitch to justice, you'd better believe I'm going to do it."

Apparently none of this came as a big surprise to William Barlow. He sat down next to Michelle and took her hand in his. "Believe me," he said, "I'm all for that."

Proceeding with the interview with Barlow in attendance wasn't Dan's first choice, either, but he forged ahead.

"What, if anything, can you tell me about Adele?" he asked.

"Who's she?" Barlow wanted to know.

"She was Ronald's first wife," Michelle explained. "She died two years before Ronald and I met. He told me that she got drunk one night, fell into their swimming pool, and drowned. He claimed that her death had been ruled accidental, but after what happened to me, I've always wondered."

That makes two of us, Dan thought. *I'm wondering the same damned thing.*

CHAPTER 31

TUCSON, ARIZONA
Wednesday, April 6, 2022, 2:00 P.M.

*THE FOURTH TIME BIG MAN AND HIS FRIENDS
shot their arrows at Beautiful Girl's brother, Hunter
jumped and went up and up into the sky. This time,
he did not return.*

*So when you are in the land of the Desert People,
if you look toward the east in the early morning, you
will see a beautiful Tohono O'odham girl smiling at
you from the sky. The People call her Mahsig Hu'u—
Morning Star.*

*And sometimes—not often—you will feel the
ground shake under your feet. The Milghan—the
Whites—would say that was an earthquake. But
the Desert People know that is only Hunter, Beautiful Girl's brother, come down to earth for a visit.*

LANI WAS AT HER WIT'S END. YESTERDAY HER
mother had been close to being her old self, but

today that conversant, storytelling Diana Ladd
Walker was once again locked inside a self-
imposed shell. She'd had to be pried out of bed,
bullied into taking a shower, and shamed into
eating a spoonful or two of the oatmeal Lani had
made for breakfast.

When Dan had told her that he was off to
Dallas, leaving Angie and Micah to be looked
after by Delia and Leo, she'd been pissed at him
for not consulting her first, but by midafternoon,
she had to admit he'd been right. With Lucy up
on the Navajo caring for her sister, there was
no denying that Diana Ladd Walker was in no
shape to be left on her own. She needed looking
after, and for that she was Lani's responsibility.

Late in the morning, and after her middle of
the night wanderings, Diana announced that she
was going to lie down for a nap. Once she retreated to her room, Lani set about doing the
dishes and laundry and straightening the house.
Then she faced down the stack of boxes. After
hauling the books destined to go to Bookmans
out to the carport, she decided to ask if either
Gabe Ortiz or Tim José could stop by to haul
them away. The remaining cartons she toted
back down to the root cellar.

She wanted to take more time to go through
her father's papers as well as through the box
containing Davy's stuff. Maybe, at some point in
the distant future, Tyler, Davy's son, would take
an interest in his father. The items his mother
had discarded as so much trash might give Tyler
a better idea of who his father had been. The
only thing she removed from Davy's box was

the rodeo queen photo. It was the only one Lani had ever seen of her mother as a young woman. Obviously Davy had treasured it, and now Lani would, too. She took the photograph to the guest room and stowed it in the bottom of her roll-aboard, right next to her medicine basket.

The whole time she was working, however, Lani couldn't shake her deep sense of betrayal. She knew all about Rita Antone's life, inside and out. Her beloved Nana *Dahd* had begun life as an orphaned child named *E Waila Kakaichu*— Dancing Quail—living in the village of *Ban Thak*—Coyote Sitting—with her grandmother, an old medicine woman named *Oks Amichuda*— Understanding Woman. At age seven Dancing Quail had been picked up by the reservation's Outing Matron and, along with a whole wagonload of kids from other villages, had been shipped off to boarding school in Phoenix. Lani had heard all about Dancing Quail's harrowing nighttime ordeal from Tucson to Phoenix where the Indian children had been forced to ride on top of the train cars because Indians weren't allowed inside. And it was only through what Nana *Dahd* had shared with her that Lani knew about the Evil *Ohb*—Andrew Philip Carlisle—the man who had come to her mother's house in Gates Pass determined to murder everyone inside.

So why did Lani know all these things about Rita Antone's life while knowing almost nothing about her mother's? Growing up, even though she'd been secure in Nana *Dahd's* loving kindness, she had always wondered why her mother seemed so distant. Was there something wrong with Lani that made her mother hold herself apart? Her father, on the other hand, had been all in from the start. Brandon Walker had loved his adopted daughter without restraint, spoiling her and caring for her in a way her mother never had. Only now was Lani beginning to realize that he had adored his wife in the same way—without restraint, something her mother had never quite been able to reciprocate.

After learning about her mother's horribly abusive childhood, suddenly all of it was beginning to make sense. As a physician, Lani understood that children raised in violent and abusive households often tie themselves to similarly abusive life partners. Diana had certainly done that the first time around when she had married Garrison Ladd. For husband number two she had chosen more wisely—or maybe Brandon Walker had done the choosing for both of them. But if Diana had never loved Brandon all that deeply in the first place, why was she so devastated by his death that she had now retreated completely into herself?

At the moment, as both a physician and a medicine woman, Lani had no answer to that question. She was utterly perplexed. Should she make an appointment with her mother's doctor and see if a prescription of antidepressants might help? Or should she simply continue the tough-love program she'd instituted yesterday? That strategy had seemed to do some good, if only on a temporary basis.

Lani had yet to reach a conclusion one way or

the other, when Kath Fellows called. "How are things?" she asked.

"So, so," Lani replied dispiritedly. "Yesterday I thought we'd made some progress, but it didn't carry over into today."

"I have some good news," Kath replied, "and maybe even some possible answers. I just got off the phone with the admissions lady at a place called Santa Rita Senior Living. Our next-door neighbor's mother, Betty, is staying there, and she absolutely loves the place. Surprisingly enough, they have an unexpected opening for a single resident at the moment, and there's no one on the waiting list."

Lani was a doctor. She didn't have to wonder about what might have caused that "unexpected" opening. Some other grieving family was enduring the hurt of losing a loved one. As for the idea of her mother consenting to go to such a place? That was a whole other issue!

"I doubt Mom would ever agree to something like that," she began, but Kath stopped her cold.

"Look," she said. "With Lucy unavailable, you don't really have a choice, and neither does Diana. You're going to have to go back to work, and your mom clearly needs looking after. The woman I talked to, Sandra Elkins, is willing to give us a tour this afternoon at four. And it's reasonably close by—on Prince just on this side of the river."

Lani tried another objection. "I'm not really comfortable going off and leaving Mom alone right now."

"Isn't there someone you could call to come stay with her for an hour or two?" Kath wanted to know.

Lani glanced at her watch. It was almost three in the afternoon. By this time of day, there was a good chance that Gabe Ortiz's classes at the U of A were done for the day. And from the time he could talk, Gabe had somehow always been able to penetrate Diana Ladd's defenses.

"All right," Lani relented. "Let me call and see if Gabe can come stay with her for a while."

When she reached Gabe and asked the question, his response was immediate. "Sure," he said. "Glad to."

He arrived within half an hour, and Diana's face lit up as soon as she saw him. "Why, Gabe," she said. "What a wonderful surprise! What are you doing here?"

While ushering him inside Lani had managed to clue him in as far as to what was going on, and he didn't give her away. "I was in the neighborhood and thought I'd stop by to see how you were doing," he said.

Breathing a sigh of relief, Lani headed out. Before arriving, Lani expected Santa Rita Senior Living to be on the grim side, and she was pleasantly surprised to learn otherwise. The surface of the facility's palm-tree-lined entrance featured redbrick pavers. After parking in a visitor spot, Lani made her way inside. Flower beds on either side of the glass sliding doors were filled with an impressive collection of blooming cacti. Just inside the lobby, visitors were welcomed by a bubbling fountain. The cool interior resembled that of an upscale hotel lobby and was far more bright and welcoming than Lani had expected. Kath, waiting near the reception desk, hurried over to meet her. "All good?" she asked.

"So far," Lani said.

Kath turned back to the receptionist. "We're here to see Sandra Elkins," she announced.

A moment later a smiling young woman emerged from a back room with her hand extended in greeting. "Ms. Fellows?" she asked. "I believe we spoke on the phone."

"Yes, we did," Kath agreed. "And this is Lani Pardee. Her mother is the one in need of assistance."

"Welcome," Sandra said. "I hope we can be of service."

The guided tour lasted the better part of an hour, and Lani was suitably impressed by everything she saw—dining room, kitchen, game room, and several craft rooms, along with both a small gym and a library. The game room was stocked with a number of tables, some of them topped by in-process jigsaw puzzles. The uniformed attendants appeared to be pleasant enough. As for the residents? The ones Lani saw, whether totally ambulatory, using walkers, or confined to wheelchairs, seemed to be content and in good spirits.

The residential units themselves were essentially studio apartments. Each had a small sitting area, and a bed, along with a tiny kitchen table. In what would have been the designated kitchen area, there was a counter with a few cupboards, a small drawer dishwasher, a coffee maker, a tiny fridge, and a microwave, but no real cooking facility.

"We like our guests to take their meals in the dining room to provide for their socialization needs almost as much as their nutritional ones," Sandra explained, "but the real truth of the matter is that, for some of our residents, their having access to a stovetop could easily pose a safety hazard for both themselves and everyone else."

Lani found herself heartily agreeing with that assessment. At the moment her mother seemed so absent-minded and disconnected that Lani didn't want her anywhere near a stove.

At the end of the tour, they retreated to Sandra's office for a discussion of the finances involved. Santa Rita Senior Living didn't come cheap, but Lani knew it was something Diana Ladd could well afford.

"What if my mother checks in and ends up hating it?"

Sandra smiled. "This isn't a prison, and we don't believe in holding people against their will. In addition, you're not required to sign a long-term contract," she said. "It sounds as though your mom might be somewhat reluctant."

"More than somewhat," Lani agreed.

"So why don't you try selling her on the idea of a monthlong stay—a landlocked cruise as it were—with no long-term commitments. I'm willing to bet that by the time the month is up, she'll be more than willing to stay."

Lani thought about that. This was Wednesday afternoon. Lucy Rojas was unavailable for the foreseeable future, and by Monday morning,

Lani herself needed to be back at work at the hospital in Sells.

"Could I put a tentative hold on the unit and let you know within the next twenty-four hours?" she asked.

"Of course," Sandra said. "But I'll need a five-day deposit in advance."

"Cash or credit card?" Lani asked.

"A credit card will be fine," Sandra said.

Kath was all smiles when they left Santa Rita Senior Living. Lani was still in a turmoil about what she should or shouldn't do and wondering how she'd manage to broach any of this with her mother. When she arrived home, Gabe reported that Diana had decided to take another nap.

"How are you?" Gabe asked. "You look upset. Is there anything I can do?"

"Yes," Lani said, "as a matter of fact there is. There are some boxes of books out in the carport that need to go to Bookmans. If you wouldn't mind dropping them off, I'd really appreciate it."

"Sure," he said. "What else?"

Clearly Gabe understood Lani was out of her depth. She took a deep breath before answering. "Tell me about Chair Man," she said.

"Chair Man?" Gabe repeated. "Why?"

"You know how Dan feels about all this medicine woman stuff."

Gabe grinned. "I believe he usually refers to it as so much 'feather shaking.'"

"Most of the time," Lani agreed, "but when he came home on Saturday, he told me he thought John Wheeler was a real medicine man."

Gabe nodded. "I think so, too," he said.

"At the moment, I'm a medicine woman in need of a feather shaking consultation from somebody else's feathers," Lani said. "Do you think you could put me in touch with him?"

"Sure," Gabe agreed. "Should I give him your cell phone number?"

"Please," Lani replied with a wry smile. "I'm pretty sure my smoke signal account has been discontinued."

GREEN CHILI MACARONI AND CHEESE HAD always been one of her mother's favorites, so Lani made that for dinner, and she was gratified that her mother ate a reasonable amount of it, but they talked very little during the course of the meal. It was as though all that unspoken family history that had created distance between mother and daughter earlier had now built a new wall between them. Given that, Lani chose to make no mention of her exploratory visit to Santa Rita Senior Living.

Diana had retired to watch television in the living room and Lani was cleaning up the kitchen when her cell phone rang with a South Dakota number showing in caller ID. Believing it to be spam she almost didn't answer, but then she did.

"Hello."

"Lani Pardee?" a male voice asked.

"Yes."

"John Wheeler here. Gabe Ortiz suggested I

give you a call. He says you might be in need of a good medicine man."

Chair Man! Lani thought, taking a deep breath. "Yes, I am," she admitted aloud. "In the next few days I need to make some decisions regarding my mother's future care, and I'm confused about how to move forward. Usually I can see my way through these kinds of issues, but this time I'm stumped."

"And you need this assistance sooner than later?"

"Correct," Lani replied.

"Gabe is a remarkable young man, and he's told me a good deal about you," John Wheeler said. "I understand you're staying in town at the moment?"

"Town adjacent," she said. "I'm out in Gates Pass."

"Do you happen to have your medicine basket with you?"

Lani's medicine basket was something that wasn't spoken of outside their immediate circle of friends and relations, and Lani was a bit taken aback that Gabe had mentioned it to someone Lani regarded as a stranger, but among the Desert People, not responding politely to Chair Man's question would have been unthinkable.

"Yes, I do," she said.

"Is it fully stocked with your crystals and . . ." He paused for a moment. "What's the correct word for your sacred tobacco?"

"We call it *wiw*," she answered, "and, yes, I have some of that, too."

"How are early mornings for you?"

After her midnight wanderings, Diana generally went back to bed and slept until ten or eleven.

"Early mornings work for me," Lani said.

"Good," Chair Man replied. "I'm sure you're familiar with San Xavier del Bac?"

"Yes."

"Good," he said. "Let's meet there about five thirty tomorrow morning. Not at the church itself, but out in the corner of the parking lot where the ladies usually make their popovers. We'll sit in my White Buffalo and smoke our Peace Smoke, because it sounds as though you could use some peace about now."

Lani wasn't sure she had heard him correctly. "Sit in what?" she asked.

Chair Man laughed. "My White Buffalo— that's what I call my wheelchair-accessible van and my wheelchair is my Iron Pony," he added. "I decided that as long as I'm stuck with them, I could just as well have some fun."

CHAPTER 32

THEY SAY IT HAPPENED LONG AGO THAT AN *Indian man and woman loved their baby very much.*

The mother took good care of her little one. She kept the baby with her all the time. Even when the woman went out to work in the fields, she took her baby with her. She never left it at home in the care of someone else.

The other babies in the village grew strong and fat and cried and pulled things. But the woman's baby never cried. All day long he lay in his cradle—his ulukud. He slept and smiled, but he never cried.

The mother arranged the ropes for the cradle very carefully. Over the ropes she put her softest blankets. She used so many ropes and blankets that the cradle looked like a big cocoon, and she made sure that the ulukud always swung in a spot that was nice and shady.

DAN LEFT THE BARLOWS' HOME TWO HOURS
later and was using the GPS leading him back
to the hotel near Love Field when his phone
rang. A glance at his phone screen told him that
Jennifer Brady was on the line. After talking to
Anna Rae Green, he had been so focused on
getting to Dallas and interviewing Michelle
Barlow that he'd never quite gotten around to
calling Jenny to let her know what a huge contribution she and Deborah Russell had just
made toward forwarding his investigation. It
was time to right that wrong. Maybe there were
rules somewhere about discussing ongoing investigations with outsiders, but as far as Dan
was concerned, Jennifer Brady was an integral
part of this one.

"Hey, Jenny," he said cheerfully. "How's it
going?"

"Did the package arrive all right?" she asked.

"Yes, it did," he told her. "It arrived safe and
sound."

"How long will it take for them to test it
for DNA?"

"I'm not sure. The first thing they did was
check it for fingerprints."

"Fingerprints," Jenny echoed. "Why would
they do that?"

"Because they were being thorough," he replied, "and it's a good thing, too. They found a
partial, and when they ran it through AFIS, they
got a hit. It led back to a man named Ronald J.
Addison."

Jenny was astonished. "Are you going to arrest him?"

"We have to find him first," Dan cautioned. "He went missing in Mexico in 2014 and was declared legally dead in 2021."

"Does that mean going to all the trouble of obtaining his DNA profile isn't going to do any good?" Jenny sounded disheartened.

"Not necessarily," Dan told her. "He may have faked his own death and disappeared with his clients' money. We're going to run the profile past Parabon's phenotyping algorithms and see what comes out."

"I've heard about that," Jenny said. "It's where they use DNA markers to create a composite sketch of how the person might look."

"Correct," Dan said, "and like a regular photograph those can be age enhanced. Our suspicion is that Addison may have altered his appearance with plastic surgery, but things like race, eye color, and basic facial structure can't be easily altered, so a phenotyped composite may come close enough for someone to recognize him."

"What's his name again?"

"Addison," Dan said. "Ronald J. Why?"

"I may go online and see what I can find out about him," Jenny said.

"You'll find plenty, but don't you have schoolwork to attend to?"

"I'm a little bummed about schoolwork right now. My professor gave me a D on my community policing research paper. I had plenty of statistics to back up what I was saying, but it's not what he wanted to hear, so he slapped me with a bad grade."

"Wait," Dan said. "You're taking community

policing? Does that mean you're a criminal justice major?"

"Guilty as charged," Jenny admitted. "Someday I hope to work for the FBI."

Suddenly Dan had a clearer picture as to why Jenny had inserted herself into the investigation—it was in her blood.

"I suppose you had to go through the same kind of crap," she added.

"No degree and just a different kind of crap," he told her. "I came into law enforcement through a back door—by joining the military first and then by spending years working with the Shadow Wolves at Border Patrol where I was eventually promoted to investigator. That's how I got the gig with MIP. So no community policing research papers for me. If I had to write one, I'd be lucky to get a D, but I'm giving you an A+ for what you've done with Deborah Russell."

"Thank you," Jenny said after a pause.

"But remember, this is now an open homicide investigation," Dan added. "I probably shouldn't have told you anything, but you're not exactly a disinterested bystander. You've made a real contribution to this case, but I'm trusting you to not pass any of this along—not even to Deborah Russell. The plan is to have the sketch go live in a big way. Having news about the DNA and the phenotyping leak out early might put our bad guy on guard enough for him to slip through our fingers."

"Understood," Jenny said. "I won't say a word, but have you talked to my mom? Does she know about any of this?"

"Not so far," Dan replied, feeling a sudden stab of guilt. "I'll probably give her a call tomorrow. In the meantime, feel free to send along anything and everything you find on Addison. I did a cursory search earlier today and didn't come up with a whole lot of detail, and having details would help. Consider it another research paper, one you're doing for extra credit."

"Extra credit for whom?" Jenny asked.

"For your future maybe?"

Back in his room at the hotel, Dan ordered a burger and fries from room service before dialing up Anna Rae. Despite the fact that it was well after hours, she was still at her desk.

"Hey, Dan," she said. "How did it go?"

He told Anna Rae everything he'd managed to learn from Michelle Barlow, including Addison's violent domestic assault and attempted strangulation of Michelle that had caused her to bail on the marriage and go running back home to Mama. He also included an account of what Michelle had said concerning her doubts about Adele Addison's death having been an accident.

"She believes wife number one was murdered?"

"Yes, she does," Dan replied. "Adele died in 2008. Her death investigation was handled by the Santa Clara County Sheriff's Office."

"Why don't I reach out to them and see what they have to say?" Anna Rae asked.

"Good idea," Dan said. *Better you than me*, he thought. "What about the DNA?" he asked.

"We've got the profile and that's being transmitted to Parabon as we speak. They understand the urgency and have given me assurances that they'll move this to the head of the phenotyping/ age-enhancing queue. I know it's a long shot, but right now it's all we've got."

"A long shot is better than no shot," he advised her, "which is where we were before."

Once off the phone with Anna Rae, Dan booked his return flight, a nonstop that would have him in Phoenix by 10:30 A.M. Arizona time, giving him plenty of leeway to be back in Sells before the kids got out of school. With his reservation in hand, he called Lani to let her know his travel plans.

"How are things?" he asked when she came on the line.

"Medium," she answered.

Dan knew that things Lani Pardee regarded as "medium" would register as unmitigated disasters for most people.

"What's up?"

Lani sighed. "I did something today that I'm probably going to regret."

"What?"

"I took a tour of an assisted-living facility— Santa Rita Senior Living on Prince Road just east of the river. Kath suggested it. Her neighbor's mother is there. From what I saw, it looks like a nice enough place. They have availability for a single right now, and I put a twenty-four-hour hold on that, but I haven't worked up enough nerve to tell Mom. I'm afraid she'll hit the roof."

"Maybe so," Dan said, "but with Lucy out of town for an undetermined time, what else can you do? You have to go back to work next week and we don't have room enough for her to stay with us. You'll have to tell her it's the way things have to be for right now."

"Easier said than done," Lani replied, "but to that end, I've made an appointment to see John Wheeler tomorrow morning."

For a moment Dan was stumped, but then he remembered. "You're seeing Chair Man?" he asked in disbelief.

"I need an outside opinion on all this," Lani said, "preferably from a medicine man who isn't me, and John Wheeler comes highly recommended—by you, as I recall. Since you generally discount all that medicine man/woman stuff, I take that as high praise. We're meeting up in the parking lot at San Xavier at around five thirty tomorrow morning. After I see what he has to say, I'll talk to Mom about assisted living."

"But Chair Man doesn't even know your mother," Dan objected.

"No, he doesn't," Lani agreed. "And that's exactly why I want his opinion."

"All right," Dan said. "Let me know how it goes."

"I will," she said.

After the call ended, Dan just sat there for a time holding his phone. He couldn't believe that Lani was going to see a medicine man on his recommendation. He had made the comment about John Wheeler in passing. He hadn't really meant anything by it. All he could do now was hope that the meeting between Chair Man and Dr. Lani Pardee didn't end up turning into a complete disaster.

CHAPTER 33

BUT EVEN WITH ALL THE MOTHER'S CARE, THE baby only seemed to grow smaller. When the cold days came, he slept more and more, and did not eat. He smiled less and less. And in those days the mother never smiled at all. She was too afraid.

Then one morning the parents found their baby was not breathing. So the mother wrapped the little one in her brightest blankets. The father called to his neighbors to come help. Then the father and their friends carried the baby up into the mountains where the dead are put in their rock homes.

They did not need much brush and stones to cover such a little thing.

Among the Tohono O'odham, a good Indian doesn' show how he feels. Especially if he is sad, it must no be shown. The Great Spirit, I'itoi, who is also th Spirit of Goodness, manages everything. To feel bad about something is to oppose the Spirit of Goodness.

But this mother had eaten nothing all that day. In her throat there was something big and hard, which she could not swallow. As she went up the mountain with her friends, she kept stumbling. This worried her husband because he was afraid she would let the water come to her eyes.

The baby was so small that they could not place it kneeling as the Tohono O'odham do. Instead, they placed the little form on his bright blankets and then carefully covered it with branches from shegoi—the creosote bush. Then they picked up the big rocks.

By now the mother could not see. She was looking at Tash—the Sun. She did not want to be a weak Indian, but she could not watch them throw the rocks on that little mound of brush. So she turned and started down the mountain toward the village. She walked very fast and stumbled often.

LANI PARDEE ARRIVED IN THE SAN XAVIER parking lot early the next morning but John Wheeler's white minivan was already there, parked in the far corner of the dirt parking lot with the front of the vehicle facing back toward the church. As she pulled up next to the van, Chair Man lowered his window.

"Dr. Pardee, I presume?" he asked.

"Yes," Lani replied with a smile, "but please call me Lani. You got here early."

Wheeler nodded. "I wanted to be here in time for the sunrise. I don't know how many of those I have left, and this is a special place to see one."

Lani glanced left to where the stuccoed walls

of the White Dove of the Desert shimmered in the early morning sunlight. "It's beautiful, isn't it," she said.

Wheeler nodded. "And very old," he added, "sort of like me. Come around to the passenger side."

Before doing so, Lani opened the back door of her dusty red Ford Fusion and removed her medicine basket. Once the van's passenger door was open, she placed the basket on the seat and started to climb in, but he stopped her.

"Take this," he said, handing her a gnarled walking stick. "This once belonged to my great-grandfather. He was a medicine man, too. He asked one of my aunties to keep it and give it to me if I ever came back to the reservation. I didn't go back, at least not yet, but a cousin brought it to me a few years ago. I've never been able to use it as a walking stick, but since it's a sacred thing, I would like you to use it to draw a single circle in the dirt around both our vehicles, yours and mine."

Lani took the stick and did as she was told without question. It made perfect sense to her that a circle drawn with a sacred stick would also be sacred. And as she drew the shallow furrow in the reddish dirt, she knew at once that she had come to the right place.

Once inside the van with her door closed, Lani handed the walking stick back to its owner. Then she sat there studying the complex equipment that made it possible for the paraplegic to not only drive the vehicle but also to retrieve and stow his wheelchair, enabling him to enter and exit on his own.

"From what Gabe tells me, I believe we should start with the Peace Smoke," Chair Man observed. "Why don't you tell me about it?"

Tohono O'odham's *I'itoi* stories are winter telling tales and can only be told between the middle of November and the middle of March. This was now early April, but Lani felt certain that *I'itoi* himself wouldn't object to her sharing the Friendly Gift story inside Chair Man's sacred circle. So while she rolled the dried tobacco into a cigarette, she repeated the story, telling how the envious villagers had killed not only Old Wise Woman but also her two grandsons—Little Lion and Little Bear.

After Old Wise Woman was dead, her spirit had called the dead boys to her. She had given them seeds and told them that, after burying her body in a certain place, they should plant the seeds there. She then explained that the plant that grew out of her grave would be called *Wiw*—Sacred Tobacco. She told them how to harvest it, dry it, and then roll it into sticks that could be smoked and passed from hand to hand in the circle, with each person saying *Nawoj*—Friend or Friendly Gift—as he handed it to the person next to him.

After lighting the cigarette with Looks at Nothing's aged Zippo lighter, Lani took a drag of the *wiw* and then handed it to Chair Man. They smoked the cigarette in silence until it was gone. Only after Lani had put out the smoldering stub and sprinkled the ash out the window and into the dirt did Chair Man speak again.

"You told me that you need to make some decisions regarding your mother," he said, "so tell me about her."

Lani did so, relating not only the things she had always known about her parents and their history together, but also about the terrible things about her mother's appalling childhood, something Lani herself had learned about only two days earlier. When she finally fell quiet, she looked in Wheeler's direction. He was sitting with both eyes closed, but he wasn't asleep.

"Did you know I was adopted, too?" he asked after a moment.

Lani didn't remember saying anything about her being adopted, but somehow Chair Man knew that to be the case. "No," she said.

"My mother was only fourteen and still in boarding school when she got pregnant. The nuns forced her to give me up for adoption. My adoptive parents were well meaning, and they weren't mean to me, but they did their best to erase my Native American origins. I didn't really start learning about that until after I ended up in the hospital here in Tucson after someone who hated Indians tried to murder me. At the time I knew next to nothing about my Lakota heritage. I almost died, but those months in the hospital gave me back that part of myself. You're lucky in that your adoptive parents made sure you never lost yours, but right now let's deal with your mother. I take it you never knew much about her background?"

"Hardly anything," Lani admitted, "and yet, the other day, when I found that old photo of her as a rodeo queen, it all came spilling out. It was as though it had all been locked up inside her for decades, and suddenly the dam broke. She was always kind toward me, but distant, too, and not only with me. She was the same way with my dad, but now that he's gone, it's like she's been turned to stone."

"Did she love your father?"

"I think so, yes, but she never really showed it. My father loved her beyond words. He's the one who made it possible for her to do what she'd always wanted, which was to become a writer. I know she cared for him, but in a way that seemed to hold him at arm's length, so I don't understand why she's so completely devastated by his loss. She won't eat; she barely communicates. It's like she's willing herself to die."

"She's not," Chair Man said. "She just can't figure out how to go on living. To survive that horrific childhood to say nothing of the Evil *Ohb*'s attempt on her life, she had to become strong and resilient—which also made her remote and distant. When your father came along, he became her rock—her foundation. He was her Good. By telling you the truth about what happened to her as a child, she finally found a way to let go of some of the Bad. Now she must learn to let go of the Good as well. I take it you're thinking about putting her in a facility of some kind?"

Lani hadn't said so aloud, but clearly Chair Man had figured that out on his own as well.

"I'm not sure she'll agree," Lani replied, "and even if she does, I'm sure she'll hate it."

"Maybe she will," Wheeler agreed. "But once she's in an unfamiliar place, it may give her the distance to start letting go of your father. But this move may accomplish something else too—something important."

"What's that?"

"It will remind your mother that she's still your mother," Chair Man said. "What's a mother's first duty?"

"To look after her children."

"Correct," Chair Man said with a nod. "You're her child, Lani, but you're also an adult with an important job that requires your attention. The same thing applies to your husband. Your having to look after your mother right now is interfering with your ability to perform your job, and it's probably impacting your husband's job as well."

"True," Lani agreed.

"You need to help your mother understand that by allowing someone else to look after her right now, she'll really be taking care of you. I'm guessing that, once you do that, you'll have your mother back—not the same mother you had before, but a better one—a mother who has finally learned to love herself."

Lani felt her eyes filling with tears. She was Tohono O'odham. She wasn't supposed to cry, but in that moment the water came into her eyes all the same, and maybe the Spirit of Goodness wouldn't mind since these felt like tears of joy and relief.

"Thank you," she whispered. "Thank you so much."

"See there?" Chair Man added with a grin. "Things are already better, and we didn't end up having to shake a single feather."

Lani was surprised to find herself laughing through her tears. As she wiped them away, Chair Man spoke again, but more seriously this time.

"You know," he said, "the Desert People are very lucky to have you. Not only are you a trained physician, you're one who is open-minded enough to acknowledge the wisdom of the old ways. Gabe told me about how your telling him that Tohono O'odham legend about the origin of Morning Star during your many camp-outs on Kitt Peak was what sparked his interest in astronomy."

Lani nodded.

Chair Man went on, "That's what I try to teach people who come to the Circle. I tell them that being able to accept both the old and the new is part of finding the right path. By the way, thank you for sharing the Peace Smoke with me and for telling me the story behind it. I may have to ask Gabe to go out and gather some *wiw* for me so I can add it to my own medicine pouch."

Realizing the consultation was coming to an end, Lani reached for the door handle. "I'm sure he'll be happy to do so," she said.

"One more thing," Chair Man added. "Would you mind giving your husband a message for me?"

"Of course," Lani replied. "What kind of message?"

"Tell him he needs to go see his father before it's too late. It may not do much for his father, but it'll do Dan Pardee a world of good."

CHAPTER 34

Thursday, April 7, 2022, 7:00 A.M.

AS USUAL, CHARLIE DRANK HIS COFFEE AND smoked his first cigarette of the day outside under his pull-out canopy. In a few hours it would be too hot to sit out here, but right now it was pleasant. Just then, Melody Baxter and her stupid mutt passed by. Naturally, as soon as Hazel caught sight of Charlie, she began to bark. For a change Charlie appreciated the racket. The dog was making so much noise that Melody didn't bother trying to chat. She simply waved and kept going.

Rosa Rios's name had vanished from the local news overnight, and that was a good thing. Identified or not, throwaway girls tended to do that, and that's why he chose them. So while he waited to hear back from his "travel agency" inquiry, Charlie wondered who he would be his time around. What would be his new backstory? Where would he be from? The last time he'd been given a textbook's worth of material to study. Fortunately he had always been a fast learner. What he wasn't good at was waiting. As the hours dragged by, he became more and more anxious. So much so that, when his cell phone rang a little past ten, he jumped out of his skin.

The RV park was a gated community, and caller ID read GATE!

"Hey, Mr. Milton," a voice said. "It's Dave down at the gate. I've got a guy here named Julio Marquez. He says he's here for your massage appointment."

Charlie hadn't ordered a massage—ever—so he knew this had to be his "travel agency" contact. "Great," he said. "Send him right up."

The man arrived a few minutes later. "You're with the travel agency?" Charlie asked.

"I am," Julio said with a nod.

Charlie held the door open while Julio carried a full load of traveling massage equipment into the RV. Naturally he didn't bother setting it up. They both knew there was no need.

"What do you have in mind?" Julio asked, taking a seat on the tiny sofa.

"A complete makeover," Charlie answered, "name, face, ID, family history—the works."

"I believe you've made use of our services before?" Julio asked.

Charlie nodded. "And it worked like a charm," he said, "but right now circumstances have changed, and I need to be someone new."

"I trust you understand that having undergone extensive reconstructive surgery previously, results the second time around may not be as . . ." Julio paused for a moment. ". . . as satisfactory."

"If you're talking about all those movie stars with fat lips, don't worry," Charlie said. "I understand. In my situation, I don't care if I end up looking like Quasimodo himself as long as I don't look like this."

Julio's response, a somewhat puzzled frown, made Charlie suspect that the man was unfamiliar with *The Hunchback of Notre-Dame*.

"How soon would you need this?" Julio asked.

"The sooner the better," Charlie replied.

"Sooner will be costly," Julio warned.

Charlie nodded. "Whatever the rush-job surcharge is, you can be sure I'm good for it."

"Very well. Dr. Madrid told me that before he would consider taking you on as a repeat customer, you would be required to make a fifty-thousand-dollar good-faith deposit with the funds to be transferred in the usual fashion. Once our bank is in receipt of the money, we will contact you with instructions on how to proceed."

"No," Charlie said. "That's not good enough. I don't have time to sit around indefinitely waiting for someone to get back to me. I'll be glad to up that good-faith deposit to a hundred thou if you like, and I'll do it today, but I need extra speed in return. I understand Dr. Madrid is a busy man, and having to readjust his schedule to allow someone to jump the line may cause some inconvenience. I'm prepared to compensate him for that."

"All right," Julio said. He reached in a pocket and pulled out a burner phone, which he handed over to Charlie. "My number is the only one in the contacts list. Call me once the transfer is complete. In the meantime, I'll discuss your situation with Dr. Madrid."

"Fair enough," Charlie said. "Working with him turned out so well the first time around that I'm sure doing business with him again will be a pleasure."

Julio left shortly thereafter, taking his portable massage table with him. Melody Baxter happened to be outside walking Hazel again as he was loading his gear into a small SUV.

"I wish I had known you had a masseur stopping by," she said to Charlie as Julio drove away. "Maybe he could have squeezed in an extra appointment. There's just nothing better than having a good massage."

CHAPTER 35

WHEN THE WOMAN REACHED HER HOUSE, the first thing she saw was one of the cradles that she had made for her baby. The cradle was swinging from the branches of a mesquite tree. For this cradle the mother had used a brown blanket. She snatched the cradle down from the branch. She folded the blanket and held it against the thing inside her that hurt so much. Then she went away from the house because she didn't want to be there when the others came back from the mountains.

The trail led down to the water among the cottonwoods. The woman could not see where she was going, but she did not care. There were many trees down by the water, but most of the leaves had come off their branches because Toniabkam—Summer—was gone. And it was almost dark down there because Tash—the Sun—had gone down.

The woman was still holding the brown cradle blanket against her breast.

Then it seemed to her that she was hearing a baby's weak voice. She looked. Just beyond the water, she saw a tiny brown cradle swinging from the branches of a mesquite tree.

The woman dropped her own blanket and ran to the ulukud from which the baby's voice had come. She took the cradle in her hands but found she was only holding some dry, brown leaves that were swinging from a spider's web.

BY EIGHT FORTY-FIVE, DAN WAS IN THE BOARD-ing area for his Phoenix-bound flight. He was about to call Lani to let her know he'd be home by the time the kids got out of school when a call came in from Anna Rae Green.

"What are you wearing?" she asked.

Dan was surprised. That kind of inquiry from an immediate supervisor seemed somewhat out of line, but he answered anyway.

"A pair of Levi's, my Tony Lama boots, and a blue plaid shirt. My Stetson's sitting in my lap. Why?"

"Because a media escort named Nancy Stuebe will be meeting your plane in Phoenix, and I need to tell her what to look for. I told her to look for a green-eyed Indian, but knowing what you're wearing will help. She said she'll be wearing an apricot-colored pantsuit."

Dan didn't have the heart to admit that he was color-blind and wouldn't be able to tell apricot from a hole in the ground, so he focused on the first thing Anna Rae had said.

"Media escort," he repeated. "Why would I need a media escort? What's going on?"

"Check your text."

Dan held the phone away from his ear as it dinged with an incoming message. What he saw was a photo of a white male, probably in his early sixties, with white hair, and blue eyes.

"This is the Addison composite from Parabon?" Dan gasped. "Already?"

"Yup," Anna Rae said. "Turns out, they don't like serial killers any more than we do. They were more than happy to help out. Our media team is doing a blanket national press release distribution on this, but I thought we should do more than that in Arizona, Utah, and New Mexico. We're booking field officers to do live news media interviews—preferably television interviews, wherever possible—and you're on tap for Phoenix and Tucson. Since your flight is due to land at Sky Harbor at 10:30, we've got two noontime appearances there already set up with more to come. Nancy has been letting us know what's feasible and isn't. Once you have Phoenix covered, you should be able to make it to Tucson in time to hit the evening newscasts there. It's going to be a busy day."

Dan held the phone away from his ear long enough to study the composite image once more before speaking again. "What am I supposed to say?" he asked.

"As you know, this is a projected image as

opposed to a real one. So we need to provide more details than we usually would with an ongoing investigation. MIP is investigating what we believe to be a serial killer who may or may not look exactly like the Parabon image. Not all of the victims involved are Indigenous, but we believe that the one commonality is some kind of connection to rodeos. That detail may be enough to ring a bell with someone. Everywhere the story appears, we'll ask that the number for our toll-free anonymous tip line be included."

"Isn't putting this much detail out in public going to result in an avalanche of tips?" Dan asked.

"Probably," Anna Rae agreed, "but if you're going to find that needle in a haystack, you need to start with a haystack. I'm hoping the tip line will give us that much at least."

Dan was still concerned. "And as soon as this goes live, won't Addison know we've got his DNA profile?"

"I'm sure he will," Anna Rae said, "and with any kind of luck, it'll spook him into doing something stupid. Dan, this arrogant bastard has literally been getting away with murder for years. I'm sure he thinks he's the smartest guy in the room. We need to prove him otherwise."

"How?" Dan asked.

"Don't go all Lone Ranger and Tonto on me, Dan," she advised with a laugh. "I have no idea of exactly how we're going to do it, but getting this phenotyped image into as many hands as possible is a first step."

In the background, Dan heard the gate agent

calling for his boarding group. "I'm supposed to board now," he said. "I need to go. I guess I'll see you on the noon news."

"Good luck," Anna Rae said. "Break a leg."

Once on the plane and unwilling to let his Stetson be crushed in the overhead bin, Dan stowed it under the seat in front of him. Then, before takeoff, he called Lani.

"I just heard from my boss," he told her. "I'm going to have to appear on some live local newscasts today in both Phoenix and Tucson. That means I won't be home by the time the kids get out of school. Can you call the school and leave a message for them to go back over to the Ortiz place this afternoon? In the meantime, I'll let Delia and Leo know that I'll pick the kids up and take them home once I get back to Sells."

"I should just go home," Lani said at once.

"We both know you can't do that," Dan told her. "It'll be a few hours later than expected, but I'll be able to handle it. But before we have to hang up, how are things on your end?"

"I'm not sure," Lani said. "Mom isn't up yet, but I'm expecting a battle royal."

"You're going to talk to her about the assisted-living arrangement?" he asked.

"That's the plan."

"Good luck with that."

"I'll need it. Do you have any idea which TV channel you'll be on?"

"All of them, supposedly," Dan replied.

"Okay then," she said. "I'll go set the DVR."

Off the phone with Lani, there was just time

enough to leave a message on Delia's phone before it was time to shut down his.

As a Shadow Wolf, Dan had been interviewed on camera a number of times, but those had always been out in the field. This would be his first visit to a television news studio for a live interview, and the whole idea made him nervous. He spent the bulk of the two-hour flight trying to frame everything he wanted to say in a concise, understandable, and effective fashion.

ON ARRIVAL AT SKY HARBOR, DAN SPOTTED A woman in a light-colored pantsuit while he was still on the escalator. Maybe it was apricot colored or maybe it wasn't, but the woman wearing it was anxiously consulting her watch.

"Nancy Steube?" he inquired.

She glanced up from her watch with a relieved smile on her face. "Dan?" she asked.

He nodded.

"Do you have checked bags?"

"Nope," he said, "carry-on only."

"Great, depending on traffic, we just might be on time for our first appointment. Miraculously I found a good parking place, and I'll bring you back to your car once we're finished."

"Fair enough," he told her.

The next two hours were a footrace—speed-interviewing as opposed to speed-dating. Folded into the front seat of Nancy's Hyundai Sonata and with no idea of where they were going or how they would get there, Dan simply settled in to enjoy the ride. Along the way he was impressed by the assertive way she steered the vehicle through traffic, all the while engaging him in a stream of casual conversation that vastly reduced his case of nerves. Once they made their first stop at a multistory building with a Jack in the Box on the ground level, Nancy was able to locate yet another primo parking spot. Inside the station, she greeted the receptionist out front like an old friend and seemed to be on a first-name basis with the producers if not with the talking heads themselves.

By the time Dan's first appearance was over, he began chiding himself for being so nervous. It turned out the remarks he had put together on the plane were more than adequate. The interview lasted something under two minutes—less time than it had taken for him to be mic'ed up and seated on the studio's leather sofa. The young woman interviewing him read her questions from a teleprompter and couldn't wait to be shuck of him the instant the broadcast went to a commercial break.

During the interview itself, Nancy had waited in what was referred to as "the green room," although Dan had no idea what color it really was. Back in the car afterward, however, it was clear that she'd been paying attention.

"That was a good interview," she remarked as she put the Sonata in gear to head for their next destination. "I could tell from what you said that you really care about what you're doing."

"I do," he told her. "Someone needs to pay for what happened to these young women, and it's my job to make that happen, although how much good a two-minute TV spot is going to do is anybody's guess."

"You'd be surprised," she remarked. "Lots more people than you can imagine are seeing this guy's face, and I think all this extra effort on your part is going to pay off."

Dan took her at her word, but by the time he finished interview number four, he wasn't so sure.

"Okay," she said. "It's almost one. Your next interview is at five at a station that's on the way into Tucson rather than inside the city itself. How are you fixed for food?"

"Hungry, I guess," he admitted.

"And how are you on Mexican food?"

"I'm way better on Mexican food than I am on sushi."

"Great," she said. "La Piñata, one of my favorites, isn't far from here."

"Does that mean you feed me, too?"

"That's right," Nancy said with a smile. "A media escort's first priority is getting clients to interviews on time, but our second responsibility is making sure they don't keel over from hunger on the way."

"Good deal," Dan said. "I had no idea."

CHAPTER 36

THEN THE WOMAN HEARD ANOTHER BABY
cry. *The cry came from among some low bushes, but
when she reached the place, there were only more dry
leaves. The leaves were curled into tiny cradles, but
the cradles were empty.*

*The woman was puzzled. From right to left and
all around she heard the cry of little babies, but when
she looked, she found only dry leaves. The leaves were
thick under her feet. The crunching noise of the leaves
was almost as loud as the cries of the babies.*

*Then, after a time, she heard someone speak to
her very softly. She knew without looking that it was
I'itoi speaking to her.*

*"The babies are here," Spirit of Goodness said to
the woman. "They are all the babies who have left
their mothers, just as your baby has left you, to come
live here with me. These tiny brown curled leaves are
the cradles in which they sleep when they are tired.*

These babies who have left their mothers are very happy here with me, and they do not like you to feel as you do. That is why they are crying now in their little brown-leaf cradles. Are you different from all other mothers?"

"No, I am not," she said. Then the woman raised her head from her hands and smiled, and from all around her came the sound of babies laughing.

LANI WAS STILL SETTING THE DVR WHEN HER mother emerged from her bedroom. "You hardly ever watch TV. What are you doing with the clicker?" Diana asked.

"Recording the evening news?"

"How come?"

"Because Dan's going to be on," she said.

"He is? Why?"

"It's about his case . . ." Lani paused. "It's about his cases," she corrected, "the ones he's working on for MIP."

Diana sat down on the sofa next to her daughter. "I keep forgetting he's no longer with the Shadow Wolves."

That's not all you keep forgetting, Lani thought.

From the time she'd returned from her visit with John Wheeler, she'd been wavering, struggling with how to broach the subject of Santa Rita Senior Living with her mother, but her brief conversation with Dan had solidified her resolve.

"Do you remember Gina Antone?"

Diana's body stiffened, as though an electrical shock had just shot through her body. "Of course. Her murder was the start of everything."

"And if a deputy sheriff named Brandon Walker hadn't worked so hard to solve her murder—and if he hadn't come back to help you and Nana *Dahd* when Andrew Carlisle came after you, none of this would be here," Lani added, waving her hand in a motion that encompassed the whole room—a room filled with precious handmade baskets and shelves overflowing with books, but a room that had always seemed furnished with love.

"You wouldn't be here," Lani finished. "I wouldn't be here."

"No," Diana agreed quietly. "I suppose we wouldn't."

"When no one else gave a damn about a murdered Indian girl, he did. And when no one else would take a child—an Indian child—who had become a dangerous object, he did that, too."

"Yes, he did."

"That's what Dan's doing now, too," Lani explained. "That's his job—caring about murdered women and girls no one else seems to care about. He's working on a case just like that right this minute. It's a serial killer case with victims dating back almost a decade. Yesterday he had to be in Dallas. Today he's here. No telling where he'll be tomorrow, and that's why I have to go home. He made arrangements for someone to look after the kids in his absence, but he shouldn't have had to. I should have been there."

Diana nodded. "Instead of being here taking care of me."

"And that's what I need to talk to you about," Lani continued. "Kath found a place where you can stay on a temporary basis until Lucy comes back."

Lani was prepared for an eruption of anger or denial—for her mother to declare that she didn't need that much looking after. But that didn't happen.

"Where is it?" Diana asked.

"Not far from here," Lani said. "It's a place called Santa Rita Senior Living. It's located on Prince, on the far side of the Santa Cruz. They have a room available at the moment, and right now there's no waiting list, so I went ahead and put a reserve on it. Would you like to go take a look?"

"I suppose," Diana said, "but if that's the case, I'd best put on something more presentable. You never get a second chance to make a good first impression."

CHAPTER 37

TUCSON, ARIZONA
Thursday, April 7, 2022, 2:00 P.M.

CHARLIE WORKED HIS WAY THROUGH THE money transfer issue as soon as Julio left, then he had nothing to do but wait. Had Charlie Milton been a golfer, he might have gone to a driving range to whack a few balls around that afternoon, but golfing wasn't his thing. Had he been a movie buff, he might have taken himself to a bargain matinee to check out whatever was showing, but movie stars these days weren't what they used to be. Besides, when those doofuses tried making thrillers? Forget it. They were nothing short of laughable. If they'd bothered to hire him as a consultant, he could have pointed them in the right direction and shown them how things should be done so their serial killer stories would have been more realistic.

As a result he spent the afternoon as he often did—going through his tie box of treasures, holding each trophy in his hand and remembering the time he'd spent with each of his victims. Adele was the only one who hadn't seen it coming. She'd been too drunk. He'd made sure of that. She had taken his total disinterest in sex personally and made it plain how unhappy she was in the marriage, but she hadn't had guts enough to leave him. She'd liked his money and living the high life. Besides, he had let her know that if she ever walked away from him, she'd end up living in far different circumstances from those to which she was accustomed. So she'd stuck it out, self-medicating along the way— consoling herself with booze and using sleeping pills to help her sleep. More than once he'd come into the living room and found her passed out in her chair in front of a blaring television set.

That night, sitting outside by the pool, he'd made sure Adele drank more than usual, and he had slipped her regular dosage of sleep aid into her first drink as opposed to her last. Then, feigning interest in whatever inane thoughts were rattling around in her dim little head, he'd kept pouring one drink after another. Adele had been so thrilled—so stupidly grateful—to have her husband's undivided attention for a change that she hadn't even noticed.

Once she passed out, he'd gone inside and stripped down to bare skin. When the cops showed up, he hadn't wanted them to find a pile of soaked shoes and clothing lying around. Then he'd gone back out to the pool. After wrapping his arms and hands in towels to prevent her from scratching him, he had picked her up and carried her into the pool.

Fortunately, like most of his other victims, Adele had been a little mite of a thing. When he dumped her face-first into the water, she'd gone under without making a sound, and he'd held her down by pressing down on the back of her head and her butt. She'd fought some, of course, but she'd been too inebriated to struggle for long. And Ronald's foresight in using the towels for cushioning meant there were no discernible bruises on her body and no scratches on his.

Leaving the bottles and glasses on a poolside table to testify about their evening by the pool, he'd gone back into the house where he'd dropped the two bath towels into the washer. In the bedroom, he'd set his alarm and placed his phone on the charger. Those actions were designed to make it look as though he'd gone to bed at his usual time—around eleven. Instead, sitting in the house with all the lights turned off, he waited for both the washer and dryer to finish running. Only after placing the newly laundered towels back in the bathroom where they belonged did he finally crawl into bed where, wonder of wonders, he'd had no difficulty in falling asleep.

The next morning, at five past six, still wearing his pajamas, robe, and slippers, he ventured out onto the patio, taking his coffee and the morning newspaper along with him. Finding Adele's lifeless body floating in the pool, he had jumped in—pajamas and all—and wrestled her out of the water. Then putting his phone on speaker, he placed a panicked call to 911, all the while unsuccessfully attempting to resuscitate her. Cops and EMS had shown up almost simultaneously minutes later with Ronald still on the phone with the 911 operator.

The subsequent police investigation had turned up nothing. Adele may have been unhappy in the marriage, but she hadn't gone blabbing to any of her friends about their marital difficulties because no one stepped forward to mention it. He told the cops that when he'd gone to bed, Adele had decided to stay outside for one more glass of wine—which he made sure she poured on her own. That way her handprint on that last bottle of merlot clearly overlaid his. He'd also made sure that when he'd retrieved some of her sleeping pills, he'd done so with a piece of toilet tissue between his fingertips and the bottle cap. He'd made a good show of being overwrought and had immediately agreed to a lie detector test. Naturally, in his emotional state, the results had come back as inconclusive, but the fact that he'd been more than willing to do so had counted for something with the two homicide cops who had shown up at the scene.

Ultimately, with no other injuries or any sign of a struggle, and in the absence of any kind of suicide threat or note, Adele's death had ultimately been ruled as an accidental drowning. The $250,000 life insurance policy Ronald held on his wife had been purchased years earlier. For people of their considerable means, having that amount of insurance was held to be reasonable.

The proceeds had been paid within a matter of weeks, including an additional $250,000 accidental death benefit. He'd squirreled that money away in his offshore accounts along with what was then rolling in from his investment scheme. In fact, Adele's death benefit was what he'd used to help cover Dr. Madrid's considerable charges the first time around.

Adele's death had been a good monetary investment, although it had been less than satisfactory as far as immediate gratification was concerned. The others were different. As he went through his mementos one by one, he remembered each girl by name and which trinket had belonged to which one. He treasured their initial relief when he had assured them, quite truthfully, that he had no intention of raping them. At that point they'd mistakenly assumed they were home free—which of course they were not. But what he loved even more was the fear that had gradually taken over when they understood what his real intentions were. He savored their abject terror when they had concluded that there would be no escape. And finally he recalled, at the very end, that precious moment when the light had vanished from their eyes. Those were the things he lived for and what he had missed out on with Adele, damn her anyway!

He still felt shortchanged on that.

Lost in thought, the hours flowed by. When evening came, it was too hot to cook, and Charlie opted to head up to Marana to his favorite watering hole for dinner. It was one of those places where he could do fusion dining by having a pitcher of sangria along with a serving of unexpectedly excellent lasagna. He settled onto his customary seat at the end of the bar. He'd just taken his first bite of the lasagna, when the five o'clock news came on. Because it wasn't sports of some kind, the volume was muted. Since Charlie couldn't hear what was being said, he wasn't really paying attention.

But then a guy on the screen, someone wearing a Stetson not unlike Charlie's, held up a poster-sized photo of someone who, although it wasn't Charlie, could easily have been Charlie. That's when he dropped his fork, which clattered noisily back onto his plate. Meanwhile something about a toll-free tip line flashed across the screen. Charlie wanted to ask the bartender to turn up the volume, but he didn't dare, because, in that moment, Charlie understood that Stetson Guy was talking about him.

He had no idea how the hell the cops had done it, but somehow or other they must have found a trace of his DNA. The poster, a computerized sketch based on his DNA profile, really did look like him—like him the way he used to look before meeting up with Dr. Madrid and a little less like the way he looked now. But still, the resemblance was there. If he could see it, what if other people could too?

Charlie waved at the bartender. "All of a sudden I'm not feeling so hot. Do you mind bringing me the tab and packing this up to go?"

"Want me to put the sangria in a covered cup and pack it in with the food?" the bartender asked. "You've barely touched it. If you put the bag in the trunk on your way home, you won't be risking an open container citation."

"Thanks," Charlie mumbled. "Good idea."

But it was all he could do to sit there long enough for the barkeep to come back with his take-out bag, because Charlie Milton wasn't just scared. He was terrified. It seemed to him as though everyone in the room was staring at him. Any minute now, someone was going to come over, point a finger in his face, and say, "Hey, aren't you that guy?"

Because he really *was* that guy, and that asshole on TV, the one wearing the cowboy hat, was coming for him.

CHAPTER 38

EARL BAXTER HADN'T ALWAYS BEEN A NEWS addict. In fact, up until he retired he'd barely watched the news at all, but that had changed five years ago when he stopped working. Now that's what he watched constantly. His wife, Melody, did not. There was far too much bad stuff going on in the world these days, and she could only tolerate so much of it.

The limited space inside the RV didn't offer much relief from the ever-present barrage of things she didn't control and couldn't fix, so she practiced a couple of avoidance tactics. One was to take Hazel for walks, which she did several times a day. The other was to plug in her earbuds, dial up her Audible account, and listen to books, crocheting like crazy as she did so. She was connected with a group of ladies back home in Indiana who sent crocheted blankets and caps to neonatal units in hospitals all over the north-eastern corner of the map. By the time she and Earl got back home, she'd have a whole drawer's worth to put into the pile.

There was one small crack in Melody Baxter's almost total news blackout. Once a day, she allowed herself to watch a local news broadcast, mostly for the weather report—not that Tucson's weather varied that much from day to day—but also to see what was going on around town. And that was how, on that Thursday afternoon, she was sitting there watching Channel 13 when the afternoon news came on at five o'clock.

Several days earlier, while viewing the same program, she'd seen the news about the burned human remains from Cochise County that had finally been identified three years later. And when the handsome guy wearing the Stetson hat—a guy good-looking enough to be a movie star—said that he was looking for a man who might be connected to those newly identified remains, Melody was all ears, because she was, after all, a true crime addict. Then, as soon as he held up what he said was a computer-generated composite of the suspected perpetrator, Melody almost jumped out of her seat.

"Hey," she demanded. "Doesn't that look like Charlie Milton?"

"You're seeing things," Earl replied. "It doesn't look like him at all."

Melody thought it did, but she knew better than to argue the point. For a long time, she simply sat there, staring at the TV screen but no longer listening to what any of the people pictured there were saying. Instead, she was thinking about Hazel. She was a sweet little pup who seemed to like everyone with the single exception of Charlie Milton. No matter how many times Hazel saw the man, she barked at him. What if her dog had some kind of sixth sense about the man—some animal instinct—that told Hazel Charlie was dangerous? What if all her barking wasn't just to be annoying? What if she was trying to warn Melody about a real threat?

During the interview, the man with the cowboy hat—Melody hadn't caught his name—had posted a toll-free number for a tip line, but at the time there hadn't been any way for her to jot it down, not with Earl sitting right there. He would have said Melody was nuts to even *think* about calling in a tip.

Although Melody hardly ever watched the news on purpose, she nevertheless was something of an expert on how the programs worked. For example, more often than not, what showed up on one channel was likely to show up on another channel that same day. She glanced at her watch. It was Thursday—spaghetti night at their local VFW—and she and Earl usually went there for supper, showing up around seven and then playing bingo for a while starting at eight.

"I think I'll go shower before dinner," she told her husband. Once in the bedroom, however, before stepping into the shower, she used the bedroom TV to record that evening's upcoming local news programs. Maybe the man she had seen before would show up again. Earl was an early-to-bed kind of guy. Once he hit the hay each night, Melody usually stayed up watching her own shows—the non-news ones. She wasn't worried that Earl would notice those newly recorded programs. He never bothered looking at Melody's list of recordings.

She showered, fixed her hair, put on her makeup, and got dressed. When she presented herself, Earl shut down the TV, and off they went. All through dinner and several games of bingo, Melody could barely sit still. Once they got home, it took forever for Earl to head for the bedroom, put on his CPAP machine, and go to sleep, but eventually he did. That's when Melody was able to have the TV set to herself.

When the intro teaser on the first newscast announced that viewers would be hearing from an MIP investigator later in the broadcast, Melody knew she was on the right track. Dan Pardee finally appeared in the last segment before the weather. He was someone local who lived in Sells and worked for a federal agency called MIP. He was investigating the deaths of several dead or missing Indian women whose disappearances seemed to be connected with rodeos. Melody felt a wave of gooseflesh crawl up her legs. Everybody in the RV park knew how much Charlie Milton loved rodeos. And when she saw the DNA-generated composite again—done with something called DNA phenotyping—Melody was more certain than ever that it looked like Charlie.

This time she watched the program with pencil and paper in hand. When the tip-line phone

number came on the screen, she jotted it down
Having done so, she immediately erased that recorded program and the others as well. Earl constantly griped about Melody not minding her
own business, and she didn't want him catching
her red-handed.

She left the TV set on, tuned to one of her
usual crime dramas but she wasn't really watching. Instead, she sat there thinking about what
would happen if she called the tip line. What
would she say? The composite looked like someone she knew—sort of, but not exactly. He was
someone who liked going to rodeos. Her dog
didn't like him and always barked when he was
around. Was that enough information to make
someone at the tip line pay attention to her or
would they act like Earl and tell her she was
imagining things?

Melody guessed that the toll-free number
would be answered by an operator located
somewhere far away from Tucson, Arizona.
What were the chances they'd just give her the
brush-off? But what about Dan Pardee, the guy
in the Stetson? On the news he had said that his
office was in Sells. Melody had never been there
but she knew it was located on a nearby Indian
reservation, somewhere off to the west of town.
If Melody could speak directly to him, maybe
he'd believe her, but what would happen then?
Would Mr. Pardee be able to do something about
it? Would the information Melody provided be
enough to give him what was called probable
cause, the thing needed to obtain a search warrant

for Charlie's RV? And even if they did a search, what if they didn't find anything?

Only a week or so earlier, on one of her true-crime programs—the ones Earl dismissed as nothing but "blood and guts," she had followed a story where, once the cops had a DNA profile, they'd had to follow the suspect for weeks before they were finally able to collect a cigarette butt he had discarded in a grocery store parking lot.

That's when Melody remembered that Charlie smoked. A lot! When she went out to walk Hazel in the mornings, instead of fresh desert air, the first thing that hit her nostrils was the stink of cigarette smoke from Charlie's patio. She didn't know for certain, but Melody suspected that Charlie did most of his smoking out on the patio rather than inside his RV. Whenever Melody and Hazel walked by, she could see that his immense black ashtray—carved from some kind of rock—was almost always filled to overflowing. And where did he empty it? She'd seen that happen more than once, too. He'd turn around on his chair, use his foot to open the lid on a nearby metal trash container, and dump his ashes and cigarette butts into that.

Garbage day at the park was late on Friday afternoons. This was Thursday. If Charlie hadn't yet taken his trash to the dumpster, all those cigarette butts might still be right there on his patio. If Melody could get her hands on one of those . . . She wasn't a cop. She didn't need probable cause to raid his garbage can. She was a private citizen calling in an anonymous tip.

Hurrying over to the window, she looked out. It was close to eleven. A light still glowed in Charlie's windows. Earl was in bed and fast asleep, but Charlie was still up, and Melody decided to wait him out, which seemed to take a very long time. At 12:15 the light in his bedroom window finally went out. Just to be on the safe side, Melody waited another half hour after that—waited and worried. What if Charlie's RV was equipped with one of those Ring camera things? The park was gated and considered to be very safe. Most people didn't bother with outside security cameras, but what if Charlie did?

Finally, she went to the linen closet, pulled out a sheet, and wrapped it around her, covering both her face and her clothing to the best of her ability. Then with a plastic sandwich bag in hand, and feeling like some kind of grown-up out-of-control trick-or-treater, she snuck out of the house.

By the time she reached Charlie's patio, her knees were knocking and her hands shaking. She held her breath as she raised the lid on the trash can, praying that it wouldn't squeak. When she plunged one hand inside, her searching fingers immediately encountered a pile of ashes and cigarette butts. Despite the terrible stink she held the lid open with her forehead while using both hands to scoop a fistful of the evil smelling stuff into her waiting sandwich bag. She performed that challenging operation inside the can itself to keep from leaving behind a telltale trail of debris on the patio.

Finished at last, she eased the lid shut and

hurried out of Milton's tiny yard and back to her own. On trembling legs she climbed up into the RV; then, almost sick with relief, she sank gratefully onto her sofa. She sat there for several long minutes, steadying her nerves and catching her breath. She'd done it, but as her breathing steadied, she finally noticed the smell. Her hands stank of cigarettes, and if she wasn't careful, soon the whole house would stink as well. If Earl woke up and got a whiff of that, the jig would be up for sure.

Taking the baggie, she carried it back outside and hid it under the dog crate they kept stored next to the RV. Back inside she washed her hands vigorously with dish soap from the kitchen sink. Letting the water run, she felt incredibly proud of herself. She'd done it. She wasn't just offering Dan Pardee a vague tip. When she spoke to him in the morning, she intended to tell him that she had actual physical evidence, DNA evidence. Tip line or not, that should be enough to catch his attention.

At that point, and after taking Hazel out one last time, Melody Baxter went to bed, but for some strange reason, it was several hours later before she finally fell asleep.

CHAPTER 39

SELLS, ARIZONA
Friday, April 8, 2022, 6:00 A.M.

AFTER THE WOMAN HEARD THE BABIES
*laughing, she took her own brown cradle blanket and
returned to the village. There she found the neighbor
women busy in her home. The ground was swept and
cleaned and a fire was burning under the cooking
ollas.*

*A friend called to her and told her not to go too
near the cooking fire, warning that the smoke would
make her eyes bad. But an old woman who had looked
at her carefully said, "Do not worry. She has talked
to I'itoi."*

*Always after that the woman's eyes seemed to be
looking a great way off. Sometimes if you see eyes
like that, ones that are big and quiet and looking
beyond—farther and farther—then you will know
that is a person who has talked to I'itoi.*

AN AWAKENED IN HIS OWN BED THE NEXT
morning to the welcome aroma of coffee brew-
ng in the kitchen. He was home, so was Lani,
nd so were the kids. The evening before, while
raveling from one Tucson television studio to
nother, he had tried calling Lani to say that
e'd stop by the house in Gates Pass on his way
ome. He'd been astonished to learn that she
erself was already headed there.

"But what about your mom?" he'd asked.

"You're not going to believe this," Lani re-
lied, "but Mom agreed to check herself into
hat assisted-living place in Tucson. We went
o look at it yesterday afternoon. She thought
seemed nice enough, but I couldn't imagine
Iom would agree to go there. But I had told her
ou were working a case and that I needed to get
ack to the hospital. She was willing to consider
without the slightest objection.

"It's not far from here," Lani continued. "It's
n Prince just east of the Santa Cruz. After
ur walkthrough, she said it was fine, to go
head and sign her up, and how soon could she
ove in?"

"Just like that?" Dan asked in amazement.

"Just like that," Lani repeated, "so that's
hat we did this afternoon. Kath and the twins
ame along, and we all went back to the house.
packed up Mom's clothing and toiletries and
hatever else she might need for a short stay,
hile Kath and the girls rounded up her com-
ter and printer. Once we got into her room,
e twins took charge of getting her Wi-Fi up
d running. And you'll be happy to know that

Richard called me. He went by the house and checked on the washer. He said it had a marble stuck in the gears, but he was able to get it running again. You can stop by and pay him whenever."

"A stray marble," Dan said. "Next time I do the wash, remind me to do a better job of checking Micah's pockets. But the news about your mother is amazing."

"Yes, it is," Lani agreed.

After the last newscast, he was headed for Sells when his phone rang. "What the hell?" Joanna Brady demanded when he answered. "I thought you were going to keep me in the loop."

Clearly Sheriff Joanna Brady was pissed, and Dan didn't blame her. He had told her he'd keep her informed, but in the rush of getting to and from Dallas, he had failed to do so. Now he had to work his way out of this mess without betraying Jenny's confidence.

"I'm really sorry," he said. "It's been a circus."

"I'll bet it has," she continued. "I just saw you on the news. Obviously you must have come up with a DNA profile."

"We did," Dan admitted. "It was on a piece of previously overlooked evidence. We also made a connection to several other MIP cases, all of them involving young women who disappeared about the time there was a local rodeo in the areas. We finally got a lead on the guy. His name is Ronald Addison, a crook who made a fortune running a Ponzi scheme in San Francisco. When the Ponzi went bust, he took off for Mexico where he staged a phony suicide and hen disappeared. Since he's obviously back in he States, we suspect that he's had some kind of surgical intervention to change his appearance."

"That's the reason for going public with the composite?" Joanna asked.

"Exactly. My boss thinks there may be enough of a resemblance between that and how he looks now to generate some tips. I'm the one who got drafted into doing the dog and pony show."

"I'm sure that was fun," Joanna observed.

"Not so much," he said. "Those newspeople aren't exactly my cup of tea."

"Mine either," she said with a laugh.

Dan found that bit of laughter encouraging. Maybe eventually Sheriff Brady would find it in her heart to forgive him.

"Any other connections among the cases besides proximity to rodeos?"

"A couple," Dan replied. "Causes of death—manual strangulation—and each set of remains we've found so far is missing several teeth."

"Just like Rosa," Joanna murmured.

"Yes," Dan agreed. "Just like Rosa."

"I talked to Kendra late this afternoon. She said that someone from a mortuary in Safford stopped by earlier today to collect her remains."

"Good. Ida will be relieved," Dan said, "sad but relieved."

"Yes, she's had a long wait."

"And I'll try to do better about keeping you up-to-date."

"Don't worry about it," Joanna said. "Sounds like you've had a lot on your plate."

"I have," Dan said, "but that's no excuse. I should have done a better job of keeping you in the loop."

Even as he said the words aloud, he understood that part of his reluctance to be in touch had been wanting to keep Jenny from getting in trouble. But once he got off the phone, he felt as though he'd done a reasonably good job of walking that tightrope of bringing Joanna into the picture without blowing the whistle on her daughter. And that night, once he was finally home, he fell asleep grateful to have his wife back home and lying next to him. That same sense of thankfulness was still there the next morning when he woke up. Pulling on his clothing, he hurried to the kitchen.

"It's good to be back home," Lani said, when she spotted him standing in the doorway.

"You can say that again."

Dan was going to tell her the story his grandmother had once read to him about the man with a goat on the roof, but his phone rang just then with an unfamiliar Colorado phone number showing in caller ID. Obviously the caller wasn't Anna Rae, but it was most likely someone from MIP.

"Dan Pardee," he said when he answered.

"This is Todd Aikens," the caller said. "I'm the shift supervisor for the MIP tip line, and have an odd request for you."

"What's that?"

"I've got a lady on the line. Says her name is Melody and that she lives in an RV park some where in Tucson. She claims she's got a tip for us on the DNA composite and maybe even some physical evidence—DNA evidence, she claims—but she'll only talk to you. Not only that, she doesn't want to do it over the phone. She says she saw you on TV yesterday and wants to meet with you in person. For the record, I don't think that's a good idea."

Dan could barely contain his excitement. A tip on the phenotyping composite this soon?

"If she's got evidence, I'm all in," Dan replied enthusiastically. "Ask her where and when."

He heard Todd speaking to someone on another line before returning to him. "She says to meet her at noon in a place called the Wagon Wheel. It's a diner in a small strip mall at Ina Road and the freeway."

"How will I recognize her?"

Again Todd went offline for a moment. "She says the people there all know her," he told Dan once he returned. "Just ask for her by name."

"And her name is Melody?"

"Correct."

"Does Melody have a last name?"

"It's an anonymous tip line," Todd reminded him. "We don't require last names."

"All right. Tell Melody I'll see her there."

"You've already got a tip?" a surprised Lani asked.

Dan nodded. "Someone named Melody. I'm supposed to meet up with her here in Tucson at noon at a restaurant called the Wagon Wheel at Ina and the freeway."

"Never heard of it," Lani said.

Dan laughed. "That makes two of us."

Once Lani and the kids set off for work and school, Dan got on the horn with Anna Rae Green. She had been made aware of the incoming tip and was already strategizing about the problem.

"We know for a fact that Ronald Addison is abusive toward women and has violently attacked at least two of them—Michelle Barlow and Deborah Russell. Unfortunately neither of them reported the attack to law enforcement. According to what I was told, the tipster in Tucson claims to have some kind of DNA evidence. If that's true, and if it's something that actually links back to our profile, that would be terrific," Anna Rae said, "but we still have a problem."

"What's that?"

"What we need is sufficient probable cause to go for a search warrant and/or an arrest warrant. The cleanest way to do that would be to link our DNA profile to an active police investigation. There's no point in asking Michelle Barlow to file a complaint because the statute of limitations on her incident has already run out. On the other hand, if Deborah Russell would agree to file a police report about the attack on her, even at this late date, we might be able to persuade the authorities in Albuquerque to issue an arrest warrant for an unknown individual matching that DNA profile. Is there any way you could make that happen?"

"I doubt it," Dan replied. "My understanding is that she's absolutely opposed to going public with any of this. Not only that, I told Jenny that I'd do my best to keep Deb's name out of it, but if it comes down to a trial, there's no way we can guarantee that. In addition, Deborah is attending Snow College in Ephraim, Utah. No matter how you cut it, it's a long drive from northern Utah to Albuquerque, New Mexico."

"Hello," Anna Rae said, "earth to Dan Pardee. Who said anything about her having to drive to Albuquerque? In the postpandemic era and in nonemergency situations, most jurisdictions are willing to have victims file police reports by phone or online rather than having officers respond in person. If she would be willing to consider doing a remote interview, I'm pretty sure we'd be able to help facilitate one of those. Would you ask her?"

Dan was almost positive that wasn't going to fly. "I'm probably not the right person to do that," he replied. "What would you think about my asking Jennifer Brady to intercede on our behalf? I know she's a civilian, but . . ."

Anna Rae cut him off. "Jennifer Brady may be a civilian, but she's also the reason we have Ronald Addison's DNA profile in the first place. If involving her in this part of the investigation would help us, I'm all for it. You reach out to her, I'll reach out to the Albuquerque PD, and then we'll meet in the middle."

"Fair enough," Dan said. "I'll give Jenny a call."

He did so right then, but she didn't answer. Assuming she was probably in class, he left a message, asking her to call as soon as possible. By ten thirty that morning, Dan was headed into town. His phone rang before he reached Little Tucson.

Jenny's name was in caller ID. "Good morning," he said.

"You left a message for me to call?"

"I did. We need your help."

"What kind of help?"

"I'm on my way into Tucson right now to meet up with an anonymous tipster who may be in possession of DNA evidence matching our profile. The trouble is, even if we identify the guy, we don't have enough probable cause to obtain a search warrant, let alone make an arrest. To do one or both of those things, we need an active police investigation, preferably one concerning the physical assault and attempted kidnapping of Deborah Russell in Albuquerque."

It seemed to Dan that Jenny should have been thrilled by the news he'd just given her, but she wasn't.

"You're saying you need Deborah to file a police report." It was a statement rather than a question.

"Exactly," Dan replied. "And you're probably the only person on the planet who might be able to make that happen."

"Don't be so sure about that," Jenny said dubiously. "Besides, Deb's nowhere near Albuquerque right now."

"That's what I thought, too, but my boss

thinks she'll be able to arrange for Deb to file the complaint remotely by means of a Zoom-like meeting."

There was a pause. "Okay," Jenny said with a sigh. "I'll see what I can do, but I'm not making any promises."

Dan wondered about her subdued reaction. After all, Jennifer was the one who had opened up this whole avenue of investigation. Now she was being invited to play a more active role. As a criminal justice major, she should have been over the moon about that. Instead she sounded almost indifferent. If that was the case, it didn't bode well for her being able to convince Deborah Russell to do something she clearly wasn't interested in doing.

"By the way," he added. "There's something else you need to know."

"What's that?"

"I talked to your mom last night. I did several newscasts in Phoenix and Tucson yesterday hyping the phenotyping composite. She was pissed that I hadn't kept her apprised of what was going on."

"Did you tell her about me?" Jenny asked.

"No, I didn't," Dan replied, "but you should. When it breaks, this is going to be a big story. It'll be better if your mother hears it from you instead of someone else."

"She's going to kill me."

"I doubt it," he said, "but you're probably a better judge on that score than I am. So do what you think is best."

"Okay," Jenny said. "I'll think about it."

Let's hope you do more than think, Dan thought, but then, resigning himself to the fact that they'd probably need to find another way around the lack of probable cause, he decided to focus on the issue at hand and kept on driving.

CHAPTER 40

JENNY WASN'T THE LEAST BIT THRILLED ABOUT having to call Deborah Russell. She was still irked by the fact that Deb hadn't bothered to let her know that she'd arrived home safe and sound late Sunday night, and the half-baked apology she'd finally sent hadn't done much to fix things.

Jennifer was a product of her upbringing. If she was traveling from Bisbee back to Flagstaff or from one destination to another, she always let her folks back home know once she had safely arrived at her destination. She felt as though Deb should have granted her the same courtesy, especially since they'd agreed to do just that.

But now, she was on the horns of a different dilemma. She had told Dan Pardee that she would make the call, and even though she didn't want to, she found Deb's number in her call history and punched it anyway.

"Jenny," Deb said when she answered. "How's it going?"

She sounded cheerful and happy, but she wasn't the one harboring a grudge.

"I've got some news," Jenny said. "I just heard from Dan Pardee. The lab got a partial fingerprint off those glasses, and they were able to ID your attacker."

"Really?"

"Really," Jenny replied. "They also got a DNA profile."

"That's great news!" Deb said. "When are they going to arrest him?"

"They can't."

"Why not?"

"Because they don't have probable cause," Jenny replied. "They have to be able to link his DNA profile to an active police investigation. At this point, there isn't one."

That statement was followed by such a lengthy pause that Jenny was afraid Deb had hung up on her.

"What are you saying?" Deb asked finally. "Do they need me to file charges against him?"

"Yes, they do," Jenny said. "That's the only way he's going to get caught. By obtaining an arrest warrant on what happened to you, they'll be able to search his residence with the hope of finding evidence that will link him to the other cases. Serial killers often keep trophies of their kills, and that's what they're hoping to find."

"And having him arrested for attacking me may be the only way to find answers for those other victims?"

"Yes," Jenny answered.

"Will I have to go to Albuquerque?"

Jenny was surprised. "You mean you'd consider doing it?"

"I have to," Deborah said, "for my mom."

Jenny went from being surprised to being mystified. "What do you mean for your mom?"

"It's why I got back to the dorm so late on Sunday," Deb answered. "After what you said to me that day, I started thinking about my own mom. So on my way north, I stopped off in Cedar City to see her. My dad wasn't home. I didn't expect it to happen, but when my mom asked how things were going, I ended up telling her everything— even about Eddie and the attack. When she asked if the guy had been caught, that's when I told her that I hadn't reported because I was afraid she and Dad would be disappointed in me if they found out about what I'd really been doing. That's when she told me."

"Told you what?"

"That she was a victim of date rape back in high school, and she didn't report it, either. She was too ashamed. But then, when my dad asked Mom to marry him, she felt like she had to tell him because he thought she was still a virgin even though she wasn't. I think she expected he'd drop her like a hot potato, but he didn't. He told her that what had happened to her wasn't her fault, and that they wouldn't speak of it again. They didn't, and she didn't, not until Sunday when she told me."

"Your father must be a really good guy," Jenny offered.

"Better than I ever imagined," Deb agreed. "But I was shocked. It never occurred to me that something like that could have happened to my own mother and, in a way, to my dad, too, but it did. So she understood what was going on with me. In fact, she told me that even though Eddie was a two-timing jerk, I should forgive him because, if he hadn't been there that night, I'd probably be dead."

It occurred to Jenny that if it hadn't been for Eddie, Deb probably wouldn't have been out there walking to the barns by herself in the first place, but she didn't say anything about that. What she said instead was, "That must have come as a shock."

"It did," Deb agreed, "but we ended up talking for hours. That's why I didn't call you— because by the time I got back to Ephraim it was three o'clock in the morning. Before I left, though, Mom told me not to worry about telling my dad. She said she'd handle that. She also said that if I decided to go to the cops and report what happened, she and Dad would back me one hundred percent. All this week, I've been thinking about that—about maybe calling in a report, but I hadn't worked up enough courage. Now that I know the guy who attacked me might be a serial killer, though, my mind's made up. Will I need to go down to Albuquerque to talk to the police?"

"I don't think so," Jenny said. "Because of the pandemic, Dan Pardee's agency may be able to arrange for you to file charges remotely. I don't know the details of all that. Is it okay if I put Dan Pardee in touch with you?"

"Sure," Deb said. "That'll be fine, but thank you, Jenny. All this time I've been so worried about what my folks would think about me if they knew what had happened. It turns out I was wrong about that—wrong about both of them—and if you hadn't talked to me the way you did, I might never have figured it out."

When the call ended, Jenny sat there for a long time—staring at her phone and thinking about her own parents. Deb had found the courage to speak to her mother, but Jenny had yet to do the same, and it turns out she still wasn't ready.

What she was ready for was another solitary ride on Maggie. Maybe that would clear her head and help push her over the edge.

CHAPTER 41

TUCSON, ARIZONA
Friday, April 8, 2022, 7:00 A.M.

EVEN THOUGH MELODY BAXTER HAD BEEN UP
most of the night tossing and turning, she and
Hazel set out on their morning walk well before seven. After closing the door behind her,
Melody retrieved the baggie of cigarette butts
from under the dog crate and transferred them
to the trunk of their Buick on her way past. Getting those cigarette butts disposed of needed to
happen before Earl woke up rather than after.

As soon as Melody caught a whiff of fresh
cigarette smoke in the air, she knew in advance
that Charlie Milton would be out on his patio,
enjoying his early morning coffee. The idea
that he'd be right there watching as she rounded
the corner made her want to turn back, but she
forced herself to keep moving. That didn't mean
she stopped worrying. What if he really did have

a security camera? What if he had seen her and knew who she was?

Naturally Hazel launched into a full-scale barking fit as soon as she saw him. For once Melody was grateful for that. She didn't have to say a word—she just waved cheerily and kept right on walking. She had copied the MIP tip line number into her phone before she left the house, so she didn't have to look it up in order to place the call. She had a very specific way in which she wanted this conversation to go, and she didn't intend to talk to anyone other than the guy she'd seen on TV the day before. If she couldn't speak directly to Dan Pardee, she wouldn't talk to anybody.

Only when she was on the far side of the RV park did she place the call. What came next was a forty-minute hassle trying to explain to a whole series of different people that she had information about their serial killer suspect and that she would share that information only with Mr. Pardee. By the time that was finally agreed upon, Hazel was more than ready to be back inside, and so was Melody. Fortunately, Earl was in the shower when she got back home, and she was able to book some last-minute appointments for a mani-pedi and a haircut before he ever emerged. Occasional beauty shop visits were Melody's one tiny extravagance, and having those in place gave her an airtight excuse for being gone the rest of the morning and well into the afternoon.

Earl was planted in his recliner and tuned into

the first of his prerecorded news programs when she deposited his plate of scrambled eggs with a side of whole wheat toast on the TV tray in front of him.

"I've got spa appointments at Elaine's today," she muttered in passing, "so I'll be out the rest of the morning."

"Have fun," Earl said. "See you when you get back. I won't be holding my breath."

When Melody left half an hour later, Hazel was planted in Earl's lap, happily scarfing down the last few bits of toast and egg.

ELAINE'S WAS LOCATED AT ONE END OF A small strip mall with the Wagon Wheel diner conveniently at the other. Calling Elaine's a spa was a vast overstatement. It was humble and affordable, making it an attractive destination for retired ladies living on fixed incomes. Melody seldom went there without running into at least one or two of her neighbors from the RV park. Usually she enjoyed the friendly banter and chitchat, but today she needed to focus on her upcoming meeting with Dan Pardee.

What if her suspicions about Charlie Milton were wrong? What if he was innocent, and she was accusing him unjustly? Or what if he wasn't innocent, and Dan Pardee didn't take her accusations seriously? What if word about Melody's attempt at being a snitch somehow got back to Charlie? If he really was a serial killer, would he come after her next?

By a quarter to twelve she was a nervous wreck,

tucked into a back booth at the Wagon Wheel and swilling down iced tea. That's when Dan Pardee walked into the restaurant, removing his hat as he did so. When the hostess pointed him in her direction, Melody had to force herself to resist the temptation to flee. If Earl had even the slightest idea about her intentions to spill the beans on Charlie, he'd be furious.

"Melody?" Dan Pardee inquired politely as he approached.

Unable to speak, Melody nodded.

"My name is Daniel Pardee," he added, handing her a business card. "I understand you wished to speak to me."

She nodded again as he slipped into the booth across from her, setting his hat on the bench seat beside him. He had barely settled in before their waitress appeared. He ordered root beer. "Are you having something to eat?" he asked Melody.

"Their hot roast beef sandwiches are good," she managed. "That's what I'm having."

"Good," he told her. "I'll have the same."

As the waitress walked away, still writing down their order, Dan turned his attention back to Melody. In grocery stores, she usually grabbed an extra plastic bag or two from the produce section. Those always came in handy, and she had used a couple of them to double wrap the baggy before removing it from the trunk and putting it in her purse. Now she removed the package, placed it on the table, and pushed it over to Dan. When he reached down and picked it up, Melody felt a rush of relief at having the bag out of her hands and safely in his.

Dan held up the bag and examined the contents, peering through the outside layers rather than removing them. "Cigarette butts?" he asked.

Melody nodded. "Charlie Milton, the man I think may be your suspect, is our neighbor at Ina RV Park. His spot is next to ours. He always smokes outside. Last night I snuck over to his house and raided the trash can on his patio. That's where he always empties his ashtray."

As the waitress returned with Dan's root beer, he stowed the bag on the bench seat next to him. After taking a sip of his beverage, he asked, "Do you mind if I record our conversation?"

Melody shrugged. "Not at all," she said. "No skin off my nose."

Dan fiddled with his phone and then laid it down on the table between them. "Okay," he said after announcing her name and his and stating the time and date. "Now, if you would, please tell me what you know about Mr. Milton."

CHAPTER 42

MAN AND A WOMAN AND THEIR BABY LIVED
the foothills of the Baboquivari Mountains. In
e summer, many of the Desert People came to
ose foothills and lived near the family in the cool
the mountains. But when the summer was gone,
e people left the mountains and returned to the flat
untry. Their homes were in the village where they
rked their fields and looked after their cattle.

There were many rocks in those foothills and also
any wild animals. When it was cold and stormy,
e animals would come to the house and ask for food.

Now the man had fields and cattle, but they were
ar the village in the valley. When he went to work
fields, he would often stay with friends in the vil-
e and not come home. That left the woman very
uch alone with her baby.

One night, as the woman was putting her baby

to bed in his little cradleboard—his ali wulkud, sl
heard a coyote cry.

It was not Ban's usual cry. When he called again
the woman knew that he needed help, so she went
look for him.

It was very dark. At first the woman could not se
but finally, over near the water, she saw a large ol
coyote, lying on his side. Ge'e Ahithkam Ban, whic
means Large Old Coyote, called to the woman to he
him. He had slipped on a rock when he was getting
drink. The rock had shifted and caught his leg.

The Tohono O'odham must always help someor
who needs help, so the woman moved the rock, an
then she gave the coyote some food. From then on
Ahithkam Hahaisag Ban, which means Old Broke
Coyote, stayed very close to the woman's house, an
they became friends.

DAN LISTENED CAREFULLY AS THE SPRITEL
old woman related her story. She wore her care
fully combed white hair in what his grandmoth
used to call a "pixie cut." Her nails were painte
a garish shade of purple, and her skin was :
white as to be almost translucent, but what s!
had to say was fascinating.

"Everyone claims that Charlie's a nice guy
she said. "Some say he's divorced, some say he
a widower, and some say he's gay. All I kno
is it makes me nervous to be around him. N
dog doesn't like him, either. Hazel's a sweet li
tle miniature poodle, and she gets along wi
almost everyone, but whenever she's arour
Charlie, she barks like crazy."

That one statement grabbed Dan's full attention. While deployed to Iraq, he'd been partnered with a service dog named Bozo. Being named after Bozo the Clown wasn't a compliment. By the time the dog was paired with Dan, he was regarded as a hopeless goofball and was about to be put down. But then the "incident" happened. Dan, Bozo, and Justin Clifford had been out on patrol in a Humvee. Justin had been at the wheel when an innocent-looking kid—decked out with a bomb-filled vest under his shirt—had blown himself up next to the Humvee's driver's side. Justin had suffered life-threatening injuries. Dan and Bozo had both come away with relatively minor cuts and bruises, but in an instant Bozo was a clown no more. From that moment on, the dog was dead serious. Over time, while they were still in Iraq and later once Bozo joined Dan with the Shadow Wolves, his low-throated warning growl had alerted Dan to the presence of danger, saving both their lives in countless instances.

If Melody's Hazel thought Charlie Milton was dangerous, Dan Pardee happened to be someone who was inclined to agree with the animal. Coming back from that set of distant memories, Dan realized Melody was still chattering away. Fortunately his phone was recording her every word.

"As soon as I saw that computer-generated composite on the news, I said to Earl, my husband, 'Doesn't that look like Charlie?' Naturally Earl told me I was imagining things and to mind my own business, but when you said that some of the cases you're investigating are connected to rodeos, that hit me hard. Charlie Milton loved rodeos. I heard him bragging once that he hadn't missed the Tucson Rodeo in years until the pandemic hit, but I know he goes to other rodeos as well. He follows them everywhere like a regular rodeo groupie.

"You said on the news that you have the killer's DNA profile, so last night, once Earl went to bed, I decided to do something about it. I waited until the lights went out in Charlie's RV, then snuck over to his place and grabbed the cigarette butts out of his trash. You probably think the same thing Earl does, that I'm a batty old lady who needs to stop acting like some kind of aging Nancy Drew, but if it turns out that Charlie is the guy you're looking for, and I said nothing, I'll never be able to forgive myself."

By then Dan Pardee was thinking no such thing. Right now there were only two strikes against Charlie Milton—Hazel hated his guts and the man loved rodeos, but if the DNA on Melody's illicitly obtained cigarette butt matched up with his DNA profile from the De Russell attack, he really was their killer.

The waitress reappeared with their orders. Once she left and between bites, Dan launched into a barrage of questions.

"Do you have any idea where Charlie was born?"

Melody shook her head. "I don't think he ever mentioned anyplace in particular."

"But he's a snowbird?"

"I guess."

"Any idea where he lives when he's not in Tucson?"

"His car and his RV both have South Dakota plates."

"How old is he?"

"Probably in his early sixties—a lot younger than Earl and me."

"So he's retired?"

"I guess. I don't think he's ever said what he did before he retired, but I get the feeling he's pretty well off financially. He doesn't seem to have to watch his pennies the way the rest of us do."

By the time the meal ended, Dan could hardly wait to get the hell out of there. Glancing at his watch, he told Melody that he was late for an upcoming meeting. No meeting was scheduled, but what he did have was an urgent need to talk to Anna Rae Green. Halfway to the door, however, he turned around and went back to where Melody was gathering up her leftovers as well as her purse.

"One more thing," he said. "You've been a huge help, but I'm wondering if you'd be willing to do me one more favor."

"What's that?"

"My direct number is on the card I gave you earlier. If you see any indication that Mr. Milton might be intending to leave town, would you mind giving me a call?"

"Of course," she agreed. "I'll be glad to."

Dan's silenced phone had buzzed with an incoming call during his interview with Melody Baxter. On the way to the car, he checked the phone and discovered both a missed call and a voice mail, from Jennifer Brady.

"I just spoke to Deb Russell," Jenny's recorded voice told him. "She's willing to file a complaint and needs to talk to you. I'm texting you her contact information."

Dan was stunned. Earlier there had been no indication that Deborah Russell would be willing to go through with filing criminal charges.

The next number he dialed was Anna Rae's.

"I've got something," he said as soon as she came on the line.

He immediately passed along both pieces of good news, telling her about Melody's bag of cigarette butts as well as Deborah's unexpected change of heart and her willingness to file charges.

"So what's our next step?" Dan asked when he finished.

Anna Rae didn't hesitate. "We need those cigarette butts here in Denver immediately if no sooner. Hold on a second."

For the next several seconds, the only sound coming in over Dan's phone was the clattering of fingers on a keyboard.

"Okay," Anna Rae said finally. "Here's one. There's a direct nonstop flight from Tucson to Denver departing Tucson International this afternoon at 4:20 P.M. I want you on it with those cigarette butts in hand."

"Wait," Dan objected. "You expect me to fly to Denver today?"

"I certainly do," Anna Rae declared. "If this is our guy, we're hot on his trail right now, and don't want him to slip through our fingers. We'll book your flight from here and text you both the details and a boarding pass. Once you land, I'll have someone meet you at the airport to take you to the office. In addition, I'll have people from the DNA lab on hand and ready to go to work on those cigarette butts the moment they arrive. All you have to do is get both those butts and yours to the airport."

Dan glanced at his watch. Lunch with Melody had taken longer than expected, and it was already verging on two P.M. His home in Sells was over an hour away. "A 4:20 flight won't give me enough time to go by the house and pack," he objected.

Anna Rae was relentless. "We'll book you on the first available return flight tomorrow, so how many clothes do you need? If you're missing something essential, feel free to expense it, but I want you here. This is our chance to solve several cases all at once, and we're not missing out on that opportunity because you need a fresh set of underwear. Understand?"

"Yes, ma'am," Dan said. "I'm on my way."

"On another subject," Anna Rae added, "I reached out to the Albuquerque PD and spoke to one Louise Acuña, the head of their sex crimes unit."

"How come sex crimes?" Dan asked. "Technically Deb isn't a sex crime victim."

"Only because she got away," Anna Rae shot back. "From what you've told me about her, she'll need to be handled with kid gloves. Louise assures me that she has twenty years' worth of

experience at interviewing traumatized teenag
ers. Not only that, she's been helping victims fil
criminal charges via remote interviews for the
past two and a half years."

"Sounds good," Dan agreed. "I'll see you in
few hours then. In the meantime, I'd better cal
my wife and let her know that I'm going AWOI
for the second time in three days."

"Name's Lani and she's a doctor, right?" Ann
Rae asked.

Dan was surprised that she remembered tha
much about a member of one of her employee
families. Anna Rae and Lani had met at the cer
emony marking the end of Dan's initial MII
training session, but still . . .

"Yes," he said.

"As I recall, she was completely in favor c
your taking this job—in fact, I seem to remem
ber her saying she was over the moon about it."

That was also true. Lani had been absolutel
delighted to think that Dan would no longer b
out in the wilds of the desert in the middle c
the night, duking it out with illegal immigran
and/or drug cartel gangsters.

"She was," he conceded.

"She may not be thrilled about the inconve
niences your job is posing right this minute, bu
if we end up nailing Ronald Addison/Charl
Milton's ass based on the work you've done, she
going to be popping her buttons with pride."

"Probably," Dan agreed.

"And speaking of Charles Milton," Anna Ra
continued, "I know you have a recording of you
interview with Melody but between now and th

time your flight leaves, please text me whatever you think will give us the most help in tracking down information on him. I already have a research team building his bio, but any information you can add will be helpful. And unless I miss my guess there won't be any trace of Charles Milton until sometime after Ronald J. Addison disappeared. That should put another nail in Ronald Addison's coffin."

"Right," Dan agreed, "and it couldn't happen to a nicer guy."

CHAPTER 43

DENVER, COLORADO
Friday, April 8, 2022, 9:00 P.M.

ON THOSE LONG EVENINGS WHEN TH *woman was alone, Old Broken Coyote brought new of the desert and of the mountains. He told her abor the places where honey could be found; when O. Gray Fox and his family had returned to their cav how a wolf had carried off a dead calf only to have stolen by a pack of coyotes.*

But sometimes before it got too cold, the woma whose husband did not come home would go out an. sit very quietly in the blue-gray light that comes aft Tash goes down. When the woman sat that way, the blue-gray light, Old Broken Coyote did not ta. to her. He knew that was a time when she want messages and talk from her own people, the ones the village.

Sometimes the woman felt very heavy insia Then she would close her eyes and with that the lig.

would always be red like the sunrise—red and bright and happy and warm—and not blue gray and cold.

Sometimes, when the messages from her people would not come, she knew they were not thinking of her, so she talked to Old Broken Coyote and to her baby. She would tell them how she loved the red light of the mountains more than any other and wished that everything was that color.

T NINE O'CLOCK THAT NIGHT, DAN PARDEE was seated in his boss's office and waiting for the DNA crew to do their stuff. The MIP research staff had spent the intervening hours working on the Charles Milton issue, and Anna Rae's suspicions were correct. The first time the name Charles Milton appeared in any public records was when he obtained a driver's license in California in March of 2015, months after the disappearance of Ronald J. Addison. His birthdate and Social Security number led back to a deceased child, an infant bearing the same name, who had passed away at six months of age in Memphis, Tennessee. That was good circumstantial evidence as far as it went, but Dan knew they still needed that DNA match.

Shortly before ten a call came in from Captain Louise Acuña in Albuquerque. Anna Rae immediately put her on speaker.

"What do you have for us?" Anna Rae asked.

"Liftoff," Louise replied. "I've conducted and recorded Zoom interviews with both Deborah Russell and Eddie Willis, the only other person

present at the time of the assault. He corrobo-
rates Deborah's version of events. He reported
that, in the aftermath of the attack and while
helping Deborah collect her scattered belong-
ings, he picked up a pair of glasses and placed
them in her purse."

"So far so good," Anna Rae said.

"I've also spoken to our prosecutor and explained the extenuating circumstances."

"By that you mean the possible connection
between your case and ours?" Anna Rae asked.

"Correct. Based on the information Deborah
and Eddie provided, the DA is willing to issue
an arrest warrant for whatever unknown individual matches the DNA profile found on those
glasses."

"So if the profile found on the cigarette butt
matches the one found on the glasses, officers on
our end will be able to place the individual currently known as Charlie Milton under arrest?"

"Yes," Louise countered, "but I'm not sure
which jurisdiction will be in charge. That has yet
to be determined. I suppose it'll be Tucson PD."

"No, ma'am," Dan replied, jumping into the
conversation for the first time. "I've already
checked. The Ina RV Park is situated just outside the Tucson city limits in Pima County."

"The arrest warrant should go to the Pima
County Sheriff's Department then?" Louise
asked.

"Yes," Dan agreed, "and since it turns out
Pima County Sheriff Brian Fellows is actually
a close family friend, I'll send you his conta-

information so you can forward the information directly to him. By the way, he's already on board with this investigation."

"He is?" Anna Rae asked.

"I spoke to him about it. Turns out Brian was working at the Tucson PD when one of our victims—Rosa Rios—disappeared after attending the Tucson Rodeo. Her mother attempted to file a missing persons case at the time, but there's no record of that. So he's aware of the situation, and he's pissed about it, too. If this lands on his desk, you'd better believe it'll be taken seriously."

"Sounds good," Louise said. "Any news on those cigarette butts?"

"Not yet," Anna Rae said. "My people are working on them. We'll let you know the moment we hear."

When the call ended, she favored Dan with a beaming smile. "An arrest warrant!" she exclaimed. "Astonishing, Mr. Pardee. I think you're a keeper."

Dan appreciated the praise, but he knew none of it would have been possible without someone like Anna Rae running the show. It was refreshing to be working for someone who was more interested in getting the job done than she was in sitting around talking about it. When it came to red tape, she was more likely to take a machete to it rather than a scissors.

Needing something to fill the sudden silence between them, Dan asked, "How much longer do you think the DNA people are going to take?"

"Be patient," Anna Rae advised. "In the old

days, getting results on something like this would have taken weeks or months instead of a matter of hours."

Dan sighed. "While we're waiting, I should probably give Lani a call to see how much trouble I'm in."

He left Anna Rae's office and placed the call from the break room.

"How are things?" he asked. It seemed like that was the question he always asked, and somehow he always dreaded her answer.

"Under control," she replied. "What's going on with you?"

"Right now we're on hold waiting to see if the lab can come up with a DNA profile," he replied. "The really good news is that the Albuquerque victim has come forward and filed an official complaint. If and when we do get a profile, Albuquerque has agreed to issue an arrest warrant for anyone whose DNA matches the profile obtained from the glasses."

"Will that work?" Lani asked.

"I hope so."

"But you still don't know for sure that the Albuquerque incident is connected to your homicides."

"We're hoping that a search of Milton's residence will turn up evidence linking him to those crimes. Once he's placed under arrest for the Albuquerque attack, we'll have grounds for obtaining a search warrant of his residence and vehicle. Speaking of his residence, you'll never guess where his RV is located."

"Where?"

"In an RV park located on Ina Road."

"He's in Tucson then?" Lani asked.

"The address actually places it outside the city limits in Pima County."

"Does that mean Brian's people will end up working the case with you?"

"Sure does," Dan replied. "I told Louise Acuña, the Albuquerque detective, that once she has the arrest warrant in hand, she should contact Brian directly. But enough about me," Dan said, abruptly changing the subject. "What's going on with you? How's your mom?"

"I talked to her earlier this evening. She was just back from having dinner in the dining room. She said the food was okay, but she was tired and on her way to bed. She said being around all those strangers wore her out."

"She used to thrive on being among strangers," Dan observed. "Whenever we saw her at the book festival she seemed to be having a ball."

"Those were the old days before Covid," Lani said. "After everything shut down, she and Dad pretty much lived like a pair of hermits. And once he was gone, it's mostly been just Mom and Lucy."

"Do you think she'll stay where she is until Lucy gets back or will she bail?"

"I'm hoping she'll stay," Lani replied.

"So do I," Dan agreed, "but I'm still not sure how you talked her into going there in the first place."

"It turns out I had some help—from you."

"From me?" Dan echoed. "I wasn't even there. How did I help?"

"By referring me to a medicine man at a time I really needed one," Lani said with a laugh. The sound of her laughter made Dan feel as though all was forgiven, but he was still puzzled.

"You really went to see John Wheeler?"

"I did."

"And he was able to tell you how to get your mother to agree to go into assisted living?"

"He did. He told me I needed to be firm with Mom and let her know that taking care of her has disrupted our lives and interfered with our work. He suggested that I remind her that she's still my mother, and that by letting someone else take care of her, she'll be taking care of us."

"That actually worked?" Dan asked.

"Evidently. As soon as I told her that, it was as though I had toggled some invisible switch. The next thing I knew she was all for packing up and going."

"Amazing."

"Chair Man had some advice for you as well," Lani added.

"He did?" a startled Dan responded. "What kind of advice?"

"He said you should go see your father before it's too late."

"My father?" a dismayed Dan repeated. "How does John Wheeler know anything about my father?"

"Beats me," Lani said. "I certainly didn't tell him, but you know how sneaky those medicine people can be—they always seem to have ways of knowing stuff they're not supposed to know."

Just then, the door to the break room slammed

open. Anna Rae Green charged into the room, giving Dan an unequivocal two thumbs-up.

"You're kidding. We've got a match?"

"We certainly do. Ronald J. Addison and Charlie Milton are one and the same. Once we have him in custody on the assault charge, we'll try to find out what else he's done."

Dan could barely contain himself. "Did you hear that?" he practically shouted into the phone.

"I did," Lani said. "Congratulations! What's the plan now?"

"As soon as I get off the phone with you, I'm going to call Brian Fellows and give him the news. Then we'll figure out our next steps. I'm booked on a flight that lands in Phoenix at 9:30 tomorrow morning. I'll rent a car there for the drive back to Tucson, but given everything that's going on, it's anybody's guess what time I'll get home."

"Not to worry," Lani told him. "I'm here, and I've got this."

CHAPTER 44

TUCSON, ARIZON▮
Friday, April 8, 2022, 9:45 P.M

AT NINE FORTY-FIVE, PIMA COUNTY SHERIF▮
Brian Fellows decided to call it a night.

"Time to take the old two-bagger to bed," h▮
said to Kath.

Bowling jargon aside, between husband an▮
wife that's how Brian often jokingly referre▮
to himself. After the accident that left him ▮
paraplegic, losing the use of his legs had bee▮
bad enough, but the prospect of having to dea▮
with ostomy bags for the rest of his life had bee▮
daunting. Years later, however, managing hi▮
two-bag system was simply the way things were▮

In the old days, Brian had showered in th▮
mornings. Now he did that just prior to going t▮
bed. After wheeling himself into his bathroo▮
and while preparing to enter his non-walk-i▮
walk-in tub, his mind went back to that fate▮
ful carjacking incident. In a split second, he ha▮

chosen to push a woman and her almost three-year-old son—Virginia Torres and Pepe—out of the path of an oncoming semi. That piece of selfless bravery on Brian's part had put him in a wheelchair for the remainder of his life while, at the same time, turning him into a local hero.

Once he had been released from the hospital and rehab, months later, he discovered that the entire community had rallied behind him and his family. When he arrived home, the front steps that had once led into the house had magically turned into a wheelchair ramp. The front and back doors had both been widened to accommodate his comings and goings, but the changes to the house's exterior were minor compared to what had occurred inside.

The two-bedroom, one-story bungalow just west of Country Club had been totally transformed. A second floor had been added, upping the bedroom count from two to three while the two original downstairs bedrooms had been combined into a fully accessible master suite, complete with a deluxe walk-in tub and shower—which Kath loved and Brian did, too, despite the fact that he couldn't actually use it the way it was originally intended.

Learning to live without legs had been one issue, but learning to live with no onboard plumbing had been quite another. With practice, Brian had learned the care and feeding of his two-bag ostomy system, but he needed to allow himself plenty of time to do so, and that was what had necessitated his nighttime shower arrangement.

Pima County's lack of preparation for dealing with a paraplegic sheriff had gone far beyond the extensive remodel of his private office. The board of supervisors had drawn the line at investing in a handicapped-accessible police vehicle, opting instead for providing a driver to transport him between home and work. Performing his complex body-prep operation in the mornings while a driver sat outside waiting for him just didn't cut it.

After undressing and using Saran Wrap to cover his ostomy equipment, Brian loaded himself onto the bathroom's permanently installed Hoyer Lift and turned on the water. A duplicate set of controls had been added, making it possible for him to turn on the water prior to lowering himself into the tub, sparing him from being hit by that initial blast of cold water from the rain-bath showerhead.

Brian never failed to be grateful for the convenience of his redesigned home. The person who was ultimately responsible for that was the same one who, almost single-handedly, had helped elect him to office. Virginia Torres—the woman whose life he had saved—had become one of Brian's most ardent supporters. Ginny had rallied Tucson's Hispanic construction community into pulling off that massive house remodel at no cost to the family. As the volunteer coordinator for his election campaign, she had worked the same kind of magic with Pima County's voters. Brian Fellows may have saved Virginia's life, but as far as he was concerned, she had more than evened the score.

He was out of the tub and drying off when his phone rang. With his phone still on the counter, he answered with his waterproof Apple Watch.

"Hey, Dan," he said. "What's up?"

"I'm calling about the Rosa Rios case and several others besides. You'll be surprised to learn that the ball has just landed in your court."

"My court?" Brian repeated. "How did that happen? You caught that case just a couple days ago, but you already have a lead?"

"It was actually a week ago," Dan corrected, "and it turns out it's more than a lead. Any minute now, a DA in Albuquerque will be sending you an arrest warrant."

It took several minutes for Dan to explain everything that had transpired since his visit to Brian's office. The story wasn't finished when Kath came in to the bathroom to undress. At that point Brian wheeled himself into the bedroom to allow her some privacy.

"If this Milton character gets wind that you're coming for him, what are the chances he'll try to take off?" Brian asked. "Should I send a surveillance crew out to keep an eye on him?"

"I don't think so," Dan said. "I did a drive-by earlier this afternoon before I left town. The surroundings are pretty much open desert. Any kind of law enforcement presence would be too easy to spot, but I wouldn't worry about his flying the coop unnoticed. His neighbor, Melody—the woman who called in the anonymous tip—lives next door to him. I have a feeling she doesn't miss a trick where Charlie is concerned. I asked her to let me know if it looks like he's making a run for it."

"And Albuquerque PD will be sending the paperwork to me personally?"

"Yes, I gave Louise Acuña, the detective on the case, your contact info, so the warrant will be routed directly to you."

"Should I go back into the office tonight to wait for it?"

"Don't do that," Dan replied. "Tomorrow morning should be fine. That's when all this will probably go down, and I want to be there when it happens. Right now the lab is still processing evidence."

"Where are you?" Brian asked.

"Still in Denver at the moment. I'm booked on a flight that'll have me in Phoenix by nine thirty A.M. I'll be renting a car to drive back to Tucson International where I left my wheels. The soonest I can be in Tucson is eleven thirty or so."

"Send me your flight information," Brian said. "I'll have a deputy meet you at the airport. A patrol car with flashing lights will get you back to Tucson a hell of a lot faster than driving a rental."

Kath came into the bedroom just as the call ended. "What's going on?"

"Dan's caught a lead on that Rosa Rios case, and the suspect is on my patch. Once Albuquerque PD issues an arrest warrant, they'll forward it to me. I should probably organize an arrest team and have them standing by."

"Do you want to go back to the office to-night?" Kath asked.

"No," Brian said. "Dan says tomorrow will be fine, but I'd better call in and let them know I'll need a driver in the morning. Luis is off on weekends. They'll need to send someone else."

"You're not planning to be part of the arrest team, are you?" Kath wanted to know.

"What do you think?"

"Never mind," she said resignedly. "I shouldn't have bothered to ask."

CHAPTER 45

TUCSON, ARIZONA
Saturday, April 9, 2022, 1:45 A.M.

OTHER THAN VENTURING OUT TO THE PATIO for periodic smoke breaks, Charlie had spent the whole of Friday inside the confines of his RV. With that age-enhanced composite out in public and on the news, he didn't dare set foot beyond the shadow of his awning. As time passed, it wasn't lost on him that being stuck inside the RV was probably not unlike being locked up in a jail cell, although the RV's interior design and creature comforts were undoubtedly much more pleasant.

Instead, he had spent the time sitting and stewing. He had immediately forked over Dr. Madrid's so-called deposit, so why hadn't anyone gotten back in touch with him? Why was the phone Julio had given him still absolutely silent? Of course, he could have dialed up Julio himself, but that might have betrayed how anxious he was, and being weak just wasn't Charlie Milton's style. Instead he simply waited, hour after interminable hour.

Then, at 1:45 on Saturday morning, the burner finally rang. Groping in the dark, he grabbed the device off the nightstand.

"Hola," someone said.

Charlie instantly recognized Julio's voice. "Took you long enough," he grumbled.

"It takes time to put these kinds of arrangements in place," Julio replied.

Especially if you don't start until after the money transfer clears the bank, Charlie thought. "Okay," he said. "What's the deal?"

"Ever been to Nogales?" Julio asked.

"No, it's never made my 'must visit' list. Why?"

"Because you need to be there this afternoon at four P.M. You're to go to a bar called El Barrio. It's on the main drag as you drive into town. Park on the street and leave your keys in the vehicle. We'll handle getting rid of it."

"I'm supposed to abandon my vehicle just like that?"

"That's right," Julio replied. "Someone inside the bar will make contact. That person will be responsible for smuggling you across the line into Mexico. Once there you'll be handed off to someone else who will deliver you to a private landing strip where you'll meet your plane for Guadalajara."

Charlie didn't mind letting go of the car. The Lexus was an older model, and he wasn't really attached to it, but the idea of leaving the RV behind was a different story. For years it had been his only home. He was comfortable inside its four walls, but leave them behind he would.

"What about luggage?" he asked.

"If you have a backpack or a briefcase, you can bring one of those, but that's it," Julio advised. "You may be leaving town, but you shouldn't look like it. And, whatever you do, don't bring along your phone or any other electronic devices, including that burner. Best thing to do with both of those would be to remove the SIM cards and ditch them out in the desert somewhere between Tucson and Nogales."

"Got it," Charlie said. "Sounds like I'm traveling light."

"You are," Julio agreed. "Remember, four o'clock sharp. Don't be late." With that, the call ended.

"Yes, sir," Charlie said sarcastically into the empty phone. "Whatever you say, sir."

He wasn't used to taking orders from someone like Julio, and the whole idea pissed him off. As for traveling light? When it came to briefcases or backpacks, he was fresh out. The only thing he had that would serve the purpose was his trusty camera bag. He'd carried it around with him for years without ever owning a camera. The bag had mostly functioned as his date-rape kit, providing both camouflage as well as portable storage for everything he needed for getting the job done—tie wraps, latex gloves, and rolls of duct tape, along with the pair of pliers he had used for removing his victims' teeth. In this instance the bag wouldn't be carrying any of its usual contents. Instead it would hold all the treasures too precious and dangerous to leave behind.

He'd never been to Nogales, so he checked with Google. From Ina Road the driving distance was probably another ten or fifteen miles over what was estimated to be sixty-nine miles. In other words, if he left the house at 2:30, he'd arrive in plenty of time. And once he closed the door on his RV for the last time, Charlie Milton's short, secondhand life would be over.

With all the uncertainty finally out of the way, the soon-to-be-former Charlie Milton was finally able to relax. He put the burner phone back on his bedside table. After reminding himself that he'd need to decommission both his phone and his computer in the morning, Charlie Milton rolled over, and went back to sleep.

CHAPTER 46

PHOENIX, ARIZONA
Saturday, April 9, 2022, 9:25 A.M.

ON ONE OF THOSE NIGHTS WHEN THE WOMAN
could not hear the voices of the people in the distant village, Coyote told her that her baby was not going to stay with her. Old Broken Coyote had been high up in the mountains and had heard the medicine men talking.

That made the woman very sad. Then, Ban told her to listen very carefully.

The woman listened. At first she heard nothing but the wind in the trees. Then, quite close, she heard a low, soft chuckle. She looked and saw her own baby sleeping quietly in his cradle. When she listened again, she heard the sound of many children laughing.

Then Old Broken Coyote told her that many, many children were playing all around her. He told her that there were many more children near her than in all the villages put together and that these children were very happy.

After that, the woman could hear the children laughing almost every night. They were so happy and laughed and played so much that she almost felt sorry for her own child who had to lie on his back in his cradle and cry a great deal.

Finally the woman's husband returned from the village. The woman did not tell him that their child was going away. She only asked that he stay a little while longer with her and their child and not return to his fields and cattle near the village.

But the man only laughed. He said summer would come soon and then there would be plenty of other people near her, but he promised to return home if Old Broken Coyote should come for him. That made the woman even sadder, but it was the best she could do.

NATURALLY, BECAUSE DAN WAS IN A HURRY, once his plane landed at Sky Harbor, whoever was supposed to be in charge of maneuvering the Jetway just couldn't get his or her act together. Dan was left standing, seemingly for endless minutes, crammed into the narrow aisle of the aircraft along with a planeload of other disgruntled passengers. That's when a text came in:

Pima County Sheriff's Department Detective Philip Hirales at your service. I'm here at the bottom of the escalator in Baggage Claim. Do you have checked luggage?

No luggage, Dan responded. How will I know you?

I'll be the guy holding a badge.

> Okay, they just now finally got
> the door open, so it shouldn't
> be too long. I'll be right there.

Dan spotted Phil—as he asked to be called—while still on the escalator.

"Glad you're good to go as far as luggage is concerned," Phil said. "I let the security guards out front know about the situation. They very kindly allowed me to leave my vehicle right outside in the passenger load zone. Let's go."

Within a matter of minutes after leaving the terminal, Phil's Ford Interceptor was speeding along I-10 toward Tucson. Their flashing lights sent them gliding effortlessly past vehicles pulled over into the right-hand lane to clear the way.

"You're obviously getting rock-star treatment," Phil observed as they sped along. "Not only did Sheriff Fellows have me come get you in a patrol car, he also had me bring along an extra vest. Word is he's putting together an arrest team, and I'm supposedly on it. What I don't understand is how you fit into the picture."

Dan began by laying out the close connections between his family and that of Sheriff Brian Fellows.

"That explains a lot," Phil allowed when he finished. "Now tell me about the case."

Dan did that, too, but it took time. They were already on the far side of the Gila River and passing the first Casa Grande exit by the time he finished. In fact, he had been so caught up in telling the story that he had failed to notice that the speedometer had nosed up to 85 miles per hour, ten miles over the posted limit. That's when his phone rang with Brian Fellows's name showing in caller ID. He put the call on speaker.

"Where are you?" Brian asked.

"Coming up on the second Casa Grande exit," Dan answered. "Why? What's going on?"

"I disregarded your advice and sent out a surveillance team after all," Brian informed him. "After doing their drive-through, it was determined that the RVs in the park are packed too closely together to risk having a shoot-out inside the property. The risk of collateral damage is too great. I've got a team of out-of-uniform deputies posted along Ina Road keeping an eye on things. They're posing as volunteers doing Adopt-a-Highway trash removal. Once Milton leaves the RV park, we'll have chase vehicles in place to initiate a traffic stop. The suspect drives an older-model white Lexus."

"How soon will this go down?" Dan asked. "Am I going to miss it?"

"You might," Brian allowed. "Tell Phil to get a move on."

Detective Hirales hardly needed urging. He gave the gas pedal another firm nudge, and the speedometer shot up to ninety.

"I called on your phone because we're maintaining radio silence," Brian continued. "On the off chance Milton is equipped with a police scanner, we don't want to give our presence away. The arrest team, you and Phil included, will rendezvous at the Circle K on the frontage road just north of Ina. Pull in north of the building. That way you'll be out of sight from anyone traveling on Ina. We won't be able to see Milton, but he won't see us, either."

"All right," Dan said. "We'll do our best to be there."

DAN AND PHIL TURNED OFF I-10 AT THE INA
Road exit at ten past eleven, a mere eighty-seven minutes after leaving Sky Harbor. Once there they joined three other patrol vehicles cooling their jets in the parking lot outside the convenience store. In addition to Philip Hirales and Dan, the arrest team consisted of four uniformed deputies. Sheriff Brian Fellows himself, accompanied by a driver, was also in attendance. Spotting Brian's mobility scooter parked in a shady spot next to the building, Phil and Dan hurried over to join him.

"What's the situation?" Dan asked.

"Our fake litter control crew is currently taking a lunch break," Brian answered. "They're doing such a great job that they're almost a half mile from where they started, but they can still tell if Milton turns left or right when he exits the RV park."

"What's next?" Dan asked.

"We wait," a resigned Sheriff Fellows replied. "Regardless of which way he goes, we stay right here until he makes a move. We've told people inside the store that we've had an anonymous tip about a huge drug buy that's supposed to occur somewhere in the near neighborhood over the course of the afternoon. That's the story, and everybody needs to stick to it. A camera crew

rom KOLD just up the road stopped by a few
minutes ago. Someone had told them about 'unusual police activity in the area.' I told them to
get lost. The last thing we need right now is for
the press to latch onto this."

So wait they did—for one hour and then for
two. After the exhilaration of that breakneck
ride from Phoenix, Dan found the enforced
pause in the action excruciating. It was hot outside, and the cops, dressed in battle gear and
vests, were miserable, while the clerk inside the
store happily did land-office business in sodas,
chips, and candy bars.

Every time Brian's phone rang, the assembled
officers went dead still, wondering if this was the
call they were expecting. Finally it came—at two
thirty in the afternoon. When the call ended,
Brian held up his hand.

"Okay, people," he said. "It's a go. The target
vehicle, a white Lexus, just left the RV park and
turned eastbound on Ina. He's two miles out.
Load up and switch on your body cams. After
we determine which direction he's going on the
freeway, Detective Hirales and Field Officer
Pardee will take the lead. They're the ones with
the arrest warrant in hand. Once they initiate
traffic stop, we cancel radio silence. If Milton
heads toward Phoenix, I'll notify the Arizona
Highway Patrol and the Pinal County Sheriff's
Department. If he goes the other way, I'll bring
Tucson PD into the picture. As soon as Milton
pulls over, all other vehicles are to converge on
the scene to provide backup. Got it?"

The assembled officers nodded in unison.

"All right then," Brian added. "Be safe out there."

That closing comment was still in the air as the officers sprinted toward their waiting vehicles.

"Are you ready to do this?" Detective Hirale asked, as he and Dan slammed their respective car doors and belted themselves into their seats.

"Damned right I am," Dan replied. "More than ready!"

"All right then," Phil added with a grin, "let' go get this guy, but remember, you may be MII out the kazoo, but you're not one of Sheriff Fel lows's sworn officers. If anything bad happens to you, he's going to be in a world of hurt. I sure a hell don't want that to be on me."

"It won't be," Dan assured him. "I'll be careful."

CHAPTER 47

THE MAN WENT AWAY AGAIN TO BE WITH HIS friends in the village, leaving the woman alone with her baby. A few days after that, the child went to sleep and did not wake up again, leaving the woman sitting all by herself with her dead baby.

At last she heard Old Broken Coyote call. She knew that she must have been sitting there with her dead child for a very long time, because her husband was coming up the trail. Old Broken Coyote had traveled to the distant village to bring him to her.

The woman gathered together the child's cradle and all the other things she had used for him. Then the woman and her husband carried the child and all his things up the side of the mountain.

When they came to the right place, the man set the little body down on the ground. The woman laid the baby's things beside him. They piled bushes over *the body and his things, and over all those they piled rocks.*

That's when the man noticed that the baby's tiny shoes, his little shu shushk, were not covered by the rocks, but he did not say anything about it.

That evening when the blue-gray light came and filled all the canyons and hollows, the woman went out alone. The husband wanted to scold her and he started to follow her, but Old Broken Coyote stopped him. Much later the woman returned bringing the baby's shoes. This time there was a string tied to them.

ONCE PHIL AND DAN WERE BELTED IN WITH the engine running, they remained out of sight behind the building until the white Lexus appeared. It paused briefly at the stop light before turning right onto the frontage road and then merging over onto the freeway's eastbound entrance ramp.

"Eastbound it is," Phil said aloud as he pulled out into traffic. "Here goes."

By the time they merged onto the freeway the Lexus was cruising along about half a mile ahead of them. At that point, due to construction, the posted speed limit on I-10 had dropped to a 55 limit, and Charlie Milton seemed to be doing just that. The roadway between the Interceptor and the Lexus remained fairly empty. Cars disregarding the change in speed limit zoomed up behind them, seemingly hell-bent on passing, but they quickly backed off once they recognized the Interceptor's distinctive cop-car profile.

"Does this guy have any idea we're coming for him?" Phil asked.

"No way to tell," Dan replied. "That age-enhanced composite has been all over local media, but I doubt he knows we've actually made the connection."

The construction zone ended, and both vehicles sped up to 60 miles per hour.

"I'll hit the lights just beyond Orange Grove," Phil said. "After that, there's not much activity on this side of the road until we're closer to town. So what's it going to be, will he pull over or not?"

"Who knows?" Dan said.

Bare minutes later, after gradually closing the distance between the two vehicles, Phil hit the gas pedal and the light bar simultaneously, but as the Interceptor shot forward, so did the Lexus.

"I guess we've got our answer," Phil observed. "He's definitely not pulling over!"

It was Saturday afternoon, and traffic on I-10 was fairly light. Even so, both Dan and Phil were well aware of the inherent dangers posed by high-speed police pursuits. Concentrating on driving, Detective Hirales had both hands glued to the steering wheel while Dan Pardee maintained a death grip on the armrest next to him.

"Just keep him in sight," Dan said through gritted teeth. "I'll call for reinforcements."

Struggling to keep the suspect in view, Dan picked up the patrol car's handheld mic. Using

that, he related that a speeding suspect had failed
to stop and was heading toward the city center
One exit after another flew past. After Miracle
Mile and while approaching Grant Road, the
Interceptor was suddenly caught up in a knot of
traffic. Phil immediately slowed, and that's when
Charlie Milton's turn signal came on. Moments
later he swerved abruptly into the right-hand
lane.

"Suspect appears to be exiting at Speedway,"
Dan said into the radio.

"We no longer have eyes on him," Phil added
"Discontinuing active pursuit. Exiting I-10 at
Speedway."

Leaving his body cam activated, he switched
off the light bar and siren as they crawled along
at a glacial forty-five before taking the exit. The
stoplight at Speedway turned red as they approached, forcing them to wait in traffic through
an entire light cycle with both of them assuming
that the suspect had ditched them for good.

"Which way?" Phil asked when they were
finally able to move forward. "Right, left, o
straight ahead?"

"He was going like a bat out of hell the last
saw him," Dan said. "I vote for straight ahead."

And that's the way they went—straight ahead
At the St. Mary's intersection, they once again
were caught by a red light. While they waited
for that one to turn green, and much to their
astonishment, the white Lexus shot out from
the Burger King parking lot and back onto the
frontage road where it quickly regained speed.

"I'll be damned!" Phil exclaimed.

Dan returned to the radio. "Suspect is back n view. He's eastbound on the I-10 frontage between St. Mary's and Congress Avenue."

Charlie Milton may have been headed for Congress Avenue, but he didn't make it past. While attempting to run the light there, he plowed into a Dodge RAM pickup, T-boning the much larger vehicle in the driver's side and completely demolishing the front end of the Lexus.

Phil and Dan arrived before the dust had finished settling and found Charlie Milton, barely visible beneath a layer of deployed airbags. While Phil called in the accident, Dan took up a position next to the smashed and still-steaming vehicle. Inside, the driver was stunned but stirring. He had some visible cuts and scratches due to flying debris, but he didn't appear to be badly injured.

"EMS is on the way," Dan said. "Are you okay?"

"I think so," Milton said. "I seem to be fine."

Except you're not, Dan thought to himself. *You're not even close to fine. You just don't know it yet.*

Phil appeared at Dan's elbow. "How is he?"

"Says he's fine," Dan replied.

"He won't be if the guy driving the pickup lays hands on him," Phil said. "That truck's brand-new and still wearing paper plates. The guy who owns it isn't hurt, and he's ready to rip your friend here a new one."

"Don't blame him a bit," Dan said. "If somebody wrecked my new truck, I'd be pissed, too."

By then the two following patrol cars caught up with the action. Shortly thereafter a Tucson PD patrol car rolled onto the scene as well. The newly arrived cop, Officer Cameron, asked one of the uniformed deputies who was in charge and was pointed in Phil's direction.

Detective Hirales began his conversation with Officer Cameron by flashing his badge. "The driver of the Lexus failed to pull over for a traffic stop a few miles north of here. We were following him but discontinued pursuit just this side of Grant when the suspect took the Speedway exit. My body cam will show that from that point on we were no longer in hot pursuit."

"Did either of you see the accident?" Cameron asked.

"No," Phil answered, "we were too far behind to actually witness what happened. According to the driver of the RAM, he entered the intersection on green when Mr. Milton here ran the red light and nailed the truck on the driver's side."

Officer Cameron had his notepad out. "Did you say Milton?" he asked.

"Yes," Phil answered. "The driver's name is Charles Milton, at least that's one of his names. Apparently he has at least one more."

"And who's this?" Officer Cameron asked, nodding in Dan's direction.

"That's Dan Pardee," Phil explained. "He's with me. He's also a field officer with MIP."

"With what?"

"The MIP. It's a new federal outfit charged with investigating cases of missing and murdered Native Americans. It turns out Mr. Milton here is one of Dan's prime suspects. In fact, you might want to have a look-see at the paperwork in his pocket."

"What paperwork?" Cameron asked.

Dan reached into his shirt pocket, extracted a document, and handed it over.

"What is it?" Cameron asked, peering up at Dan for an answer rather than consulting the paperwork itself.

"It's an arrest warrant from Albuquerque, New Mexico," Dan explained. "That's where Mr. Milton here is wanted on a charge of felonious assault. There may be several more charges coming, but that remains to be seen. So after EMS takes Mr. Milton here to an ER to be checked out, we'll be placing him under arrest."

Still in the Lexus, Charlie Milton had been listening in on this whole exchange. "Shit!" he muttered under his breath just loud enough for Dan to hear him over the noisy racket of an arriving fire truck and ambulance.

"You've got that right, buddy boy," Dan said with a smile. "Turns out you're in a world of it."

CHAPTER 48

THE NEXT DAY THE MAN RETURNED TO TH
village. Once he was gone, Old Broken Coyo
felt free to examine things. So he followed the strin
that was tied to the dead child's shoes. The strin
went straight from the tiny shoes to the dead child
grave.

That night the woman sat alone, waiting and li:
tening in the blue-gray light, but there was no soun
of baby laughter.

When the woman complained to Old Broken Coy
ote that the children did not come, he told her th
the string from the shoes to the grave must sure
be broken. He told her that of course the baby wou
want his tiny shoes, and if the string were not broke:
he would be able to follow the string and find them.

So the next morning the woman and Old Brok
Coyote went together to the baby's grave on the side

he mountain. There they found that the string had
ndeed been broken and carried away.

That made the woman feel very sad.

WHEN OFFICER CAMERON'S SHIFT SUPERVISOR
ppeared on the scene, Detective Hirales went
ack through the whole story. Brian Fellows ar-
ived a few minutes later, just as EMS was pre-
aring to place Charlie Milton's loaded gurney
nto the back of an ambulance. By then the situ-
tion had attracted some media attention, and
eporters from two local TV stations were on
he job. Both camera crews captured the action
s Sheriff Fellows wheeled up to the gurney.

"Mr. Milton," he announced loud enough to
e heard by the assembled reporters, "I'm ar-
esting you for the felonious assault of a young
oman named Deborah Russell two months
go in Albuquerque, New Mexico. Once you're
leared by the ER, you'll be transported to the
ima County jail and held there pending extra-
ition to New Mexico. In view of the fact that I
elieve you to be a flight risk, I'm sending you to
he hospital wearing these."

With that he pulled a pair of handcuffs out of
is pocket and hooked one of Charlie Milton's
rms to the frame of the gurney. When that
appened, Dan Pardee, sitting on a nearby curb
 a tiny patch of shade, was tempted to break
ut in applause, but with the media presence
 mind, he managed to keep his cool. Seconds
ter, Brian Fellows turned his back on the de-

parting ambulance and rode his scooter to where Dan was sitting.

"What are you doing over here?" he asked.

"I've been sidelined," Dan said with a shrug. "I'm a fed, and the locals don't want me any where near this investigation. That makes per fect sense, of course. I didn't witness the actual accident, and I wasn't at the wheel of the patrol car. The Tucson PD supervisor pretty much told me to get the hell out of the way, so I did."

"How are you feeling?" Brian asked.

"About locking Milton up?" Dan responded. "Relieved as hell. Once he hit that exit ramp and disappeared from sight, I was afraid we'd lost him."

"Well, you didn't," Brian said, "and congrats on that. I haven't had a chance to talk to Phil yet. Is my department going to be looking down the barrel at a hot pursuit lawsuit with the owner of that wrecked truck?"

Dan understood Brian's concern. Traffic ac cidents related to high-speed police pursuits amounted to big business for trial lawyers these days, and it made sense for Brian to worry that this incident was about to morph into a legal disaster.

"I'm not a lawyer, but I don't think so," Dan told him. "As soon as we hit traffic coming into town on I-10, Phil immediately reduced speed. Once Milton took off down the Speedway off ramp, he discontinued pursuit altogether."

"That's all on his body cam?" Brian asked.

"It should be," Dan replied. "Body cam and dash cam both. The footage will also show the

ve arrived at the intersection here after the incident occurred."

Brian heaved his own sigh of relief. "All right
then," he said, "I'd better get over there and cover
my ass by making damned sure that footage is
properly collected and taken into evidence."

Once left alone, Dan was content to simply
sit and observe. The intersection had turned
into a hive of activity as well as a traffic jam
nightmare. Some officers were still involved in
taking measurements while others were occupied with directing traffic or cleaning up debris.
As the first of the media vans departed, Dan
realized it was time to make his first phone call,
and he decided it had to be to his anonymous
tipster.

"Melody?" he asked when she answered.

"I'm sorry," she said. "You must have the
wrong number. There's no one here by that
name." With that she abruptly hung up.

Dan was mystified. He knew the number
he'd called was the correct one, and he had
recognized Melody's voice. What the hell was
going on?

A little over a minute later, when his phone
rang, her number showed up in caller ID.

"Why did you just hang up on me?" he demanded.

"I was in the house with Earl sitting right
here next to me," she said. "He thinks I'm terribly nosy, and I didn't want to talk about this in
front of him, but I'm outside now. Why are you
calling? I noticed that Charlie left a while ago,
and now there are a whole bunch of police cars

out in front of his place with some officers inside his RV. What's going on?"

"Thanks to you, Charlie Milton has been placed under arrest. The officers you're seeing on the scene are executing a search warrant."

"Oh, my goodness!" she said. "You actually caught him, really?"

"Really," Dan replied. "His arrest might not have happened if it weren't for you. He was taken into custody after being involved in a motor vehicle accident at Stone Avenue off I-10. There were TV cameras at the scene, so the story will most likely be on local news channels tonight."

"I hope they won't mention me by name in conjunction with any of this," Melody said, sounding worried.

"Not likely," Dan replied, "but there's a good possibility that you've helped take down a very dangerous individual who may turn out to be a serial killer. That makes you a hero in my book. Wouldn't you like your friends and neighbors to know about that?"

"I don't think so," Melody said after a pause. "I'd rather remain anonymous and have a happy home. As far as I'm concerned, what Earl Baxter doesn't know won't hurt him."

"All right then," Dan agreed. "An anonymous tipster you'll remain, but here's a big thank-you from me. Your gathering up those cigarette butts made for a huge break in this case."

"I'm glad," she said, "but I'm also glad you're willing to keep that between you and me."

With the call ended, and with his butt aching from sitting on the curb, Dan looked around for somewhere more comfortable to sit. By then the patrol cars had all been moved out of the intersection to clear the way for traffic. Phil's vehicle was parked in a section of shade on the far side of a nearby gas station. Dan stood up, limped over to it, and gratefully settled in the front passenger seat.

Closing his eyes, he let himself replay the whole pursuit in his head, from the time he and Phil had left the convenience store on Ina Road right through their turning off the freeway onto the exit ramp. He remembered the long waits for red lights at both Speedway Boulevard and St. Mary's. That's where they'd been when the speeding Lexus had suddenly shot out from behind the Burger King.

So what the hell was Milton doing at a Burger King? Dan thought to himself. *He sure as hell didn't have time to buy anything.*

But then, like a bolt out of the blue, it hit him. Milton hadn't been there picking something up. He had ducked in there to get rid of something, and that's exactly where the dumpsters would be located—behind the restaurant!

Dan bolted out of the car and spotted Phil standing off to the side talking to Brian.

"Are you finished here?" Dan demanded.

"Yes, but . . ."

"No buts," Dan countered. "We've got to go."

"Go where?"

"Back to Burger King," Dan said.

"You're ready for a Whopper?" Phil asked.

"No," Dan replied, "I want to take a look at their dumpsters."

Brian Fellows seemed completely mystified. "What's all this about Burger King?" he wanted to know.

"When we were following Milton, he disappeared from view for a time. We were stopped at a red light at St. Mary's when his vehicle came tearing out onto the frontage road from behind the Burger King. My guess is he dropped some incriminating evidence in their dumpster."

"Let's get a move on then," Sheriff Fellows said. "You two lead the way, and I'll go find my driver."

CHAPTER 49

WHILE THE WOMAN AND OLD BROKEN
oyote were sitting there, Tokihthhud—Spider—
me along. Spider asked what all the trouble was.
Then they told him, Spider offered to make a string
at would not break.

So Old Broken Coyote and the woman went home.
he next night, when Tash—the Sun—went down
the end of his day's journey, Spider appeared. He
d the silver thread that he had made to the baby's
es. The silver thread went all the way from the
tle shoes to the child's grave on the side of the moun-
in.

The woman felt that now her baby would surely
d his way, so she lay down and went to sleep.

The next morning, while she was sleeping, she
ard Old Broken Coyote calling to her, so she asked
m what was the trouble.

Ahithkam Hahaisag Ban answered that during

the night Koson—Pack Rat—had stolen one of th
child's shoes, but that, from now on, he would stan
guard.

Old Broken Coyote sat for a very long tim
watching and waiting for that rat. He knew that k
koson—pack rats—were sneaky, mean things. The
had no honor. They would not fight. And it was a
this very time that Koson learned to carry thing
away.

PHIL AND DAN DROVE STRAIGHT BACK TO TH
Burger King with Sheriff Fellows's car hot o
their heels. Behind the restaurant, they pulled i
next to the dumpsters, smelling the odor fror
them the moment the car doors opened.

"This is going to be fun," Phil muttere
pausing long enough to collect a pair of late
gloves from a container on the floorboard of th
back seat. "Since this is your call, I vote you d
the honors."

"Gee, thanks," Dan said, but he took th
gloves and put them on without protest.

"What do you think you're looking for?" Ph
asked.

"No idea, but I'll know it when I see it."

And he did, too. The moment he spotte
the khaki-colored camera bag, he knew th
was the target. The bag lay on top of a lay
of evil-smelling, fly-infested garbage. Nearby l
also spotted two discarded cell phones. Unfo
tunately, the trash had been recently emptie
making the layer of trash in the bottom of th
dumpster low enough to be just out of Dar

reach. He and Phil were standing there strategizing about what to do as Brian Fellows rolled
up on his scooter.

"What seems to be the trouble?" he asked.

"There's a camera bag in there along with two
cell phones," a frustrated Dan Pardee reported.
"I'm willing to bet my last dime that they all
belong to Charlie Milton, but there's no way to
reach them."

"Right," Phil said, "we were about to flip a
coin to see who goes dumpster diving."

"Hold on," Brian said. "Maybe I can help."

Earlier, while waiting behind the Circle K, Dan
had noticed a long narrow leather bag attached
to the handlebar of Brian's scooter and dangling
next to the front wheel. He had wondered about
it but hadn't asked. Now Brian reached down,
detached the bag from the handlebar, and
handed it to Dan. The leather was old and worn,
but as Dan studied it, he was barely able to make
out the faded and almost invisible words printed
there: *Red Ryder*.

"Wait," he said in dismay, "you're giving me a
damned BB gun so I can shoot any rats I find in
the dumpster?"

"It's not a BB gun," Brian answered with a
laugh, "and I didn't put my eye out, either. It's
my grabber. I use it to reach things. As for that
holster? The Daisy BB gun that came inside it is
long gone, but I kept the holster. I found them
wrapped and waiting for me under the tree the
first time Brandon and Diana Walker invited me
over for Christmas dinner."

Feeling as though he was now wielding a fam-

ily treasure, Dan turned back to the dumpster.
Needing to maintain a chain of evidence, Phil
Hirales, left without his body cam, used his
phone to video the process. It turned out Brian's
grabber was exactly the right tool for the job.
With the length of that added to Dan's already
long arms, it was easy for him to reach the bag's
handle. After hauling it out, Dan held it up in the
air, grinning from ear to ear as though he had
just landed a prizewinning trout. After dropping
it into an evidence bag, he retrieved phones.

"Load everything into my trunk," Brian ordered. "Nobody touches it again until we're back
at the department. We won't open the evidence
bags until we're in an interview room with light
and cameras rolling."

And that's what they did. Once they arrived
at the department, while Brian went to his office
to exchange his scooter for his less cumbersome
wheelchair, Dan took charge of setting up the
recording equipment in a tiny interview room
barely large enough to accommodate three people. At last, with the camera bag front and center
on a Formica table, the three men donned their
gloves.

"Okay, Dan," Sheriff Fellows said. "This is
your show. You're up."

Dan held his breath as he undid the fastener.
He brought out the phones first. Unable to un-
lock either one, he simply laid them on the table.
Next he lifted the camera bag's lid and peered
inside. The first thing he removed was a pair
of wildly colored wooden maracas. He recognized the instruments due to the fact that, a yea

earlier, during a Cinco de Mayo celebration at school, Micah had been tapped to play the maracas. He had loved practicing with them, and the constant racket had driven his parents nuts.

"What the hell?" Dan muttered, laying them down on the table so the others could see.

Phil, wearing gloves, reached over, picked up one of them, and gave it a rattle. It sounded fine to Dan, but Phil gave a disapproving shake of his head. "That's not right," he said.

"Why?" Dan asked. "What's the matter?"

"They sound wrong."

"They seem okay to me," Dan said.

"That's because you don't spend your days off doing gigs with a mariachi band," Phil answered. "I do."

"So?"

"Most maracas contain rice," Phil explained. "This sounds like it's filled with pieces of gravel."

Without waiting for a response from either Dan or Brian, Phil grasped the top of one of the maracas and gave it a twist. Philip Hirales may have been an experienced homicide cop, but once he looked inside, the color drained from his face.

"Oh, no!" he groaned.

Dan and Brian stared at him in alarm. "What?" Dan asked.

"See for yourself," Phil replied.

He tipped over the maraca far enough to allow the appalling contents to tumble out onto the tabletop where they formed a grisly pile.

"Teeth?" Dan asked faintly.

"Yes," Brian Fellows confirmed, "and human

ones at that, and unless I miss my guess, they're from several different victims."

A stark silence followed. "So this is his trophy bag!" Dan murmured aloud.

"Apparently," Brian agreed.

At that point, Phil eased the top off the second maraca with the same result. At that point, the room fell eerily silent. Finally Phil got to his feet. "I'll be right back," he said.

He left the room, returning a few moments later with a straight-edged ruler. Using that he carefully scraped the teeth off the table and into a much smaller evidence bag, counting them as he did so. The final total came to forty. When Phil sealed the evidence bag shut, he did so with the kind of reverence generally accorded to holy relics, as indeed they were. Those forty hunks of enamel-coated remains—some perfect, some chipped, some containing fillings, and some showing obvious decay—amounted to the last earthly fragments of several slaughtered women.

"With DNA we should be able to identify the victims, even if we don't have the actual bodies," Phil said at last. "The problem is, how long will that take?"

"You'd be surprised," Dan told them. "MIP headquarters has a fully staffed DNA lab up and running with no wait list, but first we'll have to get these teeth to Denver."

"Don't worry about that," Brian said. "One of my captains owns his own plane. He flies in and out of Colorado all the time—fishing in the summer and skiing in the winter. If somebody will cover his fuel expenses, he'll deliver them in a heartbeat, but let's see what else is inside that bag."

Taking a steadying breath, Dan reached inside for a second time. His hand emerged holding a silver belt buckle. Studying it closely, Dan was able to make out several words on the badly tarnished surface. He read aloud, "Silver City and Junior Rodeo."

At that point he sank back in his chair. "It's Rosa's," he managed.

"Rosa Rios?" Brian asked. "The girl whose remains were found out by San Simon? Are you sure?"

Dan nodded.

Brian picked up the buckle and examined it for himself. "There's no inscription here," he said. "How do you know it's Rosa's?"

"Jenny told me that years ago she and Rosa participated in a rodeo over in Silver City. Rosa won, and rodeo winners get buckles."

"Who's Jenny?" Brian asked.

"That would be Sheriff Brady's daughter," Dan answered.

"So did Sheriff Brady point you in her daughter's direction?" Brian asked.

"No," Dan admitted. "Jenny came forward on her own. She's a senior in college, majoring in criminal justice."

"If Sheriff Brady is in the dark about all this, she's going to be pissed."

"If I were in her shoes, I would be, too," Dan said.

"This really is the guy then?" Phil asked,

bringing the conversation back to the task at hand.

"Looks like," Brian said, depositing the buckle in its own separate evidence bag. "What else do we have?"

Dan brought out the next item—a colorful leather-backed beaded bracelet—decorated with the image of a golden eagle superimposed over an American flag. Dan had never seen it before, but he recognized it at once. While he'd been spending time on airplanes and in boarding areas, he'd had plenty of time to read through the reports submitted by his fellow MIP field officers.

Dan held up the bracelet. "This belonged to a young woman named Marcella Sixkiller, a one-time high school rodeo queen. She was living in Oklahoma City and working as a prostitute when she went missing in 2017. According to Hank Wilcox, the MIP field officer assigned to her case, the bracelet was made by her grandmother, and it was something she wore every day."

After Brian and Phil took turns examining the bracelet, that, too, went into a bag.

The next time Dan's hand emerged from the bag, it was holding a fistful of rings. One was a wedding set, which included a substantial emerald-cut diamond.

"You'd need a good reason to drop something like this into a dumpster," Dan observed as he passed it along to Brian, "but it suggests that at least one of the victims was married at some point and long enough to keep the ring."

While Phil bagged that one, Dan moved on

to the next—a class ring. He knew that a class ring from Kalispell High School had been part of Martha Little Calf's missing person report on Yolanda Larson. A careful examination revealed the tiny letters KHS at the top of the ring. On one side of the stone was a Y; on the other was an L.

"I know this one, too," Dan said. "It belonged to a girl named Yolanda Larson, a member of the Blackfeet Nation. She was born and raised in Kalispell, Montana. She was twenty years old and studying nursing in Butte at the time of her death. She disappeared in 2018 after coming home to attend a rodeo in which her younger brother was participating. Her remains were found on the banks of the Yellowstone River in 2020."

The third ring appeared to be a birthstone ring with a stone Dan didn't recognize. He handed that one to Brian.

"It's an opal," Brian determined, "so whoever wore that one was probably born in October."

When Dan turned back to the bag, he discovered that the bottom appeared to hold a shallow cardboard box of some kind, with the top resting inside the bottom. All of the previous items had evidently been contained inside.

"Looks like a tie box to me," Dan said, after examining the box long enough to spot a printed name. "Anybody ever hear of a company named Zegna?"

Brian and Phil both shook their heads.

"That makes three of us," Dan said, "but from what Anna Rae told me about Ronald Addison, he was worth a ton of money when he disappeared. My guess is that Zegna ties are for people way above our pay grade."

At that point most people might have assumed the bag was totally empty, but Dan turned it upside down just to be sure. At that point two more items fell out onto the table—a tiny diamond stud of some kind and a heart-shaped locket, neither of which rang a bell. Phil was in the process of bagging those when someone knocked on the door and pushed it open.

"Sorry to disturb, Sheriff Fellows," someone said from the corridor. "Charlie Milton has just now been transported from St. Mary's ER to the jail. He's in booking right now. Do you want him in an interview room or in a holding cell?"

"Bring him here," Brian said. "We'll give Dan here the first crack at him."

CHAPTER 50

THEN OLD BROKEN COYOTE HEARD A NOISE.
It was not Koson, that was for sure.

Ban turned and saw a crowd of children. Some were tiny little things. Some were larger, and the children were carrying the woman's baby. The baby was gurgling and chuckling and laughing as happy babies do. They were all coming straight down Spider's silver thread, which led from the baby's grave on the mountain back to the shoe, the one Pack Rat hadn't stolen.

The baby put on the shoe that was left. Then the children scattered and they began to play and dance. And everywhere the little baby's bare foot touched down, the ground turned red. Soon the children noticed this. They pointed at the red spots and began to laugh, but the baby said it was because red was his mother's favorite color.

Then the other children took off their shoes, and

they, too, began to dance. Everywhere the children's bare feet touched the ground there was color. Their colors were red and pink and blue and white and yellow—all the colors. Some of the spots were small and some were large, and nearly all of them were fragrant.

THE INTERVIEW WITH CHARLIE MILTON/RONALD Addison turned out to be a great big nothing burger. As soon as Dan read the prisoner his rights, Addison replied with the four words cops dread hearing, "I want a lawyer."

That was the end of the interview. In a way that was fine with Dan. In the course of an interview, he might have inadvertently revealed a hint or two about how much they had on the guy, including the fact that they had retrieved his camera bag. Right now, awaiting extradition on that arrest warrant, he wasn't going anywhere, and that gave law enforcement a breather in terms of building airtight cases against him.

Before Dan left the department, Brian Fellows was in touch with Anna Rae Green, solidifying arrangements for having the teeth from the maracas delivered to MIP's forensics lab in Denver. Captain William Lugo of the Pima County Sheriff's Department planned to fly out of Ryan Field early on Sunday morning and was expected to have his Cessna on the ground at Jefferson County Airport outside Denver by 9:30 A.M. Anna Rae assured Brian that she'd have someone there to meet him and take possession of the evidence.

Dan turned down Brian's invitation to drop by for dinner, in favor of heading home to Sells. He had plenty of calls to make along the way, and first up was reporting in with Anna Rae. She had heard some of the story from Sheriff Fellows, of course, but she wanted to hear the whole thing from Dan's point of view. She listened mostly in silence, but while he was going over the items retrieved from the camera bag, she called a halt when he mentioned the diamond-studded wedding and engagement ring set.

"As you asserted, this is most likely a trophy collection, and that wedding ring makes me wonder. Addison's wife, Adele, died in what was supposedly an accidental drowning incident shortly before his disappearance. I've had my research team doing a deep dive on him. At the time of Adele's death, several friends and relatives claimed that her husband was responsible. Unfortunately, the ME's determination of accidental death made it virtually impossible for their claims to gain any traction, but maybe we can change that. If you can have someone there forward a photo of the wedding ring, I'll send it along to Santa Clara County and have their investigators see if anyone in the area can tell us for sure if the ring belonged to Adele Addison."

"I'll bet he killed her," Dan said.

"I think you're right, but we need to prove it."

Dan was preparing to hang up, but Anna Rae stopped him. "You've done remarkable work here, Dan, and I want you to know how much I appreciate it. There are any number of people out there in the world of politics who were ab-

solutely opposed to the establishment of MIP.
They claimed plenty of other agencies were out
doing this job, but that's the whole point. Those
other agencies haven't been doing a damned
thing! Once you took the bit in your teeth on the
Rosa Rios case, you've single-handedly proved
all those naysayers wrong. Thank you."

"You're welcome," Dan said. "I didn't do it
alone."

"And speaking of Rosa," Anna Rae continued.
"Have you spoken to her mother?"

"Ida Rios will be my next call," Dan replied.

"Do you want me to contact Hank Wilcox and
Martha Little Calf, or would you rather do it?"

"Go ahead and let them know," Dan said, "but
if they need any additional background information before they talk to the families, have them
give me a call."

Dan called Rosa's mother next. When Ida
heard the news that her daughter's killer was finally in custody, she burst into tears. Next up
was a call to Michelle Barlow in Plano, Texas.
She, too, was thrilled beyond words to hear that
her ex had been caught.

Not wanting to repeat a mistake he'd made
earlier, Dan's next call was to Joanna Brady. He
was relieved when the voice mail prompt came
on. He left a brief message saying that Charles
Milton was in custody and being held in Pima
County's lockup. That gave him a chance to pass
along the bare bones of the situation without his
having to blow the whistle on Jenny's contribution.

By then Dan was approaching the open range

section of Highway 86 near Little Tucson, and he automatically slowed down. That was a good thing since, half a mile later, he spotted a small herd of cattle sauntering across the road. Once he passed them, he placed his next call—the one to Jennifer Brady.

"I have some news for you," Dan said when she answered.

"What?"

"A guy named Ronald J. Addison, aka Charlie Milton, has been taken into custody in Tucson. He's currently in the Pima County jail awaiting extradition to New Mexico to face felonious assault charges in the attack on Deborah Russell."

"You're kidding!" Jenny breathed.

"Not kidding," Dan answered. "Not kidding at all. Now I have two questions. Do you want me to let Deborah Russell know about this or would you like to tell her yourself?"

"I'd love to be the one to tell her," Jenny answered at once.

"And what about your mother?" Dan asked. "I just left a message letting her know that Rosa's killer is in custody, but I didn't mention your involvement. Do you want to tell her about that or should I?"

Jenny's response to that was slower in coming. "I'd better tell her," she said at last. "When Mom finds out I've been monkeying around in one of her cases, she's going to be pissed."

"More like solving it instead of monkeying around in it," Dan said. "And if she wants to be pissed at someone, tell her to come looking for me. I'm the one who should have told her."

"All right," Jenny said after a moment. "I'll tell her."

"One more thing before you go," Dan said. "You're due to graduate in a few weeks' time. What are your plans after that?"

"I've applied for several internships. So far nothing."

"Why don't you give Anna Rae Green a call?" he suggested.

"Your boss at MIP?"

"Yes, you happen to have a whole lot of ink with her at the moment."

"But . . ."

"But what?"

"I'm not Native American," Jenny objected, "not even close."

"Neither were three of Addison's victims," Dan pointed out. "Solving their homicides was an unintended consequence of solving the others. Those victims may have been outside MIP's sphere of influence, but you're responsible for helping us solve all of them. A friend of mine once told me that one of the things about circles is that there's always room for one more. So give her a call. I'll text you her number. Anna Rae Green has certainly surprised me. She may surprise you, too."

Off the phone now, Dan kept on driving. Minutes later he topped the low-rising pass that separates the town of Sells from the surrounding valley. When he'd first come to the reservation to work as a Shadow Wolf, he'd always felt like a foreign invader whenever he drove over the top of that hill and saw the lights of Sells glow-

g in the darkness ahead of him. But tonight he
o longer felt that way because now things were
ifferent. Years before he had come home from a
ar that had really never ended. Tonight he was
soldier returning from a war he had won.

CHAPTER 5

DURING HER THIRD TERM IN OFFICE, WIT
two little ones at home, Sheriff Joanna Brady w:
really striving to attain a better work life ba
ance. To that end, she was attempting to carv
out real family time, especially on the weekend
Once she left the office on Friday afternoor
when Chief Deputy Tom Hadlock was on ca
she turned her phone ringer to silent, put it c
the charger, and left it in the bedroom. If the
was a real emergency at the department, som
one would have to drive out to High Loneson
Ranch to get her.

So last night, and today, had been all fan
ily. Once again, Butch had grilled steaks. Aft
dinner, while he'd cleaned up the kitchen, J
anna had taken charge of bath time. Saturd:
evenings were now designated as television-fr
zones, so bath time had been followed by sto:

me. Now with the kids in bed it was time for st the two of them. With that in mind, they ere sharing a bottle of merlot.

It had been a tough week at work and her home fe had been on the bumpy side as well. Both she nd Marianne Maculyea had been summoned the principal's office at Greenway School—a éjà vu experience for both of them since, as rade-school pals, they and their respective parnts had been dragged into the principal's office n more than one occasion.

This time, however, the circumstances had een slightly different. Now they were the parnts, and the miscreant children in question were heir respective sons—Joanna's Denny and Marnne's Jeff. Although a year apart in school, the vo boys were best friends, and they'd had the merity to show up on the school playground med with—horror of horrors—water pistols!

Both mothers came from an era when pril had always been open season for squirt uns in Bisbee, Arizona. Back then, almost eryone—boys and girls alike—had one. As a p, Joanna knew all about the now ever-present reat of mass shootings in schools. In fact, er department had recently participated in a ultijurisdiction training operation involving tive school shooters. Even so, she was a bit ovoked that these days everyone was willing hit panic buttons and lower the disciplinary om on a pair of little boys for packing entirely nlethal squirt guns.

In the end both boys had been handed threey suspensions, which meant that the parents

were being punished far more than their kid
were. Naturally Joanna and Butch had give
Denny a stern talking-to, warning him tha
he'd pretty much be dead in the water if he eve
pulled that stunt again. For his part, Denny ha
served out most of his sentence by spending th
unexpected bonus of free time by riding Jenny
retired barrel-racing horse, Kiddo. Truth b
told, Joanna, too, had regarded that as a win-wi
situation. The extra riding time had been goo
for Denny and good for Kiddo, too.

Butch's phone, however, was not on silen
and it rang at five to ten. After answering, h
handed the phone over to Joanna. "Who is it:
she asked.

"Jenny," he answered.

"Why are you calling?" Joanna wanted t
know once she was on the line. "I thought yc
and Nick had a big date planned for tonight."

"We did," Jenny said, "but I came home earl
I need to talk to you."

The way Jenny said those words set off alar:
bells in Joanna's head. Was something going c
between Nick Saunders and Jenny? They ha
been boyfriend and girlfriend since their fresl
man year at NAU. Joanna liked Nick a lot. F
was smart, motivated, and good-looking, too.
they were breaking up, it would be awful f(
both of them. And then there was the other sic
of the boyfriend/girlfriend coin. What if Jeni
was pregnant? What would that do to her pla
for going into law enforcement and his of b
coming a vet? Not that Joanna herself could s:

nything about that or even ask a question without risking being labeled a total hypocrite.

"Why?" Joanna asked, trying to mask the oncern she felt. "What's going on?"

"They've arrested a suspect in Rosa Rios's eath," Jenny said. "His name is Ronald J. Addi-on, and he's being held in the Pima County jail waiting extradition to New Mexico."

Joanna felt like she'd just plunged down the teep incline of a roller coaster. If Rosa's killer ad been arrested, that was wonderful news. But ow was it that Jenny knew about that when oanna didn't? What the hell did Dan Pardee hink he was doing?

With that in mind, it took a moment for Jo-nna to reply. "What amazing news!" she de-lared finally. "But how on earth do you know oout it? Was it on the news?"

Jenny cut her off. "Dan told me."

"Dan?" Joanna repeated. "Dan who?"

"Dan Pardee, the guy you told me about, the ne who works for MIP."

"How on earth do you know Dan Pardee?" oanna demanded.

"I know him because I called him," Jenny re-lied. "He just now called to let me know the iller's been arrested."

Joanna's surprise quickly morphed into anger. He called you without calling me?"

"He told me he'd left you a message. That's hy I called Dad's phone—because you turn ours off on the weekends. So is Dad still there?"

"Yes, but . . ." Joanna replied.

"No buts, please, Mom," Jenny interrupted "Put the call on speaker. This is a long story, an I don't want to have to repeat it."

As advertised, it was a long story. As she lis tened, Joanna's emotions were all over the map Why hadn't Jenny told her about what was goin on? Why had she taken it upon herself to contac Dan Pardee instead of involving Joanna? Bu even as all those internal objections surfaced Joanna couldn't help but be impressed by th way Jenny had taken similarities between th two separate incidents—Deborah's and Rosa's— and helped bring them together into an arres worthy case. Not only that, the careful way sh had handled that critical bit of evidence—th assailant's glasses—had been nothing short o masterful. By the time Jenny finished, Joann was left feeling nothing but pride.

"So," Jenny said at last, "are you mad at m or not?"

"Not mad at all," Joanna replied. "You're n even a sworn police officer, and you've alread helped take down a serial killer. From where I' standing, Jennifer Ann Brady, you're going to b one hell of a cop."

CHAPTER 52

SELLS, ARIZONA
Saturday, April 9, 2022, 11:00 P.M.

WHEN THE SKY IN THE EAST BEGAN TO TURN
ink, all the children joined hands and ran away.

Old Broken Coyote watched them go and smiled.
He knew that they were all very happy. Then he put
his head down on his paws and went to sleep.

When the woman came out the next morning and
looked around, she was happy. She had heard the chil-
dren in her dreams and knew they were nearby. And
now she saw that the children had left their footprints
for her.

Some people call these footprints of the spirit chil-
dren "flowers." But Indians who are wise know what
they really are. And the Tohono O'odham, the Desert
People, know why the desert flowers are so sweet and
why they come in so many colors, even when they are
very close together.

And sometimes, if you listen very carefully in the
desert when the flowers are blooming, you can still

hear the sounds of those happy children, laughing an
playing.

AT ELEVEN O'CLOCK THAT NIGHT DAN AND LA
were still seated at their kitchen table bringin
each other up to speed on everything that ha
happened, when a pair of arriving headligh
flashed in through the living room window.

"Who would turn up at this hour?" Da
asked, pushing his chair away and heading f
the door. He returned a few minutes later wi
Gabe Ortiz in tow. As soon as Lani saw tl
expression on the young man's face, she kne
something was wrong.

"Are you okay?" she asked.

Shaking his head, Gabe sat down heavily
one of the kitchen chairs. "It's Chair Man,"
said.

"Chair Man," Lani echoed. "What's going on

"He didn't show up at Circle today," Ga
said. "The popover ladies were there, and
were lots of other people, all of them hopir
to see Chair Man and listen to what he had
say. Finally, I sort of stepped up to the plate a
took his place. I did the same thing he usual
does—I tried to put everyone at ease and
them talk about the things they needed to ta
about—what's worrying them, what's botheri
them, what's driving them crazy. Finally, when
was over, I went by Chair Man's place to che
on him. The White Buffalo was there, but
didn't answer the door."

Dan was mystified. "White Buffalo?" he asked. "What's that?"

"That's Chair Man's handicapped-accessible minivan," Lani explained. "That's what he calls it—his White Buffalo."

But Gabe remained focused on his story. "I was afraid he was lying inside there sick or dead," he continued, "so I tracked down the building manager. He told me they'd taken Chair Man to the VA hospital by ambulance the day before yesterday. I went straight there. He's in intensive care. No visitors allowed other than relatives. The problem is, he doesn't have any relatives."

Lani stood up at once. "I'll go," she said. "I may not be a relative, but I am a doctor. I'll be able to get in to see him."

"Wait," Dan objected. "It's the middle of the night. What are you thinking?"

"I'm thinking John Wheeler needs me," she shot back. "I'm going, and I'm taking my medicine basket with me."

Dan understood that since this was a medicine woman call, there'd be no talking her out of it, so he quit wasting his breath.

"Drive carefully," he said. "There's a herd of cattle loose on the highway over by Little Tucson."

Once in the car, Lani couldn't help but remember one of the last things John Wheeler had said to her the first time they met—something about not wanting to miss any sunrises because he didn't know how many of those he had left. Had he already known something bad was about

to happen the same way he had known Dan ha[...]
a troubled relationship with his father?

Heeding Dan's warning, Lani lowered h[...]
speed to a mere forty-five as she drove past Litt[...]
Tucson. Sure enough she spotted several head [...]
cattle grazing on the shoulders of the highwa[...]
and meandering back and forth. Once back u[...]
to speed, she returned to thinking about Cha[...]
Man. He had told her that he appreciated th[...]
idea that, in a modern world, she continued [...]
honor the old ways. And so, as she drove pa[...]
Ioligam, I'itoi's sacred mountain, Lani let the o[...]
ways flood through her and did what the Dese[...]
People have always done in times of trouble—
she began to sing, using the words that came [...]
her heart.

> Hear my voice, Spirit of Goodness
> Listen to this medicine woman
> Calling to you out of the darkness,
> Hear me while you rest in your sacred caves
> And know that I am calling for help
>
> Another medicine man is in trouble,
> A Lakota who has wandered into your lands
> And stayed here to help others.
> But now he is the one who needs the help
> And that is why I am calling.
>
> This is an honorable man who has suffered
>   greatly
> But instead of thinking of his own troubles
> He has spent his time helping others find
>   their way.

So help him find his own way now in this time of
   trouble.
If it is his time to go on to another place,
Please comfort him so he may go in peace.

When the song ended and as Lani drove on,
she discovered that somehow she, too, had been
comforted. Once at the VA hospital, after a quiet
talk with the receptionist at the front desk and a
flash of her ID lanyard from the hospital in Sells,
she was directed to an ICU waiting room. Stepping across the threshold, Lani glanced around
the room and realized she wasn't alone.

A much older woman with her chin resting
on an ample chest dozed in a chair in one corner of the room. Her wrinkled brown features
looked as though they might have been carved
from an ancient oak tree. She was dressed in
a voluminous, colorful smock that fell almost
to her ankles. On her feet were a pair of worn
beaded moccasins. Her gnarled hands, resting
in her lap, loosely held a string of rosary beads.
Since Gabe had said that only relatives were allowed to see John Wheeler, Lani assumed there
was some kind of familial connection between
woman and patient.

Not wanting to disturb her, Lani slipped into
John's room. He appeared to be sleeping peacefully, but the monitors stationed at his bedside
told another story. Lani suspected he had already
fallen into a deep coma. The end was most likely
only hours away rather than days or weeks. An
IV drip was attached to one arm and his ostomy
bags were fastened to the side of the bed. But the

most glaring thing in the room was the brigh
orange sign affixed to the wall over his bed.]
read: DNR—Do Not Resuscitate. Knowin
DNR directives had to be handled well in ad
vance of a crisis gave credence to Lani's initia
suspicion that Chair Man had known he wa
on his way out well before their early mornin
meeting in the empty parking lot at San Xavier

Retreating to the waiting room, Lani took
seat, but the old Indian woman, seemingly sens
ing her presence, stirred and looked around th
room. When her eyes landed on Lani, she bri:
tled. "Who are you?" she demanded.

"Dr. Lanita Walker," Lani replied. "I'm
friend of John's from out on the TO west (
town?"

The woman frowned. "TO?" she repeated.

"The Tohono O'odham Nation," Lani ar
swered. "It's west of here, and you're Lakota,
presume?"

The old woman nodded. "My name is Car(
line Bridges. I'm John's auntie. His birth moth∈
was my baby sister, Charlotte. I've come to tal
him home."

"How did you know he was here?" Lani aske
"We only just now heard."

"I'm on his emergency contact list," Caroli∎
replied.

"Do you mind if I ask what happened?"

Caroline shrugged. "Sepsis," she answere
"from an infected bedsore. It's from sitting
that chair all the time. He should have come
the hospital sooner, but he didn't. The doct∎
says he probably won't make it."

Having already figured that out, Lani drew
n her breath. "I'm sorry," she said. "He's a
good man."

Caroline nodded. "He was adopted out of the
ribe when he was just a baby, but with the help
of an old Navajo he met here in the hospital, he
finally found a path back to the Lakota way."

"Yes," Lani said. "He told me about his being
adopted."

"Charlotte was only fourteen and away
t school when she got pregnant," Caroline
xplained. "She said a priest did it to her, but
he nuns didn't believe her. They told her she
was a wicked girl and would go to hell for lying.
My parents didn't even know the nuns had
shipped her off to a home for unwed mothers
until after the baby was gone. When Charlotte
ame back to the res, she was in a bad place.
he died of a drug overdose before she turned
wenty."

Lani wanted to weep. The world was rife with
imilar horror stories about what had gone on
t Indian boarding schools back in the old days
when countless Native American children, both
oys and girls, had been irreparably damaged
y members of the clergy. The violated child
ictims were almost always left with no defense
nd no recourse while the perpetrators went un-
unished.

"That's horrible," Lani murmured.

Caroline nodded. "We never knew where
Charlotte's baby went," she continued. "We
idn't know if she had a boy or a girl or even
the infant was born alive. Then a few years

ago, John wrote me a letter. He said he had
been in a bad accident and was just learning to
read and write again, but someone had helped
him track down his adoption records. Once he
knew his mother's name, he was able to find me.
I begged him to come home to the reservation.
I'm a widow. I told him I would take care of
him, and if he needed more help than I could
give, his cousins would pitch in. But he said
no, he needed to be close to this hospital because the people here had taken such good care
of him. Besides, he said, he had people here who
needed him."

"You know about his work then?" Lani asked.
"About the Circle where he ministers to disaffected Indian youth?"

Caroline nodded. "We heard. Word about
what he does for The People—especially young,
troubled ones—got back to the res," she said
with a small smile. "It came in over the smoke
signal telegraph. We're all very proud of what
he's done."

Lani appreciated that bit of understated Native American humor. Being able to smile in
the face of adversity was a trait that seemed to
encompass members of all the tribes no matter
where they lived.

A text alert dinged on Lani's phone. Unwilling to read the message in front of an audience,
Lani found a way to excuse herself. "Would you
like me to go down to the cafeteria and get you
something?" she asked.

"A Mountain Dew would be nice," Caroline
told her.

Lani left the room. As soon as she was out in the corridor, she saw a text from Dan.

Call me!

So she did. "What's going on?" she asked.

"You're not going to believe it," Dan said. "I've just identified another one of Addison's victims."

Before Gabe had turned up at the house, Dan had been laying out everything that had happened in the case, not just what had gone on that day, but over the last several days as well. Right now, though, the excitement in her husband's voice was unmistakable.

"How's that possible?" she asked.

"After you left I had a chance to go back through my mail. I've been away so much that there was a whole stack of it waiting."

"I know," Lani said. "Who do you think has been moving it from place to place?"

"I just opened the envelope from Detective Tucker up in Yavapai County. They had a missing persons case—a woman named Annika Wallace—who disappeared sometime over Fourth of July weekend in 2019 while the Prescott Rodeo was going on. I called about it because of the rodeo connection and asked Lauren to send me what she could about Annika's next of kin. She did that, but she included a copy of Annika's driver's license photo. You'll never guess what she's wearing—a heart-shaped locket."

"Like the one you found in Addison's camera bag?" Lani asked.

"I can't say for certain, but it sure as hell looks that way. It's the middle of the night, so I haven't called anybody about this—not Anna Rae and not Lauren Tucker, either, but I had to tell someone, so I chose you. Now tell me about John Wheeler."

She did. Realizing how serious the situation was, Dan took things in stride. "I'm guessing you won't be home any time soon?"

"I don't think so. His auntie is here all alone. Someone needs to be here with her, and I'm it. If I end up being too tired to drive back out to Sells, I can always stop off at Mom's place."

It wasn't until after she said the words that she remembered her mother was no longer at the house in Gates Pass, but since Lani had a key, she'd be able to let herself in.

When Lani returned to the waiting room, Caroline had abandoned her chair in the corner. She was now in John's room itself, seated next to his bed. When a nurse came and took his vitals, he didn't stir.

As the nurse exited the room, Lani asked, "How long?"

The nurse frowned. "Who are you?"

"I'm a doctor from the hospital in Sells," Lani answered. "I'm also a friend of the family."

"Not long," the nurse said.

"That's what I thought."

After handing Caroline her Mountain Dew Lani returned to the waiting room alone, leaving Caroline at John's bedside. Lani customarily carried large purses, ones big enough to accommodate her medicine basket, and tonight as no exception. Alone in the waiting room, he opened the basket and retrieved the leather ouch that held her crystals. From where she was ated, the door was cracked open far enough to low her a tiny view of Chair Man lying in he bed.

Because all of nature goes in fours, the bag eld only four crystals. One at a time she held hem up and stared through them, trying to ocus on John Wheeler's comatose features. The rst three times she saw nothing at all. What she w the last time caused a catch in her throat. lear as a bell, she saw a white buffalo, standing knee-high grass staring back at her.

Lani's immediate instinct was to laugh. For ie first time ever, it appeared as though her ystals had a sense of humor. She had used them hopes of gleaning some information about hair Man's condition. Instead the crystals had sponded with a joke about his minivan.

Several more hours dragged by. Caroline was leep by her nephew's chair, rosary in hand, hen the monitors alerted the hospital staff that hair Man's life had come to a peaceful end. he doctor pronounced John Wheeler dead at 33 A.M. on Sunday morning, April 10, 2022.

Looking out the window Lani saw the still rk sky overhead. Yes, this was the first sunrise hn Wheeler would miss.

The doctor was still in the room when Carone asked, "What happens now?"

"The body will be transported to the Pima ounty Morgue."

"How long before it can be released?"

"Mr. Wheeler clearly died of natural cause so I see no need for an autopsy. That shoul make things fairly cut and dried."

"Can you get me an exact time?" Carolin pressed. "I need to know when so I can make ar rangements."

"I'll do my best," the doctor said.

Caroline waited until he was out of earsho before she spoke again. "That isn't true," sh said.

"What isn't true?" Lani asked.

"John didn't die of natural causes," Carolir answered bitterly. "If that kid hadn't pushed hir under a train, John would still be with us. H didn't die of natural causes. He was murdered."

"You're right," Lani agreed with a no "He was."

"Do you know where the morgue is?"

"Yes," Lani replied.

"Will you take me there?"

"Yes, but why?"

"Because he's Lakota," Caroline answere simply. "I need to wash his hair."

CHAPTER 53

TUCSON, ARIZONA
Sunday, April 10, 2022, 3:00 A.M.

CHARLIE MILTON—HE STILL THOUGHT OF HIMSELF as Charlie Milton—lay on his bed and waited for the noise around him to diminish. That took forever. The steel-framed cot was hard as a rock, and so was the bag of corncobs that was supposed to be a pillow. The cell never went completely dark, so from where he was, he could see the cell's only furnishings—a stainless steel sink and toilet, both of them glowing in the dim light. His cell happened to have one of the jail's narrow slit windows. It was dark enough outside that it might have been possible to glimpse the stars overhead had it not been for the infernal glow from the streetlamps in the parking lot below.

Lying there, Charlie couldn't help thinking about Dr. Octavio Madrid. He'd just come into a hundred-thousand-dollar windfall for doing absolutely nothing. That was too bad, but it hardly mattered. At least Charlie had had some say in how that money was spent. What would happen to the rest of his funds—and those added up to a considerable sum—was anyone's guess. Most likely, if they lay dormant long enough, they would wind up in the treasury department of the Cayman Islands. Or else—and this seemed more likely—they'd end up lining the pockets of some treasury department agent. But, that was no longer Charlie's problem, and he didn't care.

He had always known it would come to this sooner or later, and he had known from the start that he didn't want to be paraded through some packed courtroom where he'd have to stand before a judge and be found guilty by a jury of his peers. He didn't have any peers. No one could come close to him, so the members of the jury would have no business judging him.

Fortunately for him, they would never have that opportunity. All those years ago when he'd told Dr. Octavio Madrid what he wanted, initially the doctor had straight out refused. But Charlie had still been Ronald J. Addison back then, and what he said went. He'd added another ten grand into the bargain as a little carrot to ensure Octavio did as he was told.

When the jail was finally quiet enough, he used a thumbnail to pry off the cap Dr. Madrid had installed over one of his back molars. Then he calmly bit down. It took only a matter of moments for the broken cyanide capsule to do its work. No one was there to mark the time when it was over, but had anyone been in attendance, they might have noticed that although Ronald J. Addison and John Wheeler had never met, their times of death were exactly the same—3:33 A.M., Sunday, April 10, 2022.

CHAPTER 54

TUCSON, ARIZONA
Sunday, April 10, 2022, 4:30 A.M.

BEFORE LEAVING THE HOSPITAL, LANI HAD T
wrestle Caroline's enormous suitcase up and int
the back of her Ford Focus. It barely fit. At th
Pima County Morgue, she sat on the sideline
while Caroline Bridges carefully unzipped he
nephew's body bag. Then, with loving care, sh
washed, dried, and combed John Wheeler's lon
hair before zipping the bag shut once more.

"There," she said. "It is done. Now what?"

"We wait until they tell us when they'll re
lease the body," Lani told her.

After that they sat in a small lobby outsid
the ME's office waiting until the assistant M
on duty came out to speak to them. "There's n
reason the body can't be released immediately,
he said. "Have you contacted a mortuary to co
lect the remains?"

"A mortuary?" Caroline repeated. "Why would I need a mortuary?"

The ME looked perplexed. "The mortuary's vehicle will transport Mr. Wheeler to wherever the services will be held."

"The services will be in South Dakota, and I'll be taking him with me," Caroline stated flatly, placing both hands on her sturdy hips. "All I need is a pickup truck."

"You can't drive him cross-country like that," the ME argued. "You'll need a casket at least."

"I'm not driving him cross-country, and I don't need a casket," Caroline declared. "I only need to get him to the airport. The tribe is chartering a plane to come get us, and since John is a powerful Lakota medicine man, he'll be going home wrapped in a white buffalo robe."

And that's when Lani realized that her crystals had been right all along. That's also when she figured out what was in Caroline's huge rolling suitcase.

"My godson Gabe Ortiz has a pickup," Lani suggested. "He and John were good friends. I'm sure he'll be glad to help."

ACTUALLY, GABE ORTIZ AND TIM JOSÉ DID more than just provide transportation. They put out the word to members of Chair Man's Circle about what had happened. By the time the chartered Embraer Legacy 450 landed at the general aviation end of Tucson International Airport in the afternoon, more than a hundred people were waiting inside Signature Aviation's very crowded lobby. Before the aircraft finished refueling, another fifty or so had jammed their way inside.

Gabe, Tim, and four other young men volunteered to do the honors. They were the ones who carried Chair Man's body from the FBO, across the tarmac, up the air stairs, and into the aircraft itself where they strapped the robe-wrapped body onto the sofa. Gabe told Lani later that he couldn't believe how light the body was—that he thought the robe weighed more than John did.

Caroline waited at the bottom of the stairs for the pallbearers to finish. When Gabe and the others emerged, she thanked them each individually, but when it was Gabe's turn, she took his hand for a moment before dropping it and hugging him instead. Then she leaned in close and whispered in his ear.

"John told me months ago that if anything ever happened to him, he hoped you'd take over the Circle. I think he was right."

Then Caroline turned to Lani and hugged her, too. "Thank you for your kindness," she said. "All the best to you and your family."

Lani accepted the hug and then kept her head lowered as she stepped away. A good Tohono O'odham woman shouldn't let the water come to her eyes, but tears of sorrow were definitely there that afternoon, and she didn't want anyone, most especially the Spirit of Goodness, to see them.

CHAPTER 55

FOR DAN PARDEE, THE REMAINDER OF APRIL and all of May flew by in a flash. He'd had to upgrade his wardrobe, because he was now a media icon and not just in Tucson, Arizona. Anna Rae was using the bombshell Charlie Milton/Ronald Addison case as a media bonanza to turn MIP's name and purpose into household words. Dan's distinctive good looks and his ease in front of TV cameras made him a natural spokesman for the agency. He'd also updated his vehicle, finally trading in his old Tahoe for a new four-door crew-cab Silverado.

Everyone in the country had awakened on Sunday morning, April 10, to the shocking news that a suspected serial killer named Ronald J. Addison, aka Charlie Milton, had committed suicide inside his Pima County jail cell after being arrested on suspicion of murdering six young women and assaulting another. He had perished after swallowing a cyanide capsule that had been concealed under a cap on one of his teeth. That had grabbed headlines everywhere. Over the next several days more than one network media crew had made the long trek out to Arizona to do live, in-person interviews with the man of the day—Dan Pardee. All the stand-ups were conducted in front of the carport at the family's modest home in the housing compound of Sells Indian Hospital.

The makeup artist for one of the network morning shows, a very young Milghan woman named Brittany, who came complete with head-to-toe tattoos and body piercings, was tasked with doing Dan's makeup. She helpfully suggested that, if he was going to do many more media appearances, he might want to consider getting braces. Dan had responded to her rude comment with one of his own. "Have you been on a reservation before?"

"Never," she admitted. "In fact, you're the first real live Indian I've ever met."

Which wasn't news to Dan Pardee. He could have gone on to explain that the economic realities of reservation life made orthodontist visits out of the question for most Native American children. Instead, he let it pass.

"I'll think about braces," he said, but he knew, even as he said it, that he wouldn't.

Over time, while the media circus died down, at MIP headquarters work in the DNA lab was ramping up. One at a time the teeth found in Ronald Addison's camera bag were processed for DNA. Results verified the identities of the young women Dan had already attributed to his suspect's list of victims—Rosa Rios, Marcella Sixkiller, Yolanda Larson, and Annika Wallace. In addition, the owner of the opal birthstone ring turned out to be a girl named Coreen Tyson, a Cheyenne River Sioux from the Eagle Creek Reservation in South Dakota. She had been reported missing in August of 2017 after attending the Jimmi Rose Memorial Barrel Races in Huron, South Dakota.

The big surprise was locating what appeared to be Addison's first victim after murdering Adele, Makayla Brown, an African American eighteen-year-old from Bakersfield, California, who had been reported missing in 2009. Her family had been tirelessly searching for their missing loved one ever since. Her mother, Mariah, had recently entered her own DNA into NamUs as a last resort. That's where MIP got the hit—from the NamUs database.

When Dan reached out to Mariah, to give her the news that her daughter had been among Addison's victims, he had asked if her daughter had worn a nose stud.

"Yes, she did," Mariah answered with a sigh. "I didn't approve, by the way, but she got the stud on her eighteenth birthday, so there wasn't much I could do about it."

"And, just out of curiosity," Dan asked, "did there happen to be a rodeo going on in Bakersfield at the time your daughter disappeared?"

"Why yes, there was," Mariah answered, sounding surprised. "The Midwest National

Black Rodeo was in town. The last time we saw her, that's where she was going with a bunch of her friends—to the rodeo. How in the world did you know that?"

"Because that's the one common denominator in all of Addison's homicides," Dan explained. "Each one had some kind of rodeo connection."

As a result of his involvement, Dan was invited to and attended each of the scheduled funeral and/or memorial services. Whenever a grieving relative had hugged him and thanked him for giving them answers if not actual justice, he had been overwhelmed with gratitude in return.

In Annika Wallace's case, no body had been found and no relatives had bothered to step forward, either, so several of her pals organized a memorial service held at the Lucky Strike on Prescott's Whiskey Row. The event had turned into a raucous party, but Dan had gladly attended that one, too. And he was especially touched to meet Annika's sole survivor—an elderly Chihuahua named Pepito—who had been permanently taken in by one of Annika's drinking buddies.

With each of those interactions something changed inside Daniel James Pardee.

"What's going on with you?" Lani asked one evening late in May. "You seem different from the way you used to be."

"No, I'm not," he said. "I'm exactly the same as I ever was."

But that wasn't true. Dan Pardee *was* different—even if he was the last to notice. He was searching for something, but he wasn't sure what it was.

Then summer came around. Years earlier, in 2019, Dan and Lani had promised to take the kids to Disneyland for summer vacation the following year. Once Covid reared its ugly head, that hadn't happened—not in 2020 and not in 2021, either. Over the winter, they had discussed the situation, hoping that the twice-postponed trip might finally become a reality in 2022. In early April, however, Diana Ladd Walker's complex care situation had once again put everything related to Disneyland on hold. With that resolved, by June the trip was back on.

To everyone's amazement, most especially Lani's, Diana's negative attitude about going into an assisted-living facility had miraculously undergone a sea change. Diana's first night at Santa Rita Senior Living on a trial basis had not gone well. After so much time of Covid-enforced solitude, she had objected to being among so many strangers. But then, the next morning Betty Livingston, Kath Fellows's next-door neighbor's mom who lived there, had shown up, knocking on the door to Diana's unit and inviting her to breakfast.

It turned out Betty Livingston happened to be one of Diana Ladd's most ardent fans. She had taken the new arrival in hand, leading her from table to table and introducing her to everyone in sight. By the time Betty was finished, the people in the dining room were no longer strangers, and neither was Diana. As Santa Rita Senior Living's only bestselling author, Diana soon morphed from being a wary, out-of-place newcomer into the reigning queen bee.

By the time Diana's supposedly one-week trial period was over, she was ready to settle in on a permanent basis. Weeks later, when a two-bedroom unit became available, she had switched over to that and had asked Gabe Ortiz and Tim José to strip some of her furnishings—and lots of her basket collection—out of the Gates Pass house and bring them to her new digs. By the middle of May, Diana Walker was happy as a clam and busy, too, teaching two separate classes—pottery making in one of the craft rooms and a family history writing class in the library.

As a result of all that, the Pardee family's much-delayed Disneyland trip finally came to fruition. Early on the morning of June 9, 2022, they loaded their luggage into the bed of Dan's new pickup and headed out. As they tooled along I-8 through the empty desert landscape between Gila Bend and Yuma, the kids begged their mother to tell them a story. They especially wanted to hear the one about the lonely woman and Old Broken Coyote.

"No way," Lani told them. "It's June and way too late in the year for winter telling tales. The snakes and lizards who are out might overhear the story and bring the storyteller harm."

"Come on, Mom," Micah begged. "*I'itoi* made up that rule a long time ago. We're driving in a truck right now. How is a snake or lizard going to be able to hear you?"

"Sounds like a solid argument to me," Dan said, giving Lani an amused glance, and eventually she relented.

"All right," she said, "one story but only one."

As she related the tale, Dan, although listening right along with the kids, was thinking about that uncaring husband who had gone back to the village in the valley instead of staying in the foothills with his wife and child. At the same time he was remembering what Chair Man had told Lani about Dan's needing to go visit his own uncaring father. The fact that John Wheeler had mentioned Dan's father at all was spooky enough. What made it even spookier was that he'd somehow known there was something amiss between them.

Initially Dan had rejected the whole idea. He had zero interest and even less need to encounter Adam Pardee. Nonetheless, the dying medicine man's haunting charge had somehow burrowed its way into the back of Dan's head and remained there, like a dog worrying a bone.

As a consequence, prior to their leaving on vacation, Dan had availed himself of some of MIP's search capabilities and discovered that his birth father now lived in an assisted-living facility called That's a Wrap. It was located in West Covina and catered to Hollywood's older and more impoverished nonelites—retired stuntmen, cameramen, makeup artists, and bit players.

ON SATURDAY MORNING, THEIR FIRST DAY FOR going to the theme park, Dan awakened early in the hotel room. While everyone else still slept, he did a quick internet search and discovered

That's a Wrap was located less than ten miles from their Disneyland hotel.

As Lani and the kids got ready to head for the park, Dan bailed on them.

Micah was incensed. "But you promised to go on a roller-coaster ride with me," he said accusingly.

"And I will," Dan said, "but there's something I need to do first. I'll catch up with you later."

Lani was the last one out the door. "Your father?" she asked.

Dan simply nodded. While she and the kids took the shuttle to Disneyland's main gate, Dan climbed into his truck and keyed That's a Wrap's address into the Silverado's GPS. Then, with his shoulders squared, he put the truck in gear and prepared to bite the bullet.

The GPS directed him to a repurposed motel that was anything but posh. When Dan checked with the front desk, the attendant there said it was almost lunchtime, and he had just spotted Mr. Pardee heading for the dining room. Dan went there, too, and he caught sight of his father the moment he entered.

Adam Pardee was on the far side of the room, seated in a wheelchair, and talking up a storm with a much younger woman. From her uniform Dan realized she was most likely a dining room attendant. That didn't surprise him. Even though he hadn't been near his father in decades, Dan somehow knew that Adam Pardee was now and always had been a womanizer.

Then came the electric moment when two

airs of matching green eyes met across an ex-
anse of several cloth-covered tabletops. Adam's
ace quickly morphed into a wide grin.

"Why, I'll be damned," he exclaimed loudly.
If it ain't that damned little half-breed son of
mine come to pay his poor old dad a visit. What
rings you here?"

The word *half-breed* caused Dan's fists to curl
into a pair of tight balls, but he kept his tone
even. "I was in the neighborhood and decided to
rop by," he said.

"Well," Adam replied, wheeling his chair
oser, "if you're here looking for a handout or a
an, you're out of luck. The last time I worked, I
stove up my back pretty good and ended up in
ere. As you can see, it ain't exactly the Ritz."

"No, it isn't," Dan agreed, "and I'm not here
oking for a handout or a loan. Lani and I are
ing just fine."

"Lani," Adam repeated. "That'll be the In-
an squaw you married?"

Dan had no idea how his father knew any-
ing about his life now, but he supposed inter-
t searches worked in both directions.

"Her name is Lani," Dan said tersely, barely
anaging to contain his fury. "Dr. Lanita
Valker-Pardee. She's the chief medical officer at
e hospital in Sells, Arizona."

"And a squaw," Adam crowed. "What else
ould she be? Like father like son."

"I'm not at all like you," Dan said between
enched teeth.

"You still haven't told me why you're here."

"I wanted to tell you about my new job," Dan said. "I'm a field officer for a new federal agency called the MIP Task Force."

"Right," Adam said with a knowing nod. "That's the outfit that's supposed to solve cases about murdered Indian women. One of the people here saw something about it on TV and asked me if the two of us were related. I told him yes we were. I said, 'That's my boy.'"

The man's tone was so cocky that Dan wanted to punch him in the face. "Did you happen to tell him that my job at MIP is tracking down people just like you?" he asked.

"Come on," Adam cautioned, his voice rising. "No reason to bring up any of that crap. It's all ancient history."

"Not to me, it isn't," Dan countered. "I'm the one whose mother was murdered. For me it could just as well have happened yesterday."

"What were you, five or six when that happened?" Adam asked.

"I was four!"

"Well, guess what?" Adam said. "Stop harping. It's over and done with. I went to prison for that and paid my debt to society."

"You never paid your debt to me!" Dan retorted. "My mother's still dead! But every time I'm on the job and have a chance to slap a pair of cuffs on the wrists of some murderous scumbag like you, that's who I'll be doing it for—Rebecca Duarte Pardee—my mother, the beautiful young Apache woman you tormented, beat up and murdered."

"So that's why you came today?" Adam demanded. "You wanted to bring up all that bad old stuff and cause trouble for me with my new friends here?"

"Actually it is," Dan replied, "and every time I put one of those assholes in prison where he belongs, he'll have you to thank. But I wanted to thank you, too."

"Thank me for what?"

"For helping me find my life's purpose," Dan replied, "something I can be passionate about, and to let you know that every morning when I get up and go to work, I'll be thinking about you."

By now every eye in the room was focused on those two men with matching green eyes—the older one seated in a wheelchair while the younger one glared down at him in absolute fury.

Suddenly a light went off inside Dan's brain, and he finally understood what Chair Man had meant. Dan had somehow assumed John Wheeler had been urging him to visit his father to give Adam Pardee some kind of closure before he died. Belatedly, Dan realized the closure was for him—that he needed to do this before it was too late for *him*!

"Well, great, then," Adam replied. "Pin a rose on you! At least I won't be forgotten."

"And I wanted to say one more thing," Dan continued.

"What's that?"

"I hope you rot in hell, and now that I've told you that, I'm going to go meet up with my fam-

ily at Disneyland. I promised my son a ride on
roller coaster. Unlike some people I could name
I'm a man who keeps my promises."

With that Dan Pardee turned on his heel an
stalked from the room. When he emerged from
the lobby into the California sunlight, he fel
as though a huge weight had been lifted from
his shoulders. He had taken the job with MII
primarily out of respect for his mother an
what had happened to her. In tracking dow
Ronald J. Addison, the killer of those dea
girls, Dan had thought he was bringing jus
tice to them and to their families, but now h
understood that something else had happene
along the way. Taking down the killer of his lo
girls had somehow freed him from his fathe
The fact that Adam Pardee was still alive an
breathing no longer mattered to him, no longe
haunted him. That was the blessing his lost gir
had given him.

And *I'itoi*, the Spirit of Goodness, would hav
been proud.

AFTERWORD

n the aftermath of the Civil War, a young
oman married a fellow she thought to be a war
ero. He turned out to be a scoundrel. When
e died a few years later, the father abandoned
eir children, leaving them to fend for them-
lves at a very young age. Two brothers man-
ed to eke out a living by painting houses with
ad-based paint while sleeping under haystacks.
s a result they grew into adulthood with per-
anently damaged lungs.

One of the brothers, a young man named Har-
d who had always wanted to become a minister,
as eventually taken in by a family who helped
m make his way through seminary. As a young
inister, he wrote a story with the intention of
ading one chapter a week to his congregation.
ventually they prevailed on him to publish the
ory as a book, and that became Harold Bell
right's first published novel—*That Printer of
dell's*. His second published book, *Shepherd of
e Hills*, became a massive bestseller, making
m the first fiction million-copy seller in his-

tory. By then, thinking he could reach mor
people by writing than he could by preachin
Wright abandoned the ministry and devote
himself to writing.

Although he was a contemporary of Heming
way and Faulkner, he was completely ignore
by the literary establishment. For one thing, h
publisher was in Chicago rather than New Yo
City. For another, his books were sold throug
Sears and Roebuck catalogs, which is how the
ended up in farmhouses all over the countr
That's where I first encountered Harold Be
Wright's name and work—among the few bool
hidden away in the attic storeroom at the to
of the stairs in my grandparents' farmhouse i
South Dakota. And the book I read that ho
muggy summer? *Shepherd of the Hills.*

The next time I encountered Harold Be
Wright's handiwork, I didn't even know
When I went to work as a school librarian o
what was then the Papago Indian Reservatic
in Sells, Arizona, in the late sixties, there was a
olive file folder on the shelves behind the des
In it was a tattered typed and mimeograph
Tohono O'odham legend, the story of *I'itoi a
Eagle Man.* I learned that story by heart an
told it during my twenty-six weekly story time
much to the delight of the K–6 kids who heard

One year, however, I made the mistake of te
ing that story in early April. The next time
visited that school, the principal called me in
her office and told me she had received a co
plaint from a parent. That's when I learned th
Tohono O'odham stories are winter telling ta

nd may only be told between the middle of No-
ember and the middle of March. If those stories
re told after the snakes and lizards are out, they
an swallow the storyteller's luck and bring him
arm. Once I heard that rule and with only one
otable exception when it comes to oral story-
elling, I've been careful to abide by it ever since.

In the late eighties, when I was preparing to
rite the first Walker Family book, *Hour of the
unter*, I had been away from the reservation for
venty years. In order to re-up my reservation
tuff," I did what any right-thinking librarian
ould do. I went to my neighborhood library
nd submitted over seventy interlibrary loan re-
uests.

Among the books that came my way was one
lled *Long Ago Told* by Harold Bell Wright—a
ollection of legends from the Tohono O'odham.
hat's where I learned that the typed and tat-
red copy of *I'itoi and Eagle Man* that I'd found
the Indian Oasis Library all those years ear-
r was, in fact, an exact copy of one of the leg-
ds in *Long Ago Told*.

I later learned that in the early part of the
entieth century, Mr. Wright was urged by a
octor to take his damaged lungs to a dryer cli-
ate. Not surprisingly, he ended up in Tucson.
nce there, he made friends with the locals, in-
uding Tohono O'odham storytellers, many of
om suffered from lung problems similar to
s own. He listened to their stories, though, and
ved them. Then, concerned they might disap-
ar completely once that generation of story-
lers passed away, he made a concerted effort

to preserve them. He went to the reservati
with a shorthand-equipped secretary along f
the ride. He listened to the storytellers tell t
stories, which were then repeated by a transl
tor, while the secretary took dictation. After th
Wright returned home to Tucson and edited t
secretary's transcribed stories before retur
ing to the reservation where his edited versio
were read back to the original storytellers by t
translator.

Those stories were collected and publish
in *Long Ago Told*. Most of Harold Bell Wrigh
books had print runs that numbered in t
hundreds of thousands of copies. *Long Ago T*
had an initial print run of five thousand co
ies and was never reprinted. Having read t
stories, I made the decision to include sor
of Mr. Wright's versions of those ancient ta
in *Hour of the Hunter* and in each succeedi
Walker Family book as well, including *Blessing*
the Lost Girls.

After reading the book, I thought it to be su
a treasure that my husband tracked down one
those rare five thousand copies and gave it to r
for my birthday that year. Believe me, it is one
my best-loved and most-used books.

Hour of the Hunter came out in the early nir
ties. In 2001, someone called and asked i
would come to Tohono Chul (Desert Corne
an arboretum in Tucson, and read the Toho
O'odham legend about the origin of the nig
blooming cereus from *Hour of the Hunter*
the night of the annual bloom. Naturally I s
yes. Then, belatedly, I realized the bloom wo

occur sometime during the summer, so I called my hostess back and told her sorry, no can do.

It turns out Tohono Chul keeps a medicine man on call. They checked with him and he said, "We no longer tell these stories in the villages. These are the real stories. I can't imagine I'itoi himself would object to Mrs. Jance reading that story on the night of the bloom." Of course, the fact that they were the *real* stories had far more to do with Harold Bell Wright than it did with me.

Feeling as though I had the medicine man's *Good Housekeeping* seal of approval in the middle of my forehead, I went ahead and read the story at the bloom party, which happened in the middle of July that year. I know the snakes and lizards were out that night because the on-duty snake handler relocated fourteen of them away from the crowd and to other parts of the park. However, none of the rattlers must have overheard the story since my luck seems to have come away intact. I can also tell you that once you've sampled the sweet fragrance of a night-blooming cereus, you never forget it.

Harold Bell Wright wrote the stories down in hopes of preserving them for future generations, and I am one of the grateful recipients of that effort. I've used his stories in my books for the same reason—to pass them along to succeeding generations. I've made very few revisions in the stories because . . . the stories are *the* stories.

As always, while writing this book, I was fascinated to see how those ancient tales seamlessly wove themselves into the very fabric of my book.

Because that's the magic of legends and stories—they're timeless. They cross the artificial boundaries of ethnicity and language and reflect our common human experience down through the ages. Some of my readers, intent on plot, may have skipped all that "Indian stuff," and that's fine, but it's possible they missed something special—something they never knew before.

Harold Bell Wright's works may not have been good enough for the literary establishment of his time, but they're good enough for me, and I'm grateful.

Some two years ago, while I was busy writing another book, a friend from Oregon told me about the passing of one of her longtime friends, James. In the process, she told me a fascinating story.

James was a Lakota who lived life to the fullest. In his youth he rode boxcars, traveling all over the country and working in railroad yards when he needed funds to continue his journeys. In the nineties, someone else was hopping trains—a serial murderer who eventually became known as the Boxcar Killer. He was someone who was into hate crimes before hate crimes became a thing, and he despised Native Americans. His specialty was locating victims and shoving them under moving trains.

James's encounter with the Boxcar Killer happened in Klamath Falls, Oregon, when he was shoved under a moving train and dragged for a mile and a half before the engineer was able to stop. Law enforcement was summoned. They pronounced him dead at the scene, zipped

him into a body bag, and shipped him off to th
morgue, which was located in the basement of
local hospital.

A nurse who worked in the hospital who hap
pened to be Lakota heard about the inciden
That evening, after finishing her shift, she wer
down to the morgue to wash James's hair—
time-honored Lakota custom. When she un
zipped the body bag, an arm rose out becaus
he wasn't dead. Once stabilized enough, he wa
life-flighted to Portland, Oregon, where he un
derwent the first of countless surgeries. That
where my friend first met him when she wa
called to his bedside along with several other
including native elders. Because his docto
didn't expect him to survive, this was suppose
to be a deathbed blessing, but rather than goin
in peace, James surprised everyone by wal
ing up.

His numerous surgeries left him a paraplegi
and the recovery process took years. He had t
relearn how to speak and read. Before the i
cident, he had been a talented painter. Becaus
his dominant arm had been amputated, when
came time to relearn how to write and paint, h
did so with his other hand.

Before James regained his ability to read, m
friend read books to him, and because she love
my books, mine were among the ones she rea
aloud to him, including her favorite, *Hour of t*
Hunter. He loved it.

James wasn't a medicine man or a shaman, b
he was a talented storyteller, who knew and to
the traditional Lakota origin stories. Once he r

gained the ability to speak, he began doing that again, only this time his audience was different. Using his own personal history with alcohol and drugs, he spent the next twenty years of his life reaching out to disaffected urban Indian youth in the Portland area, urging the young people he met to return to the right path.

Twentysome years after the Boxcar Killer's fateful attack, James finally succumbed to his injuries. The last time my friend saw him, James told her, "Tell your friend she needs to write another Walker Family story. There aren't enough Indian heroes in books." When he passed away shortly thereafter, he was returned home to the reservation not in a casket, but wrapped in a buffalo robe.

I know there are people who don't read beyond the last word of any given novel. Sadly those folks will miss out on learning about the inspiration for this book. James may not have been regarded as a medicine man by the Lakota, but in my humble opinion and from my distinctly Milghan point of view, he was indeed a medicine man, and a powerful one at that. I regard what he said to my friend about my writing another Walker Family book as a sacred charge, and *Blessing of the Lost Girls* is the result.

James told my friend that there aren't enough Indian heroes in books, but if you've met my character John Wheeler, you know that when it comes to heroes, now James is one.

READ THE
JOANNA BRADY
MYSTERIES

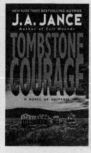

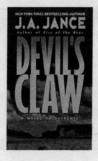